W9-BTO-013

the Silence that Binds Us

JOANNA HO

HARPER TEEN
An Imprint of HarperCollinsPublishers

HarperTeen is an imprint of HarperCollins Publishers.

Library of Congress Cataloging-in-Publication Data

Names: Ho, Joanna, author.
Title: The silence that binds us / by Joanna Ho.
Description: First edition. | New York, NY : HarperTeen, [2022] | Audience:
    Age 14 up. | Audience: Grades 10–12. | Summary: In the year following their son's
    death, May Chen's parents face racist accusations of putting too much pressure
    on their son and causing his death by suicide, and May attempts to challenge
    the racism and ugly stereotypes through her writing, only to realize that she still
    has a lot to learn and that her actions have consequences for her family as well as
    herself.
Identifiers: LCCN 2021051004 | ISBN 9780063059344 (hardcover)
Subjects: CYAC: Suicide—Fiction. | Brothers and sisters—Fiction. | Racism—Fiction.
    | Chinese Americans—Fiction. | Asian Americans—Fiction. | Family life—
    California—Fiction. | High schools—Fiction. | Schools—Fiction. | LCGFT:
    Novels.
Classification: LCC PZ7.1.H596 Si 2022 | DDC [Fic]—dc23
LC record available at https://lccn.loc.gov/2021051004

Typography by Joel Tippie
22 23 24 25 26   PC/LSCH   10 9 8 7 6 5 4 3 2 1
❖
First Edition

For Julia

My mom has her own personal arsenal of silence, and she wields it like the Force, bending me to her will. Her silence can be a flashing yellow light, warning me to proceed with caution, or a magnifying glass she uses to study me like I'm some kind of alien species. Most often, her silence is a hippo, pregnant with disappointment. She can brandish that hippo at me while gracefully hosting a dinner party, chatting up guests, and offering them tea.

Which is what she did on the night Danny died.

Just as the Wus arrived for dinner, Danny bounded down the stairs with all the grace of a six-foot water buffalo in basketball shorts, bellowing, "May-May! Have you seen my Star Wars socks?" He froze when he saw the Wus, then burst out laughing. "Everyone loves Star Wars, right?" Then he whipped around and ran back up to his room. He was extra scatterbrained his last few months, which was a little weird.

My mom emerged from the kitchen, perfectly pressed, with pearls of steam glistening in her hair. She just shook her head and laughed.

Her eyes flitted over to me, taking in my usual ripped jeans and hair, a cinnamon roll splat on top of my head. I was wearing my nicest hoodie, but that didn't stop my mom's right eyebrow from twitching, though her smile never wavered as she greeted our guests. "你越來越漂亮啊。"

She didn't say anything to me.

I glanced at Celeste, who of course looked perfect. Her hair glistened in a silky, straight waterfall down her back. She wore a loose black dress that hit modestly above her knees, the shapeless kind that would look like a potato sack on me but made her look like a model. Celeste had a figure made for qipao: slender, tiny really, with just the slightest suggestions of curves in all the right places.

When my mom greeted her, Celeste smiled, dipped her head, and said, "謝謝, Āyí." Her Mandarin didn't have the telltale ABC accent; it sounded like she grew up in Taiwan.

Five minutes later, Danny came back down the stairs, dressed this time and still chuckling. "Hi, Uncle. Hi, Āyí. Hey, Celeste."

Pink cherry blossoms bloomed on Celeste's cheeks and I rolled my eyes. *You and every other girl at school*, I thought. My mom made a sucking sound against her teeth and cut her eyes over at me.

2

While my dad herded everyone into the dining room, I slipped upstairs and changed into a pair of skinny high-waisted jeans and a cream-colored cardigan with lacy detail on the sleeves. My mom got it for me a while ago and I hadn't even taken the tags off. Because, not a hoodie. I brushed my hair, but it stuck out in haywire angles from being twisted up all day, so I tied it back up carefully, attempting to wrap it into a neat knot.

When I walked back into the dining room, tugging at the edge of my cardigan, Danny coughed into his noodles and arched his eyebrow at me. I gave him a death stare and he stifled a smile by blowing determinedly on his steaming bowl of niú ròu miàn.

My mom set a bowl in front of me and said, "熱的，趕快吃啊。"

It was too hot to eat, but too tempting to wait. The meat was so tender it melted as it touched my tongue. In between bites and burned mouths, everyone praised my mom for the beef noodle soup. She tried not to look too pleased and said, "還好而已。It's only okay. I forgot to make the suāncài so it's not as good today." Then she changed the subject. "How's school, Celeste?"

Celeste looked up, chopsticks frozen in the act of depositing noodles into her mouth. "It's good, Āyí."

Auntie Wu jumped in. "I heard you did very well on your math test last week, May."

"Not as well as Celeste," my mom said. "I heard she got the top score!"

Celeste shifted uncomfortably. I don't know where my mom gets her information, but she has her ways, and she takes a special interest in math because she's an engineer. It's just another reason for her to summon that pregnant hippo. Math is whatever to me; I'd rather be writing.

My mom directed her praise to Uncle and Auntie Wu. "真屬害。"

"She stays up so late to study, sometimes we worry about her," said Auntie Wu, shaking her head. "I say to her, 'Go to sleep or you will ruin your eyes.' But she just keeps working."

"不要擔心。Studying hard is a good thing."

"I tell her to relax a little. An A-minus never killed anyone!" Uncle Wu laughed and looked at my dad. "If I'd ever brought home an A-minus, my mom would have thrown me a party."

"You couldn't have afforded the bribe to get an A-minus. You spent more time in the principal's office than in class," my dad retorted. They looked at each other and laughed harder, past memories filling the space between their eyes.

Uncle Wu and dad grew up together in San Francisco's Chinatown. When Uncle Wu came over, they slipped in and out between Cantonese and English—amphibians of language comfortable in both habitats. I loved seeing my dad morph into his teenage self: the swagger, the laughter, the slang all came back when Uncle Wu was around.

"What would Joe think of us now, all cleaned up? With kids?" Uncle Wu said while slurping up a bite of noodles. "He wouldn't believe it."

"He'd love it." My dad's smile drooped as he looked toward the living room, where a faded picture of Uncle Joe sat on a bookshelf. "This is all because of him."

4

"Ai-yah, you were such troublemakers," said my mom, tilting the subject back toward humor with her mock exasperation. "I'm glad I met you after your Chinatown days."

She started scooping more noodles and soup into our bowls. I shook my head a little and croaked, "I'm good, Ma. I'm full."

"Full? You barely ate, Maybelline." My name was my mom's idea. When she was a young graduate, fresh out of Taiwan's top university, she saw a commercial for Maybelline makeup products that sang, "Maybe it's Maybelline." She thought it sounded beautiful and refined, everything she hoped her future daughter would become.

She's the only one who actually calls me by my full name.

My mom tried to sound chipper in front of our guests, but chipper on my mom is like a fake tan on a Minnesotan in winter. As she ladled soup and meat into my bowl, she said, "I thought niú ròu miàn was your favorite." Her eyes flashed a silent warning: *Don't embarrass me.*

I really was stuffed but gave up protesting. It's just safer to keep my mouth shut. Every time I retreat into my cave of silence, I spruce the place up. At this point, I've basically decorated myself a room complete with Pocky, books, a couple leafy plants, and a bed. I'm comfortable here.

As everyone tucked into beef noodle soup, round two, my mom looked up like she'd just thought of something, though I got the sense she'd been waiting for this moment all day. She said, "Danny, tell everyone the news!"

Auntie Wu sat up. "是啊! Wasn't today the day that—"

Danny's eyes widened, and I glimpsed a flash of something

drowning behind them. He choked. "Not now, Ma."

"Now is a perfect time! We're like family here."

Danny stared for a long second at his noodle bowl, then re-arranged his face so quickly that no one else noticed. He said, "I got into Princeton." He smiled and showed the high dimple on his right cheek—it always looked as if someone had pinned it out of place.

Congratulations burst around the table, and someone asked, "Did you hear from Stanford yet?" Danny shook his head. He kept smiling, but his dimple faded. He looked lost as he disappeared beneath best wishes and well-intentioned questions.

I watched him closely and frowned. Something was wrong. I tried to catch his eye, but he wouldn't look at me. He knew I was trying to telegraph a million questions to his brain.

"We have some exciting news to share too," said Auntie Wu, looking at her daughter. Celeste gave her mom a look that said, *Shut up, Mom,* and shook her head faintly. Auntie Wu kept talking. "Celeste was accepted into a summer internship program at Google! It is supposed to be for graduating seniors, but she got in even though she'll only be a junior next year."

Auntie Wu practically exploded out of her skin she was so dang proud. My mom clasped her hands, a speechless smile spread across her face. She never looked at me that way, a lantern glowing with pride. That look was always saved for Celeste.

"May, 你呢? What will you be doing this summer?" asked Auntie Wu.

The smell of jasmine wafted beneath my nose as Celeste looked down and refilled teacups around the table before pouring her own. I looked at Auntie Wu and said lamely, "Oh, uh, I don't really know."

Obviously, not the right answer.

"May is an amazing writer," Danny chimed in, always there to step in for me. Then he grinned. "She's also a pretty dope break-dancer."

I choked on a chunk of beef but let Danny keep talking. He continued, "Back in the day, she thought she was going to become a member of the Jabbawockeez, and she spent all her time working on her moves."

He glanced at me quickly and gave me a lightning-fast wink. I smiled back, grateful for his deflection. He knew I hated the sensation of other people's eyeballs resting on my face, watching me. Sizing me up. When people look at me, I feel like their eyes highlight all my deficiencies. I hate that feeling so much I almost failed seventh-grade English because I refused to give the final presentation in front of my class. I only passed because Ms. Johnson let me redo the presentation alone after school. I've gotten a little braver since then, but not much.

"Danny used to practice with May in her room," said my dad, bobbing his head in a terrible mimicry of our dance moves.

"Whoa, please stop, Bà. She clearly didn't get her dance genes from you," said Danny. My dad socked him in the shoulder. Everyone laughed as the conversation skipped right over me.

My mom collected bowls and chopsticks as she cleared the table. She didn't say anything. She didn't have to. The hippo at her side shaking its head at me said it all.

After dinner, my dad perched atop a ladder, changing the lightbulbs in the entryway. My dad has a thing with lightbulbs. If he
sees them on sale, he buys a box, or two, or twelve. We have a
small closet in the upstairs hallway filled with bulbs of all shapes
and sizes. LED, fluorescent, halogen, neon, CFL, incandescent—
he has them all. He changes lightbulbs around the house the way
people watch their favorite shows: regularly scheduled, with an
occasional bingefest. I swear, his dream is to make a wall full of
lightbulbs in our living room.

I squeezed his big toe and called up, "There is a terrible stink
in the house, Bà. Didn't you wash your feet before people came
over?"

"Foot washing is for the weak. Real men have stinky feet," he said. I pinched my nose and scrunched my face. I had a sneaking suspicion he posted up by the door to catch me heading to my room. He knew I was bugged because of dinner, and lightbulbs tended to get changed near me when I wanted privacy.

"You almost done?" I asked.

"Just your room left," he answered cheerily as he climbed carefully down the ladder. His lean frame was softening at the edges.

I poked the soft roll near his belly button.

"That's called dad-bod," he said. "Your brother started it, and you made it grow."

"It's the best pillow." I grinned.

"Ai-yah. It's not that big yet." He walked off in a huff. My dad had a little swagger in his step, even when he was stalking up the stairs in his socks. Signs of his childhood on the streets of Chinatown clung to him like cigarette smoke. He loved siu yeh, a midnight meal. He only ate egg tarts from Golden Gate Bakery on Grant. He always sat with his back to a wall where he could see all the entryways to a room. I asked him about this once, and he changed the subject.

He was already messing with my lights when I got upstairs.

"Yam, pass me that bulb," my dad said, balanced precariously in the air, one foot on my bed and another on the bookshelf. *Yam* is *May* spelled backward. My dad thinks he is a comedian.

"You changed that one last week," I said.

"I got these new LED bulbs. They save energy and were on sale. Don't worry, I'll keep the other bulbs in my emergency box."

His slipper caught on the edge of the bookshelf and he wobbled.

"Careful, Bà."

"I'm fine," he said lightly. Then he added in a low voice, "How are you doing, Yam?"

"Eh." I knew he wanted to cheer me up, but I didn't want to talk about dinner. Or Mom.

My dad was quiet as he twisted a bulb into place. Then he said with a slightly over-the-top conspiratorial tone, "Hey, last time I changed this bulb you told me about that boy, what's his name? John, Joe, Jacob—"

"Josh."

"Oh yeah, Josh. Football player but quiet. Big-shot VC dad. See? I remember. He passes you funny notes in class."

"Yeah, he folds them into little triangular footballs."

"Tell him you can't date until you're forty-five."

"Date? Who dates? That's for old people, Bà. These days, people just hook up." I pretended not to see my dad's eyebrows shoot up in alarm as I climbed onto my bed to dig around for my phone; it was always getting lost under the covers or wedged in between the wall and the mattress. "Besides, I don't like him like that. He's just a friend."

"He'll stick to funny notes if he knows what's good for him. There, all done." My dad hopped to the floor with a thud. He patted me on the back, then turned around at my bedroom door and said casually, "Your mom's downstairs in the kitchen. I bet she'd love someone to talk to."

* * *

When I walked into the kitchen, my mom nodded, but she didn't say anything; she just kept packing up the leftovers.

I loaded the dishwasher and started a cycle. The hum of the machine and the rush of water from the faucet were the only sounds in the kitchen. That stupid pregnant hippo tromped around me in circles like a well-trained circus animal as I soaped up the sponge and started scrubbing pots.

Finally, my mom broke the silence.

"Celeste 真的很孝順," she said. 孝順, or *xiàoshùn*, is like my mom's favorite word. I looked it up once, and the internet said it means "filial piety," which looks and sounds like gibberish to me. There really isn't a good translation. It's like obedient, respectful, caring, and every other desirable quality rolled into one intimidating word. All good Chinese kids should be 孝順.

It bothered me that I had been thinking about my mom all night, but she had been thinking about Celeste. Granted, I wasn't thinking very nice things, but at least I was thinking about her. "Yeah, she's pretty perfect, Ma."

I told myself not to say anything more. My mom looked up sharply, her rudeness radar on full alert. "What's wrong with you, Maybelline?"

"Nothing."

"Celeste knows what is best for her future and she works very hard. You can learn a lot from her."

"I work hard, too, Ma."

"Do you?" She snapped the lid onto a glass container. "Celeste 很厲害, but you could have a Google internship too."

"I don't want a Google internship."

"Then what do you want?"

I felt like this was a trick question, so I kept my mouth shut.

"When Danny was your age, he was already joining clubs and leading the basketball team."

I scrubbed the pot in my hand like I was trying to clean off the Teflon. I could hear her from past conversations: *I should have signed you up for camp or a summer program. I never had to do that for Danny; he was already so involved.* My mom's pregnant hippo plopped itself beside me and stared up with unblinking disapproval; she let it convey all her disappointment as she kept cleaning. I made a face at it, then turned my back to string up some lights in my cave of silence.

She wasn't done, though. "You're smart too. So smart you don't study hard. You're just going along. Floating along."

"I get good grades, Ma."

"Good grades aren't enough, Maybelline." She put a food container in the refrigerator and turned around. "You need to be doing more for your future."

"Okay, Ma." My hands scrubbed away with a life of their own. I closed my eyes and sucked in a lungful of air. Slowly, so it wouldn't seem like I was trying to be attitude-y.

I could feel her eyes on my back for a long minute before she sighed. "I am trying to help you, Maybelline."

I didn't respond. Speaking up would just make things worse.

As the minutes stretched forward, I peeked at the pot in my hands to make sure the Teflon was still intact before stacking it on the drying rack. Then I got to work on the larger bowls that didn't fit in the dishwasher. After bowls, I did the chopsticks and spoons. There's nothing satisfying about washing utensils, so I always wash them last. When I finished, I wiped my hands on a dish towel and brushed wordlessly past my mom.

3

I changed into a pair of baggy sweats and an oversized T-shirt before throwing myself onto my bed. It welcomed me with open arms, and I buried my face in a pillow. Its fluff softened the rougher edges of my frustration.

I reached under my mattress and pulled out my journal. I flipped past old doodles, poems, pages filled with the extremes of my emotions and memories, and started scribbling on the next blank page.

A beam of light stretched across the room as the door opened and a shadow slipped inside. I hurriedly tucked my journal back under my mattress. I never let anyone see my writing, not even my big brother.

Danny snuck in while whispering lyrics that graduated into

a dramatic rendition of Sam Smith's song "Lay Me Down." He drew out the vowels for effect: "Can I lay by your side? Next to youuuuu ooooo oooo ooo oooo oooooo, yooouuuu ooo ooo ooo ooo ooooooo. And make sure you're alriiiiiightt?"

I smiled. "Wow, Danny. I didn't know you could make it sound even worse than usual."

He plopped down next to me and rolled up in the comforter. "You okay, May-May? I didn't hear the whole thing." Danny's nickname for me was a play on my name and mèi-mei, the Mandarin word for "little sister."

"It's the usual. It's worse when Celeste is here." I curled into his side, and he patted my head like I was a poodle.

He sighed. "The Google thing didn't help."

I threw up my hands. "Of course she got a Google internship. How perfect of her. She's on the fast track to valedictorian and getting invited to fancy internships, and what am I doing? Throwing away my life because I have no summer plans yet.'"

He made a *pppfffft* sound through his mouth and said, "There are worse things you could be doing."

"Like having a baby."

"Flunking weekend Chinese school."

"Getting a nose ring like Calvin's."

"Dude, I heard his mom tried to rip it out," Danny said as he winced and rubbed his nose.

"Of course she did." I mimicked my mom's voice: "Because 'nose rings are only for pigs and cows.'"

"His nose must be made of steel." We chuckled together, then lay quietly in the cradle of our laughter.

I paused before I rolled over and asked, "Why didn't you tell me about Princeton, Gē?"

Danny got serious. He stared up at the ceiling and shrank into himself. "I dunno," he whispered. "I wasn't that excited."

"Not excited? It's *Princeton*."

"I know. I should be excited, right? Everyone else is."

"But you're not." I turned and studied his face. His eyes were closed, and his chest rose as he sucked in air.

He shook his head. "I feel nothing."

"Well, maybe you're not meant to go there. You're a shoo-in everywhere else if you got into Princeton."

He shook his head again, then lay quietly for a few minutes. I asked, "You heard from Stanford again, didn't you?"

He nodded with his eyes closed. "I didn't get in." He paused. "I didn't want to ruin the mood at dinner. Everyone was so happy about Princeton."

Stanford had been Danny's dream ever since a couple of its basketball players visited our elementary school when he was in second grade. I was only in kindergarten, so I don't remember their visit at all, but Danny begged my parents for a Stanford sweatshirt, and he wore it so much it smelled funky even after it got washed. He applied early last fall but got deferred.

"Oh, Gē, I'm so sorry." I wrapped my arm around him and snuggled in. "They have no idea what a colossally bad decision they made."

He grimaced and said quietly, "I should be happy about

Princeton, right? But I really wanted Stanford."

"You worked so hard. You deserved Stanford! The only kids from Sequoia Park High who get in to Stanford are the ones whose parents went there or work there. The whole system is stupid, Danny. It's their loss." I pounded my hand into a pillow. "You okay?"

Danny didn't respond; he just stared at the ceiling again. His silence was a black hole, so I kept talking to fill the void. I poked him and forced a smile. "You'll love Princeton, Gē. They don't know what they're in for."

He lifted himself to his elbow and smirked as he gestured to his six-foot frame. "They won't be able to handle this."

I laughed. He patted my head again. "Don't be upset about Ma," he said. "She just worries too much. She'll always watch out for you . . . even if you get a nose ring like Calvin's." He hooked two fingers in his nose and stuck out his tongue. Just like that, he was himself again.

I blinked at the transformation. It happened so fast, I started to wonder if I'd imagined Black Hole Danny a moment ago. "Danny, you didn't answer my question. How do you feel?"

His phone vibrated and he checked the glowing screen. "It's Marc."

His fingers flew as he typed a response. "People are going to Annette's tonight. Her parents are out of town. I think Tiya's riding with Marc." He reached over the mattress and started making sweeping motions on the ground under my bed. "Where's your phone, May-May? Tiya's probably blowing it up. I think going out will cheer me up. You wanna come?"

I patted around the bed for my phone too; I swore I'd just had it. I am pretty sure my phone has legs because it is always wandering off and hiding itself in the weirdest places. Once, after hunting around the house for hours, I found it in the refrigerator.

I finally found it—not under the pillow, but somehow tucked in a corner inside the pillowcase—and Tiya had indeed been blowing up my phone.

Mayday, first night of spring break!

Let's go out!

Mayday

Mayday

Mayday

Where you at??

Celeste and her family were over for dinner

How'd that go?

Eh, the usual

Party at Annette's tonight

Let's go and dance our faces off

By faces, I mean booties

It'll make you feel better

Nah, gonna stay in

Joooosssh will probably be there

Ugh. You know it's not like that

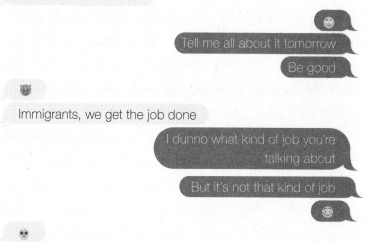

Well, he wishes it was

Tell me all about it tomorrow

Be good

Immigrants, we get the job done

I dunno what kind of job you're talking about

But it's not that kind of job

P.S. Check your vm

I checked my voice mail and found Tiya's message. I hit play and put it on speaker so Danny could hear it too.

"LET'S GO OUUUUUTTTTT TONIGHT! I have to go OUUUUTTTTTT tonight!" Tiya's voice blasted through the tinny speakers of my phone as she sang Mimi's song from *Rent*. I knew the song because Tiya had been into musicals since freshman year and she'd taken it upon herself to school me on Broadway. She liked them because she could sing along hella loud and sound amazing. I liked them because I loved listening to her sing.

Tiya Marie Duverne and I have been best friends since seventh grade. We were partnered together for a project in social studies, and we did a dance routine about world religions. The rest is history. My mom loved Tiya because she earned excellent grades and ate everything Ma put on her plate. Her mom loved me for the same reasons. Turns out immigrant Haitian parents and immigrant Chinese parents aren't all that different.

Danny's phone vibrated again. He winked. "Marc says you should come too."

Tiya's brother Marc has been Danny's best friend since some basketball league in elementary school. They were the only kids of color, and they stuck together. Even though Danny was a year older than Marc, they were co-captains of Sequoia Park High School's basketball team, and they balled together almost every day. They were like a pair of broken-in basketball shoes: one didn't function without the other.

I shrugged. "Do you want me to go? I'll go if you want me to. Or you could stay home and we can eat a crap ton of ice cream and trash-talk Stanford all night."

"You're no fun at parties unless you're in the mood. I don't wanna babysit your grumpy butt all night." Danny threw up a couple peace signs and smiled at me before heading back to his room. "Let's do ice cream and trash-talking tomorrow."

Alone again, I flopped back into bed with my arms and legs out like I was about to make a snow angel on the comforter. I lay still, then I grabbed my journal again and started scribbling. Writing helps me process the mess inside my head. Somehow ideas come more easily, more clearly through my fingers than they do through my mouth.

I heard Danny rustling around, and he stopped by my room

one more time before he left. He was wearing jeans and a plain white T-shirt, and I could see his Star Wars socks peeking out over his shoes when he moved. He had on his KT3s, which was a little strange because he usually only wore them for basketball. They were blinding white; I bet he'd cleaned them for the party.

On his eighteenth birthday, Danny jumped and screamed like a banshee when he saw the KT3 box underneath the blue-and-gold Warriors wrapping paper I'd picked out. Klay Thompson's Anta basketball shoes were all he wanted on his big day, so I saved money to get them. Most of the time, he kept the shoes in their box in his car, ready to ball anytime, anywhere. Tonight he held the shoebox in his right hand—probably to put it back in his trunk—and a jacket hung over his wrist.

"Ooooh," I whispered. "I'm going to tell Mooooom. You're wearing shoes in the house. You're gonna be in *big* trouble."

"What she doesn't know won't hurt her, May-May." He grinned as he did one of his fast-feet basketball drills in my room. I threw a pillow at him.

He stepped toward my bed and tripped over a shoe in the middle of my room.

"May-May," he said, shaking his head. "You gotta get a handle on your closet."

"Go ahead and handle it for me," I said as I threw another pillow at him. He got on his hands and knees and started shoveling clothes into the closet corner where things end up when I don't feel like cleaning. Which is all the time. He set the offending shoe on top of the big pile and dusted off his hands.

"The things I do for you . . . ," he mumbled as he came over and squeezed me hard.

"You sure you don't just want to hang with me here? I can think of other things for you to clean, you know."

"Nah, I'm good."

"We could watch *Star Wars* . . . ," I said in my best tempting voice, but he just laughed and mussed up my hair. I wanted him to stay, but it was like trying to hold on to a cloud, its wispy mist slipping softly through my fingers. He slung his jacket back over his arm as he turned to go. He paused, then came back and planted a kiss on my forehead. "I love you, May-May," he said. He looked me in the eye and held my gaze with his off-center dimple and sideways smile.

Then he was gone.

4

The train blasted its horn over and over, slicing through my sleep. Piercing sirens wailed through the night and my dreams fluttered beneath half-closed eyelids. The sirens' high-pitched wailing faded in and out, muted then screaming then muted. Over and over again. Groggily, my mind took note. There were a lot of sirens flying by.

I must have fallen asleep writing because I knocked my journal off the bed as I reached for my phone to check the time. It was actually on my nightstand where I thought it was. I rubbed the blur from my eyes and held the phone up to my face so I could see it. No point in looking for my glasses in the dark.

It was three a.m. I'd missed five calls, three voice mails, and a bunch of texts from Tiya.

Mayday

Mayday

Mayday

WAKE UP!!

Danny left the party early

Is he home yet?

Marc said he was acting weird

Just wanted to make sure he got home safe

I'm sure he's fine

But can you check?

After reading Tiya's texts, I shuffled over to Danny's room to make sure he was in bed.

It was empty.

A shard of ice stabbed into my stomach.

Where was he?

Come home, ge

Where are you?

Are you okay?

This isn't funny

Danny, answer your phone

Text me

Where are you?

I'm freaking out

Please come home

6

The ice in my stomach traveled up to my heart and sent frigid waves through my body. My fingers and toes were twitchy with nervous, dreadful energy. I headed downstairs. The lights were already on, and my mom was sitting at the dining table. My dad was pacing, adjusting wall fixtures, and running his hands over windowsills. Just hours ago, we sat here eating dinner with the Wus. Now it felt like an interrogation room, the darkness too big, the light too harsh. Crooked shadows leaped from every angle.

My parents barely glanced up when I walked in and sat at the table. "Maybelline, why are you up? You should be sleeping. Go back to bed," my mom murmured. I ignored her and stared out the window.

My mom muttered to no one in particular, "He usually comes home by midnight." Her hand tapped the table anxiously. "I've been calling. He's not answering." Her right leg bounced up and down. "He always calls."

The silence in the room swelled with waiting and worry.

I alternated between staring out the window, willing Danny to walk in the door, and staring at my phone, hoping his name would pop up on the screen. My mom was right. It wasn't like him to stay out without calling or texting.

"I am going out to look for him," my dad announced. No one mentioned the sirens.

"He'll be home soon," my mom said too confidently. "He'll be back soon."

My dad went upstairs to grab a sweatshirt. While he was upstairs, red and blue lights flashed from the street outside. Moments later, we heard a sound at the door.

Knock.

Knock.

Knock.

My eyes met my mom's. My stomach turned inside out and all my muscles went numb.

My mom made her way to the door and placed a trembling hand on the knob. My dad came running down the stairs just as my mom took a deep breath and pulled the door open. An ashen-faced police officer with dark circles under his eyes stood stiffly on the front step.

"Mr. and Mrs. Chen?"

"Yes, where is our son?" The words tumbled from my dad's mouth.

The officer stood with an unnatural straightness to his back. His tag read *J. Jeffries*. He was young and too inexperienced to wipe the emotion from his face. I could see he didn't want to be on our doorstep any more than we wanted him there.

"You may want to sit down, sir . . . ," he said.

"Please. My son. Where is he? Is he okay?" my mom whispered.

"It may be best if you sat down, ma'am." Officer Jeffries swallowed and paused. No one moved.

"Where is our son?" My dad's face was pale, his body a coiled spring of fear and anxiety. He reached out and put his arm around my mom's shoulders.

"There's been an . . . accident."

My mom buckled into my dad; the words "Please tell us he's okay" escaped, barely audibly, from her lips. Officer Jeffries frowned and started again, his back curved as the effort to be strictly professional wilted to reveal real sadness. "I meant to start by saying this is the hardest thing I've ever done. I'm so sorry." His voice caught. "Your son, Danny, was hit by the train. He . . . he did not survive."

My mom screamed. It was an animal sound, a primal sound. It sounded like every fiber binding her soul to her body ripped violently apart.

Her body collapsed. My dad caught her, and they crumpled into a heap on the floor. A second officer stepped in and helped

28

my parents to the table. I hadn't noticed her before. I stood and stared at both officers. I stared as the air pulsed around my head. I stared as my ears started to ring. I stared and stared and stared at their mouths moving, but I heard nothing.

Silence filled my mind, a thunder so loud it was deafening.

Then sentence fragments fell out of Officer Jeffries's mouth and jarred my brain even more.

. . . possibly suicide . . . autopsy . . . with your approval . . .

No no no no. I retched onto the floor.

And the world turned black.

7

I was unmoored. Without my anchor, I floated on an endless ocean under a starless sky. I bobbed up and down. Up and down. I drifted with no thought or direction. Darkness here was the same as darkness there.

There was darkness everywhere.

8

My dad came home with a blue-and-gold rubber-band bracelet, a Warriors key chain, and a scuffed-up basketball shoe.

A KT3.

The pieces of Danny that had survived his death.

His suicide, said the final report.

Dad cradled his treasure, carried it upstairs, and closed the bedroom door.

9

I tugged at the scratchy lace collar of the white dress my mom made me wear to the funeral. White as is the custom, she said. White like the huge chrysanthemum wreaths with fluttering banners that lined the walls of the funeral home. White like Danny's shoes when he left my room that night.

Everyone else was in black, staring at us like we were out of place at our own funeral. Staring and whispering words of pity I couldn't hear but felt on the nape of my neck like swarms of mosquitoes pricking my skin.

I couldn't stand up and walk by the casket. I stayed glued to my seat as my parents got up, my immobility a gaffe in my family's perfectly poised presentation.

I wouldn't go close, but I couldn't look away.

He couldn't be lying in that box.

He couldn't be gone.

10

People didn't know what to say, so they brought food. Our kitchen was filled with food. Fruit overflowed from bowls, and golden bananas draped themselves across the counter like suntanning beachgoers. They reminded me of summertime trips to Santa Cruz with Danny. We'd lie out on the sand, attempt to get in the freezing-cold water, then make a mandatory stop at Marianne's for a scoop of 1020—caramel ice cream with swirls of Oreo and fudge.

This year, summer barely made it through our closed curtains.

The bananas' bright yellow peels were too happy for our home. They fit in better when they turned black. Our kitchen table was covered with muffins and bagels and more plastic-wrapped plates of homemade cookies than a bake sale display. Our fridge was stuffed with meals stored in glass containers. Meals covered in tinfoil. Meals in takeout boxes. Meals clamoring for attention, piled one on top of the other.

It all went bad, nearly untouched.

Eventually, the food stopped coming.

11

There was a woman in a pink blouse.
A counselor.

Talk to me when you are ready.

How could I ever be ready to talk about this?
There was a woman in a blazer.

Sign on the line.

Paper packets from school piled up,
Cold and lifeless
like me.
Like my brother.
Then instinct took over—
school above everything—
and I filled in lines,

colored in bubbles,
and the packets disappeared
with the school year.

12

I slept
    when the world was awake.
I slept
    when the world went to bed.
Sleep meant darkness
and dreams
and nightmares.
But no nightmare could be worse than reality.

13

AWHOOOOO!

AWHOOOOO!

The train blasted its horn over and over, slicing through my sleep. My heart began to pound, and a sick feeling sent trembling waves through my body. I saw Danny standing on the tracks, the train racing toward him. *Get out of the way, Danny!* I screamed and screamed, but no sound came out.

I barfed over the side of my bed.

Trains traveling between San Jose and San Francisco passed by my house around ninety times a day. I never used to notice them rumble by

. . . until I did.

14

My dad and I were ghosts. Translucent, almost invisible, but somehow held together; we were wavering outlines of ourselves, going through the motions in a life without Danny. Faint wisps of desire to find peace tied us to the world and kept us alive, if just barely.

Not my mom.

She always said becoming a mom changed the way she walked in the world. Danny was her firstborn; he changed her. He was the one who made her a mom and gave her life new meaning. Without him, she cracked into a million lost and scattered pieces.

She was too broken to even be a ghost.

All her memories were fragmented by questions and tainted by Danny's death; nothing meant what she thought it meant, so there was nothing to tie her together, no desire for peace to bind her to the world. Her body was there, but she was gone.

She lay in bed, not speaking, just staring. My dad and I flitted around, feeding her, bathing her, mumbling in her ear, stroking her hair. Every once in a while, in the recesses behind her pupils, a light sparked, then faded.

Little by little, two ghosts tried to glue my mom back together.

But who tended to the ghosts?

15

A cool hand on my forehead.
My eyes fluttered
and glimpsed a gentle smile.
Tiya
sat next to me
lay by me
cradled me in my darkness.
She would not let me drown.

16

Basil-scented spray wafted up from downstairs, carried on a breeze that smelled like sunshine and late summer. The windows were open for the first time in months. Tiya, hair wrapped with patterned fabric, hugged my dad and kissed my mom as she wielded a broom and hummed show tunes under her breath. Marc, wearing rubber gloves like boxing mitts, faced off with the dishes piled in the sink. They hollered and screamed dire warnings when my dad or I tried to help. Eventually, we gave up, and I forced my cheeks to lift the corners of my mouth into a smile.

Marc, elbow-deep in soap bubbles, watched me from across the room. Tiya danced over and dipped the broom into my lap like it was her tango partner. They cleaned and scrubbed and sprayed and rubbed until the house felt new.

Except Danny's room.

They didn't go in there.

I woke up in the middle of the night and shuffled over to the bathroom.

I flipped the light switch.

Click.

Nothing turned on. I tried again and again.

Flip. *Click.*

Flip. *Click.*

Still nothing.

I registered confusion. The lightbulbs were all burned out.

I padded over to the hallway closet and fumbled through my dad's lightbulb collection. I didn't know what was what, so I grabbed the most generic-looking bulb I could find, padded back to the bathroom, and felt my way over to the counter. I climbed up, accidentally turning on the faucet and kicking over a soap dispenser in the process, and changed the lightbulb.

I flipped the light switch again.

Click.

The light was blinding.

18

Mayday, you ready for tomorrow?

Nope

You can do this

Marc and I will pick you up at 8:30

Imma be curled up in bed

I'll throw water on you

You know I will

Be ready

Uggggh

Fine

19

Danny was a magnet, and people were drawn to me because I was an extension of him. I followed in the smooth path of Danny's wake, protected from the choppy social waters of school, and I was always careful never to make any waves that might upset this delicate balance.

Danny parts waves for me when he is gone as he did when he was alive. But his magnet has flipped, creating an invisible force pulsing against the rest of the world, pushing people away. As I walk to class, Taylor Harlow sees me and starts walking toward me with her arms outstretched. "May, where've you been? I haven't seen you in so lon—" she begins. Her face flushes and eyes widen as she remembers. Her arms fall to her sides and she turns her face. "Oh crap, I'm so sorry."

Taylor stands awkwardly before mumbling something indiscernible and backing away. As I round the corner, a group of freshmen drop their voices and talk behind their hands. I catch the bits and pieces of their whispers. ". . . her brother . . . suicide . . . train . . ." People part in front of me, unsure what to say or how to react. Some lift their hands and offer wavering smiles, some turn away, some step toward me with words frozen on their tongues. I swallow and duck into class.

After Danny died, I finished last year on independent study. Pencil-paper packets that I barely remember filling out. I disappeared when Danny disappeared, and now it's a new year—my junior year—and I'm back. I'm a reminder of the trauma and grief everyone at Sequoia Park High School wants to forget.

The students don't know what to do, and the teachers are no better.

Some are overly welcoming. *Maybelline, it is SUCH a pleasure to have you in my class. So excited you're here.*

Some are overly accommodating. *Maybelline, don't worry about this first assignment if you're not ready. Just do what you can.*

One flat-out ignores me.

One chokes on my name as tears come to her eyes. *Maybell— oh! [Grabs tissue.]* She used to be Danny's teacher too.

I soldier through the morning, but by the time the lunch bell rings, I'm packed and ready to find Tiya. She is already waiting outside my door, out of breath with words tumbling willy-nilly out of her mouth. "Mayday, you won't believe this but they messed up my schedule. I have to go get it worked out right now. I'm so mad. I wanted to eat together today. How's it going so far? How are your classes? *How has it been?* I'm so sorry. Do you want to come with me? Or you could sit with Marc and wait for me. Or you could come with me. Hang on . . ."

She puts a hand on my shoulder and bends over to take three dramatic, heaving breaths. "Oooooh! I'm out of shape. Anyway, what was I saying? Oh yeah, lunch. Do you want to come with me to the office? I hear lunchtime in the office is real special around here."

I smile for her. "It's good, Tiya Marie. I'm going to head to our spot. The main office sounds like zero fun."

"You sure?"

"Go get your stuff figured out. Come find me when you're done."

"You know they're slower than the DMV up in there."

"Then I'll meet you by our lockers after school. Go handle your business and don't worry about me."

Tiya flies up to the office, ready to do battle with whoever messed up her schedule. I start wandering toward our spot, a tree that grows between the English and history buildings on a small, grassy hill framed with bench-height concrete walls. Its branches stretch out like hugging arms. Tiya and I have eaten lunch there since freshman year. I wonder who she ate with last year when I stopped coming to school. I've never even thought to ask.

Everything on campus is almost exactly the same. Buildings grouped by subject. Red-shingled rooftops with awnings for huddling under on rainy days. Raised flower beds between build-ings. Stressed-out, high-achieving energy in the air. But I'm not the same. My life is not the same.

It's jarring.

As I walk toward the hugging oak, I think, *Danny used to walk here.* I imagine him leaning up against a wall, surrounded by people and waiting for the bell. I see him dribbling through the halls, head-faking and spinning around friends who attempt to steal his ball. *That's my brother,* I used to think proudly. He always seemed so happy. I don't understand how I missed the signs that pointed to suicide.

I pass his old locker, the corner where he sometimes stood to check on me between classes. Every place that Danny once stood, once laughed, once breathed is now a gaping hole.

Lost in my thoughts, I am surprised to hear laughter as I near the history building. A group of white girls in flowery sundresses—did they coordinate their clothing on purpose?—circles the corner near my tree. They're like a slow-motion movie: hair swirling around faces, sunlight catching on smiles, giggles popping in bubbles all around them. I cringe and wonder, *How can people laugh like that? Don't they know what happened?*

My mind struggles to process as I realize it's been four months and life went on for everyone else. Life did not stop for them when it stopped for Danny.

The circle of girls shifts as a tall, broad-shouldered white guy with sandy brown hair stands up. He looks up and I realize it's Josh McIntyre. He's wearing a green T-shirt with *Sequoia Park*

Football written across the chest in silver block letters.

I have a vague recollection of my dad saying Josh should stick to funny notes if he knew what was good for him. It seems like another lifetime ago, though that doesn't stop me from full-on creeper-status staring at him and all those sunny-smile sundress girls. My mind feels like it got stuck in a freezer and won't fire on all cylinders. Staring happens to be a by-product of freezer brain.

Josh starts when he sees me, and his eyes don't leave my face. I wave half-heartedly and wander back through campus; I don't feel like talking to anyone right now. I walk toward the patio, a wooden deck surrounded by grass in the center of campus. It's where Danny used to sit with his friends. As I pass the library, I run right into Marc.

"Mayday, I was just looking for you. I saw Tiya heading up to the office and didn't want you eating alone today." He smiles and points up at the patio. I notice he's got a fresh cut. His low fade hugs his head, and the midday sun highlights the warm reds in his brown skin. "Come sit with me."

I let him take my backpack and follow him across the grass. People scoot over and I sit close to him, finding safety in his space. Someone passes around a bag of chips and he offers me some before taking a couple and handing them back. Someone else cracks a joke, and Marc throws back his head and laughs. A couple girls walk up and hug everyone on the patio before sitting down, and suddenly, I need to get out of here.

Seeing Marc acting so sunshiny and *how-was-your-summer*

and *so-good-to-see-you* on the first day of school sparks anger in my chest. How can *he*, of all people, act like nothing's changed? Marc is sitting here eating chips and cracking jokes and hugging girls. Danny was his best friend. How could he forget so quickly?

I stand up abruptly and walk away. I hear Marc call, "May!" but I don't turn around.

There are three minutes until the bell, but I'm the first one in class, still repelling people with my invisible magnetic force field. I put my head down on my desk and shut my eyes as students trickle in. I look up to watch the seconds tick by on the clock. There is a sign underneath it that says, "Time will pass. Will you?" Hardy har. Where do teachers come up with this stuff?

"MAYDAY!"

I look up and there is Tiya, resplendent and glowing with a thick goddess braid circling her head and resting over her shoulder. Her skin is the same rich brown color as Marc's. "Mayday, I got myself switched into your class. Call me a miracle worker!"

"Best news of the day, Tiya Marie. Sit here."

I pull her into the seat in front of me. We learned a long time ago that it is easier to whisper in class sitting front to back, not side to side. She sees her friend Ayanna a few rows over and waves, then she swivels around just as Josh walks in to a chorus of, "Yaaaas! J-Mac! Over here!" Tiya looks at me with her eyebrow raised. I ignore her. Josh sits with his friends across the room and immediately looks over at me. Ava Prince slides into an open seat next to Josh, sees me, and waves both hands excitedly, like, *So glad we have a class together!* I smile at her until Celeste walks in and my stomach drops.

Ms. Daniels sweeps into the room a second after the tardy bell rings, talking a mile a minute. "Sorry, class, late on the first day, what a way to start the year! But honestly, you wouldn't *believe* how hard it is to hold your pee from lunch to the end of the school day." She is a whirlwind of movement, but never stops talking even as she opens her laptop, fiddles with its keys, and connects it to the projector.

"I thought I could do it, but my bladder had other ideas. We only have a five-minute break between classes, as if that's enough time to beat back the hordes on the way to the teachers' lounge. It's inhumane, I tell you." She pauses as the class giggles. "Anyway, TMI, amiright? Welcome to American Lit."

She stands at the front of the room, hands on hips, commanding the space with a smile. All that movement and she's not even breathing hard. Rose undertones glow through her brown skin and a patterned turquoise band is wrapped around the dark curls piled in a pineapple on top of her head. She wipes her forehead with the back of her hand. I like her immediately.

I whisper to Tiya, "She's like an adult version of you."

Tiya nods and holds up a heart symbol with her hands. Ms. Daniels gives us an in-class writing assignment and we settle down to write. No laptops allowed, only old-school pen and paper. At the end of class, when I walk up to turn in my essay, Ms. Daniels puts her hand over mine, looks into my eyes, and says firmly, "I've heard so much about you, Maybelline. I'm expecting a lot from you this year."

I meet her eyes and nod. When I walk back to my desk, I show Tiya the heart I make with my fingers.

Marc looks at me quizzically as I climb into his car after school. He asks, "What happened, May?"

"Nothing," I say, avoiding his eyes.

"Where did you go? Are you all right?" He starts the car and backs out of the parking spot.

"You seemed busy. I didn't want to interrupt." The image of Marc on the patio talking to his friends rekindles the anger in my chest, so I fold myself into a little bundle by the back-seat window. As if making myself smaller will hold in my feelings.

Sitting shotgun, Tiya looks between us and frowns. She makes a silent *What's up?* gesture and I shrug.

"My day was great," says Tiya, cutting in. "I think AP History is gonna be a beast, though. We already have an essay due next week. But in other news, I got myself transferred into Mayday's American Lit class. Guess who our teacher is."

"Aw, you got Ms. Daniels?" Marc lights up.

"Yup. I couldn't believe it." Tiya turns around to look at me. "Ms. Daniels is our Black Student Union advisor. She's the best."

"You joined the BSU?" I ask.

"Yeah, Marc got me to go to some meetings last year when you"—she pauses, considering her words—"were at home. Ayanna, Mikayla, and I started going together. You should come check it out, Mayday. It's open to anyone."

55

Marc watches me in the rearview mirror and says, "Yeah, you should come through, May." But as soon as he opens his mouth, all I can hear are the popping sounds of angry firecrackers bursting behind my eyes.

Before-Danny-died May is confused and a little scared by this uncharacteristic rage. What's wrong with Marc eating chips and laughing with some friends? I should be glad he's healing. But I'm not. I want him to hurt like I'm hurting. To miss Danny like I miss Danny.

After-Danny-died May feeds the anger because it makes me feel alive.

Lost between the warring factions of my mind, I retreat into my silent cave and don't respond. I ride the rest of the way without speaking.

20

I make it through the first week of school, and when I get home on Friday afternoon, I notice someone has filled a cup with strawberry Pocky and fanned them evenly against the rim. Did my mom set these out for me? She used to do this for us when we came home from school. Danny and I would try to come up with new ways to make faces at each other while my parents made dinner. Danny's specialty was a walrus face. He would poke one stick into both sides of his mouth and snorffle at me—that's the only word we could come up with to describe a walrus sound after we looked up a video online. Once, he made the face and I laughed so hard, milk and chewed-up Pocky came out of my nose.

That afternoon, my mom spun around when she heard

everything spew out of my face and immediately snapped, "May-belline, 你在幹嘛? Don't play with the food."

Before I could respond, Danny had jumped in for me, saying, "Ma, May-May didn't do anything; it was me. Look!" And he stuck two new Pocky sticks into his mouth and made another walrus face. He really hammed it up as he snorffled at my mom, and she laughed so hard she had to clutch her stomach to hold herself together. Then she grabbed some cooked mǐfěn and draped the noodles across his upper lip like a mustache and we all fell apart laughing.

I nibble on a Pocky, thinking about the way Danny could bring out Mom's goofy side and wishing I had that special power too. I could really use it now. My mom hasn't been back to work yet, hasn't really left the room much since Danny died. I think she's on medical leave. Dad is probably still at work, helping his students after school. I fill a glass of water, peel an orange, and put some crackers on a plate. I take the snack upstairs and set it on my mom's nightstand. These days I feel more like the parent in our family, taking care of her and the house. I text my dad.

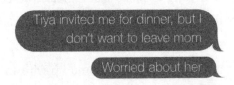

Tiya invited me for dinner, but I don't want to leave mom

Worried about her

While I wait for my dad's response, I brush my mom's hair, rearrange her blankets, change her woolly socks, and run a load of laundry. It's sweat-through-your-shirt-while-standing-in-the-shade weather, but my parents' room feels like a cave and my mom is always shivering.

My phone vibrates.

> Don't worry, Yam.
> Go to Tiya's.
> I'll be home in a few hours and we can talk.
> Love you.

I hold my mom's hand for one more minute. Then I grab a jacket because before Danny died, my mom would have pestered me to bring one, even in the summer.

Mrs. Duverne kisses both my cheeks, then gathers me in her arms and pulls me into her bosom. She smells like warm bread and ripe mangoes, and I sink into her like she's made of pillows. "Let me look at you, cherie, come here," she says, cupping my face. "How you doin', May?"

I burrow deeper into her arms and she squeezes me hard. Then she yells, "Tiya Marie! May is here! Get her some food!"

Tiya's feet clatter down to the kitchen as she belts out "On My Own" from *Les Misérables*. She's wearing basketball shorts and a big Warriors T-shirt that she stole from Marc. "Singing isn't going to get you into college, Tiya Marie. Get your head out of the clouds." Mrs. Duverne throws up her arms. "Didn't I tell you to get May's plate ready?"

"I'm getting it ready, Maman!" Tiya calls from the kitchen.

"Sorry we didn't wait to eat together," Mrs. Duverne says, shaking her head as we walk toward the kitchen. "Dr. Duverne got called back to the hospital, so we ate real quick before he left."

"It's okay. Thanks for saving me some food," I say, mouth watering. Tiya hands me a heaping plate and I inhale it all. "This is amazing, Mrs. D."

"I'll teach you how to cook, cherie." Mrs. Duverne sucks her teeth and cuts her eyes at Tiya. "I've given up on this one. She can't cook for nothing."

"I can make rice!" whines Tiya, grinning at me and ducking as her mom's hand flashes lightning fast to whack the back of her head. Mrs. D has a degree from Harvard Business School and used it to start a popular catering company back in the day. I heard she almost opened her own restaurant but put those plans on hold when she had kids. She put catering on the back burner when Marc and Tiya were younger, and now she picks and chooses the gigs she wants. Mrs. D plants a kiss on my forehead as Tiya hauls me upstairs.

Tiya's room is draped with white Christmas lights that hang over walls covered in a mosaic of color. Magazine pictures of places she wants to travel one day, photos, pieces of fabric, beads, ticket stubs, receipts, anything that reminds her of her dreams, she tacks onto her wall. Pictures of activists are mixed in with everything else. She's got pictures of Maya Angelou, Yuri Kochiyama, Dolores Huerta, Tommie Smith, and the three founders of Black Lives Matter: Alicia Garza, Patrisse Cullors, and Opal

Tometi. Tiya made me learn their names when she put up the magazine cover with their photo.

She has a huge poster of Audra McDonald, the "goddess of Broadway" according to her, and another poster that says, *The hottest places in hell are reserved for those who, in times of great moral crisis, maintain their neutrality.* Her walls are a haphazard, colorful, layered canvas of patterns that make perfect Tiya sense.

"You survived the first week back, Mayday," Tiya says as soon as we shut her bedroom door. She sits at her desk and doesn't waste any time with small talk. "How do you feel?"

I sit on her bed and grab a fluffy pillow. "I don't know. Like a machine?"

"What do you mean?"

"I'm handling my stuff. I'm functioning, getting it done, you know?

"But . . ."

"No buts. That's it."

"So, you're saying you feel nothing about coming back to school after Danny . . . ?"

"I can't go there, or I won't be able to do all the things I need to do."

Tiya eyebrows pull together. "That doesn't sound healthy, Mayday."

"What's healthy about any of this?" I squeeze the pillow in my hand.

Tiya thinks for a moment before she responds. "You know there were grief counselors at school after it happened. We had groups and presentations and all that, like we did after Christian and Becca and the others died by suicide. But the school stepped it up even more after Danny—"

"He's the fifth—"

"Yeah, in eighteen months. Christian and Becca from our school, the senior and alum from Los Arboles High. People are starting to call it an epidemic, and they're freaked out. Plus, it was *Danny.* So the school did a lot. Kids could leave class and talk to someone if they wanted. A lot of kids talked to those counselors. I talked to a counselor." She reaches up and pats her hair. "It was really helpful, Mayday. You should think about talking to someone."

I shake my head. I'm barely holding it together as it is. The thought of unbuttoning my heart for a stranger and wading back through the darkness sounds unbearable.

"It was helpful, Mayday, I swear. Marc talked to someone too."

"He did?"

"Yeah, girl. Danny was like our brother too. We were at the party that night. What if we could have stopped him?"

I've asked myself that same question every day for months: What if I could have stopped him? I feel like there is so much I didn't know. I haven't had the courage to ask about the party yet, and here's an opening I can't ignore. The words leave my mouth haltingly. "Tiya . . . what . . . happened . . . that night?"

Tiya sighs and looks around her room. "To be honest, Mayday, everything I know I heard from Marc. I was over there dancing with Ayanna and Mikayla, and he was with Danny. I wasn't paying those boys any attention."

I lie down on the bed as she keeps talking. "Next thing I know, Marc was grabbing my arm asking if I've seen Danny. I guess D was drinking a lot more than normal, then he said he was going to the bathroom and never came back. We tried calling, but it went straight to voice mail. I think he turned off his phone."

"And that's when you texted me."

"Yeah. I'm so sorry, Mayday."

"You didn't do anything wrong," I say. "It's not your fault."

"We should have stopped him from leaving."

I shake my head, but there are nights I can't stop the should-haves from barreling through my own mind. They screech back and forth on the same worn tracks. I should have made him stay home. I should have made him talk to me more about Stanford. I should have gone to the party with him.

I should have taken care of him the way he took care of me.

Would he still be here if I had done those things?

"You know I haven't cried since it happened, Tiya? I just get mad all the time."

Tiya treads carefully with her words. "I know you were mad at Marc on the first day of school. But you gotta know, Marc's having a hard time, Mayday. He has nightmares. When he's asleep, he screams for Danny to come off the tracks. He blames himself for everything."

"He is? He does? But he was laughing and acting like everything was fine."

"Well, yeah. Fake it till you make it, right?" She moves my

backpack to the edge of her desk and lines it up perfectly with hers. "But he hasn't made it yet."

I chew on this new information. "I need to apologize."

"Don't worry about that big meathead. He's not holding grudges." She comes over and wraps her arms around me. "The grief counselors said anger is normal. They said healing is messy. Marc's the least of your worries. He's not going anywhere."

"How are you so wise? You're only like two months older than me, but you talk like a grandma."

Tiya shimmies her shoulders. "I got you, Mayday. If you want, we can go find Marc. He worries about you. He doesn't like being shut out." She stands up and walks to her bedroom door and grins. "He's nosy like that."

Marc can't suppress a smile when he sees my contrite-looking face poke around the door. "Marc?" I ask a little nervously before Tiya shoves me into the room and follows right behind. "I'm s—"

"Aye, come here, May." He sets down the book he was reading faceup with the pages open—he's always reading something—stands up, and pulls me into a hug the way his mom did. But he's not made of pillows like she is. He's all lean basketball muscle. Hugging him is like finding the perfect avocado—firm and a little soft without being squishy. That sounds weird, but whatever. It's true.

"I am sorry for getting mad, though, Marc," I say midhug. "I just . . . I don't know . . ."

"I get it, May." Marc steps back and looks into my eyes like he's reading the mess behind them. "I should have been more thoughtful. Bringing you back to Danny's spot on your first day was probably too much."

"It wasn't that; it's just, you seemed so . . . so . . . like you're doing just fine."

"Oh, that part. It's day by day. I gotta take it one day at a time."

"Fake it till you make it, right?" I wrap my arm around Tiya's.

"But I haven't made it yet." He looks at me, and just beyond the glisten on the surface of his eyes, I can see there is an ocean that feels a lot like mine.

"What did I say?" Tiya plops down on Marc's bed and pulls me next to her. Marc's room is the opposite of Tiya's. Everything is on a monochrome grayscale color palette with wooden accents. His bed is perfectly made, and the only thing on his wall is a photo collage of five framed pictures that hang at perfectly right angles and are spaced exactly 1.76 inches apart. The pictures are of the Duverne family, Marc and Danny in their middle school basketball uniforms, Marc and Tiya making goofy faces, the four of us at the beach, and Marc holding up an award. Some kind of plant with vertical leaves stands against a wall. Despite the precision and muted colors, his room feels warm and inviting.

"What are you two doing tonight?" Marc asks abruptly. He slides a bookmark between the pages of his book and snaps it closed. His bookmark is shaped like a fist.

"That was a smooth subject change if I've ever heard one," Tiya snorts.

"No one's ever accused me of being smooth"—he cocks

his head—"except on the court."

"We're probably just hangin' here, watching movies," says Tiya. "We could watch a Pixar movie if you want to chill with us."

Marc taps his finger on his mouth. "Tempting, very tempting. But I heard people are going to Josh McIntyre's tonight. His dad's out of town and they have a big ol' house up in the hills. Isn't he a junior? You know him?"

Tiya gives me a quick side-eye. "Yeah, he's in our American Lit class."

"I was gonna go with some of the guys. Come with us."

Tiya looks over at me. "We could stay here and watch movies with my mom. Or we could go dance a little."

"I dunno," I say. "I *like* watching movies with your mom."

"Up to you."

"Come," Marc says. "I'll drive you home as soon as you want to leave."

Tiya asks me with her eyebrows. "Maybe it will help take your mind off everything. Dancing always makes you feel better."

I consider this new proposition. I haven't gone out since it happened, and I've never been to a party without Danny. Sometimes we went together and sometimes he showed up later with his friends, but he was always there to watch out for me. But Tiya's right; dancing *does* make me feel better. It's like writing, but with my body. Plus, I will probably always regret the last time I said no to a party. "Fine," I decide. "Just for a little."

Marc smiles and starts gathering his things. Tiya says, "He needs us there because we make it fun, Mayday."

I smile, then turn away so she won't see the creases on my forehead.

I can do this. I can go to a party without my brother.

And if I can't . . . well.

I guess that's what alcohol is for.

21

Josh lives in Sequoia Hills, the super-rich neighborhood above Sequoia Park that is, obviously, up in the hills. His house is enormous. It is surrounded by trees at the top of a driveway that winds into a curved loop. It occurs to me that anyone with a driveway this extravagant is really flaunting their money; I could probably fit the floor plan of my entire house in Josh's driveway, which isn't saying much, but it says something.

My parents bought our little house almost twenty years ago; they could never afford to buy it now. Housing prices blew up when giant tech companies moved to the area. I've heard my parents complain that even people with decent jobs at those tech companies live in trailers on the street. My family feels like we're barely scraping by on my mom's engineer salary and my dad's teaching one, but we stay because the public schools are supposedly some of the best. An outhouse around here could sell for a bajillion dollars, so Josh's house is really next level.

We walk up the driveway past people milling around the front yard in various states of intoxication. Couples pull away from larger groups and find their way into the shadows. People laugh too loudly at each other's drunken antics. The football players manning the front door clasp hands with Marc and pull him into quick chest bumps. One of them does a nearly imperceptible double take when he sees me and says, "Haven't seen you out in a minute, May." He nods toward Tiya. "The dance floor's not the same without you two."

"We better get down there, then." Tiya laughs as we start down the hall. She's wearing a cropped T-shirt with some skinny jeans and walks in like she owns the place.

The other guy calls after us, "Cups in the kitchen! Drinks in the back!"

The house smells like beer, sweat, and weed won a wrestling match against an expensive candle. We squeeze by people hovering in the hallway and make our way through a raucous game of beer pong. Tiya grabs my hand and pulls me through the crowd as we follow the music to the outdoor patio. Everyone is too focused on their own socializing, flirting, drinking, mingling, and gossiping to spare a thought for me. I don't mind. The turned faces not paying attention to me feel different from the turned faces awkwardly avoiding me at school. I almost blend in here.

Sione Vainikolo and Wes Snyder, a couple of Danny's good friends from the team, call for Marc from across the room. Marc touches my arm lightly before heading over to find them. Sione is Tongan and Wes is white, and the school was always using pictures of Danny's little crew for flyers and publicity. They checked all kinds of diversity boxes for Sequoia Park High. If Danny was here tonight, he would probably be over there laughing and dancing. The thought squeezes air out of my lungs.

I tap Tiya's elbow and say over the music, "Cups in the kitchen."

"You sure? You don't need to drink, Mayday. We can just dance."

"C'mon." I pull her toward the beer.

We grab red plastic cups and fill them at the keg outside. I don't know how a bunch of high school students get kegs at a party, but around here there's always a way. Sometimes the parents hook it up for their kids. I can't imagine that. My parents would rather have all their fingernails pulled out with tweezers than see me drinking—my mom because she thinks good girls don't drink, my dad because he knows they do.

The beer tastes like pee. Not that I'd know how pee tastes, but the liquid in my cup tastes the way pee smells. I down my beer in gulps so the flavor doesn't linger.

"Damn, Mayday, chill," says Tiya when she looks over and realizes my cup is empty. She takes it and tosses it in the trash. "No more for you, lightweight. I'm cutting you off right now."

I feel the alcohol in my face before I feel it anywhere else. My eyes start to puff up and my cheeks flush. I don't think I've ever finished a whole beer, so it doesn't take much for me to feel that Asian glow. "I'm fine, Tiya. Let's dance."

The music thumps and vibrates through the air. We avoid the tangle of bodies in the middle of the dance floor and find a spot with a little room to breathe. We like to dance in the sweet spot between the center and the edge of the crowd, where we're in the group but there is still space to move. We don't dance for anyone but ourselves. And we really love to dance.

The first few songs warm up me up, and I step with the beat, shaking out the rust. Then the song changes, and whatever song comes on—it must be a new one because I don't recognize it—gets me going. Tiya starts to sing along, and her voice makes me smile. Ayanna and Mikayla join us—their families are friends with the Duvernes, and I think Tiya hung out with them more when I was home last year. I loosen up when we all dance together. I let the rhythm flow into my blood and work its way through my body. The beat winds into my muscles, like fingers running through hair. My hips, arms, legs, chest, toes, fingers, ears . . . everything is feeling it.

"Aaaaaayyyyyyyyye, Mayday!" calls Tiya as she dances next to me. We flow, vibing off each other's moves, letting the music conduct our bodies. People fade, the darkness fades, everything fades. The world around me disappears and I'm lost in the harmony between music and dance. I feel alive.

Happy.

As soon as I recognize the feeling, everything freezes. There shouldn't be space for happy in my heart. Guilt crashes over me and I feel sick to my stomach.

I motion that I'm taking a break and Tiya starts to follow, but I shake my head and yell over the music, "I'll be right back." I feel Marc's eyes on me as I break away from the dancing mass. He's like the *Mona Lisa*. His eyes follow me wherever I go, checking up on me.

I walk to the edge of the patio and take in the unreal view. The lights of the Bay twinkle in a glittering ribbon below Josh's house. I gaze into the distance and try to gather my thoughts. If I felt happy, does that mean I'm forgetting Danny?

I have to hang on to him.

Danny was at a party just like this the night he died. He drank more than normal. When he left the party, did he know it was goodbye? I'm here at this party—why didn't I go to that other one with him? Would he still be here if I had?

The questions assault me and I have to make them stop. I head back inside and grab a red cup from the kitchen. I fill it at the keg and hide in the crowd while I gulp down another beer. Then one more for good measure.

I don't want to worry Tiya, so I wander back inside the house and eventually end up in an unlit hallway. The world starts to tilt a little, so I lean against the wall and knock a picture askew. I freeze as the sundress girls walk past the hallway. I feel like I'm intruding somewhere off-limits and a don't-get-caught instinct kicks in. I shut my eyes like a little kid. If my eyes are closed, no one can see me.

"May? Are you okay?" A soft hand rests on my forearm. I open my eyes and Ava Prince's peachy-white face hovers in front of mine. Her hazel eyes are full of concern. I nod. "You sure?"

Ava and I were attached at the hip when we were in elementary school. I loved going to her house because her mom always prepared snacks for us while we played. She served homemade cookies, animal crackers, string cheese—all kinds of things I didn't eat at home.

Ava and I drifted apart in middle school when she became part of that sundress crew and I met Tiya, but we stayed friendly. She is involved in everything—student council, tutoring, fundraising for disaster relief, organizing protests about all kinds of things. I've always admired that about her.

I nod again at her question. "Jus' takingabreak." My words are a little smooshed together, but I wave her back to her friends. She looks at me with concern, pats my arm softly, and says, "I'm going to get you some water. Wait here." As she walks back toward the kitchen, she looks over her shoulder, eyebrows sitting heavy on her eyelids.

When she leaves, I stand up to straighten the picture I bumped. It is a framed image of a woman with golden curls tumbling over her shoulders. Light glows around her face as she kisses a swaddled baby. A smiling man embraces them from behind. This must be Josh and his parents. My eyes slide over to the next photograph: the three of them laughing, captured in an epic food fight with frosting smeared all over their faces. Josh must have been about six. The next image is of Josh and his father, a few years older, standing side by side in matching suits. There's one of Josh in middle school, posing in his football uniform. Josh and his dad at a fancy restaurant. Josh and his dad skiing in Tahoe. Josh and his dad golfing in matching Yale shirts. Josh and his dad lounging on a tropical beach.

The room starts to spin faster, and I stumble deeper into the hallway. I feel like I'm on one of those barf-inducing rides at Great America. There must be a bathroom down here somewhere. I need a good place to hide in case I have to empty my guts.

"May?"

I blink rapidly, trying to clear my vision as a face floats in front of me. I'm expecting Ava, but it's Josh. He asks, "Are you all right?"

"Mmfine, jush needed ab rake." I bump back into the wall.

He wraps his arm around me and holds me up. I let myself sag into him. "Yeah, me too. Do you need to sit down?"

In response, I lurch unsteadily forward and trip over his feet. He guides me into a room and helps me sit down on the bed. Somewhere beneath the woozy fog of my brain, a little red warning light blinks at me. *Proceed with caution.* I shake my head and the fog swallows up the signal.

Josh sits down next to me hesitantly. He seems just as out of his element as I am. After a couple minutes, he asks, "Do you need water?"

I nod and Josh disappears. I look around and make out football posters on the wall, trophies on a bookshelf, and a neat desk with a laptop placed perfectly in the center. This must be his room. I am sitting on Josh's bed. Danny would not approve of this AT. ALL.

But he is not here.

Sharp pain and anger bubble up with the thought. Why wasn't I enough to keep you here, Danny? The force of my anger surprises me. I fall back into the bed, sinking into the downy comforter. I curl onto my side, and my eye catches on the shoes neatly lined up against the wall. Each pair looks like it has never been worn and sits atop a pristine shoebox. Converse. Vans. Air Jordans. Nikes.

KT3s.

They are on top of a white shoebox just like the one Danny carried that night. Even here in Josh's room, galaxies away from my world, I cannot evade the black hole that is Danny's death. My acute awareness of his absence makes him present everywhere I turn.

Tap. Tap. There's a soft knock at the bedroom door.

Josh comes in with a glass of water and helps me sit up to drink it.

"Thanksh," I mumble, sinking back into the bed. My head feels so heavy. Josh lies down beside me and the moon floats through the shutters, casting a striped glow across his face. I close my eyes for a second but pry them open when he starts talking.

"How much did you drink, May?"

I hold up two or three wobbly fingers. I'm not entirely sure which.

"That's it? Dang, you really are a lightweight." He puts his hand on my forehead. "Your head spinning?"

I nod queasily. "Mm-hmm."

"You about to barf on my bed?"

I let my face sink deeper into his comforter. I rotate it back and forth. "Mmm-mmm."

"I hope not." The corner of his mouth turns up. "When I heard you came to the party tonight, I came looking for you. I've been wanting to talk to you." He shakes his head in disbelief. "But clearly you're in no condition to be talking."

Josh reaches over and lightly brushes the hair out of my face. His fingers are cool as he tucks a strand behind my ear. He says, more to himself than to me, "Another time . . . when you're not wasted. Right now, we gotta get you home, May."

He slides his right arm underneath me and steadies my head. He grips my waist with his left hand and gently begins to lift me upright. He is so close I can feel his breath evaporate into the air between us.

Slam! The door swings open and a glaring light floods the room.

"WHAT THE HELL, JOSH?" roars an angry voice.

22

Tiya barges into the room, grabs Josh by the shoulders, and throws him off the bed. It's possible that Josh rolled off on his own in shock, but everything is a blur and I can't tell. Tiya is half Josh's size, but her fury makes her seem twice as big with muscles to match. Marc pauses in the doorway, his face expressionless. He is *Mona Lisa* taking in the scene. Watching me.

I catch a glimpse of Ava holding a glass of water, hovering in the hallway a few feet behind Marc.

"What are you doing, Josh!?" Tiya is a tornado whirling around the room. She picks up my shoes. I don't remember slipping them off. She crawls up on the mattress, slings my arm over her shoulder, and bundles me off the bed. Marc is there, and he wraps his arm around me to steady my step. His hand grips my waist firmly. My face burns.

"Mayday, you reek. How much more did you drink?" Tiya mutters at me under her breath. Then she rounds on Josh. "SERIOUSLY, JOSH. HOW COULD YOU?"

"I was trying to help her, Tiya!" Josh's face is red and his hands are clenched.

"Help yourself into her pants, you mean! Don't you think she's been through enough?"

"For fuck's sake, Tiya, it's not like that!" says Josh. "I would never."

"Not like what, Josh? Not like trying to get with a girl who's probably too drunk to remember how she ended up in your room?"

Josh opens his mouth and closes it. He looks at me.

"Cat got your tongue?" Tiya steps closer to Josh, disintegrating him with her eyes. "I thought so."

"Tiya, c'mon. Let's get outta here." Marc's voice cools Tiya's protective wrath just as she is about to launch into another tirade. He does not acknowledge Josh.

My head feels so heavy. Do I really hold this thing up all day long? I must have neck muscles like Hercules because my dome weighs at least a million pounds. It rolls itself into the spot just under Marc's shoulder and stays put. As we walk by Ava, I hear her mutter, "I was looking for her, but I couldn't find her anywhere . . ."

Tiya responds, "Thanks for coming to get me, Ava."

Then she looks back at Josh and says, "We all know you've

liked her since forever, but this is all wrong. If she wanted to hook up with you, it would have happened some other way."

I lie across the back seat of Marc's car and close my eyes. Marc and Tiya have not spoken since we left the party. When I start to doze and my breathing slows, I hear Marc turn around to check on me. I keep my eyes closed.

"You should have followed her off the dance floor," Marc says sternly to Tiya.

"She told me not to. She said she'd be right back," says Tiya, her voice taut. "You should have gone after her when you saw her go back inside the house."

"Since when do you listen to drunk people?"

"She wasn't that drunk then. She only had one beer." Tiya sounds defensive.

"You know she's a lightweight."

"Well, why didn't *you* stop her when you saw her getting more?"

"I didn't see her go back in for more." Marc wipes his forehead with the back of his hand.

"Celeste told me she downed at least two more cups before going inside."

I groan before I can stop myself. Hearing Celeste's name makes me forget I was fake sleeping. Tiya mumbles, "Even when she's passed out, that name triggers her."

"Two more cups? Jesus. You have to be more responsible, Tiya. You should have kept your eye on her."

"Responsible? You're the one who talked us into going to the party, remember?" Lightning crackles dangerously through her hushed voice.

I peek through my eyelids. They are both sitting stiffly upright, staring straight ahead. Neither speaks for a few minutes.

"Clearly, it was a mistake," answers Marc softly. His hands grip the wheel tightly as he maneuvers the car down the winding road.

"Not at first," says Tiya, her lightning extinguished by Marc's remorse. "She seemed happy, like herself again. I don't know what happened. One minute she was tearing it up on the dance floor. The next, she was gone."

Marc puts on the blinker. "I saw her checking out the view, but I didn't see her back at the keg."

"It's not like her, that's why. It never even crossed my mind that she'd be with . . . you know."

Marc hesitates before asking, "Does she like him?"

Tiya looks over at Marc, like she's seeing him for the first time. "No," she says firmly.

Marc noodles on this as he drives. We're out of the hills and driving back through Sequoia Park when Marc jerks the car to a stop. *CLANG! CLANG! CLANG!* The red lights of a crossing gate flash through the car windows, and moments later a train passes by. I feel the rumble of every wheel turning over the tracks like slow-motion earthquakes tearing me apart.

The gates lift and our car bumps over the rails. The three of us exhale in unison after we cross.

"Sorry I got mad," Tiya whispers. "It's just when I couldn't find her, I couldn't stop thinking, what if May went to the tracks . . . ?"

"I know, sis. Me too." Marc squeezes Tiya's hand.

"She never would have gotten so wasted before. She never would have ended up in that room before . . . it's not like her."

"I know." Marc sighs. "I know."

"I'm worried about her."

"Me too."

Suddenly, it gets harder to breathe and I need to get out of the car. I don't want to be *that* person—the one everyone's whispering and worrying about behind her back. I don't want to be a burden on anyone else.

Marc reaches over and tugs Tiya's ear, their gesture of a thousand words. They do it when they're mad (more a yank-and-twist than a soft tug). They do it when they play. They do it when they show affection.

A jealous pang tightens my heart and I hug my knees.

I miss my big brother.

23

How you feeling?

Headache

😫

But better

Thanks for getting me last night

Josh is on my shit list forever

Why?

What do you mean why?

He tried to hook up with you

He didn't

He was trying to get me home

Hot girl he's liked forever passed
out on his bed?

I don't buy it

82

He didn't need to be all up
on you to do that

Someone could profess undying
love to your face and you wouldn't
know he was trying to get with you

I mean . . .

When people are constantly
professing their undying love
you stop noticing

But seriously

He was trying to help me get
home

You keep telling yourself that

He's still on my shit list

Fine

You gonna tell your dad?

Heeeelllllli no

It would just make more
problems

Not worth it

You're worth it

Love you

I'm picturing Mr. Chen pulling
up to Josh's with a bat

Shut up

83

24

My parents and I slip into the gym and sit by the door. The bustle of people moving around the room, exchanging greetings, and finding seats allows us to slip in mostly unnoticed. My mom is wrapped in a shaggy brown coat shaped like an upside-down paper bag. She looks like she's geared up for a snowstorm. My dad, more appropriately dressed for the late-September weather in khakis and a blue short-sleeved button-down, is sitting beside her with his hand in her lap. My mom grips his fingers tightly, and together, they seem to press themselves into the walls. My dad has a clear view of the room, and the door provides a quick escape, if needed. Old habits die hard.

Tiya flaps her hand at me to get my attention and points to her phone. She wants to text during the meeting.

I show my parents Tiya's last text and point her out across the room. My parents look up and Tiya is waving at them with a huge smile on her face. The right corner of my mom's mouth tilts upward briefly; I can't remember the last time I saw her do that, Tiya can work her magic on anyone.

Ms. Matthews, a tall white lady who wears Patagonia like a uniform, hurries by and spots my parents. She is Danny's old math teacher and one of our class advisors. She stops and grasps their hands, saying, "I'm so glad to see you here." My parents stand up, polite porcelain smiles painted on their faces. Then Ms. Matthews is off, troubleshooting last-minute technological issues before the meeting starts.

A low whisper ripples through the room when Josh and his father, Nathaniel McIntyre, a big-shot venture capitalist, walk in. According to Marc, people's dreams live and die by Mr. McIntyre. He decides which start-ups get funding and his choices affect technological innovation around the world. Or something like that. He's not a national household name or anything, but around here, he's a low-key celebrity.

As he walks in, Josh's eyes fly quickly around the room. A lady in a tight pencil skirt and flowy blouse motions to three empty seats beside her and Josh follows his father across the room. They sit next to pencil-skirt lady, just a few rows in front of Tiya and her family. Mr. McIntyre whispers something to

Josh, and they share a private chuckle. Ava walks across the room and sits next to them; Pencil Skirt must be her mom. Whoa, I totally didn't recognize her. She's lost like thirty pounds since I last saw her.

I heard Ava's parents got a divorce in eighth grade because her dad had an affair. That was after she started hanging with the sundress girls, so I only heard through hallway whispers and never asked her about it. Mr. McIntyre leans over and greets them familiarly. Ava says something that makes him laugh.

Josh shifts in his seat and spots me by the door. I look away. In English last year, Ms. Perez showed us a portrait by Picasso and had us journal about it. What did we think was going on in the painting? What did we think it meant? At the time, I had no freaking idea what to write; it just looked like a mixed-up face. Now when I see Josh, I feel like I'm that Picasso painting. I'm a bunch of mixed-up emotions thrown abstractly on canvas: a color block of embarrassment here, a stroke of gratitude there, a solid background of confusion behind everything else.

Celeste and her parents slide in the door and scoot into the open seats beside us just as Ms. Matthews and the other junior advisors start the meeting. My heart clenches when I see Celeste, perfect as always, even in a hoodie and leggings. I nod in greeting.

"Mic check. Mic check," begins Ms. Matthews as the microphone emits an earsplitting squeal. "Oops! Sorry about that! Thank you all for coming out to the Junior Jam. I'm Ms. Matthews, the lead junior advisor. With us tonight is the junior advisory team: Ms. Daniels, Ms. Chin, and Mr. Gonzalez. We are excited to get started."

Ms. Matthews opens the projector and bright slides appear on the portable screen. "Junior year can be an incredibly stressful time. College applications are just around the corner, and the Acronym Attack, as we like to call it, really hits hard: APs, GPAs, SATs, etc."

She moves the slides with her clicker. "We started holding the Junior Jam to help us get prepared for the coming year. It can be a real doozy. I don't need to tell you that the pressure to succeed at Sequoia Park High is unparalleled. We all want what is best for our kids . . ."

Blah, blah, blah . . . I assume this is more of the same mumbo jumbo we've been steeped in since elementary school, and I start tuning out. There are only so many different ways to tell kids to work hard because if you don't get into the right schools, your life is over. Teachers might not say it like that (though some parents might) but we all know what they mean. It's in the air we breathe. I glance to my left and see Celeste hunched over the polka-dotted notepad she always carries with her, scribbling away with a dark pencil. She *would* be taking notes right now.

Celeste catches me mean-mugging her notes and smiles sheepishly. She tilts the notepad and shifts her hand. She's drawn a mirror image of Ms. Matthews with the mic. My eyes widen in surprise. Celeste flips back one page and there's a funny carica-ture of a man snoring. She points to the left side of the gym and I see Alan Johnson's dad with his head tilted back, mouth open wide enough to be a cup holder. Poor Alan is simultaneously try-ing to cover his tomato-red face and poke his dad awake. Celeste and I share a silent giggle behind our hands.

I reach for her notepad and she passes it over. I start flipping through. It looks like she draws anything and everything: intri-cately detailed flowers, swirly loops, chubby animals, students in class, people eating ice cream, flying dragons, a laundry machine. I mouth to her, *This is amazing.* She smiles.

I start paying attention when Ms. Matthews passes the mic to Ms. Daniels, whose pink batik dress and matching hair wrap are giving her smile some competition in the brightness depart-ment. Ms. Daniels says, "As Ms. Matthews mentioned, we've noticed a pretty dramatic increase in anxiety, stress, and depres-sion in our students over the past few years. Especially after the tragic losses we've suffered in our community. We hope the Junior Jam can start a dialogue about supporting not just the academic achievements of our students but more importantly, their social-emotional and mental health as well."

This is not what I was expecting. I thought this would be another PowerPoint lecture about the massive checklist of things we need to do to prepare for college. Ms. Daniels begins leading us through a discussion protocol similar to ones we've used in her class. We turn our chairs to face our parents. Students and parents each get two minutes to answer several question prompts. No interruptions.

The first prompt for students is: What are you most proud of? Showing up to school in my underwear could not be more uncomfortable than this. I shuffle through my thoughts, trying to think of something, anything, to share. There was the time in first grade I found an abandoned baby squirrel and cried for three straight hours until my mom agreed to take me to the wildlife center with the furry creature in a box. I'm pretty sure I saved its life, but my mom was not pleased about the drive. In eighth grade, I got voted Easiest to Talk To. When I showed my mom the yearbook picture, she said, "What does it mean if you are the easiest to talk to? 没有意思，看。" She pointed at the picture of Celeste, who was voted Most Likely to Succeed, and said, "This is a good thing. Why didn't you win this one?"

Last year, Ms. Perez submitted a story I wrote to a local writing contest, and I won third place. I didn't bother telling my mom, but Danny called me Maxine Hong Kingston for a month and made all his friends read my story.

Ding! Ms. Daniels rings her chime and time is up. I couldn't think of anything to say.

"Great job in the first round!" Ms. Daniels calls, looking right at me. "Okay, parents and families, it's your turn. Your prompt is: What makes you proud of your child? The timer starts . . . now. Go!"

My dad coughs into his hand and my mom fidgets in her seat. Around us, parents gush like Yosemite waterfalls in the spring. Praise spills like snowmelt over parents' lips and I see tears in some of my classmates' eyes.

My mom's gaze lingers on my face as she studies me. I could be the answer to a prayer or have a cockroach crawling over my forehead; there's no way of telling from her expression. She asks, "Maybelline, why you didn't put on a jacket? It's cold outside."

I bite my lip and glance over at Celeste. She's scowling at her shoes. I look across the room at Tiya and she's frowning too. Her parents must be on her case about pursuing singing again. She wanted to audition for the school musical this year, but they wouldn't let her because it would be a distraction. I pull my phone out to text her as my mom continues softly, "你變瘦了。你吃不夠嗎?"

She's right. I've lost weight and I haven't been eating enough. Everything tastes like sand, especially the frozen meals I've been eating for dinner. Most nights, my dad comes home from teaching and we microwave food together. I scoop some on a plate for my mom and try to make it look fancy. I read somewhere that pretty food is more appealing and actually tastes better. It doesn't work on my mom, though. Like me, she barely touches anything.

My mom gets up, mumbles something I can't hear, then disappears from the room. She's no Yosemite waterfall in the spring. She couldn't even pass for a barely-there trickle of late summer. Any pride she feels about me, if it exists, is snow stuck in an eternal winter, frozen on the mountaintop.

My dad touches my knee and says, "She's trying, Yam. I know it's hard to tell, but she is."

I purse my lips. "It shouldn't be *that* hard to come up with ONE thing she's proud of, Bà."

He says, "You know one time I was proud of you?" I shake my head and he keeps talking. "You were three and Danny was five."

"The last time you were proud of me was when I was three years old?"

"Oh, come on, of course not. Just listen, will you?" He pauses, but when I look at him with a salty expression, he continues, "We were at a playground and I was watching you two play. You were at the top of a big slide and Danny was headed for the swings. A bigger kid ran in front of him, pushed him out of the way, and took the last open one. When Danny started crying, you shot down that slide before anyone could stop you, ran over, and shoved the big kid off the swing, yelling, 'That's my brother's!'"

I stare incredulously at my dad as he chuckles. "I did that?"

"You used to do stuff like that all the time."

"I did?"

He laughs and pats my knee again. "You were the most protective baby sister the world has ever known."

I process this information slowly. My dad takes my hand. "Yam, Danny was there when you needed him, but you were there for him too. He needed you too."

"I needed him more, Bà."

"You don't realize you made him stronger. It wasn't just the other way around."

A tear forms behind my right eye and I blink quickly. "Then I didn't do my part. I didn't make him strong enough."

My dad takes both my hands, and his voice cracks a little. "Look at me, Yam. It is not your fault."

I study the stitching on my yellow Converse. Bà and I sit in silence for a few minutes and miss all the other prompts from Ms. Daniels. Finally, I look at him and ask, "Did he get the swing?"

My dad claps his hands once and smiles. "You made sure he did!"

An angry screech from the microphone interrupts our conversation. Mr. McIntyre has somehow gotten ahold of the mic and is standing near his seat. "With all due respect," he begins in a tone that says *I respect no one*, "I think we've had enough of this touchy-feely stuff. If you ask me, we should cut right to the chase and address the real cause of all this so-called increasing anxiety."

The rest of the room holds its breath in anticipation. My mom chooses this moment to reappear in her seat; her eyes are red-rimmed and a little puffy. Mr. McIntyre continues, "If student anxiety and depression are on the rise, it doesn't have anything to do with my ability to talk with my son. Everyone knows that the real reason our kids are more stressed is because of all the Asians moving into our schools."

What the—

The angry embers that seem to always be in my chest roar into crackling, scarlet flames.

My phone starts buzzing in my pocket and I silence it. I see Tiya's fingers tapping furiously on her screen. The teachers are stuck to the ground in shock, eyes wide, mouths agape. Pencil Skirt and several other parents nod. Ava looks down at her feet and covers her face with her hands. Josh is frozen, staring through his father at the wall.

Mr. McIntyre is just getting warmed up. He says, "These Asian parents push their kids so hard. All they care about are good grades and Ivy League schools. Asian kids don't play sports. They don't have social lives. They're machines. Those parents put so much pressure on their kids that our kids can't compete. Of course stress and anxiety has gone up!"

Ms. Matthews grabs the microphone and says, "Now, Mr. McIntyre, I don't think—"

"He's right!" calls a parent from the other side of the room. "Our kids don't stand a chance against the Asians. That's why we're moving. It's too competitive here."

"N-now, Ms. Chambers . . . ," stammers Ms. Matthews. She's like a rag doll trying to control a bucking bull. She's about to go flying off. Around the room, heads nod more vigorously.

Ava looks up, eyes wide, when her mom stands up and says, "Asian parents send their kids to Chinese School on Friday nights. Friday nights! They all play the piano and do extra homework over the weekends and summer. I heard there's a Chinese girl in this class who already got an internship at Google. I mean, it's ridiculous. These tiger moms and dads are making life harder for all of us. Let's stop beating around the bush and call it what it is." She puts her hand on Mr. McIntyre's shoulder and smiles at him. He reaches up to squeeze her hand and smiles back. "Thank you for speaking up, Nate."

Some people start clapping. Uncle and Auntie Wu bow their heads and Celeste's eyes have turned to steel. I can practically see the smoke coming out of Tiya's ears.

Mr. McIntyre stands up again. "You want to talk about 'the tragic losses we've suffered in our community'? Everyone knows we're talking about the suicides. There's been five in the year and a half just between the two high schools in Sequoia Park. This never used to be a problem before. It only started happening when Asian families moved in. We all know that last year, some Asian kid got into Princeton and then killed himself on the tracks. I mean, come on. What did his parents say to him? If Princeton isn't good enough for these people, then what is?"

The color drains from Josh's face, leaving him ashen. He looks at me with desperation and I stare back, flinging fireballs at him with my eyes. His dad says, "Everyone is too worried about being politically correct, but I'm not afraid to say that the Asians are the real problem here. I know most of you are thinking it too."

The flames in my chest erupt violently upward. I'm ready to haul ass across the room and punch Mr. McIntyre in the face.

Then I see my parents.

The fragile facade they've worked so hard to piece together has collapsed beneath the blame and accusations hurled their way. They look like they're about to crumble to pieces on the concrete floor.

I need to get them out of here.

I pull my parents to their feet and my legs nearly buckle when they both lean on me. We step forward and shuffle slowly out the door. One foot at a time, with everyone's eyeballs glued to our backs.

How dare he talk about my parents and my brother that way? Just when my mom has worked up the strength to get out of bed. What will this do to her? I begin shaking at the thought and my ball of fury grows, but I can't focus on it right now. I need to get my family home. I tamp down the flames leaping inside . . . for now.

25

My parents wrap themselves in silence. It swaddles their thoughts and binds their bodies in wide, tight strips. I lead them upstairs to their room.

I help my mom change into pajamas and ease her into bed. I tuck the comforter tightly around her body, mummy-style, the way she used to do it when I was small. I kiss her forehead. My dad shuffles out of the bathroom in his furry, old-man bathrobe. Danny and I gave it to him for Christmas four years ago and he wore it so much it got embarrassingly thin. Earlier this year, Tiya and Marc were over and Dad came downstairs in that thing; Danny popped off the couch so fast he knocked over his Gatorade, hollering, "Whooooaa, Bà, PG only down here! Bring the peep show back up the stairs!" Danny hustled Dad to his room, using his body as a shield. We forbade him from ever wearing it in front of our friends again.

I remember that night Danny had a hard time choosing which movie we should watch. We all assumed it would be a Star Wars marathon, but for some reason, he couldn't decide between Star Wars and something else. We made fun of his sudden indecisiveness because with Danny, Star Wars was a given.

"Bà, are you okay?" I ask hesitantly.

He walks me to the door and rubs my back. He says, "Let's talk later, Yam." Then he closes the door gently behind me.

When I get to my room, I throw myself into bed and skim through Tiya's live texts from the Junior Jam.

What the hell!?

What just came outta his mouth?!

I'm about to reach over and grab the mic

Or maybe I'll just sock him in the jaw

That'll shut him up

Oh really? Asian parents push their kids too hard?

Pretty sure you had Josh in football camp as soon as he learned to walk

But Asians are the problem here

Riiigght . . .

Ms. Matthews needs to shut
this down

Grow a backbone, woman!

Oh, Ava's mom got something
to say now?

Ava's got private tutors for ACT
and SAT prep

And math

And English

Not to mention year-round sports
clubs

And student council

But Asians are the tiger parents

Okaaayyy

WHAT THE @#&$*! did he just say

That racist dirtbag doesn't know shit
about your family

Mayday

Check your parents

Forget that fool

Text me as soon as you can

Love you

Her live texts rekindle the anger I tamped down when we left
the meeting. I replay the whole thing, feeding the flames with
words and phrases that are now seared in my mind.

Asians are the real problem.

They're machines.

Tiger moms and dads.

They . . .

They . . .

They . . .

Some Asian boy got into Princeton and then killed himself . . .

Some Asian boy.

His name was Danny.

I grab my notebook and start scribbling, but the words are rushing out faster than I can write. I open my laptop and let the rage flow through my fingers. They fly over my keyboard. That man doesn't get to talk about my parents like that. He doesn't get to desecrate Danny's memory.

I write and write and write until the crackling red flames wane into pulsing embers. I look it over and make some revisions. On impulse, I paste the whole thing into an email. Then I look up the contact info for the *Sequoia Park Weekly* and put it in the recipient box. Just as my finger hovers over the send button, I hear my bedroom door creak on its hinges. "Yam? You still up?" asks my dad.

His shoulders are stooped, and white patches pepper his once-jet-black hair. He looks decades older as he pads into my room in the fluffy hotel slippers he snagged on our last family trip.

"Hey, Bà. You should go to sleep," I say.

"I couldn't sleep."

"Me either."

"Yam, what that man said. Do you think . . . Does everyone think . . . ?" My dad can't finish his sentences.

"Of course I don't think that. No one who matters thinks that. It's like you told me earlier, it's not your fault, Bà. It's not Ma's fault."

He says, barely audibly, "That's what they told me about Joe too."

"What do you mean?" I have no idea what he's talking about.

My dad exhales and sits on the edge of my bed. He bunches the yellow comforter in his fists. I pat the back of his hand, and he seems to remember I'm still here. He says, "I just don't understand. There weren't any signs. At least, none that I ever noticed. It came out of nowhere."

He squints as he flicks on my reading light, then turns it back off. "I've been thinking maybe Danny was depressed, Yam. I think maybe he hid it from us, and we never realized." His voice cracks and he presses the heels of his hands to his eyes. "Or maybe we didn't want to realize. What if . . . What if that man was right?"

"No, Bà. Mr. McIntyre knows nothing. He was wrong about everything and especially about us." I mean what I say, but something in my dad's words brings up other memories about Danny. The random days he'd lock himself in his room. A few nights when he didn't feel like eating dinner. The days he slept in later than usual. His face that night when he told me about Princeton, then Stanford.

On their own, these don't seem like a big deal, but do they paint a different picture when I put them all together? How could I have known?

How could I have *not* known?

I wrap my arms around my dad; they feel too small and weak to hold up the ghosts and burdens weighing him down. My arms are overcooked spaghetti noodles trying to support the sun. But they're better than nothing. "*All* those people at the Junior Jam were wrong. Every single one. Don't think about what any of them said, Bà. Promise?"

He squeezes my biceps and smiles. "You been working out, Mèi-Mei? When did you get so strong?"

"I've always been ripped, Bà. Don't change the subject. Promise me."

"Okay, I promise. But you promise me something too."

"What?"

"Promise you won't do anything. No shooting down a slide and shoving the bully off the swing this time." He pats my arm. I glance quickly at the email open on my laptop. "Before she fell asleep, your mom asked me to talk to you. Let's let it go and move on. She can't . . . I can't handle . . . It's just too much."

I squeeze my dad again and rest my head on his shoulder.

The silence stretches between us, a canoe filled with promises we can't keep.

26

Silence is the space
    between my mom and me—
    a chasm
    over which we throw words
    that make the distance
    wider.

It is the smile
    with a crooked dimple to the side
    that hid my brother's pain
    so well
    it strangled him
    while we watched.

Silence is a bow
so low
our foreheads touch the ground
in submission
under the heels of powerful men
and their lies.

It is a blanket
we pull over our heads
to hide from the world—
where difficulty breathing
is the price we pay
for an illusion
of safety.

My parents want me to be silent.
But

Silence is death.

Forgive me, Ma.
Forgive me, Bà.
I cannot be silent.

27

I hit send.

28

When she was twenty-two, my nǎi-nai left her elderly parents and swam through the shark-infested waters of Dàpéng Bay to flee the horrors of the Cultural Revolution and beatings from the Red Guards. Nǎi-Nai didn't have papers to leave China, and if she could make it to Hong Kong there were no jobs for her. She was too old to enroll in school, too illegal to find a job, too female to be hired into manual labor. A distant relative in Hong Kong arranged a marriage for her with a Chinese man from America who was looking for a wife. Staying in China meant humiliation and death, so her family sent her off to find a better life. This was her only way out.

But she had to get to Hong Kong first.

Nǎi-Nai kicked and paddled her way across four miles of treacherous water, clutching a basketball as a flotation device.

A moonless midnight offered cover from the soldiers guarding the border but could not mask the gasps and screams of people drowning or being attacked by sharks. She kept her eyes forward, knowing that if she turned them to either side, fear would overwhelm her. Nǎi-Nai never stopped kicking her feet even after they went numb with exhaustion. When she pulled herself onto the Hong Kong shore, she collapsed and kissed the ground.

In Hong-Kong, Nǎi-Nai met my yé-ye, her arranged husband. He was a restaurant worker in San Francisco's Chinatown. Unlike many men who spun tales of golden mountains to win their wives, he was honest about life in America. He told her that jobs were scarce, that he was poor, and that racist discrimination limited their opportunities. But these challenges seemed small in comparison to reeducation camps and shark-infested waters, so Nǎi-Nai sailed with him across the ocean.

My nǎi-nai was a badass. They could make a movie about her life and all her badassery. But they won't. At least they won't do it right. If Hollywood made a movie about her life, she'd be some submissive, silent babe in a qipao, too weak to hold her own chopsticks. In their version, she might have some dope kung-fu skills (mostly so they could show more leg), but she'd need some buff white dude to come and rescue her from everything. Even herself.

Thing is, anyone who thinks Asian women are submissive and silent has never truly known one. Asian women are matriarchs of the earth.

Nǎi-Nai came to California with just the clothes on her back. She traded her tore-up shoes for some meat and flour while Yé-Ye salvaged old pots and nicked spices from the restaurant where he worked. Somehow Năi-Nai turned their meager ingredients into dumplings and sold them on the streets. She made enough to buy new shoes and her own food cart. Eventually, she was able to open a small dumpling shop. She and Yé-Ye built a humble life in Chinatown with their two boys: my dad and my uncle Joe. Năi-Nai didn't just run the house; when she was alive, she was a neighborhood force.

Năi-Nai was fierce, but she's not the exception. She's the rule. If an Asian woman is silent, it's not because she's submissive; it's because she's watching. Watching and learning.

Like a warrior.

Today, the Monday after the Junior Jam, my mom put on a navy skirt with a ruffled hem, a cream-colored blouse, and a matching navy blazer. She combed her hair, dabbed some makeup on her face, reminded me to wear a jacket to school, and went back to work. She walked out the door, head high, like she'd been going all this time.

I watched her, my hand stalled in midair holding a knife loaded with peanut butter. A giant glop of brown goo splatted on the countertop before I realized my mouth was hanging wide open. Naturally, I texted Tiya.

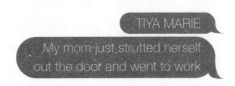

TIYA MARIE

My mom just strutted herself out the door and went to work

> Like it was nothing

What? What?

Did she say anything?

> Nope

Because of the Junior Jam?

> Yup.

> Like a big f-you, Nate McIntyre

> Only she'd never say that

👏👏👏, Mrs. Chen!

Good for her

Did she wear the upside-down
paper-bag coat

> Skirt, blouse, blazer, makeup!

Oh damn. She means business.

👏👏👏

Also, you have some explaining
to do.

> What? Why?

Check The Weekly.

A small sulfur pond burbles in my stomach. Did they actually print it? I open my laptop and find the website for the *Sequoia Park Weekly*, and there it is, just below a short article titled: "Silicon Valley Leader Spouts Anti-Asian Sentiment at Sequoia Park High School." The article outlines the purpose of the Junior Jam and its ensuing "discussion." My piece is printed in large font, just below the article.

HE'S NOT SOME BOY
By Maybelline Chen

"Some Asian boy got into Princeton and killed himself on the tracks," he said.

Some Asian boy.
> A talking point—
> not a life
> a person
> a brother
> a son
> worth honoring.

Some Asian boy.
> A wrapper
> tossed on the floor,
> a blemish
> on the sidewalk.
> > Expendable.

Some Asian boy.
> As if he didn't have friends
> and family
> sitting right there in the room,
> listening as he was
> thrown back onto the tracks
> again.

"What did his parents say to him? If Princeton isn't good enough for these people, then what is?" he said.

These people.

> As if my parents
> are aliens
> colonizing the land
>> like a couple white settlers
>> in America.

These people.

> As if the birth of their first child
> didn't restitch the seams
> on their souls
> and redefine love
> in their lives.

These people.

> As if my parents
> drove their firstborn child
> to the tracks
> and
>> killed him themselves.

"The Asians are the real problem here," he said.

The Asians.
  As if the entire community
  doesn't marinate
  its babies
  in Ivy League intentions.

The Asians.
  As if a little five-spice
  ruins chicken-noodle soup—
  like a few barbecue pork buns
  threaten
  your white bread life.

The Asians.
  As if rewriting
  my family's story
  absolves you
  of responsibility
  in this narrative.

I read it two, three, ten times, skimming the words like I'm watching strangers at Stanford Shopping Center. I can't believe I wrote this. I can't believe I sent it in.

I can't believe they actually published it.

What would Danny say? I think of the way he used to lean over my shoulder when I wrote essays. He would talk with a nasally English-teacher voice and ask me about diction and punctuation and say things like, "Now, what kind of evidence do you have to support that claim?" Sometimes, Bà would join in his for-real English-teacher voice and he'd add, "Vary that sentence structure. I'm not really seeing your thesis. What's the main point of this paper?"

Then, when I got up to use the bathroom or get a snack, Danny would type extra sentences into my assignment while my dad giggled with glee. If I was really rushed, I sometimes forgot to check my work before turning it in. Once, a paper I wrote about *Romeo and Juliet* came back with an entire paragraph about the feeding habits of hippos highlighted bright pink with a big question mark in the margins. When I showed Danny and my dad, they just looked at each other and cackled.

Would Danny call me Maxine Hong Kingston and make his friends read this? Or would he tell me I should have listened to Bà?

29

It's lunchtime and we sit in our spot under the hugging oak. The breeze chases its way through the oak tree's leaves, catches the hem of Marc's shirt, and ripples the cotton. Then it whips a strand of my hair until it sticks onto my lips.

Marc is lying on his side in the grass, wearing a *BLACK LIVES MATTER* T-shirt. He has one arm draped across his torso; the other props up his face. He watches me wrangle my hair into a flopping knot on top of my head.

"That hair is still stuck to your mouth, May," he says, grinning.

"Then why'd you watch her put it all up before you said something?" says Tiya, sucking her teeth. Today she's wearing a short denim skirt with a zip-up hoodie draped over her shoulders. Her T-shirt says *BLACK GIRL MAGIC* in big letters, and her hair frames her face in wide curls. "Useless. That's what you are."

"I wanted to see if she'd get it." Marc laughs. He turns back to me. "I mean, did you lose feeling in your lips, or what?"

"Or what, obviously," I say huffily as I dismantle the knot, shake out my hair, hook the wayward strand with my pinkie, and twist the mass back into place. "Tiya, did you finish that essay for AP History?"

"Ugh, barely. Stayed up until almost three a.m. writing that thing. Good thing nerd-boy over here was up working on calc and some college applications. He kept throwing stuff at my head or else I would have been snoring on my keyboard."

"Where are you applying, Marc?"

"A bunch of UCs, Harvard, Columbia, Penn, Howard, Morehouse, Florida A&M—" starts Marc.

"Is that a state school outside California?" I interrupt.

"It's an HBCU," explains Tiya as she picks a few blades of grass off her skirt.

"What's that?"

"Historically Black colleges and universities," says Marc. "I'd really like to go to one."

"Even if you got into Harvard, Penn, or Columbia? You'd go to an HBCU over an Ivy?"

"Definitely. Don't tell my parents, though."

"Why?" I scratch at a spot behind my ear. I've never heard him talk about college before and this is all news to me. In fact, getting into an Ivy or Stanford or Berkeley and choosing to go elsewhere feels like sacrilege around here. Especially if it's not for financial reasons, which it's not for the Duvernes.

Marc leans back on both hands and looks up into the branches of the hugging oak. He thinks a while before he asks, "Did you know my mom used to have one of the most popular catering businesses in the Bay?" I nod and he continues, "Did you know she put her career on hold when she had me and Tiya?"

I nod again. Marc looks at me. "Do you know why she did that? My parents could have hired an au pair or nanny or someone to help out."

"She told me it was because she wanted to spend time with her babies," I venture.

"Yeah. She did. But she wanted to be home so she could teach us. She started teaching me letters before I could walk. She would hold up a letter while I sat in a high chair and smeared food on my face. She'd practice with me until I remembered it, then she'd move on to the next letter. I knew how to read by the time I turned three."

"That's amazing, Marc. You really are a nerd-boy." I turn to Tiya. "You too?"

"Three *and a half*," says Tiya. "Don't let him rub it in."

"She was a slow learner," says Marc, immediately shielding his face with his arms as Tiya rips out a handful of grass and dirt and chucks it at him. "My mom did the same thing with math. She would teach us concepts using beans and old egg cartons. We thought we were playing, but she was getting us ready."

"Ready for what?"

"For school. She knew we had to start way ahead of the curve or else teachers would assume we were behind. She always told us, 'You need to be twice as good.'"

"I don't get it. What does that have to do with going to an HBCU?"

Marc says, "I want to go to college somewhere I don't need to be twice as good just so people don't think I'm slow. Somewhere where being Black isn't the only way other people define me." He sighs and shakes his head. "I want to blend in for a change."

I don't think Marc could blend in anywhere; he's just too . . . nerd-boy brilliant and perfect-avocado-built fine. But there's no way I'm saying *that* out loud. I'm horrified and embarrassed I thought it at all. I'm not sure how to respond, so I nod and let his words settle in. I've never talked with Marc or Tiya about being Black at Sequoia Park High School. Or about being Black. So I go with, "What will your parents say if you get in and don't go Ivy?"

Marc glances at Tiya, who stops unzipping her backpack and looks back at him quietly. I wonder what they're communicating back and forth in the space between us. "They won't be happy about it. They think an Ivy on my résumé is the only way. It's how they made it."

"But they didn't grow up in white spaces like we did," adds Tiya. "Marc wants to swim in different water for a change."

Marc nods. "I guess we'll worry about it if we need to in the spring, huh?"

"But what about—" I start before Tiya interrupts.

"Oh no no no you don't, Ms. Maybelline," says Tiya. "Don't try to weasel your way out of explaining today's *Weekly*. We want to talk about your poem. I didn't even know you wrote it."

I busy my fingers with my backpack, clicking and unclicking the straps. Danny used to buckle his chest strap when he wore his backpack. I'd laugh and say it looked like a backpack wedgie. He'd say it was better for his back. Eventually, everyone at school started buckling their chest straps too. "I don't even know what to say, Tiya Marie. I wrote it the night of the Junior Jam. That was two weeks ago."

I keep clicking and unclicking until I remember I brought rice with ròusōng for lunch. The label on the round ròusōng container translates it as "meat floss" and I really think someone needs to update English translations of Chinese food terms. I mean, "meat floss"? That sounds disgusting. But it's not. It's delicious, fried, shredded pork.

"I was mad. I didn't really think it through. I didn't think they'd actually publish it." I pull out my rice and the box of strawberry Pocky I grabbed off the kitchen counter. I add, "By the way, are you two matching on purpose today?"

Tiya rolls her eyes. "For the record, I was dressed first. He copied me."

"I didn't even see your shirt until we got to school. You had your hoodie on," retorts Marc. "This is my mood today, that's all."

"Why?" I ask with a bit of rice in my mouth.

"Haven't you been following little André Johnson's story?"

I shake my head. Marc offers me a bite of his lunch and says, "You should come to our BSU meeting tomorrow. We're gonna finalize plans to protest this weekend."

"What happened?" I offer Marc a Pocky.

Tiya and Marc look at each other. "He's the Black kid the police shot outside the midtown 7-Eleven last week," says Marc.

"Did he steal something?"

Tiya cocks her head at me and narrows her eyes. "*That's* your first reaction? He was a little kid, Mayday."

"And no, he didn't steal anything," adds Marc curtly.

"Then why'd they shoot him?"

"Are you serious, May? Since when do they need a reason?" Tiya snaps. She and Marc both look hard at me for what feels like an eternity.

"Since when is it okay to shoot a child for *any reason*?" Marc says with a heavy sigh. "He had a big backpack is all."

"I don't get it. Why would the police shoot someone over a backpack? There must be a reason the police were there."

"They were there because some rich white lady called the cops on a fourth grader, May. It's been all over the news," says Marc. "It's not like this is new."

His words drop through the air with a finality I don't really understand, and Tiya looks away. It's clear they both have a lot more to say, but neither of them wants to discuss this with me anymore.

A few long minutes pass before Tiya says slowly, "Let's talk about that another time. I can't today. Bring it back to the *Sequoia Park Weekly* and the Junior Jam. We weren't done with that yet."

"I wish I had been there," says Marc. "I would've said something."

"I'm glad you weren't there *because* you would've said something. It would have blown up into a whole other kinda mess and you know it. I'm not trying to wear a T-shirt with your name in a hashtag, Marc Duverne. You don't need to be next," says Tiya, and she tugs at the hem of her skirt. They do that sibling ESP again where the silence between them becomes a private thought conductor.

Marc reaches over and tugs her ear as he nods in understanding. "Well, someone had to check him. If he's saying stuff like that *in public* about 'the Asians,' what the hell does he think in private?" He chews on his Pocky stick, strawberry side first. Then he waves his free arm in the air for emphasis. "How many Asian-run companies do you think he backs? I bet not very many. And if he feels like that about 'the Asians,' can you imagine what he says about Black folks?"

"That's what I said to Ayanna! It's always the supposedly liberal places that are the most racist," Tiya cuts in.

"Seriously. How many companies started by 'the Blacks' do you think McIntyre funds? Probably none," adds Marc.

"Why do you care who he funds?" I ask.

"Why *don't* you care, Mayday?" Tiya cuts in. Her usual joking tone is all the way gone. "Who Nate McIntyre funds determines the future of technology and affects people all over the world. Plus, your mom is an Asian woman who works in Silicon Valley. Do you think she's getting a fair shot with people like him in charge? Ayanna's mom says she's the only Black person left on her team because the other three Black folks quit within a year."

As I'm trying to wrap my head around what she's saying, Marc says, "My dad's dream is for me to start my own company one day, and it's practically impossible to get funding as a Black man in Silicon Valley. On top of that, people who look like me have to worry about getting shot at 7-Eleven . . . or walking down the street, or trying to get into our own homes, or just sleeping in our own beds."

Tiya taps Marc with her foot. "Another time. I really can't today." Marc nods at his sister and says quietly, "I know. I'm sorry, T."

"Is starting a company in Silicon Valley your dream too?" I feel like I missed something, and my question feels out of place now.

"It's my dad's dream," says Marc. His fingers brush my arm as he reaches for another Pocky. I hand him the box, suddenly aware of the tingling on my skin.

I rub my arm as Marc catches my eye with his steady gaze. "All we're trying to say is that it's good you spoke up. You should do it more. If Danny were here . . ." His voice trembles like a car going too fast on the highway. He pulls it back, reining himself in from his uncharacteristic outburst. "If Danny were here, he woulda given you a spike drop."

I think back to freshman year, when I watched Danny and Marc shoot around with some guys after school. During one play, Sam Fletcher drove the ball toward the net and went up for a shot. As the ball rose, Danny leaped and swatted it away from the hoop. Danny's teammate, Miguel Rosas, snatched the ball, crossed over left then right, head-faked, and passed the ball back to Danny, who had somehow gotten open behind the three-point line. He caught the ball and shot it in one swift motion. *Swish.* The ball never even touched the rim.

I remember the jubilant *Oooooooooooh!*s of his teammates as Danny did a slow-motion spin, raised his arm above his head, and made an exaggerated mic-drop motion as Miguel and Marc clapped him on the back. That was the day Danny's mic-drop meter was born.

After that play, Danny mic-dropped anything that made his eyes pop with approval: witty trash-talking, a funny joke, delicious food, a well-reasoned argument. He had his own increasing scale of mic-drops, from the tiny, two-fingered mic drop—for making fun of me or for stuff that was "all right"—to a full-fisted mic drop to the ultimate: the spike drop. The spike drop was when he pretended to slam a mic into the ground—reserved, as he said, "only for mind-blowing awesomeness."

"A spike drop? You think so?" Doing something to earn one of those makes me smile, even now.

"Yeah, I do." Marc lies back in the grass, his leg an inch from mine.

"Marc's right, you know, Mayday. Someone had to check Mr. McIntyre," says Tiya quietly, which makes my goose bumps sit up again. She's absentmindedly helping herself to a spoonful of my lunch. "He has a lot of power. When someone like him is openly racist, other people think it's okay to be that way too. You heard the rest of the fools at that meeting."

"What they said was hella messed up, but I already wish I hadn't sent it in." I eat another bite of rice and ròusōng. "When we got home from the Junior Jam, my dad specifically told me not to say anything, and clearly, I didn't listen."

Tiya reaches for my hand. She does it without thinking, curling her fingers between mine, like we're sisters. "All I'm saying is speaking up isn't a bad thing. You're the best person to step to Mr. McIntyre after the Junior Jam."

"In the moment, all I could think about was defending my family. I thought it was the right thing to do." I rub my forehead and think of the expression on my dad's face when he asked me to let this go. "Now I'm afraid this will just hurt them more." I want to crawl back into my cave of silence—the one usually reserved for fights with my mom—and wipe my little excursion beyond its walls from memory.

The breeze has paused and the leaves are still. The world holds its breath, watching me. I hate that feeling; it makes me want to hide in the shadows behind the tree.

"You can't let fear trap you into silence, May. You'd regret it more than anything else," Marc says. "Nothing will change if you don't speak up."

The problem is, I responded to Nate McIntyre to defend my family. I never really thought through what I was trying to change. I am not sure I really know.

30

I'm walking from physics to English when a shoulder smacks into mine and whirls me around. Instinctively, my right hand flies up to the throbbing area, and my face begins arranging itself into a don't-worry-about-it smile as I see Alvin Lo's black North Face backpack disappear around the English building. He didn't even turn around. Maybe he didn't realize his shoulder almost knocked my arm from its socket.

I wince as a hand grabs my shoulder from behind. I turn to see Tiya wiping sweat off her brow. She must have run all the way here from her class on the other side of campus.

I forget about Alvin and turn to Tiya. "Are you okay? What's wrong?"

"Wrong? Nothing's wrong. What makes you think something's

wrong? My lung just exploded, that's all." She straightens up, readjusts her skirt, and bats her eyes at me. "I just wanted to see you before class, obviously. I had to tell you what happened in Ms. Hartog's class."

I laugh and say, "Aww. I just saw you at lunch. It's only been one class since then."

But Tiya's talking so fast, I already missed the first half of her story. ". . . then Ms. Hartog schooled Sarah for texting under her desk. I swear, some teachers have eyes on the backs of their heads. They see everything." She looks at me expectantly. When I look at her blankly, she sighs dramatically and says, "You weren't listening."

"I didn't realize you were still talking."

"Girl, my mouth was moving. Words were coming out. Come on now." Tiya puts her hand on her hip and purses her lips.

"I mean, sometimes you drone on and o—"

She makes a smacking sound with her lips and whacks me in the back of the head with her notebook.

As we walk toward Ms. Daniels's class, Tiya tells me her story for a second time. I humor her and laugh loudly in all the right parts. Then she sings me the "What Is This Feeling?" song from *Wicked*. It always makes me laugh when she jumps back and forth singing the two different parts. I know she's pulling out all the stops to distract me from the uneasiness prickling under my skin. She knows I am still worried about my piece in the *Sequoia Park Weekly*.

As we get close to Ms. Daniels's door, Ava catches up to us and calls, "Hey, you two!" She's wearing a white Bohemian-style shirt with eyelets along its ruffled sleeves.

"What's up, Ava? Cute shirt," says Tiya. "You going to the protest this weekend?"

"Of course I am. I've been so pissed about everything. I might try to get some student council members there too."

"You should have them cosponsor. It shouldn't just be the BSU organizing when Black folks are murdered," says Tiya. I bite my lip. This must be the André Johnson thing they were telling me about at lunch earlier. Ava's pretty involved in just about everything, so I'm not surprised she knows about it. Still, I feel a twinge because Tiya didn't want to talk to me about it at lunch but feels fine talking to Ava about it now.

"Yeah, that's a good idea. I'll talk to them about it at our meeting tomorrow."

Tiya nods approvingly and the three of us pause outside Ms. Daniels's door.

Ava turns to me and says, "May, I've been meaning to talk to you about the Junior Jam. I'm so sorry about everything my mom said. I can't imagine how it made you and your parents feel. I was mortified."

Just as my automatic *it's okay* response starts forming, the tardy bell rings. We rush into class, and Ava says quickly, "Can we talk sometime soon?"

I murmur agreement as I hurry to my seat.

"Welcome, ladies," Ms. Daniels says to us in a warm honey

voice. She gives us a sly grin and raises her right eyebrow as we hurry to our seats, muttering apologies for our almost-tardiness.

Ms. Daniels walks around the classroom, bright yellow skirt swishing around her ankles. She says, "Oh, don't mind me, I'm just walking around the room for fun. Not because I want to start class or because I'm checking for the phones you're hiding under your desks . . . ahem . . . Hunter."

Hunter sheepishly puts the phone deep in his backpack and zips the pocket. Ms. Daniels smiles at him, showering him with a sarcastic but friendly "Welcome to class, Hunter." A few students snicker. Ms. Daniels doesn't even turn around as she continues, "I wouldn't laugh too hard, Noah Kelly. Or you, Maddie. I see your fingers poking at the phones sticking out of your pockets." She turns and faces the two texting culprits with her trademark smile. "That really is a skill, you know. Sight-free texting on a touch screen. Back in my day, we had real buttons. Feel free to put those phones way down deep in your backpacks too."

As Noah, Maddie, and a few others stow their phones, Tiya rotates slowly in her seat and opens her eyes wide at me. Then she spins forward again, makes circles with her thumb and index fingers, and holds them on the back of her head like glasses.

Just then, Josh walks in and the bottom falls out of my stomach. He hands Ms. Daniels a note and waits while she reads it. Without turning around, Tiya reaches back and holds out her hand until I give it a squeeze. When Ms. Daniels nods, Josh walks across the room to his desk, ignoring the whispered chorus of greetings that always seems to accompany his arrival anywhere. When he glances at me, our eyes meet for a split second and I have flashbacks: I see myself drunk on his bed, blurry images of his face inches from mine. I remember Marc standing in the doorway watching everything and my cheeks flush; I wish he hadn't seen any of it. I hear Mr. McIntyre's voice: *Some Asian boy got into Princeton and killed himself on the tracks. What did his parents say to him? The Asians are the real problem here.*

Gone are thoughts of Josh's funny, football-shaped notes and friendship; I just have memories of things I regret and someone I want to punch in the face. It's all mushed together in my mind.

Ms. Daniels twirls to face my side of the classroom, and her yellow skirt unfurls and wraps in the other direction around her legs. She says, "Today we're starting a narrative unit. Autobiographical." Several soft groans waft up into the air. "Aye—did I hear *groans*? You're gonna thank me for this unit later. Learning to tell your own story will be one of the most important skills you will learn in *life*. Especially because you will all be writing college essays next year."

The class groans even louder. I hear Ava say to no one in particular, "Don't remind us! I'm already so stressed about the PSATs and the ACTs!"

When are the PSATs? I think they're coming up soon. I haven't been as focused on that stuff as I probably should be. It just doesn't seem as important anymore. Ms. Daniels swishes by my desk and sticks a Post-it on top without breaking stride. It says, *Courage. Lunch anytime.*

She must have read the the *Weekly* today. Is she commending me for my courage? Or telling me to have it?

When I refocus after spacing out, Ms. Daniels is showing the class a few examples of "I Am From" poems. She passes out a worksheet with question prompts in case we get stuck. I skim the worksheet and get hung up on questions about my grandparents. There are just a couple basic questions: *What are your grandparents' names? Where are they from?*

I don't even know my grandparents' real names. Don't know the phonetic sounds and have zero idea how to write them in Chinese. To me, my dad's parents were just Nǎi-Nai and Yé-Ye. When they were alive, we visited them up in San Francisco every other week.

My mom's parents were Amah and Agong. The last time I saw them was on our trip to Taiwan when I was ten. They didn't speak Mandarin—not that it would have helped; my Mandarin sucks, as my mom often reminds me—they only spoke Taiwanese. I didn't know how to talk to them, so I played around their feet, smiled, ate a lot of food, and read them books in English as they nodded proudly. When they called, my mom used to make me "talk" to them. But all I could say in Taiwanese was "I'm reading" and "I'm hungry" and "I have to go to the bathroom." All I could understand were bits and pieces like, "Study hard," "Listen to your mom," and "Have you eaten yet?" I always tried to pass the phone to Danny as fast as I could because um-ing and ahh-ing and "Okay, Amah"-ing through a conversation I couldn't really understand was so awkward.

Now they are all gone. Maybe that's better. They didn't have to go through the pain of losing Danny too. Hopefully they're with him on the other side.

Tiya once told me it used to be like that for her on the phone with her grandparents in Haiti, so I poke her to see how she's doing. She's so busy scribbling, she doesn't even notice. I look over to see if Celeste is having the same struggle as me. But of course, she's busy scribbling too. No surprise there.

While I'm looking around, a small piece of notebook paper appears on my desk. It's folded into a little triangular football, and immediately, I know who it is from. The harder I try to ignore it, the more I keep looking at it. Finally, I unfold it slowly.

Can we talk?

My body tenses and my fingers start to tingle. I crumple the note with a slight shake of my head and slouch down as I grab the "I Am From" prompts again.

I stare hard at the list of questions and try to refocus my mind. What smells are you from? What sounds are you from? What memories are you from?

Every memory I have is attached to Danny.

My parents told me Danny used to translate for me when I was just learning how to talk. My dad said he used to hide when changing my diaper because if I cried, Danny would run over and tackle him. My parents have a video of Danny helping me stack pillows to escape from my crib. We used to practice break-dancing together, and we'd stage epic wrestling matches in the living room. When I started kindergarten, Danny made sure everyone at school was nice to me, and he spent his whole recess playing with me. He had a sixth sense and always knew when I got into it with Mom; he'd come in my room singing his awful rendition of "Lay Me Down."

I don't know how to walk through the world without him.

I can only remember a few times he didn't seem like himself. Those were the days he shut himself in his room and didn't leave. There was one time he forgot to lock his door and I found him curled up in bed, staring at the wall. I just thought he didn't feel well. He probably didn't, but maybe it wasn't the kind of not-feeling-well I thought it was. He had been uncharacteristically scatterbrained for a few months and slept in a lot more. But it was his senior year, and he was doing school, playing basketball, and working on college applications, so it seemed natural that he was distracted and overly tired. How could I have known he was struggling so much if the signs were camouflaged so well against the backdrop of teenage life?

Gentle music wafts from Ms. Daniels's antique CD player, drawing out memories and hidden feelings. I glance around the room. Heads are bent over desks. Hands are busy pouring poems onto pages. Muffled sniffles, like muted popcorn, make their rounds around the classroom.

All I can think of is Danny.

I stare at my paper until the end of class.

As soon as the bell rings, Josh grabs his backpack and heads in my direction, but Ava asks him something and he stops to answer her question. By the time he gets through his group of friends, I'm long gone.

31

When I get home, I throw my stuff into my room and walk down the hallway back to the closed door of Danny's room. No one has been inside since he left us. The door stays closed and we don't go in, as if keeping everything just how Danny left it means A) it will be ready for him when he comes home, B) our memories of him will never fade, C) we're afraid of what we might discover if we look inside, or D) all of the above.

Correct answer: D) all of the above.

I put my hand on the doorknob.

Maybe I can find a clue. Something, anything, that might help me understand.

I open the door.

Everything looks just as I remembered, though it smells a little dusty and faded. It's so much Danny in one place, my feet stop moving. My chest tightens and I can't breathe. My palms start to sweat, and I wipe them over and over again on my jeans. I feel like Danny's going to walk in the room and throw his backpack on the ground or pop out from behind his bed and yell, *Surprise!* But he doesn't. He won't ever do that again.

I force two deep breaths into my lungs and wait until my airways open up a bit before walking over to the desk where Danny's laptop sits next to a Steph Curry bobblehead. I boot it up and start opening and closing desk drawers. I find pens, Post-its, an old pack of gum, and a few stray paper clips in one drawer. In the next, I dig through some old receipts, the ticket stub for a Warriors game, and a small notebook with nothing in it. I poke around on his computer, but all I find are school assignments, songs, video games, and a couple saved movies.

I slide his closet open, grab an armful of his clothes and pull them to my face. I pretend I'm holding Danny. I pretend these shirts aren't hanging here lifeless, that Danny's arms extend through the sleeves and hug me back. There are some old shoeboxes, hats, a couple basketballs—why he ever needed so many, I'll never know—gym bags, and a dusty fan on the closet floor. That's it.

I look under his bed. In his dresser. In the drawers of his nightstand. But I find nothing. Nothing surprising and no clues.

I don't know what I was hoping to find. A note? A journal with some detailed entries? Drawings of the train? If I had found something, would I feel better or worse?

I head back to my room with a strange mixture of disappointment and relief. Is it possible to heal without ever really understanding what happened?

32

A sweet, sharp scent tickles my nose. It's been so long since the smell of cooking has filled the house; the plasticky, preservative smell of microwaved meals doesn't count. This smell is both familiar and forgotten, a mysterious blend of soy sauce and spices. I must investigate, even if it means facing my parents and talking about what I wrote.

I peek into the kitchen and see the hotpot bubbling in the middle of the table, surrounded by a mouthwatering display of raw foods. There are plates of thinly sliced meats, folded and layered in neat rows. In a small bowl, enoki and wood ear mushrooms lean against piles of cubed tofu. Fish balls, fish cakes, shrimp, folded-up tofu-fish thingies, and more unidentifiable foods that I eat and never question are balanced on mismatched plates in precarious piles. There is an enormous bowl of dōngfěn (aka glass noodles, a food translation I can accept), and another bowl overflowing with Chinese cabbage. My mom, still in her work clothes, is bustling around, opening jars of chili oil, sacha spicy barbecue paste, soy sauce, black vinegar, and sesame oil. She scoops sugar into a small bowl and arranges everything on the end of the dining table. Her cheeks are flushed, and a strand of hair falls across her face. A smile plays wistfully at the right corner of her mouth. She looks twenty years younger. Softer.

I don't want to interrupt. I haven't seen my mom so peaceful, or functional, since before it happened. But my stomach growls at me, unhappy to be ignored, so for a moment, I set aside my worries about the *Sequoia Park Weekly*. I open my mouth. "Hi, Mom."

She looks up, surprised, and my heart sinks as I watch the world crash back onto her shoulders. Creases appear around her mouth, dark bags pull the skin under her eyes, and her shoulders slump forward. Is it me?

My mom closes her eyes like she's steeling herself for something, then checks her watch and says, "Ah, Maybelline, 來幫我一下。"

"Sure."

I rearrange the table to make space for our bowls. Then I set out a wire hotpot spoon and a pair of chopsticks at each seat. Three settings, not four.

As I finish setting the table, my mom says, "I'm going to change, okay?" She slips upstairs and I hear her opening and closing dresser drawers. I move my mom's floral purse from the counter to the sofa in the living room and see a copy of today's *Weekly* folded tightly and stuffed inside.

She's read it.

"Lǎopó? Yam? I'm home!" calls my dad as he walks through the front door and tosses his shoes off dramatically. Before he finishes his grand entrance, he tilts his nose up in the air. "What is this aroma in my nose?"

"Your feet?"

"Real men. Stinky feet. How many times do I have to remind you?" He musses my hair. "So, what's cooking?"

"Huǒguō, Bà. Obviously."

My dad grabs my hands and whirls me around. "Oh happy day! I can't remember the last time we had hotpot!" He reaches his hand into the plastic bag he's carrying and pulls out some lightbulbs with small remote controls. "I knew it was a good day to pick up some color-changing bulbs! Should we try one out in your room later?"

I smile in spite of myself. "I'm ready to eat and Ma's upstairs changing. You better hustle, or I'll eat all the food." I make a shoveling-food-into-my-mouth motion and then add, "Also, you shouldn't be using plastic bags!"

"I forgot to bring my reusable one." My dad wags his index finger in warning before sprinting up the stairs, hollering, "I have a photographic memory. Don't touch anything on that table."

"What if the huǒguō explodes?"

"Then the food will cook faster!" He runs up the stairs and calls over his shoulder, "No touching!"

We sit around the table, mixing our own concoction of sauces at the bottom of our bowls. I like lots of sacha spicy barbecue paste, a little sugar, and some soy sauce. My mom and dad load up on the chili oil; just looking at their bowls makes my nose run and eyes water. I fill my wire spoon with meat and dip it into the water, balancing the handle on the edge of the hotpot. Meat cooks fast, so I have to keep an eye on it. I keep waiting for them to say something about my poem in the paper, but my dad is focused on fishing out a shrimp and my mom is busy putting a piece of meat and a tube-shaped fish thing into the boiling water. She uses her chopsticks to pick out some cooked mushrooms and puts them in my bowl. Then she adds food to my dad's bowl before filling her own.

We cook and eat and eat and cook, constantly refilling our spoons and adjusting our sauces as we inhale the food. My mom keeps fishing out things I like and dropping them in my bowl, saying, "吃多一點。"

She doesn't need to remind me twice. For a few contented minutes, I eat and forget about the paper and everything else.

"So, Yam. How was your day?" asks my dad with a mouthful of food. "What did you learn at school today?"

He hasn't asked me that question in a hundred years. I narrow my eyes and go with it. "Come on, Bà. You're a teacher; you know no high schooler will answer that."

"Come on . . . not even for your old man?" he pleads.

"Oh, fine. Uh . . . we started a unit on autobiographical

narratives in English." I don't mention the bit about leaving my paper blank.

"Is that sooooo? I could teach you a thing or two about narrative writing," my dad says in his annoying teacher voice.

"Teach me anything in that voice and I'll die of boredom." I roll my eyes while I poke around in the hotpot for mushrooms. "How do your students survive?"

"My students love me."

"That's what *you* say, Bà."

"Why are you writing autobiographical narratives again?" asks my mom. "You do that every year."

"Ms. Daniels says learning to tell our own stories is one of the most important skills we will learn in life," I say, wondering if I'm talking myself into a trap.

But my mom just nods and says, "I think this will help you write college essays next year too."

My dad adds, "Is Ms. Daniels your English teacher? I like her already. Maybe I should reach out to her and compare notes."

"Oh please, no, Bà. You'll embarrass me."

My dad puts his hand on his chest in mock horror. "Me? Embarrassing? I can be very professional." My mom covers a laugh and spoons more food into both our bowls. "In fact, today one of my students told me you are lucky I'm your dad. Because I'm so cool, obviously."

My mom almost spits out her food at my dad's declaration. "Ai-yah! Cool 個屁。" Her words literally translate into, *Pfft! Cool a fart.* Or in other words, *What nonsense.*

My dad ignores her. "She also said it gives you an unfair advantage."

"Unfair advantage?" Aha, I find a clump of mushrooms and scoop it into my bowl. "In what?"

He mimics my earlier tone and eye roll. "In English, Yam. What else? They were admiring your writing skills, that's why."

"Writing skills?" All the food I've been stuffing into my mouth congeals into a heavy weight at the pit of my stomach. "How would they know how I write?"

"Oh—" He glances quickly at my mom, who breathes heavily out her nose.

"They must have read the paper today," she says slowly as she folds a piece of meat into her wire spoon. "I'm sure many people have seen it by now."

"I don't know," fumbles my dad. "I think they just meant, in general, you're lucky to have such a cool, hip dad." He smiles, hoping I'll take the bait.

"You heard Mom. Cool 個屁。" I try to play along, but can't resist asking, "So, did you read what I wrote?"

"I did . . ."

The pregnant hippo bursts into the room and two seconds later my mom cuts in. "We asked you not to say anything, Maybelline. Why didn't you listen?"

"I couldn't let Mr. McIntyre get away with what he said . . . ," I mumble. I had good reasons, I know I did. But I can't remember anything with my mom's hippo back in the game.

"Let's talk about this another time, okay? Let's just enjoy

dinner tonight." My dad tries to reroute the conversation before it heads down the same familiar tracks.

"好啦。好啦。" My mom nods in agreement and takes a bite of food. But just like me, she can't help herself. When she gets flustered, her English sometimes slips a little and her verb tenses get mixed up. "He already get away with it, Maybelline. How is your poem going to stopping him?"

"I mean . . . I just thought . . ."

"You just thought about yourself. But what about your parents?"

"I *was* thinking of you; that's why I had to respond."

"You didn't listen to us."

"What he said wasn't right, Ma! He made it sound like everything was your fault!" I slam my chopsticks on the table and the hotpot wobbles precariously. "I was trying to do the right thing."

"The right thing is to listen to your parents, Maybelline."

"Yam, Mom is just worried." My dad tries to prevent World War III from erupting at the kitchen table, but he's ill-equipped without Danny, who was always able to bridge the gap between Mom and me. "We just want to forget it happened. The paper is so *public*."

"Well, yeah. That's the point!"

"You're not thinking, Maybelline." My mom balances her chopsticks across the top of her bowl.

"A minute ago you said I was only thinking of myself, Ma," I interrupt. "Which one is it?"

"Ai-yah!" She exhales her frustration loudly and looks at my dad.

"Hang on, everyone. Let's just take a step back and calm down. We were having such a nice dinner." My dad reaches toward both of us, but we ignore his hands. I don't know how Danny did it. He was a May-May–Mom translator when we seemed to speak in different languages. Which was all the time.

The three of us simmer in a tense silence like food cooking in the hotpot.

Eventually, we busy ourselves by snatching up slippery noodles. After I scoop a clump of dōngfěn into my bowl, my mom adds even more for me. She knows they are my favorite. I eat them even though I've lost my appetite. My mom adds vegetables into the pot, and the cabbage shrinks into the hot water. It has become a fragrant soup, infused with flavor. When I drink it, I barely taste anything.

After dinner, homework is a welcome distraction, but eventually I get thirsty. And hungry. Danny used to call me the bottomless pit. He'd carry around extra snacks for me in case I didn't bring enough food to school. I shuffle downstairs and pause on the steps.

My parents are still in the kitchen sitting around the hotpot, though now it's unplugged and the soup still. My mom cradles her head in her hands. She speaks in Mandarin, its warm, lilting tones shedding her armor from the day. Her voice is slightly muffled as she says, "Maybelline doesn't know what she is doing."

My dad puts his arm around my mom and pulls her into his chest. He cradles her and buries his nose in her hair. She reaches up and grasps his arm, saying, "They will hurt her. You know what always happens . . . Don't forget your brother . . ."

A tear, then three, then ten, become rivers gliding silently down my dad's cheeks. His voice cracks as he responds in English, "I know. How could I forget?" He wipes his tears and says, "You're right, Ying. She is young. She doesn't understand. But it was a good letter."

"She's a good writer." My mom starts stacking the dishes on the table and my dad lets go of her waist to help. "But someone else should have written it. Not her."

"Who else could have written it?" I can tell my dad is torn between Mr. Chen, the English teacher trying to inspire his students to action, and my ba, the father who wants to shelter me in a soundproof, bulletproof bubble.

"People will twist what she said to benefit themselves," my mom continues. "They will never interpret things the way she means them. She will get hurt."

My dad nods. "I'll try to talk to her again." He pats her arm and stops her from stacking more plates. After a moment, he asks gently, "Did your boss say anything about the letter?"

"Not yet. But he is close friends with that McIntyre man. I don't know how this will affect the promotion I wanted. We could use the money." A promotion? I didn't know about this.

"I know."

My mom puts her head back in her hands. "I don't know what to do, lǎogōng."

My dad wraps both of his arms around her again. "What do you mean?"

141

"What kind of parents are we?"

"Ying . . ."

"Look what happened to our son. You heard what the McIntyre man said. How did we let it happen to him?"

Tears begin to trace lines over the curves of their faces. Neither one moves or speaks. They are submerged in an ocean of silence that is not big enough to contain their grief.

"I'm afraid, lǎogōng. I don't know how to protect her. I don't know how to talk to her." My mom looks into my dad's face. He uses his soft sleeve to pat her cheeks. "I cannot lose her too."

My dad doesn't respond. My mom turns her body and wraps her arms around his neck. When I get up from the stairs, they're still sitting there holding each other without speaking.

33

Tiya Marie

Do you think your mom and dad parent out of love or fear?

Whoa that is deep

It's too late for that kind of question

Ask me again in the morning

Love or fear?

I dunno.

What's the difference?

I dunno.

34

A week later, I see Josh standing around near my locker. He paces back and forth, ignoring kids who are trying to get his attention. As he paces, he shakes his head and pinches the bridge of his nose. He clenches his fists.

I slow my step, trying to figure out what to do. Why is he there? Images of his bedroom, then his father, flash in my mind. I don't want to talk to him.

He sees me and makes a beeline to where I'm standing. I panic and turn on my heel in the other direction. What am I, a child? I'm literally trying to run away. I mentally slap myself in the forehead, but my feet keep moving.

"May, wait!" he calls. He doesn't care if people hear or see. Students turn their heads and watch; people are always down to glimpse a little drama unfolding. I turn down a narrow walkway between the English and history buildings. The buildings are so close their roofs seem to touch. It feels like a covered hallway and it's dark. No one is here.

I slow down, take a deep breath, and turn around just as Josh catches up and nearly runs me over. Instinctively, he reaches out to steady me with both hands. I freeze and he looks down. He lets go and rubs his hands on his jeans. "Sorry, May. I didn't mean to grab you like that. I shouldn't have—"

We face each other awkwardly, silent seconds ticking on. My thoughts tangle themselves into knots with no clear starting point. This is the guy who used to write me funny notes in class. I miss those easy laughs and shared smiles. Then I remember his breath on my nose. Even though he was trying to help, the memory prickles against my skin and sends a shudder through my arms. I hear his dad's voice in my head: *Some Asian boy got into Princeton and killed himself on the tracks.* My chest tightens.

"May, I don't . . . I don't even know where to start. I'm sorry for my dad and what he said. For my party. I wasn't trying to . . . you know . . . do anything." He closes his eyes and scratches the back of his neck.

For some reason, I'm thinking about Marc. How his eyes burned through Josh that night. How my head settled so safely in the perfect-avocado nook under his collarbone.

I do that thing where I get lost in my thoughts and forget to talk. When I realize I've just been staring at him like I'm spaced out in pre-calc, I open and close my mouth like a fish, hoping something will come out. Nothing does, so Josh keeps talking.

"I guess . . . I just wish we could go back to how it was before. Before the party. Before everything."

Wouldn't that be nice. I wish everything could go back to how it was before . . . everything. I feel the angry flame start to flicker below my ribs.

"May?" he asks tentatively. "I don't know what's going on in your head. I just wanted you to know I'm really sorry."

The flame shrinks and I feel myself soften slowly. He was trying to help me at the party. He isn't his dad. I start to say, "It's all ri—"

"Yo, J-Mac!" A huge white dude from the football team sees Josh from across the floral planter down the walkway. "I saw your dad's letter in the *Weekly* this morning! Hell yeah!"

Josh's cheeks burn as he yells, "Shut the fuck up, Evan!"

Evan sees me and says, "Oh shit . . ." Then he walks away, hooting.

I whip my phone out of my back pocket (thank goodness it's there and not lost somewhere in my backpack) and pull up the online site for the *Weekly*. I've scrolled down and seen part of the headline that reads, "Nathaniel McIntyre Responds to—" when Josh grabs the phone from my hand.

"What the hell, Josh? Give me my back my phone!"

"You don't want to read this, May."

"Don't tell me what I want, Josh. Give it back." I hold out my hand. "What are you going to do? Steal my phone? You can't stop me from reading it."

Josh's eyes are tortured as he reluctantly passes the phone back to me. "I don't agree with him, May. You have to know I don't think like he does."

I barely hear him. Crackling flames leap up angrily inside me. Underneath the hot flames, I'm nervous, scared. I grab my phone and turn away so Josh can't see my face. My hands tremble as I begin to read.

NATHANIEL MCINTYRE RESPONDS TO ACCUSATIONS OF RACISM

Last week in this paper, I was accused of being racist and saying terrible things about a troubled Asian boy who took his own life. Let me start by being clear: I am not a racist.

If I am to be accused of anything, accuse me of being a concerned and loving father. I am worried for my son. The stress and pressure he faces in this community are far worse than anything I experienced at his age, and I graduated at the top of my class at an elite private school on the East Coast. I became one of the most influential venture capitalists in Silicon Valley through hard work and sacrifice. I am familiar with the cutthroat business world, I've seen start-ups rise and fall, I know failure and perseverance, and I have never seen anything like the culture in Sequoia Park schools.

The culture in our community has changed. To know why, we need to look no further than the story of Danny Chen, the Asian boy who died on the tracks near his home last spring. By all accounts, he was a popular senior and a co-captain of the basketball team. He had just been accepted to Princeton University. He had everything going for him, but he took his own life. One must wonder why.

It is no secret that Asian families place a strong emphasis on academics and an unhealthy amount of pressure on their children. They are self-proclaimed tiger moms. As more Asians have moved into our community, they have turned our schools into competitive minefields. Danny is the fifth student suicide in the last eighteen months. How do we expect our children to succeed in an environment where Princeton is not good enough? How can our kids compete?

These questions are not the product of a racist mind. In fact, I have great admiration for the Asian community. I have Asian friends and work with many Asian people. I have traveled all over Asia for work and pleasure. I know the culture deeply. What I write is not racism. It is reality.

I just want a world where my son has a fair chance.

I am appalled by the accusations leveled against me. The reputation I have worked a lifetime to build has been smeared and trampled. My business has been hurt. And still, my heart goes out to the Chen family for their loss. I hope Maybelline Chen gets the help she so clearly needs.

I read it once, twice, three times. Each time the flames leap higher and grow hotter. I think about my parents and the flames incinerate my heart into a glowing coal. After I read it for a fourth time, I turn on Josh and say through gritted teeth, "How. Could. You?"

"What? How could I what? I know it's bad, but I didn't write it."

"How could you let him write this? How could you let him publish this?" There's a teeny-tiny part of me that realizes this is not entirely fair, but I don't care.

"What do you mean? How could I stop him? He's my dad. I didn't even know he wrote it until the paper came out. I was hoping you wouldn't see it."

"You think this goes away if I don't read the paper this week?" I wave my phone in his face. "You heard what your dad said at the Junior Jam. What all those racist people said about me and my family. What they said about my brother."

Josh takes a step back, as if my words are a storm he can't withstand. "Wait a second, May. I know they said things that hurt you, and I'm sorry for that, but they're not racist. They just weren't thinking. They're good people at heart."

"Ha!" The sound barks out of my mouth before I can stop it. "I'm sure they're good to you, Josh. It's hilarious you still don't think they're racist." I step closer to Josh. "Your dad thinks you don't have a fair chance in life? You have GOT to be kidding! You have more of a chance than anyone at this school. Than most people in the world. You don't just have a fair chance, you have a step stool to the good life. No, forget the step stool. You have a freaking fireman's ladder, and the entire fire department is scrambling to lift it higher for you."

"That's not fair, May. I work as hard, if not harder than most people. I'm not just going to get into college for doing nothing."

"Oh really? You're gonna pull the bootstrap defense like your dad? He went to an elite private school on the East Coast! He wasn't exactly pulling up some penniless boots, and neither are you. Didn't he go to Yale? It's called legacy, Josh. You're going to get in to at least one Ivy just because your dad went there. Throw in a new library for another school and see what happens. I can see it already." I hold up my arm and slowly move it to the right like I'm reading the name of a building. "McIntyre Library."

"I'm working hard to get into college."

"So is everyone else. But we don't have the fireman's ladder."

Josh reaches back to scratch his neck again. He clasps both hands behind his head, like he's trying to keep it from spinning. He opens his mouth and closes it again. Apparently, only one of our mouths will work at a time.

I stare at him; the silence between us is a knife peeling skin off an onion. My eyes burn as I see him. *Really* see him. Josh finally gets his tongue powered up and asks, "So what now, May?"

"I don't know. Why do you care? You're at the top of the ladder. You're on the winning team."

He closes his eyes. "Don't say that."

"Why not? It's true."

"Because I don't want the ladder. I don't want to be on opposing teams."

"Well, your dad's the captain, and I don't think he sees things the same way."

"I know," he says softly. "Are you going to write something back?"

I hear my mom's voice: *Maybelline doesn't know what she is doing.* She wants me to put my head down and shut up. But how can I let this man have the last word?

"I don't know what I'm going to do, but I'm going to do something."

"I'm sorry about this, May."

"You should stop apologizing and do something too."

35

I knock on Ms. Daniels's door at lunch. While I wait, I pull my hood over my head and shift my weight back and forth between my feet. Ava walks past and stops when she sees me. "Hey, May, you doing okay? I saw the paper today."

"Eh. I'm all right." I shrug.

"We never really got to talk after the Junior Jam."

"Don't worry about it. It's fine."

Ava hesitates slightly before responding. "It's not fine, May. My mom shouldn't have said all those things. It's terrible. I really wanted to talk to you after; I just didn't know if you wanted to talk to me."

I raise my hand to knock on Ms. D's door again but stop it in midair. "I was at your house like twenty-four-seven throughout elementary and part of middle school. Is that what your mom was thinking every time I went over?"

"No! My mom loves you and your parents."

"She sure has a funny way of showing it, then. I mean, is this why we stopped hanging out?" I didn't mean to be so blunt, but I hadn't connected these dots until right now, and I'm not sure if I'm connecting the dots in order. Maybe I'm connecting what was supposed to be a dog's eye to its hind leg.

"What? No! Just a lot of stuff happened in eighth grade. It was a really hard time," Ava says.

"Your dad?" Despite my questions, we fall into talking like old friends. It's been a while since we've been close, but I guess that is what we are, after all: old friends.

Ava shoves her hands in her back pockets and nods. "I ended up talking to Ellie about stuff because something similar happened to her too." She pauses, then adds, "I didn't know how to tell you."

It's my turn to shove my hands into my back pockets. "I didn't even know about your dad until high school, Ava. It must have been horrible."

"Yeah, it really sucked. I don't talk to him anymore." She pulls out her phone to check the time. "Now, after her little performance at the Junior Jam, things are weird with my mom too."

"You were always so close, though." I keep shifting my weight back and forth on my feet.

"Well, you heard what she said. It was so racist. We got in a huge fight about it that night." She hugs her elbows to her chest.

"Then I went to the protest for André a couple weekends back, and she wasn't happy about that either."

Did that already happen? Tiya never mentioned anything.

"I was looking for you. I thought you'd be there with Tiya and Marc. I saw them with Ayanna and Mikayla, but I didn't see you," says Ava.

"I, uh, didn't go. I haven't really wanted to leave the house much these days."

"That makes sense. You need to take care of yourself first."

"I'm sorry stuff is hard with your mom, though. It's different, but I know how that goes."

"I'll figure it out. I just really wanted you to know I'm sorry about what she said." Ava tugs at the top of her shirt, then pulls out her phone to check the time again.

"That means a lot, Ava." I smile at her. "Do you need to be somewhere?"

"I'm supposed to be at a student council meeting right now."

"Don't be late because of me. We can talk more later."

"Yes, I'd love that." She smiles that toothpaste-commercial smile and bounces on the balls of her feet. "I'm headed over the ramp to Sequoia Grove after school today. I tutor some kids over there at the Boys and Girls Club. Wanna come?"

"Can't today. Maybe another time?" I'm tempted by the idea of spending a little more time with Ava.

"I've got PSAT tutoring every weekend until the test, and a huge project for AP Environmental Science due next Friday. I'm so stressed out. I probably won't go next week, but maybe after that?"

"Yeah, just let me know."

"I'm glad we got to talk a little, Maybe." It's the nickname she used for me in middle school. We thought it was funny that the first five letters of my name spelled a different word. I miss the days when the randomest everythings seemed so hilarious. "I'll see you in class later." She smiles and waves as she walks off, ponytail swinging behind her.

I knock on Ms. Daniels's door again, but no one comes. I text Tiya and start to head for the hugging oak when the door swings open and slams into the opposite wall.

"Oops, sorry!" Ms. Daniels laughs with a smile that pulls me into the room. "Have you been waiting long?"

"Just a couple minutes."

"I'm glad you're here. I was beginning to wonder if you'd ever come through. I was hoping you would." She smiles at me again.

"Yeah . . . I just, I was hoping you could help me."

"Anything. What can I do?"

"Have you seen the *Weekly* today?"

"Not yet. Hang on." She disappears through the back door of the classroom and returns a few minutes later with a copy of the paper. "Had to borrow this from Mr. Oliver's desk. Don't tell him. I'll put it back just as soon as I—" She stops when she sees the headline. Ms. Daniels clucks her tongue as her eyes scan back and forth. Her eyes travel back up the page and work their way down a second time before she folds up the paper, sets it on her desk, and smooths it out. "How do you feel, May?"

"Mostly pissed off, I think." I throw my backpack next to a desk in the front row and plop into the seat. "I can't believe he said, 'I hope Maybelline Chen gets the help she so clearly needs.' Like, what is that?"

"The whole thing is a pretty predictable response."

"It is? But what do I do about it? I feel like I should respond, but I don't even know where to start." I rest my feet on top of my backpack and lean back. "I want to write something so freaking good it makes him shut his big, stupidhead mouth."

Ms. Daniels laughs and sits on her desk, facing me. "Do you think anything you write will make him shut his 'big, stupidhead mouth,' or change the way he thinks?"

"I don't know, I guess not. What should I do, then?"

"What do you think?"

Gah. I hate it when teachers answer questions with questions. I know they're trying to mine my brain for deeper thoughts, but I just want them to tell me the answers already. I shrug. "I don't know."

"If you knew, what do you think you would say?"

Gah again. She's not giving up on her tricksy brain-mining techniques. This time I think before I answer. "I would say he got it all wrong. That he got the story twisted."

"Okay, so think about that for a sec. Why do you think he got it twisted?"

"I don't know. He has a thing against Asian people."

"*He* doesn't think he does."

"Well, obviously he does, Ms. D!"

"I'm not saying he doesn't, May. But what do you think he gets out of telling Danny's story this way?"

That one gets me for real. I shake my head. "I don't know."

"You know I don't accept 'I don't know.' *Think*, May." She hands me her borrowed copy of the paper and says, "Here, go back into the text and find answers."

I take it and skim Mr. McIntyre's letter again and again. A few lines start to stand out: *The stress and pressure my son faces in this community is far worse . . . The culture in our community has changed . . . As more Asians have moved into our community, they have turned our schools into competitive minefields. Danny is the fifth student suicide . . .*

I set the paper down and look at Ms. D. "He sets us up."

"What do you mean?"

"He's scared. He needs someone to blame for the suicides."

"Why?"

"I don't kno—" I shut up when Ms. Daniels cuts her eyes at me. She crosses her legs and her right foot bobs up and down like she's got some internal soundtrack playing in her head. She waits quietly while I process. "He blames us for changing the culture of the community and making schools too competitive. But *all* the parents here are competitive. I mean, everyone's got tutors and sports and volunteering and test-prep classes and summer activities and stuff."

"Go on . . ."

A lightbulb finally flips on in my brain. "Blaming us means he doesn't have to change. *They* don't have to change."

"What do you mean?" Ms. Daniels leans back on her hands, foot still bobbing to its own beat.

"Well, if he can make it seem like the competitive culture in Sequoia Park is our fault, he doesn't have to reflect on the ways he's contributing to the problem. No one in the community has to examine their part in it. They can just point the finger at Asian people without doing anything different themselves."

Ms. Daniels beams at me like she knew I'd get here all along.

"But that brings me back to square one." I rub my temples. "I don't know where to start."

"Something you said stands out to me." Ms. Daniels grips the edge of her desk and leans forward in my direction. "You said, 'He got the story twisted.'"

"Yeah, he did."

"So what's the story?"

"You're saying I have a story."

"Everyone has a story, May."

"You're saying I should respond with my story."

"You said it, not me." She smiles.

I feel like she just Jedi-mind-tricked me. Ms. Daniels hops off her desk and says, "You don't need clever arguments to shut down Mr. McIntyre. They probably wouldn't work anyway. But people who won't listen to arguments or facts can still be changed by stories." She grips my shoulders and looks me in the eye. "Just be sure you know why you're doing this. This isn't going to bring Danny back, May."

I fall back into my seat as icy fingers wrap themselves around my heart. I know what she says is true. But it hurts. "I know, Ms. D. I just feel like I need to make things up to him. For all the things I didn't do when he was still here. If I had been a better sister, maybe . . . you know." I put my head down on the desk.

"Uh-uh, May. Look at me. I need you to hear what I'm saying," she says sternly. I lift my eyes and look back at her. She shakes her head slowly and says, "This. Is. Not. Your. Fault. Danny's death is not your fault, you hear?"

I nod weakly.

"If you haven't yet, you need to talk to someone when you're ready. You can always come talk to me, but I'm not a professional counselor. They can help, May."

I nod again. "Okay, Ms. D. I'll think about it."

"Good. I support what you're doing about Nate McIntyre. You know I do. But this isn't going to heal that hole Danny left."

I don't respond. The idea that healing is possible seems like a complete fantasy.

"Okay, then." Ms. D switches back to teacher mode. "What's your story, May?"

I feel overwhelmed by the task. "How do I boil down my whole life into one letter?"

She grabs a stack of papers from her desk and holds them up. "I noticed you haven't turned in your 'I Am From' poem yet."

I turn away, my cheeks tomatoes. "I know, I had a really hard time . . . I didn't know how to—"

"Maybe you can start there."

I look at her suspiciously. "Waaait a minute. Was this whole

159

conversation really just about getting me do my assignment?"

Ms. Daniels laughs and grabs the lanyard of keys off her desk. She takes me down to the department computer lab and unlocks the doors, saying, "I'm not supposed to let you stay here alone, but I know you need some space. I'm going to keep my door open so I can hear you if you need anything." She squeezes my hand like she did on the first day of school. "You got this, May."

She winks at me and then disappears back to her classroom.

I find a computer in the middle of the lab, sit down, and stare at the keyboard. I type, "I am from . . ." on the first line and wait for the words to come.

The words start out disjointed, more a stream-of-consciousness brainstorm than a story. I am from beef noodle soup. I am from strawberry Pocky arranged like a fan in a mug. I am from shark-infested waters, a floating basketball, and stinky feet. I am from the dreams of farmers in the mountains of Taiwan. I am from the streets of Chinatown. I am from languages I never learned to speak and grandparents who communicate with their eyes. I am from music that moves my soul and dance that speaks when I don't have words. I am from a stomping hippo. I am from Sam Smith. I am from Lay Me Down. I am from the feathers under my big brother's wings. I am from midnight trains and sirens screeching. I am from a world that crumbled to dust while I screamed silently beside the tracks.

Each sentence further dislodges the clogs in my brain. Eventually, the words flow through my fingertips. I play with the structure of the "I Am From" poem, making it my own.

That night, I sit at my desk and keep writing. I dive into memory and meaning. I revise and reorganize. My story begins to take shape on the screen.

36

TAKING BACK THE NARRATIVE
By Maybelline Chen

I am from pillows.

Couch pillows,

throw pillows,

bed pillows,

back support pillows

carried

one by one by

Danny

up to my room

as I watched from my crib.

We piled them in the corner

and he pushed my diapered butt

up

 the

  pillow

   hill,

an escape ladder

to freedom.

In the videos

I hear my parents' muffled giggles.

I imagine them hiding behind the door

trying to capture

precious moments

as we grew too quickly

out of childhood.

I am from pillows

tied securely around my body

one in front | one in back.

Soft ones

pilfered from my parents' bed

were best.

Danny, pillow-padded too,

faced off | against me

in the living room,

the scene of many epic wrestling matches.

My parents' laughter

was louder than ours.

I am from pillows

duct taped

over hard edges

and sharp corners,

    anywhere I might bang my feet

    and wrists

    and ankles

in my attempts to windmill

and headspin

and flare,

back when I thought maybe

just maybe,

I could join the Jabbawockeez

one day.

Even when I kicked over a bookshelf

and almost lost my head,

Danny patted me on the back

and said,

    You can do this

while my parents

clapped enthusiastically

each time I tried a move

and didn't die.

I am from pillows

with Star Wars cases.

Danny's favorite

was the Millennium Falcon.
One day, I burst into his room
and found him,
lying with his head
in the middle of the ship,
staring up at the ceiling.
I lay down next to him,
on the Death Star,
and squeezed his thumb.
There were a few days,
when he locked his door
for too long.
I wonder now,
was he was trying to
keep me out
   or himself in?

I am from pillows
that cushioned my head
while Danny cheered me up
with a song.
The last time I ever saw him,
he sounded like a goose
with a cold as he sang,
   Can I lay by your side?
   And make sure you're alright?
I wish I could

go back.
I wish I could have
    said the right things.
I wish I could have
    held on to him
    and changed his mind.
I think he already knew
    what was coming.
But he lay on my pillows
making sure I was all right
even though
he
    definitely
        wasn't.

I am from pillows
I fluffed for my mom
when she couldn't get out of bed.
The world was so dark
it didn't make sense to move,
because darkness here
was the same
    as darkness there
was the same
    as darkness
everywhere.

Without Danny,
my world,
my family's world
has no pillows.
We have nothing
to make the hard edges
        and sharp corners
    of the world
feel soft.

This is my life
        our story
and I am
taking back the narrative.

37

The morning the next *Sequoia Park Weekly* comes out, I get up early and make breakfast for my parents. Eggs with Maggi sauce, bāozi with butter and ròusōng, orange juice, tea, and bacon. Because bacon makes the world go 'round.

When my parents come downstairs already dressed for work, they inhale the aroma of sizzling bacon with pleasure. Especially my dad. He says, "Yam, you've outdone yourself today." I roll my eyes at him and snort. Eggs and bacon isn't exactly rocket science.

My mom wrinkles her nose and says, "Turn on the fan and open the windows; that smell is going to stink up our whole house."

They help me set the table and we all sit down together, trying not to look at the clock as it rushes us out the door. I pass out the bāozi, careful not to let ròusōng fall all over the place, and put a couple pieces of bacon on their plates.

They haven't mentioned Mr. McIntyre's letter from last week at all. I'm hoping they haven't seen it, and they're probably hoping I haven't seen it, but I'm positive we've all seen it. Pretending there is nothing to talk about means we can preserve the fragile steps we've taken toward functioning as a family since our hotpot dinner two weeks ago.

I suspect my parents are still hoping everything will just blow over. They're willing to be seen as villains, to absorb the force of Mr. McIntyre's accusations and the judgment from others as long as it protects me and keeps me safe.

If the *Weekly* prints what I sent in, nothing is going to blow over anytime soon.

My mom pushes the last bite of egg around her plate to soak up more Maggi sauce and says, "Thanks for making breakfast, Maybelline." She looks at me and smiles.

"You must've got your cooking skills from me, Yam," adds my dad. "This hits the spot."

"What cooking skills, Bà? You burn everything you touch."

"Nah," he protests. "What about that time I made fish?"

"You mean the time you tried so hard not to burn dinner that you served it to us raw?"

"Is that what happened?" He glances up from his bāozi with a look of exaggerated disbelief.

I stick my finger in my mouth and gag. That night, Danny put the fish in his mouth and coughed it into a napkin, a technique we perfected as kids when we didn't want to eat something on our plates. He looked at my dad like, "You didn't tell us you were making sashimi tonight, Bà."

Without thinking, my dad jokingly threw a piece of fish at Danny's face, and it hit him square in the nose. My dad knocked over his chair trying to give Danny a napkin, saying, "Ah! Sorry, Danny! I didn't think I'd actually hit you! Who knew my aim was still so good?" Then my mom scolded my dad for wasting food.

Danny sat still as an emperor as my dad wiped his face and said, "Now you have to eat it, Bà. I'm pretty sure that was the rule when we were little, right? We have to eat what we throw?"

And that's when my dad gathered up all the fish, tried to cook it again, and burned it instead.

My mom chimes in, "I remember! That night, we ate pàomiàn."

"Eh, lǎopó, whose team are you on?" My dad covers his heart with his hands. "Besides, instant noodles are a delicacy."

My mom smiles. "I'm on every team."

"She's on team doesn't-have-memory-issues, Bà." I shovel the rest of my eggs into my mouth. "That's my team."

"Okay, okay, I know when to surrender. I can't win with you two ganging up on me."

We're desperate to preserve this moment, so we act like sitting down together for breakfast on a weekday has no more signif-icance than brushing our teeth or tying our shoes. There is a bāozi, a slice of bacon, and a couple bites of egg left on the table, but no one wants to be rude and take the last bite. So we all start offering food to each other. "Dad, you take the bacon; you love bacon," I say, holding the plate out to him.

He pushes the plate back at me. "I already ate too much bacon. You love it too. You take it."

"No thanks. Mom, you only had one piece, you take it."

"不要 不要。" She shakes her head. She takes the plate with the bāozi and hands it to me. "Mèi-Mei, take the bāozi. 你吃不夠啦。 Need to eat more."

"No no no, I'm really full, I can't eat that whole thing. Dad, do you want it?" Now I have two plates, and I shove the one with bāozi at my dad.

"Yam, you take it. And take the last bite of egg too."

And so it goes until finally, we decide my dad will take the bacon and eggs, and my mom and I will split the bāozi. We gulp down the last few bites as the clock ticks too quickly ahead. It's past time for all of us to leave.

My dad glances down at his phone and sighs. "I have to go. My kids are writing an in-class essay today and I can't be late." He winks at me. "They need all the time they can get."

He gets up and takes our plates to the sink and rinses them. He walks back over, wraps his arms around me, and squeezes tight. "Thanks for breakfast, Yam."

My mom checks her phone and frowns. "I need to go too. My boss just emailed to see if we can meet this morning." I freeze in the act of shoving a few last-minute snacks into my backpack. Could this sudden meeting have to do with today's edition of the

Weekly? Is it about that promotion she was going to apply for?

My dad looks steadily at my mom and says, "Good luck, lǎopó."

My mom throws on her jacket and tries to cover her worry with a smile. "Thank you, Mèi-Mei. It was a nice way to start the day." She walks over with her arms extended. She's coming in for a hug. I try to position my arms to fit hers, but she switches positions last minute, so I readjust. Then she readjusts, so I readjust, back and forth, like two gangly middle schoolers trying to dance for the first time. Finally we fit our arms around each other—with a textbook distance between—and she pats me loosely on the back before we turn away.

That was awkward. But I'll take it.

We walk out the door together and I watch them pull out of the driveway in their cars. Their eyes linger on me just a little longer than usual, reading my movements and energy. I smile and wave and dance around, making a bunch of cutesy poses with my hands. I make peace signs next to my cheeks, peace signs around my eyes, and a frame around my face. It's over the top, but it makes them laugh.

My mom calls, "Go inside and put on a jacket! You will catch cold!"

I'm already wearing a purple sherpa hoodie, but I give her a thumbs-up and keep posing.

My cheesy poses extend the moment. I hang on to this one like it's a basketball floating through Dàpéng Bay. The peace signs and winky eyes squeeze smiles from the morning, but they don't fool anyone. I know, and my parents know, that the *Weekly* comes out today, and we're all wondering what will be inside. We know today's breakfast might be more than a happy way to start the week. It might be the calm before the storm.

38

There is a note, folded into a square with two overlapping diamonds, stuck in my locker. My hands tremble as I unfold it, careful not to tear the intricate folds. It's a picture of Totoro and two mini Totoros raising plants out of the ground. It is not signed, but I know who left it. I make a mental note to find her today.

On my way to class, a shoulder smacks into mine and whirls me around. My hand flies up to the throbbing area and my face begins arranging itself into a don't-worry-about-it smile, when suddenly, I realize this is like déjà vu. Only this time, Alvin Lo saunters slowly down the hall, laughing with a couple buddies from the football team. His gray T-shirt is ever so slightly stretched over his stocky frame—just enough to accentuate the muscles in his arms and chest, but not enough to be tight. This time, Alvin barely breaks his stride as he looks over his shoulder and says, "Oh, sorry, May," before he keeps walking with his friends.

What's up with him? I feel like there are tiny fault lines running through the school. Maybe I'm being paranoid because the *Sequoia Park Weekly* comes out today and my poem might be in the Letters to the Editor section.

I realize it's definitely in the *Weekly* when I hear Marc call my name. He breaks away from Sione and Wes and walks straight toward me. He wraps me in his arms, backpack and all, and lifts me off the ground. "I'm sure big-mouth Tiya already told you it made me cry," he whispers in my ear. It tingles down to my toes.

"Like you just watched a scary movie cry? Or like you just watched a Pixar movie cry? Those are two very different things." I bite my lips together and roll my shoulders. Marc's hands stay on my arms after he sets me down.

"Excuse me." He holds up a finger. "There's nothing wrong with hating scary movies."

"Except you think movies that aren't even scary are scary."

"Some Marvel movies are legit scary, okay? That's a hill I'll die on today," says Marc, clenching his hands like he's ready to fight.

I look up at him with my eyebrows raised so high they're trying to fist-bump my hairline. "What kind of crying, Marc?"

"Pixar crying."

"Which kind? Like when Miguel sings 'Remember Me' to Mama Coco, or the scene in *Up* when the old lady dies?"

"What's the difference?" He crosses his arms over his chest.

"When Miguel sings, it's sad, but also happy and hopeful. When Mr. Fredricksen's wife dies, it's just heartbreaking."

"Like the scene in *Up* where the old lady dies."

"Oh, that's serious. It got you like that?"

"Like that plus the scene when WALL·E shoves the plant into the holo-detector."

"What does that even mean?"

"It means it's heartbreaking and horrible like when Mrs. Fredericksen died, but also I wanted to cheer like you just changed the future of humanity."

"You're such a nerd. Who even knows that machine is called a holo-detector?" I shake my head in mock disbelief.

"Whatever." Marc waves me off with his hand. His voice grows soft as he takes a step back. His dark eyes lock on mine. "I know you didn't want to write it, but I'm glad you did. What you shared was poetry."

I don't know what to say, so I just look at him stupidly, then I look at my shoes, then I look at his hands.

Marc laughs. "You can respond when your brain turns back on, Mayday. I gotta head to class, but I'll see you later."

I'm still processing too slow for a smart-ass response, so all I say is, "Yeah, okay."

"Turn your brain back on before then, all right?"

I smile as I shove him back toward Sione and Wes.

I feel like the whispers increase with every passing period. Students walking with heads bowed over phones or lowering their voices as I pass by set my body on high alert. I feel like everyone is reading my poem online and talking about me. I want to disappear down a manhole. I tell myself students walk with their heads over their phones all the time, but I can't help feeling like a trash can where everyone is tossing dirty looks.

I see Josh walking with Ava, and I resist the urge to duck behind the nearest tree. It would have required climbing up into the planter, so it wouldn't have been the most inconspicuous move I've ever made. Plus, I need to stop running away. They see me at the same time, but they have very different reactions. Ava breaks into a smile, while Josh looks down.

Right then, I spy Celeste's faded blue Herschel backpack bobbing in the sea of students flowing toward class. She's Sharpied a few subtle designs along the bottom of the small front pocket. I wave at Ava, ignore Josh, and hustle to catch up with Celeste. I tap her backpack and say, "Hey, thanks for the drawing in my locker."

The cherry blossoms bloom on her cheeks as she smiles. "I was worried it might fall out before you saw it. How'd you know it was me?"

"I've seen your polka-dotted notebook, remember? Totoro doesn't exactly look like Alan Johnson's snoring dad, but it's pretty close."

Celeste laughs and snorts. I fight back a laugh, unsure if it will embarrass her. But she throws her head back, laughs even harder, and snorts again. This time I can't hold back my giggles. Who knew perfect Celeste was a snort-laugher?

When we finally settle down, she says, "It's not a lot, but I saw what you wrote and felt like I had to do something."

I tug my backpack straps up and say, "Thanks. I was nervous about coming to school today; I saw your drawing right when I got to campus and it helped." It's strange—after so many years of putting up a jealous wall between us, I suddenly really want to know what she thinks about all this. She's known my family forever. She was at the Junior Jam. She's Chinese. Does she think I'm doing the right thing? The question catches in my throat. "What did you think?"

"What did your parents say?"

"Ah, they didn't want me to do anything stupid. After the Junior Jam, my dad specifically asked me not to say anything, but obviously I didn't listen." Celeste stops walking and looks at me like what I'm saying is so important she can't be distracted by moving her feet. I continue, "I was so mad, I wrote that first letter and hit send. I didn't think it through."

Celeste sucks in a deep breath. "I was mad at the Junior Jam too. I was mad at my parents because they didn't stand up and say anything. I was mad at myself for sitting there and taking that bullshit too."

She swears? The surprises just keep coming. I say, "I looked at my parents and wanted to sock everyone in the face for hurting them. I didn't feel scared until after the *Weekly* actually published my first letter."

"What did your parents say when they saw it?"

"My mom was upset. Said I didn't care about them, that writing wasn't going to change anything."

"Sounds about right," says Celeste, nodding knowingly. It's

nice that she gets it without needing an explanation. "My mom said some similar things about my art when I told her I didn't want to do the Google thing."

"I didn't know you didn't want that. It just seemed so—"

"Perfect, right? That's what my mom said too. Perfect for a future I don't want in tech." She mimics her mom's voice. "You going to eat your drawings? Art is not paying the bills, Celeste."

"Wow. I had no idea. I'm sorry."

"It's okay." She grins and brushes her hair over her shoulder. "My mom doesn't know about my secret plan to get connected to the Google Doodlers. Maybe I can do work with their team."

"That would be amazing! It sounds like your mom and my mom need to get together and have lunch . . . Oh wait, they already do." We both laugh. Then I remember my mom hasn't left the house for anything but work and errands since Danny died. I add, "Or used to, anyway."

That kills the laughter, and we walk quietly toward class. I say, "I overheard my parents talking in the kitchen later that night. They say people will twist my words and that I'll get hurt."

"They're afraid."

"Yeah, I guess so."

"I think that's how my parents would feel too. Wanting me to shut up because they're scared for my safety. Scared what people will say." Celeste runs her fingers through her hair, flipping it out of her face. The silky strands cascade to the side like a waterfall changing course around a boulder. "But what you wrote was powerful, May. Whatever your parents say."

It means a lot coming from her. "Thanks, Celeste."

"I'm not the only one who thinks that either. A lot of my friends feel the same way." She hangs out with an Asian crew I don't know well. "It's not how we're taught, you know? It's nice to see someone break the mold."

She pulls little cylinders of Haw Flakes from her backpack and hands one to me. I peel the paper off the mini firecracker-shaped package and put one of the small wafers on my tongue, savoring the sweet, tangy flavor. Tiya would love these. I fold the wrapper over a few wafers and save them for her.

As we walk past the hugging oak, I look down at Celeste's shoes and see that she's covered them in black Sharpie doodles and lettering. I should have her draw something on mine. We practically grew up together, but I barely know her; I've been so jealous, I haven't really wanted to try. I've definitely been missing out. I say, "I remember riding in the shopping cart, eating these with you at Ranch 99 while our dads bought groceries." I picture our feet swinging through the leg holes and Danny standing up in the main cart yelling for someone to go faster. "I spilled mine all over the floor, and your dad made you share yours with me."

Celeste laugh-snorts. "I remember that. I was so mad I threw them on the floor so you couldn't have any." We both giggle. She offers me another Haw Flake before popping the rest of the sweet discs in her mouth.

The warning bell rings. We speed up and hurry into class. Mr. Gonzalez wants us in our chairs and ready to work when the bell rings, otherwise he marks us tardy. Celeste and I smile at him sweetly as we slip into our seats just in time.

39

When I get to the hugging oak for lunch, Tiya and Marc are already there, waving their hands in the air, talking animatedly. I overhear Tiya saying something about last week's PSATs. I didn't practice and prepare like everyone else; I just can't seem to make myself care the way I used to. Tiya asks Marc something about his UC application and they mention a weekend dinner with Ayanna's and Mikayla's families, but they stop talking when they see me.

"So what's up with that candy you promised me, Mayday?" Tiya wastes no time getting down to business.

I pull the Haw Flakes out of my pocket. Tiya pops the candies into her mouth and her eyes get big as the tangy flavor spreads across her tongue. "Why've you never introduced these to me before?"

"I haven't had them since I was a kid! Celeste gave me a pack today."

"Well, thank goodness for her."

"Hey! What about me?" asks Marc. "Don't I get any?"

"Nope. I ate them all." Tiya rubs her belly dramatically in Marc's face. He reaches over and twists her earlobe. She yelps, "Ow!"

"Actually, Celeste gave me a few more," I say, digging into my bag. I pull out two more tiny packs and give one to him. Marc puts a few of the small disc-shaped sweets in his mouth and grimaces. "Ughh, what *is* this? These are nasty!"

"What? *You're* nasty!" I say, looking at him sideways. He checks me with his elbow.

"Your taste buds are wack. Give 'em here." Tiya grabs the rest of the pack from Marc, peels off the wrapper, and eats the rest. "Ooh, I almost forgot. My mom packed you some food, Mayday."

Tiya pulls a container out of her backpack, then another and another and another. Containers of all shapes and sizes pile around her like clowns jumping out of a car.

"Tiya Marie, I thought you said 'some food,' not an entire lunch buffet." I examine each container, feeling the drool pool under my tongue. "Not that I'm complaining."

She doesn't even look up, just grabs Marc's backpack and starts unloading. "You know my mom. She thinks we're all too skinny and worries we're on the brink of starvation. I tried telling her just one Tupperware was fine, but I think she packed up our entire fridge for you."

The three of us laugh as we dig into pate, rice and beans, and pikliz. There is so much food I stop looking at what I'm eating and just sample bites from different containers.

"Here, did you get this one?" Tiya hands Marc a round container with pieces of fried pork. She reminds me of our moms, air-traffic controllers making sure overflowing amounts of food land on everyone's plates. Or in this case, on our reusable container lids.

Marc nudges me with his elbow and hands me a container, saying, "Take this one, Mayday. You'll like this."

We trade food as shouts ring between the building rooftops. Wes and Sione bound up. "Aye, Marc! We thought we might find you here!"

Marc nods to his boys and sits up quickly as Wes and Sione plop themselves down into the grass behind him and start digging into the food.

"Marc, you submit your applications to Howard or the UCs yet? I hella procrastinated," says Sione through a mouthful of rice. "Pass me that pork. This food has been calling my name all day."

"I just gotta look 'em over one more time," says Marc, trying to snatch a fork out of Sione's hand. "That's mine."

"Mine now," says Sione. "Damn, this is so good."

Tiya cocks her head to the side, purses her lips at Sione, and scolds him. As they bicker, Wes leans over to me and says softly, "Hey, May, I read that thing you wrote in the paper. Do you think Danny was depressed?"

I shrug with my hands raised. "I don't know. He didn't show it, not even at home. But I wonder now."

"I should have known," Marc mumbles. He inhales, holds his breath, and lets the air out slowly. He blinks quickly before wiping his eyes. I remember what Tiya said that day in her room; he's faking it until he makes it. But he hasn't made it yet.

"I feel the same way," I say, putting my hand on Marc's for a second.

"I just . . . I just didn't see any signs. I had no idea. Then one day he was gone," says Wes, rubbing his hands together. "Sorry. We don't have to talk about this right now."

"It's okay." I feel better knowing I'm not the only one still torn up about Danny. It's easier to talk about him here than at home. At home, the pain presses too forcefully behind the concrete walls we've built to contain it. At home, talking about Danny feels like it will break the dams when we've barely started pulling ourselves out of the water. But here? This feels all right.

I say quietly, "I didn't see it coming either. Looking back, I wonder at little things. You know how he was more scatter-brained, forgetting things, losing things? Or he looked more tired and he slept in later. But who isn't exhausted senior year? It didn't seem strange at the time."

"If there were signs, I missed all of them," Marc says again softly.

"I couldn't believe what Mr. McIntyre wrote," says Wes. "It's so messed up. How can he use tragedy—shit, I mean *Danny*—to push his own agenda like that?"

"Because he pretty much owns the world," Marc says with a frustrated exhale. "People like us are disposable to him."

184

"Where does Mr. McIntyre even get off?" Sione asks. "The other kids who died weren't all Asian, were they? . . . I mean, not that it matters."

"One of them was," says Marc. "But it shouldn't matter. The man is just scared and looking for someone to blame."

"I've been over there for dinner a few times. He's friends with my parents," says Wes, rubbing the back of his hand across his mouth.

"Your parents are Mr. McIntyre's kind of people." Tiya leapfrogs her way into the conversation. "You know, the rich, white kind."

Wes wipes his mouth with his sleeve again, and we all frown disgustedly at him. He doesn't notice. He nods and says, "I already told my parents I'm never going there again. And I gave Josh a piece of my mind this morning. He *knew* Danny. We all balled together in middle school."

Marc's eyes get steely at the mention of Josh's name. He says, "Josh is just as bad for trying to excuse his dad with the whole, 'my dad wasn't thinking and is a good person at heart' crap." I notice he remembers almost word for word what I told him about my run-in with Josh.

"My ass McIntyre wasn't thinking. He knew exactly what he was doing," says Sione. Tiya claps her hands in approval because her mouth is full.

"I'm not trying to defend Josh or anything; I think he deserves whatever piece of your minds you want to give him," I say, trying to find the right words from the jumble in my brain. "But how is what he said to me just as bad as everything his dad said?"

"I think it's worse," says Tiya, finally finishing her bite of food.

"Why?"

"Because he thinks he can play both sides without owning anything," she explains as Marc and Sione nod. "Josh thinks if he just tries to be nice to everyone, he's all good."

"Right, like being nice makes him not racist," adds Sione, rolling his eyes.

"Exactly," says Tiya.

Marc is leaning against the tree, listening. He always considers everything, bakes it in his mind, and only pulls his thoughts out when they're ready. "Well, what do you think? Is it enough to be nice?"

"That's some Ms. Daniels Jedi-mind-trickery right there, Marc," I groan. "I hate it when she answers a question with a question."

"Come on now. I just came for some Mama Duverne professional home cooking, y'all," says Wes, squeezing his temples.

"Tiya brings up a legit question, though." Marc looks around the group, challenging us to think harder. I know Dr. Duverne wants Marc to own his own company one day, but I seriously think Marc should consider being a professor instead. He looks like he's in his element. I remember what he said about being a Black man in Silicon Valley and wonder if it's any easier to make it as a Black professor. I doubt it. I focus on the discussion again when Marc asks, "Does being nice make someone not racist?"

Everyone looks down, wheels turning. I think about the

186

contradictions in Josh's apologies. How he seemed to mean well, yet defended his dad and the other parents in the same breath.

"It's not enough," I say finally. "You can act nice and still be racist. You can be kind to others and still support racist ideas and actions."

Tiya jumps back in. "I was talking about this with Ayanna and Mikayla the other day and one of them said it like this: Being nice doesn't change racist systems. Fighting back does. To people who support those systems, fighting to dismantle them—or dang, just pointing out injustice at all—doesn't feel *nice*."

"So you're saying not only is being nice not enough, but trying to be nice to everyone is actually counterproductive," I respond, trying to manage my confusing jumble of emotions. I hear Tiya's words, but I'm stuck on the idea that she has conversations like this with Ayanna and Mikayla but not with me. Except now. This is the first. No. It's the second if I count the cut-off conversation about André Johnson a while back.

Tiya scoots all the way up into my space until her side is smooshed against mine. "That's why writing back was the right thing to do, Mayday. Even though you weren't sure."

Marc spoons more food onto my lid and nods. Wes and Sione are nodding too. I feel like someone released a million filled but untied balloons in my head and they're just shooting around making fart noises. There is too much to process; my brain hurts and wants to laugh at the same time.

"Yeah, seriously. I should've asked you to help me with my college essays, May," says Sione.

"Nah, you should have written them a month ago instead of waiting until the last minute to get it all done," says Tiya, snatching the fork out of Sione's hand.

"You're right, you're right. Don't start on another one of your lectures," says Sione, holding up his hands in surrender. Tiya and Sione start back up again, while Marc chats with Wes. I can't help picturing Danny sitting here with us in the grass. He would have hogged all the food and probably mic-dropped Marc for his *Does being nice make someone not racist?* questions. I wish he were here so I could talk to him about all the things.

The farting balloons run out of air eventually, and my brain settles down a bit. The sun peeks between the leaves and warms my face. I look at my friends talking and laughing under the hugging oak. For the first time since Danny died, I feel peace even though I miss him so much my stomach hurts.

Everyone is here talking and eating because of something I wrote. Tiya's right; I had to do it. I couldn't sit on the sidelines and let Mr. McIntyre use my family to push his agenda.

I couldn't let him tell our story.

My words are sword and shield.

40

No one is home when I get back from school, but there is a light on in the kitchen. My dad always leaves one or two lights on when we're not home. I make myself a snack and head upstairs to start my homework.

As part of our narrative assignment in Ms. Daniels's class, we have to research our family history, but I'm not sure where to start. I open up my laptop and search "SF Chinatown" and start skimming the sites that pop up. There are a lot of tourist information sites, mommy-blogger posts about the top ten things to do with kids in Chinatown, and tips for foodies about what to eat and where to go. Not super helpful.

I change my search terms to "SF Chinatown history" and find more relevant articles. I start reading and watching videos and going down all kinds of rabbit holes discovering things I didn't know about Chinese people in the United States.

The shadows outside my window lengthen as the sun pulls its light beyond the horizon. Brushstrokes of color brighten then fade as the sky darkens. My dad used to tell me the sun was rolling up in its blankets and getting tucked in to bed. The setting sun reminds me it's dinnertime, but no one else is home yet. Where are my parents?

I text them both, then prop up some pillows on my bed to keep reading. I find an article about one of San Francisco's worst mass murders caused by Chinatown gang feuds in a restaurant called the Golden Dragon. I start reading articles about the gangs and my head starts to spin. This is not the Chinatown I thought I knew. Then, buried toward the end of one of the articles, a single sentence catches my attention. It reads: *Joe Chen, a sixteen-year-old high school student whose family owns a local dumpling shop, was killed in the crossfire during a gang-related shootout.*

Uncle Joe.

I frantically type in every search combination I can think of to find out more information about Uncle Joe's death, but that's it. That's all I can find. One sentence at the end of a newspaper article few people even read.

By the time I look at my phone again, I realize it's almost ten o'clock. I pad downstairs.

In the kitchen, the stove light casts a pale yellowish glow over the burners, and a small note in my mom's handwriting is stuck on the fridge—how old-school, I think. She could have just texted me. It says, *Leftovers in fridge or frozen pizza in freezer.*

The food she brought home is easy to spot because it's not hidden away in old plastic takeout containers or reused fermented-tofu jars. It's a mystery wrapped in foil, shaped like a bird. I feel bad taking apart the bird's head and neck as I peel apart the crinkled silver sheet, but hunger wins the day. Inside, I find a few stalks of perfectly proportioned asparagus and half a breaded pork chop. Where did she get this fancy stuff?

I cut a tiny piece from the pork chop and nibble at a piece of asparagus. My parents would have a fit if they saw me standing here, eating food straight out of the fridge with the door wide open. I take a few bites, then wrap up the food again in case my mom wants to bring leftovers for lunch tomorrow. I turn on the oven and hunt for the frozen pizza. When the oven is preheated, I pop in the pizza and twiddle my fingers as I wait for it to bake.

Then I realize my mom came home, put this in the fridge and wrote me a note, but never came to check on me in my room. That's super weird. And where is my dad? A sick feeling starts in my stomach and gnaws its way to my fingers until they feel numb.

I take the steps two at a time to my parents' room and lift my arm to knock on their door. I stop when I hear urgent whispers inside.

"Who else went to dinner?" My dad's voice is pulled tight like the strings on a tennis racket. Drawers open and close softly.

"It was my whole team. They introduced us to the man they hired for the senior manager position."

"I still can't believe they didn't give it to you."

"It was a long shot, lǎogōng. I was out for a few months . . ."

My dad makes a sound in his throat before he says, "You've been there your entire career. You're the most experienced and most skilled out of anyone on that team. You should be director-level by now."

I can hear my dad shuffling around the room, but my mom is still. She must be sitting on their bed. I hear him walk to the bed and I imagine him sitting next to her. He asks, "So what happened?"

"When we arrived at the restaurant, Mr. McIntyre was there waiting for us." Her voice shudders.

"What? Why?!" The bed frame groans, and I hear a thud on the floor as my dad leaps back onto his feet.

"The guy they hired was his intern a few years ago, so Mr. McIntyre wanted to congratulate him, I guess."

My dad freezes, and I don't hear his feet pacing back and forth. "Ying, how old is the man they hired?"

"Late twenties? He's blond, so it's hard to tell his age by looking for white hairs."

It's all I can do to hold myself back from busting in their door, but I'll learn more out here than I would if I went in. "They hired a child instead of promoting you." I barely recognize my dad's voice, he's so angry. "Did Nate McIntyre say anything to you?"

"He asked about our family. He said it was cute that we used to video the kids when they played with pillows."

"I don't even want our kids' names in his mouth. Who does he think he is? You shouldn't have gone, Ying."

"How could I have missed a team event, Tianyu?"

My dad catches himself and calms his voice again. "I'm sorry. It's not your fault." He pauses. I fidget. Standing like this with my ear to the door feels wrong; this is clearly not a conversation they want me to hear. But I can't move. I have to know more.

My mom goes on, "He said, 'Your daughter is a powerful writer, Mrs. Chen.'"

Did my dad just swear? I press my ear closer to the door. I ball my fists, digging my nails into the palms of my hands.

"So he wanted you to know he read her letters. What else did he say?"

"That's it. He didn't bring her up again." She pauses as my dad mutters under his breath. "What could I do, Tianyu? There was nothing I could say."

"I want to give him a piece of my mind," says my dad, cracking his knuckles. I can practically see the steam coming out of his ears. It pours out of the crack under the bedroom door and swirls around my feet. He asks, "Then what?"

"Then they talked about our company. Business stuff. About ideas this new senior manager has for reorganizing to save costs."

"Reorganizing, huh? So they're going to let people go."

"I don't know if that's what it means, Tianyu."

"I bet they gave you some spiel about efficiency, innovation, and doing what's best for the company." The bed groans as my dad sits back down.

"Well, actually . . . just like that."

"It's a warning, Ying." He says under his breath, "That's some first-degree Chinatown intimidation right there."

I want to tell my mom not to let Mr. McIntyre bully her. I can't stop myself anymore and I burst into their room. It's like a slow-motion freeze frame.

When I'm a fourth of the way in, I realize I'm about to respond to something I shouldn't know.

Halfway in, I debate pretending like I didn't hear anything and acting relieved to see them home.

Three-fourths of the way in, I question my acting ability because I'm positive I looked pissed when I busted in the door.

Then I'm standing sheepishly in their room and all three of us are rearranging our faces trying to figure out how to respond. I can see my mom's face alternating rapidly between a shocked open-mouthed look, an attempted smile, and resignation. My dad is a little harder to decipher. In the blink of an eye, he cycles between furrowed brows, a goofy grin, and balled-fist anger before settling on an unreadable stone-faced expression. I'm trying to erase my fury and hide the guilty droop tugging at my ears.

"You're home!" I attempt to pretend like I heard nothing. "Where've you been?"

"Yam! Sorry! I had to stay late and help students with their essays. Did you get my text?" Apparently, my dad decides acting like nothing's wrong is also the way to go. My mom tries to follow suit.

"I had a work dinner, Mèi-Mei—"

"Is that where that fancy tinfoil duck is from? I snuck a couple bites—I hope that's okay." I smile what I hope is a natural-looking smile.

"Eat it all," says my mom.

"So, how was dinner? It looks like it was a pretty fancy place." I do another cheesy smile. I am royally sucking at this pretend-everything-is-fine thing.

"It was fine, Maybelline. Did you finish all your schoolwork already?" My mom sucks at this pretend-everything-is-fine thing too.

"Who was at dinner?" I ask.

My parents look at each other. I wait. My mom starts to say something, but it catches on her tongue. My dad fills in, "Ma had dinner with some coworkers and her boss tonight, Yam."

"That's all?"

He hesitates and it bugs me. Why does he want to hide it? I'm not a little kid. Finally, he says, "Nate McIntyre was there too."

I don't even bother acting surprised. "Why?"

In the voice I loved when I was little, the one that meant everything would be okay, my mom says, "Mèi-Mei, we don't want you to worry."

I shed the fake smiles. "All I do is worry, Ma. What's going on?"

"Mom didn't get the promotion she applied for. They had a team dinner to meet the guy they hired instead." My dad tries to keep his voice even and steady. "And now they're threatening her job."

"How can they do that?"

195

My dad levels his eyes at me like two lasers. "You know Mom's boss is good friends with Nate McIntyre. Hiring a new manager is the perfect time for some reorganization, which means they can let Mom go easily."

"But she's been there forever. They need her." I put my hand on my hip and lean my weight to one side.

"You need to stop responding to Mr. McIntyre. Stop putting him on blast, Yam. This isn't a joke. Your letters are a liability for her now," my dad says, the edge in his voice growing sharper. His tone is flint striking sparks onto dry wood.

"I'm not going to stop, Bà." I remember what Tiya said at lunch today. "Fighting back is the right thing to do."

"You're a good writer, Maybelline," my mom says. Once upon a time, I would have died for a compliment like this from her, but right now it feels like a slap in the face. "But you've done enough. You have to stop."

"How can I stop? Mr. McIntyre made it sound like you killed your own son!" I hold out my hands, palms up, and shake them for emphasis. A faint beeping sound comes from downstairs. "We can't just pretend it never happened!"

My dad looks at me; the dark bags under his eyes look like they're filled with sand. "We just want it to stop, Yam."

"It won't stop, Dad! I thought you of all people would get that. Aren't you always telling your students to stand up and speak out? Well, why not me too?" I fold my arms across my chest.

"They threatened her job, Yam. Ma might lose her job. What do you think will happen to our family then?"

"So everything you teach your students is a lie? Or do you not care what happens to them or their families?"

My dad's eyes flash and he steps toward me. "Be careful, Maybelline."

"Mom can get another job. Why would she want to keep working for Mr. McIntyre's buddy anyway? He's probably racist too."

"Listen to yourself, Maybelline. What are you saying? You think it's so easy to find a job?" My mom's back is ramrod straight, and she grips her comforter in both hands. I still hear beeping somewhere. "Do you even care about your family?"

"I'm fighting for my family!"

"You are young, Maybelline. You don't understand," my mom says. That stupid pregnant hippo is back acting like I know nothing and she's surprised she expected anything more. "We don't want you to be hurt."

"You don't want me to get hurt? Or you don't want *you* to get hurt?" Anger has become a wildfire and everything bursts into flames. My mom's expression doesn't change, but she shrinks into herself. Broken pieces that never came close to mending crumple inward.

"MAYBELLINE CHEN!" Dad's voice snaps like a whip across my face. He's never used this tone with me before. I've crossed the line.

I don't care.

"How else can they hurt me? Danny's gone. Nothing could be worse than that. I can handle a few mean words."

"A few mean words?" My dad coughs the words out. He looks

at me, eyebrows raised. "You think that's what this is about? You should know by now that men like Mr. McIntyre can hurt you with much worse than that."

"How?" I grip the doorknob and swing the door back and forth. Somewhere in the recesses of my brain, I register that the beeping has stopped. "Are you afraid someone will come after me? Shoot me like they shot Uncle Joe?"

The room freezes. My dad asks slowly, "Who told you that?"

"Not you," I say, tilting up my chin.

"You don't know anything, Maybelline." In one breath, my mom finds the strength to insult me and stand up for my dad, who is leaning against the wall; they stand up for each other even when they're broken and tired. Why won't they stand with me?

"You don't understand, Maybelline," says my dad, his hands balled into fists like mine. "You think Chinatown is a fun place to eat and watch mismatched old ladies pushing grocery carts. You don't know what it was like growing up there."

"How can I understand when you never tell me anything?"

"I didn't want you to know! I didn't ever want you to know what it was like. I got out of Chinatown so you wouldn't have to live that life." Dad's voice stumbles, then stands back up again. "I survived so you wouldn't have to go through what I went through, wouldn't know what it was like to lose your brother—"

"I KNOW EXACTLY WHAT THAT IS LIKE!" The flames feel so real I smell smoke filling my nostrils.

Dad stares at me, unmoving. He can't stop the emotions from battling across his face. His shoulders slump forward, and he rubs the bridge of his nose. After a long silence, he says softly, "I could have stopped it. I should have been there for him." I don't know if he's talking about Danny or Uncle Joe. He looks up at me, eyes glistening. "Is that how you feel about Danny, Yam?"

I nod, tears springing to my eyes. I wipe them away before they fall. My dad says, "Oh, Yam, I never realized . . ."

His fists have uncurled, and his hands hang lifelessly at his sides like a deflated life raft. My mom sniffs the air. "What is that smell?" she asks distractedly.

The smell? It's real?

Oh crap. I forgot about the pizza.

I run downstairs ready to call 911, expecting to see our kitchen in flames. There is a smoky haze, but otherwise the kitchen looks the same, and the yellowish light still glows over the stove. I throw open the windows to air out the smoke. Inside the oven, I find a disc of smoking charcoal that was formerly a frozen pizza.

I toss the burnt thing into the trash and pour myself a bowl of Peanut Butter Cap'n Crunch. Then I stew alone at the kitchen table and eat.

41

I'm lying in bed scribbling in my journal when my dad opens the door, lightbulb in hand.

"We never put in these new color-changing bulbs I got the other day," he says, holding it up. "You can change the colors on command; isn't that cool?"

I roll over and turn my back to him without responding. He sits down on my bed and puts his hand on my back. "I'm sorry I lost my temper tonight, Yam."

I pull the blankets higher around my neck. My dad comes around the bed and sits where he can see my face. "I should have told you about your uncle Joe. I don't know how you found out, but you should have found out from me."

I mumble, "I was doing an assignment for my lit class. I saw an article with one sentence about him."

My dad wipes his brow. He says, "I remember that article. It's the only thing about Joe they ever printed in the paper. His entire life reduced to one sentence."

I roll onto my back so I can see him. "What happened to him, Bà?"

He lets out a long breath and looks down at me. He cups the top of my head in his palm. "He was shot by one of the Chinatown gangs."

"Why?" I frown.

"Ahhh. I didn't explain it well earlier, but Chinatown has history you didn't see when we visited Nǎi-Nai and Yé-Ye. You and Danny used to get so excited when we went up there. You'd beg me for all those fun souvenirs, especially those little poppers you throw on the floor. You little knuckleheads would throw them at my feet and scare the crap out of me after I forgot you had them." He chuckles at the memory. "I loved that you two loved Chinatown. But growing up there was hard."

"Because you were so poor?"

"Being poor was part of it. But everyone was poor, so we didn't know any different."

"What made it so hard, Bà?"

He taps his finger on his lips for a moment, then asks, "What do you know about Chinatown history?"

"Just what I read tonight when I was trying to do some research."

"You have to understand the history to understand why it was hard. Buckle up for a Mr. Chen history lesson, Yam."

I sit up when my dad starts way back, explaining Chinese

history in the United States: sugar plantations, indentured servitude, coolie labor, the Gold Rush, the transcontinental railroad, and the Chinese Exclusion Act. We haven't gotten to this stuff in AP History yet, but I'm sure it'll barely be a paragraph in the textbook. We bust out my laptop so he can show me some of the political cartoons where the Chinese were labeled barbarians, heathens, and the "lowest, most vile of the human race." He says that not too long ago, anti-Chinese attacks—beatings, arson, murder—were common. Chinese people weren't allowed to live near white people and couldn't find jobs outside the restaurant or laundry industries; that's why Chinatowns were formed.

"Nǎi-Nai and Yé-Ye came here from Hong Kong right when the gang rivalries in Chinatown were really heating up." My dad starts telling me about the Wah Ching, the Chinese Underground, the Joe Boys, and the Hop Sing Tong, but I can't keep them all straight. Something about American-born Chinese versus Hong Kong–born Chinese versus different crime syndicates, and they all get mashed together in my brain.

My dad pulls up an old picture of the Golden Dragon Restaurant, and I point at it, saying, "I just read about this! A lot of people were killed there, right?"

He looks at me curiously and says, "Our dumpling shop was a five-minute walk from this spot, Yam."

I look at him, surprised. "You were alive when it happened?"

"I was only three, but I remember. Gunmen with sawed-off shotguns ran into the restaurant and shot it up, trying to kill some local gang leaders. They killed five innocent people, but no gangsters."

I'm starting to realize how much I've never learned about my own history. It's weird and also cool learning it from my dad. When we read about historical stuff in class, it's like learning about another planet, but when he talks, it feels real. History didn't happen as long ago as I thought; it happened to people I know.

"But if you were only three, then Uncle Joe was only two. Were these gangs still around when you were in high school?"

"For a while, it was like open warfare in the streets, but after the Golden Dragon Massacre, they kind of cracked down on the gangs. A lot of them went underground," my dad explains. "But there was another flare-up when we were in high school. More street shootings."

"Was Uncle Joe in a gang?" I ask cautiously.

My dad shakes his head emphatically. "He would *never*. They tried to recruit him and even offered the dumpling shop protection if he joined. But he wouldn't do it. He wasn't about that life."

"I don't get it."

"He wouldn't do what they asked, so they shot him in an alley one night when he went to run an errand for the shop. They made him an example." My dad pinches the bridge of his nose and doesn't move for a solid minute. I put my hand on his arm. "When he didn't come back right away, I went to look for him, but the alley was so dark I couldn't see. I didn't find him until it was too late."

He stops again and steadies his voice. I look at the lightbulb in his hand and think of his collection in the closet. "I held him until he died."

"Bà . . ." I throw my spaghetti noodle arms around him. He

pats my elbow softly. I don't know what else to say.

"One of the rival gangs came for me next. Wanted me to retaliate," he says. "So I moved in with my English teacher, whose family lived outside Chinatown. I stayed there for more than half a year."

"Really? I never knew that. Năi-Nai and Yé-Ye let you do that?"

"Oh, they were so grateful, Yam. They thought Ms. Powell saved my life." My dad smiles as he remembers her. "She didn't mess around, that woman. She's the reason I decided to become a teacher."

Thinking of my dad as this whole other person with a whole other life before me is strange. "Really? I just thought you liked to torture teenagers."

"Ha, ha." He flicks my ear. "Well, maybe I do. I used to make Uncle Wu come to Ms. Powell's house and study with me. That guy was the worst at school," he says, laughing outright. "But we put our heads down and studied our way out of Chinatown."

He gets up and removes the bulb from the lamp by my bed. As he works, he says, "That's why I choose to work in Sequoia Grove. I get to teach students who remind me of me and Joe . . . and students who remind me of the gangsters who killed him. Maybe I can make a difference for someone."

He holds up the color-changing bulb before twisting it into place. He fiddles around until he figures out how to make it change colors, then he shows me how to do it too.

"Isn't it cool?" he asks proudly.

"Yeah, so cool, Bà." I shake my head. "You better not waste that other perfectly good bulb."

"Yeah, yeah, yeah, don't worry."

I nestle back down into my bed and say, "I'm sorry I yelled at you, Bà. I didn't mean what I said about your teaching."

He tousles my hair and starts to tuck me in like a mummy. "Yam, what you said earlier . . . about feeling like you should have been there for Danny, thinking you could have stopped him. Don't do that to yourself. You were the best mèi-mei Danny could have asked for."

I look down at my white comforter. My dad continues, "It never occurred to me you felt that way because to me, it's obviously not your fault. I should have known you would feel that way, though. I've been there." He smooths my hair and brushes a strand out of my face.

"Do you feel that way about Danny, too, Bà?"

Now he looks down. He nods slowly. "I do, Yam. I know I shouldn't. But I do."

I reach out of my mummy blanket-wrap and take his hand. "You were the best dad Danny could have asked for, Bà."

He smiles sadly and pats my arm. "I just wish I understood. I wish I could have done more."

"Me too."

I lie back down and stay still as my dad tucks in the blankets tightly again. Then he says quietly, "You would have loved your uncle Joe. You remind me of him, so determined to do the right thing. Joe knew he was doing the right thing, and that's all that mattered to him." He smiles sadly, then says, "I just wish doing the right thing always led to the right results."

"Are you saying you wish he had joined the gang?"

"No. But sometimes I wonder, if he had joined the gang,

would he still be alive?" He shakes his head as he talks and I get the sense this is a conversation he's had with himself many times. "But even saying it out loud sounds ridiculous. What kind of life would he have lived if he had been in a gang? There's no guarantee he would still be alive. I just want him back, Yam. I miss him every day."

"I know how that feels, Bà."

"I think what I'm trying to say is that there are other ways to do what is right. Maybe there could have been another way for Joe. I found another way because of what happened to him." He kisses my forehead and stands up. "I hope you can find another way. A safer way. For all of us."

I can't sleep after my dad leaves. His words run around my brain like a toy train on an oval track. He wants me to lie low, ignore everyone, and study my way out of this. Like he did when he was in high school. He wants me to be safe.

If my mom loses her job, our family will be screwed. Mr. McIntyre is probably friendly with a lot of local business leaders; what if my mom can't find another job? We couldn't live in Sequoia Park on my dad's teacher salary. What am I fighting for if I'm just hurting my family more?

Maybe my dad's right. Maybe I should listen to my parents and let this go.

MAYDAY.

Guess what I found out about myself tonight?

I might be distantly related to one of leaders in the Haitian Revolution!

🔥🔥🔥🔥🔥🔥

Hello?

Hello?

DID YOU HEAR WHAT I SAID.

LEADER OF HAITIAN REVOLUTION

PAY ATTENTION, MAYDAY.

OF COURSE YOU ARE

WHO'S SURPRISED?

NOT ME.

His name was Jean-Jacques Dessalines

Born into slavery and commanded armies that overthrew France

He abolished slavery in Haiti

I learned that on Wikipedia

(Don't tell Ms. D I researched there)

Over here busy learning about my own self

There's SO MUCH I didn't know

I know exactly how you feel

43

I tap my pen distractedly on Tiya's back as Ms. Daniels gives us directions for today's discussion.

"Push your desks to the side of the room and come sit down on the floor in a circle—Hey hey hey, not yet! Wait until I say go!—crisscross applesauce, if you can still do that," Ms. Daniels says as she moves her own table out of the way. "Don't forget to bring any notes or materials you collected while researching your family history. Go!"

When all the chairs and desks are pushed aside, Ms. Daniels plops down on the floor and adjusts the bright batik fabric of her skirt.

Tiya and I sit together next to Ms. Daniels. I motion for Celeste to come sit with us, and she sits to my right. Ava points at the carpet near me, eyebrows curved in a question mark. Tiya and I wave her over too. We scoot over and she sits between us. Tiya flaps her hand for Ayanna to come over, but she's already settled in her spot by an open window.

A few of Josh's friends laugh as they push each other around before sitting down. Josh makes space for Noah Kelly, another football player, and they share some inside joke. Josh grabs Noah's ankle and Noah crashes to the ground. Josh glances at me quickly. We haven't spoken since the day his father's letter came out.

Ms. D clears her throat, and the class settles down. "Okay," she says brightly, "I know the Halloween Dance is this Friday and you're all distracted out of your minds, but let's get focused, folks. This is important. You know the drill. Our kick-off question is: What's something that surprised you about your family history?" She gestures with her hands and turns up the wattage on her smile. "Who's the brave soul who will get us started?"

Long seconds of uncomfortable rustling pass before Noah says loudly, "Well, I learned that my ancestors were a bunch of drunk Irishmen!"

"No surprise there," Ava whispers to me and Tiya, as Noah's friends laugh loudly and reach over for high fives.

"Well, that was certainly one stereotype of Irish immigrants," Ms. Daniels says, unfazed. "What else did you learn?"

Noah scratches his head and checks his notes. "Oh yeah, my ancestors came to America because of the famine." He checks his notes again. "They helped to build the Transcontinental Railroad."

Andrew Young looks up and shakes his caramel-brown hair out of his eyes. "So did mine."

"Word? Luck o' the Irish, bro!"

"Nah, it's my Chinese side," says Andrew. "My great-great-great-grandpa on my mom's side—I forget how many greats there are—worked on the railroad too."

Ms. Daniels says, "Tell us more, Andrew."

"My family actually went to Utah to be part of this flash-mob thing a few years ago. This photographer organized descendants of Chinese rail workers to re-create the Golden Spike photo. Chinese workers weren't allowed in the original." Andrew holds up two pictures. One looks familiar, like something I've seen in a textbook. It's a black-and-white photo of white rail workers celebrating around two trains. The other is posed similarly, but it's in color and everyone in the photo is Chinese. He passes the photos around.

"Maybe there weren't any Chinese people in the original because there weren't that many of them," says Noah.

Andrew gives Noah a look that could wither flowers in the planters outside. "The Chinese were the majority of the Central Pacific force, dude. They did the most dangerous stuff."

"Oh." Noah clamps his mouth shut as he passes the pictures on.

Celeste gets into the mix. "My dad told me that Chinese people—rail workers included—weren't allowed to live near white people. That's why Chinatown was created. He grew up there." She tucks her hair behind her ear and keeps talking. "There were lynchings and murders of Chinese people. My dad's family was really poor and there were a lot of gangs—"

"*Chinese* gangs? What did they do, throw books at each other?" Cal Thomas snickers from the other side of the room.

"Shut the hell up," Celeste snaps. I wonder what my mom would think if she heard Celeste like this. I kinda love it, so Ma probably wouldn't.

"It was just a joke," Cal mutters.

"Racist jokes aren't funny." Celeste glares.

"Agreed. We can't have this conversation if we can't keep this space safe. It would be a shame if anyone had to leave the discussion because they can't follow norms." Ms. Daniels looks around the circle, and we all sit up straighter. "Now, where were we?"

"Chinatown," Celeste says, nudging my knee. She leaves me an opening without realizing it.

"My dad and Celeste's dad grew up together." I stop and study the designs on Celeste's Converse. Do I really want to share what I learned last night? I mean, it was definitely a surprise. "My uncle was murdered by one of the gangs."

Tiya and Celeste compete for Most Likely to Break Her Neck as they whip their heads toward me. "What?!" they both say at the same time. I guess Celeste's dad never told her either.

"Why? What did he do?" Josh asks. He's sitting with his arms draped over his knees.

"What's it to you, Josh?" Tiya asks, always ready to come to my defense, especially against Josh. She'll probably never forgive him for his party. "Why do you all always have to make it sound like the victim is at fault?"

I rub Tiya's back in thanks and remember asking her

something similar when she and Marc talked about protesting André Johnson's death six weeks ago. Holy hell, I'm a fool. Now I get why she and Marc didn't want to talk to me about it, why they went to the protest without me.

"A gang tried to recruit him and he wasn't about it. So they killed him," I respond icily.

"Oh shit, I'm sorry, May," says Josh. His elbows rest on his knees, and he props up his head between his hands. He looks at the carpet and shakes his head back and forth.

"*Language*, Josh." Ms. Daniels looks at him sternly before turning back to me. "Do you want to add anything more, May? You don't have to if it feels too personal."

"My dad told me that Chinatown was always portrayed as a hot spot for crime, even before there were gang issues there. The police were always raiding places and harassing people. So, get this." I pause, because this was another surprise from last night. "Chinatown leaders hired a *PR firm* to spread an image of Chinese kids who loved to study and followed rules."

Noah scratches his head and looks like a cartoon caricature as he asks, "Why?"

"Have you been tackled too many times or something, Noah?" Celeste bites her upper lip and corrects herself before Ms. Daniels can cut her off. "I mean, so white people would start treating them—us—like people, obviously."

"Maybe we should hire a PR firm for Black folks around here," says Tiya, tapping her chin with her index finger.

"Right?" agrees Ayanna. She sweeps her braids over her

shoulder and turns her head toward Ms. D. "Back in the day, when my grandparents moved up here, they wanted to live in Sequoia Park, but the realtor—he was white—kept driving them over the bridge to Sequoia Grove. They didn't want Black families in Sequoia Park. That's how we all ended up in the Grove."

"But the Grove is mostly Latinx now," says Ava. "At least most of the students I tutor there are. I wonder how that change happened?"

"Actually, the Grove used to be land plots owned by Japanese and Italian farmers. That was before realtors bought their land, jacked up prices, and then sold their homes to Black folks like my grandparents." Ayanna tilts her head. "After what Celeste just said, I wonder if the Japanese and Italians were there because they weren't allowed to live other places."

"Before the Italians came to be considered white, huh?" Ava scratches a spot behind her ear.

"Our histories are connected." Tiya leans forward. "Something like what happened to Ayanna's grandparents happened to my parents when my dad started practicing at Stanford. People asked to see multiple documents as proof he actually worked there before they would even show my parents an apartment. Other people just pointed them over to the Grove. They'd say stuff like, 'You could probably afford it better over there.'"

"Now he's the chief of his department and he's won all kinds of awards," I add.

"Facts." Tiya brushes lint from the carpet off her jeans. "But it doesn't matter. Some patients still refuse to be seen by a Black doctor. Like, they'd rather die than let a skilled, renowned Black man help them out."

"I don't think a PR firm is enough for that crap," says Ava.

"Probably not," Tiya agrees. "People who are willing to get sick and die in order to hold on to racist ideas aren't going to be swayed by a PR campaign."

"I don't think the Chinese PR campaign worked either, though." Ava leans back on her hands.

"What do you mean, Ava?" Ms. Daniels hardly says anything during these class discussions; she just throws out a question here and there, and somehow she really gets people talking. I wish other teachers could work it like she does.

"Judging by Cal's dumbass comment earlier, it seems to have worked just fine, right?" Ava turns and gives Cal a death stare. "But look what people like my mom and Josh's dad said about May's family and 'the Asians' at the Junior Jam. They took the idea of studious Asian kids and twisted it into a threat."

Josh's face flushes red at the mention of his dad. He crosses his arms over his knees and hides his face in his arms. Celeste mutters, "We're a threat no matter what we do."

"Hey, welcome to our world." Tiya tilts her chin toward Ayanna, who opens her eyes wide like *yuup*. Tiya twists the frayed ends of a hole in her jeans. "There's a theme in all these stories, though."

"Theme? Look at you throwing in some English vocab. Bonus points for my girl, Tiya!" Ms. Daniels interrupts. She clasps her hands by her face and smiles. "Okay, but seriously, what do you mean?"

"Like I said, it's all connected. In every story, we're getting pushed around so that white folks can hold on to power. They control where we live, what's in our history books, what we learn and don't learn about each other and ourselves." Tiya looks over at me quickly before shifting her focus back to Ms. D. "Last night, I learned that I'm a descendant of Jean-Jacques Dessalines. He was one of the leaders of the slave revolt that led to the Haitian Revolution—enslaved people rose up, ended slavery, and overthrew the French government. Thomas Jefferson and the Americans were so terrified they passed the Fugitive Slave Act in response; they didn't want the same thing to happen here. The only part of this I've ever learned about in school was the Slave Act part. I knew almost nothing about the Haitian Revolution until last night."

When Tiya stops to take a breath, Ayanna jumps in. "White folks control the whole narrative. They don't want us to know our own power, how connected we really are. That's why people tried PR campaigns to fight back—"

"And those PR campaigns didn't work," Ava reminds us.

"Because it's not just people like Ava's mom and Josh's dad and the racist realtors. It's white supremacist systems and policies and history and *everything*." Tiya finishes, and I make a mic-drop motion for her to see. Ayanna nods emphatically. Josh's head is still buried in the crooks of his elbows.

"Whoa, come on now, white supremacists? We're not all KKK members. It's not *all* white people," protests Noah.

Ava talks to Noah like he's two inches tall. "White supremacy isn't just the KKK. It's exactly what Tiya is talking about: systems and policies that always put white people on top. You might not *think* you're racist, Noah, but you don't have a problem upholding racist systems that help you out. You probably don't even realize you're doing it."

"But we're not all bad," Noah insists. "I'm not racist. I'm a nice guy."

"It's not enough to be nice," I say. Marc's voice is taking up space in my head again.

Silence is a thief that snatches up the class's collective breath, and Ms. Daniels lets us marinate in the discomfort. She looks like she wants to jump into the discussion, but she inhales deeply and says, "Family history is personal, so naturally, strong feelings come up when we talk about it. Especially when we talk about the ways our stories intersect. Thank you to everyone who participated by sharing or listening. I appreciate that we were able to start a challenging dialogue in here today."

She untangles her skirt from between her feet and starts to stand up. "I'd like you to go back to your seats and reflect. Check the questions on the board: What's an insight you had today? What's something that surprised you? What are you still thinking about? What's a question you still have? Answer as many of the prompts as you want . . . and yes, you have to answer at least one." She smiles at Noah. "I know you were about to ask."

A beam of light from the window creates a bright glare across the prompts written on the whiteboard. I cup my face in my hands as I replay the discussion in my head. Lines around me begin to pull in different directions. Seams begin to stretch, and the costume of the world starts to tear away. I catch glimpses of things I've never noticed before.

The first thing I write is:

Narratives have always been controlled. It didn't start when Mr. McIntyre twisted up Danny's story; it's been happening through-out history.

I tap my pencil against Tiya's chair while I think. Then I write:

We can't let them control the narrative forever.

44

Something tells me to leave it alone, but the Comments button glows seductively from my laptop screen. It's early November and I've resisted looking for weeks, but I just reread my poem on the *Weekly*'s website and now I'm staring at this button, my finger poised to click. Don't do it, I tell myself, but curiosity wins the day.

I regret it immediately.

Blovin92: Boo hoo about your pillows. No one cares about your pillows, chink. Go back to China where you belong and take your whole damn family and your nasty diseases with you.

ScottY: Go back to the horse's ass where YOU came from. This girl lost her brother. Show some respect.

Blovin92: She wouldn't have lost her big brother if he hadn't jumped his ass in front of the train. Whose fault is that? McIntyre had it right.

MattGa1234: I heard that her parents forced him to study until 4 am every day, made him take piano lessons and extra math classes, and then slapped him around if he got an A-. If it wasn't for them, he'd probably still be around.

MrsForester: I know a Chinese couple that grounds their kid if he isn't first in his class on every assignment. Their kid is in kindergarten for goodness sake. Nathaniel McIntyre was right about Asians stressing out our kids. Suicide wasn't an issue before they moved in. Nate was still gracious after her terrible accusations. This girl should be ashamed.

Jillian_P: It's just terrible what this girl is doing to Nathaniel's reputation. Calling him a racist when there are no facts to support her claims. She's the racist one. Just imagine what this is putting Nathaniel's family through.

MrsForester: I'm so glad there are other people with sense in this town. That poor man and what he's had to endure. I can't believe The Weekly is even printing her letters. She's probably just writing them so she can use them on her college applications.

Jillian_P: I thought of that too. Her parents probably made her do it. These people will stop at nothing to get their kids into Ivy League schools. Shame on them. Between what happened with their son and what their daughter is doing now, it's clear they could use a lesson on parenting.

ScottY: Raise your hand if you actually read her poem? Danny was depressed. His family clearly loved him and now they have to deal with their tragic loss. Meanwhile, you are over here talking about poor Nathaniel McIntyre?! Seriously, WTF is wrong with you people?

Queen650: I'm with ScottY. Your racism is showing, people. How are you going to blame a community mental health crisis on "the Asians"? It took a lot of guts to write these poems knowing people like you are out here. Good for her.

YaZhu88: Thank you, ScottY and Queen650. Everyone in this community starts extracurricular activities at a young age and many hire private tutors and counselors to prepare for college. It's not just Asian parents. People are trying to blame Asians for stress in schools because they don't want to self-reflect.

EezyMac_45: Ching chong wing wong long duc dong! What are you saying? We speak English in America.

EileenE: YaZhu88's English is better than yours.

DrJones: The fact is, Chinese families are ruining our city and schools. They don't just want their kids to do well in school, they push their kids until no one else can compete. I know too many great families who have moved elsewhere because the competition and pressure here are too much. I believe in diversity, but not at the expense of our kids.

It keeps going on and on and on. I can't tear my eyes away from the screen even though I keep telling myself, *stop reading stop reading stop reading.* The bile in my stomach bubbles toward my esophagus. Just as I decide to close the tab, my eye catches on a comment thread tucked in toward the end:

QTGirl123: I think it's disgusting how Maybelline writes this sob story and pretends to be so innocent when she's actually going around hooking up with people at parties. Everyone knows she got with J. Mac right before the Junior Jam. Pillows huh? That's poetic. She knows a lot more about pillows than she writes about here.

> **LalaCutie428:** What do people see in her anyway? She's not even pretty.

> **Legs4Dayz:** Some guys have yellow fever. I don't know why, since it's like a deadly disease or something.

> **LalaCutie428:** Yeah, I guess slanty eyes and no boobs are a thing.

> **D8ddyO:** Azn girls are freaks that's why.

I slam my laptop shut.

I want to puke and scream and rage and laugh and cry all at the same time. It's all so absurd. I wrote my truth, just like Ms. Daniels suggested. Yet this disgusting mess came out of what I wrote. They say you should never read the comments. Now I know why.

My mom said people would twist what I wrote to benefit themselves. She said they wouldn't interpret things the way I meant them.

She was right.

45

The comment threads, my mom's job, Mr. McIntyre's letter, the class discussion, the train tracks all clamor for attention in my head, and I can't deal. I curl up on my bed, wishing Danny were here. I could use a really terrible rendition of "Lay Me Down" right now.

I think about Danny looking for his Star Wars socks the night he died. He had a pair of Star Wars socks for every day of the week and a lucky pair with Obi-Wan for big games or special occasions. We used to have Star Wars marathons where we'd watch the original three movies back to back to back. Well, more accurately, he used to bribe me with food to sit through Star Wars marathons with him.

I never really understood his love for Star Wars. Maybe he

loved how the heroes always beat the villains. How the light always beat the darkness. I wonder if Star Wars gave him hope when he was really down. Sometimes he'd even make me listen to the soundtrack in his car.

His car.

I roll out of bed.

Danny's clunky old Camry is parked in our garage. I don't remember where they found it or how it got home, but it's been sitting here for over half a year, untouched. We've all avoided the garage like we don't want to wake his Toyota..

Staring at the car feels like I'm messing with the sacred, like I'm admitting A) he's not coming back, B) my memories of him might change, C) I didn't know Danny (or anything, apparently) the way I thought I did. Maybe it's D) all of the above.

I stare for a long time, but eventually something pulls me to open the back door and look inside.

The particular smell of stale In-N-Out and Danny's deodorant blasts me in the face, and I step back. Danny's car always smelled like stale burgers because he was obsessed with In-N-Out. He was constantly dripping food on the seats and leaving wrappers in his car. My heart backflips in my chest and I blink away the burning sensation in my eyes. It smells just like it did all those days he drove me to school, like the time we drove downtown to meet Marc and Tiya for gelato, like the night he drove me to San Francisco for the best birthday surprise ever. Just the smell makes my knees buckle with memories. Maybe this isn't a good idea.

I try to back away, but it feels like something, someone—Danny?—is pulling me into the car. I breathe deeply, sucking in the smell until it turns to nothing in my nose. In the back seat, I find a basketball, a hamburger wrapper, and a crumpled napkin. I scan the front seats, poke around in the glove compartment, and open all the nooks and crannies. All I find are some car manuals, a stale pack of gum, a black Sharpie, and the hand-cranked flashlight my dad made Danny put in his car for emergencies. I'm backing out of the driver's seat when my eye catches on the lever that opens the trunk.

There's probably nothing, but I pop the trunk and peek in.

It's empty.

I slump onto the ledge of the car. Who was I kidding? I wasn't going to find anything here after the police already searched the car. Am I disappointed or relieved? Maybe both? I think I was secretly hoping for another piece of Danny. One more thing to hold on to. Something that might give me answers or help me through. But I also exhale, breathing out the worry that I might find something that makes it harder. A clue that confirms the worst of my thoughts: *this is all my fault.*

I stare at the trunk and realize the KT3 shoebox Danny always kept in here is missing. My stomach churns as something else stirs in my mind.

Another memory.

That night, Danny came into my room holding the shoebox with a jacket draped over his arm. I remember thinking his shoes were extra white and that he was probably putting the box back into the trunk.

I don't remember him holding the shoebox when he left my room.

I slam the trunk closed and bolt upstairs, combing through my memories in an effort to locate the shoebox. I vaguely remember throwing a pillow at him. I remember Danny tripping on something, then getting on his hands and knees to shove clothes back into my closet. He made some snarky remark, and I think I threw another pillow at him. He hugged me, told me he loved me, kissed me on my forehead, and left with his jacket, but no box.

The closet.

I take the rest of the stairs in sets of threes and fling open my closet door as soon as I get to my room. Clothes tumble off the enormous pile of stuff growing in the corner. I feel some disgust that I haven't sorted this behemoth in over six months, but I can't worry about that now. Must. Find. Shoebox.

I start pulling clothes and random items off the pile and tossing them into my room. There's that jacket I've been looking for. There's a mug crusted over with dried tea. Gross. There's the shoe Danny tripped over that night. I slow down and get on my hands and knees and start digging from the bottom. My fingers touch something smooth squashed into the very back of the closet and I suck in a big gulp of air.

I carefully extract the shoebox from its hiding spot and pull it onto my lap. It's shiny white and tied shut with a shoelace.

Now, one of those once perfectly white shoes is upstairs in my parents' room. Who knows where the other shoe is. What happened to it after the train . . .

I can't think about it.

My hands shake as I pick up the box. Something rolls and clunks around inside. Scribbled across the lid in faded black Sharpie are the words *For May-May.*

It's Danny's handwriting.

I imagine him writing my name across the box and shoving it into my closet before he . . . before he . . . Did he have this all planned out? Or was it an impulsive decision?

It's hard to glean any information from Danny's handwriting. My mouth twists into a partial smile. It's like his handwriting never graduated beyond third grade. No matter how carefully he wrote, it always looked like chicken scratch.

I stand up and set the box on my dresser. I sit on my bed and glue my eyeballs on it from across the room. My heart pounds in anticipation, and I realize I'm barely breathing. I take three steps across the floor and touch the box. I flip the fraying shoelace back and forth in my fingers. I go back and sit on my bed. Then I go back and touch the lid. Back and forth across my room.

What's inside?

I thought I wanted to know, but now that the box is staring back at me, I realize I don't. I'm not ready for what's inside. What if it only gives me more questions and no answers? If I open this box, there will be nothing left to discover about Danny. Nothing more he can show me or teach me or give me. There will be nothing left of him for me. This box helps me keep Danny alive.

Pressure builds behind my eyes, but the tears stay in their ducts as I hug the shoebox tighter. I shuffle, box and all, over to Danny's room.

I cradle it in my arms as I climb into Danny's bed, wrap myself in his blankets and bury my face in his Millennium Falcon pillow. Maybe it's weird to snuggle a dirty shoebox, but I don't care. I just want to hold him next to my heart.

Everything still smells like him. Like fabric softener and Old Spice and sweat. I wish my lungs were bigger, so I could inhale this smell forever.

I breath in deeply and exhale slowly, savoring every scent molecule that travels through my nose. Inhale. Exhale. Inhale. Exhale.

Inhale.

Exhale.

I fall asleep in Danny's bed with his smell curled around me, holding me. I almost believe Danny is here, snuggling me again, singing me to sleep.

46

The next morning, Tiya and Marc show up, banging down the door of Danny's room. My parents must have let them in and told them where I fell asleep. Ma and Bà must be worried about me if they're asking people to barge into Danny's room.

"Get out of bed, Mayday!" Tiya, her hair in a small Afro and wearing overalls only she could make cute, leaps onto Danny's bed and literally kicks me out of it. I scramble for the shoebox and shove it under the bed before they see it. Marc hovers by the door, gazing around the room, clutching a brown paper bag. I'm sure he's reliving memories with Danny in here. He chews his lower lip as the emotions come in waves. Tiya calls, "Marc, help me out!"

He pushes his thoughts aside and waggles his eyebrows at me. He pulls something out of the paper bag and says, "G'morning, sunshine! We brought scones!"

I am still in clothes from yesterday and Tiya notices immediately. "Oh girl, that outfit looks disgustingly familiar. Did you actually *go to bed* wearing those clothes?"

I look at her and puff my stank morning breath in her direction. That's what she gets for waking me up before my alarm. She sputters, gags, and frantically waves her hand around her face. "Oh no, Mayday. You need help." She pulls me to my feet, shoves me out of Danny's room, and shuts me in the bathroom. "We've been texting you all night. Good thing we came by to check on you this morning!"

I bang on the door half-heartedly and call out, "But my shower day is not until *next* week!"

"Hmph. I'm holding this door shut until I hear that shower turn on and some teeth getting brushed. This is for your own good." I test the door, and yep, she's actually pulling it closed. Resigned, I load up my toothbrush and bring it into the shower with me. Brushing my teeth in the shower makes them feel extra clean. Also, it's more efficient. I holler with a mouth full of toothpaste, "You better not touch my scone before I get out! I want that blueberry one!"

When I'm all fresh and clean, I wrap my towel around my body and shuffle down the hall. I hear Tiya singing "Seasons of Love" from *Rent* softly in my room. I peek into Danny's room and catch my breath when I see that Marc and Tiya have made the bed and put everything back into place. I run in to check for the shoebox. It's still there. I'll move it back to my closet later when I'm alone.

As I leave the room, I see a little Nerf basketball on the edge of the desk. I recognize it as the one Marc and Danny use to play around with at the Duverne home. Marc must have set it there for Danny.

I shut the door carefully and proceed to knock politely on mine. Tiya opens it a crack and gives me a once-over to make sure I didn't just turn on the water and stand by the tub without getting in. She points at my mouth, and I blow air into her face as I walk by so she can smell my minty breath. Satisfied, she lets me in. Marc freezes when he sees me in my towel. "I'll, uh . . . I'll, uh . . . wait in the car," he stammers, sticking his eyes to the wall and seeing himself out.

"Leave the scones!" I call. But I'm too late. He's vanished.

Tiya has laid out an outfit on my bed. She's picked out a pair of ripped jeans, a loose white T-shirt that says *FEED ME CARBS*, and a chunky sweater cardigan thing. She must have dug deep to find it. I would have thrown on a hoodie; cardigans are for fancy occasions. She's even set out a pair of sneakers and a set of hoop earrings. It feels too dressed up for school, but otherwise, very me.

After I throw on the clothes, Tiya commands me to stand still while she fusses around me. She tucks in the front of my T-shirt and weaves a belt around my waist. Where did she get that? Then she cuffs my jeans and even brushes my hair as I moan and groan. Tiya interjects, "Oh hush up. Now sit down so I can do your hair."

"What is this, prom? You don't need to do my hair. I never even brush it!"

Tiya ignores me and settles onto my bed as I sit on the floor. She tugs and pulls, and it is surprisingly relaxing. I mumble, "I better not look like Princess Leia when you're done, Tiya Marie."

She keeps ignoring me while her fingers send little tingles over my scalp. When she finishes, she walks me back to the bathroom and hands me a mirror so I can see the back of my head. I didn't even know I had a handheld mirror; where does she keep finding this stuff? She's pulled my hair into a messy fishtail braid at the nape of my neck. The braid only goes about halfway, then loosens into a regular ponytail. She's pulled out a few strands of hair around my face and at the edges of my hairline. It looks casual, like I threw my hair up and it magically turned into a braid. I study my outfit too. It's just like my hair: me, but with more style.

Tiya pulls out a little bag of makeup and I beeline for the door. "No, makeup! Imma look like a clown!"

She grabs my collar and shoves me into a sitting position on the bed. She points at her face. "You saying I look like a clown today, Mayday?"

I sulk with my lips zipped together while she paints gunk on my face. According to her, it's just a little eyeliner and mascara. She holds up the mirror again, and she's right, I can barely see it. It's still me, but my eyes pop.

I strut my way back to the bedroom and spin around slowly. Tiya claps. I complain, "People are going to wonder what the big occasion is."

Tiya rolls her eyes and clucks her tongue. "No they're not.

You're wearing ripped jeans, a T-shirt, and a cardigan, Mayday. Most people have to try way harder than that to look as good as you do."

I remember the comments I read online yesterday and frown. "You have to say that because you're my best friend."

"You know I'd tell you if you looked busted. Now hurry up or we'll be late to school."

She hustles me to the car, where Marc has been waiting. The sounds of NPR Code Switch drift out when we open the door. He turns it off as we pile in.

"No, no, don't be embarrassed by your nerd radio. By all means, let's nerd out together." Tiya laughs as she climbs into the back seat where he can't retaliate. Marc makes a swipe at her ear, then gestures for me to sit shotgun. He does a quick double take and says, "Are you wearing makeup, Mayday?"

I whirl around and glare at Tiya. "See? I told you I'd look like a clown."

Marc studies my eyes in a way that tickles the inside of my stomach. "Nah, you don't look like a clown," he says finally as he puts the car in reverse. He turns the radio back on before I can respond. Was that *you don't look like a clown*, like *you look good*? Or was it *you don't look like a clown, but you're a little late for Halloween*? I keep checking myself in the mirror, perplexed.

After a couple minutes, Marc says, "So what's up, May?"

"Scone, please." I hold out my hand. Marc shakes his head, but I see the grin hiding in the corners of his mouth. I lean over him and snatch one out of the bag.

"Yeah, what happened after school yesterday?" Tiya leans forward and pokes her face between me and Marc. "You fell off the planet."

I gulp as I think about the evening I wasted. "I read the comments section. Then I crawled into bed." I don't mention the shoebox.

"What? Lemme see." Both of them whip out their phones, but I grab Marc's arm and pull his phone from his hand. I feel his muscles tighten beneath my fingers and his eyes catch mine before he pulls his arm away. I snatch my hand back, confused.

"You can't look, Marc, you're driving. Tiya can read them out loud," I say, rubbing my hands together.

Tiya starts reading and immediately makes gagging noises. Marc's gaze turns to stone. He mutters a string of curse words under his breath. When Tiya gets to the thread from QTGirl123, she chokes a little.

"Seriously? Are we in middle school? What kind of name is QTGirl123?" Tiya turns off her phone. "I think we've read enough. No wonder you crawled into bed."

"That's some bullshit," mutters Marc. "Those people mob online, but they don't even know you. Or your family."

"I know. I can't fight back against all of them. Anytime I say something, it's like Mr. McIntyre grows heads." I keep checking myself out in the side mirror. I peek over at Marc. Why am I so stupidly self-conscious around him? He's known me since I had ginormous plastic-rimmed glasses that were half the size of my face and my idea of fashion was wearing Danny's oversized basketball T-shirts to school. Not that my sense of fashion has evolved noticeably since then.

He fiddles with the temperature knob. "McIntyre doesn't even have to do anything. All these other people jump in, and he keeps his hands clean."

"Maybe it's because Mayday's the only one hitting back. People can dogpile one story, but maybe they couldn't if there were a lot more of them . . ." Tiya's eyes light up.

"I know that look. What are you thinking, sis?" Marc looks at Tiya through the rearview mirror.

"We're working on personal narratives in Ms. D's class, and we had this discussion the other day where people shared surprising stuff they'd learned about their family history. Somehow, by the end of the discussion we were talking about how white supremacy isn't just the KKK." Tiya leans forward next to my face again. "Ava, Ayanna, Celeste, and Andrew were on point, don't you think?

"And you!" I add.

"I was, wasn't I?" Tiya brushes her shoulder a bit and grins. "Anyway, now I'm thinking: What if we could find a way to respond to Mr. McIntyre with *a lot* of stories?"

I start catching on. "Like what happened in class . . . but bigger."

"Yeah! Mr. McIntyre and his minions—no offense to the cute yellow ones from that one movie—can't dogpile you if there are tons more people backing you up," says Tiya.

"You don't mean back up, though." Marc taps his fingers on

the steering wheel. "You mean like we come back with a wave of stories that washes them out. I like that, but sharing a bunch of stories isn't going to stop people from being racist. It's not going to change *systems*."

Tiya taps her lower lip. "It's a start, though."

"We'd be taking back the narrative. That has to happen before people will see that systems need to change." I turn to face Marc, but he doesn't look over. It takes an unholy amount of mental power to stop touching my face and hair. "Before I wrote that second poem, Ms. D told me, people who won't listen to arguments or facts can still be changed by stories."

Marc lets his thoughts turn golden brown before he shares. "All right, then whatever we do has to be big. Bigger than sending a few stories in to the *Weekly*. How are we gonna get that many stories, and what should we do with them?"

"We can start by asking some folks from Ms. D's class for their essays," I answer.

"That's a start." He scratches his chin. "Seniors are writing personal essays for college. I could ask Wes, Sione, and Mikayla, and we could get other people from our class. What else we got?"

"Marc, you and I could talk to Ms. D about getting the BSU involved," says Tiya.

Marc turns the idea over in his mind. "Ms. D would be hyped, but I'm not sure everyone in the group would be. We can ask."

"Ijemma doesn't matter," Tiya snaps. Tiya never liked Marc's ex. She practically threw a party when Marc broke up with Ijemma Aku last year.

Marc looks into the rearview mirror to glare at Tiya. He says, "I wasn't thinking about her. She probably wouldn't like the idea, though."

I try to bring us back to the original topic; the mention of student groups gives me an idea. "Oh! I could check with Celeste. Maybe she could talk to her friends and the Asian American Student Association. I'm pretty sure she's part of that club."

Tiya starts to bounce in her seat. "We could get the *Weekly* to print an edition of our stories."

"Forget the *Weekly*; we could make our own magazine. Then we could make all the decisions ourselves. I know some people on the magazine staff," Marc says. He hasn't looked at me since I touched his arm.

"Like some kind of 'Take Back the Narrative' issue."

"Hell yeah!"

We keep shouting out ideas like we're at a design thinking workshop.

"We could make posters and hang them all over town."

"Hack the school email and send out daily stories to every student and teacher."

"And parents!"

"Create a social media account to share stories. Go viral!"

"Hold some kind of school rally where we all get up and share our stories!"

"Walk out of classes and hold the rally in the middle of campus."

"Get the news stations to cover the rally."

"What if we held the rally *and* organized a protest of companies Mr. McIntyre backs?"

"What if we did the rally and dropped our stories from a hot-air balloon over the crowd?"

"Oooh oooh! Let's skydive from an airplane and make a grand entrance while broadcasting our stories!"

"We could invite the Jabbawockeez to perform an interpretive dance of our stories!"

"They could make a whole show in Vegas about us!"

We brainstorm all the way to school, each thought getting wilder as we laugh and scramble to build on previous ideas. Worries about my mom's job and my dad's words about doing the right thing not leading to the right results nag at me, but I don't mention anything. I'm caught up in the excitement of possibilities.

My words were sword and shield.

Together our words can be an army.

47

We start by telling Ms. Daniels and swearing her to secrecy. That afternoon, she leaves a Post-it on my desk that says, *Hearts and minds are changed through stories.* I fold up the note and put it in my coat pocket.

We don't have anything planned, but we just want to feel out who—if anyone—would want to help out. When I mention the idea separately to Celeste and Ava, both jump (literally) at the idea. Celeste says her friends would definitely want to get involved, and Ava promises to talk to the student council about it.

Celeste stops by the hugging oak with three of her friends during lunch the week before Thanksgiving break. Olivia Kim, a girl in my first-period class, hooks her right foot around her left ankle and squeezes her hands together. "Celeste told us you were planning some kind of event or something to push back against Nate McIntyre."

"Or something," Tiya and I say at the same time. Tiya adjusts her slouchy sweatshirt. My mouth turns up as I watch; she looks—and sounds, of course—like her name should be in glowing letters on Broadway one day. She waves me away with her hand because she's a mind reader.

"We're not really sure what we're doing yet," I explain.

"Well, whatever it is, we want to help."

Another girl—I think her name is Yumi—laces her fingers through Olivia's and adds, "I missed the Junior Jam but heard what Mr. McIntyre said. I read what he wrote. We want to speak up too."

A girl wearing black tights and a chunky pink sweater says softly, "When I moved here from China in second grade, kids made fun of my English, but my parents told me to ignore them and study harder. I studied until my English was better than my classmates', but I cried every night. When I read your letters, I told myself I couldn't stay quiet this time."

"People sometimes tell me to go back to China and my family's not even from there. I'm Japanese, obviously," says Yumi, rolling her eyes. "And I was born in Fresno."

We all shake our heads because it's a familiar experience for all of us. Right up there with *Where are you from?*, *What are you?*, *Your English is so good!*, *Do you eat dogs?*, and *I'm into Asian girls.*

I flick my own ear to see if this is really happening. They're still standing here in the flesh. "We've just been trying to see if we can get enough stories—"

Celeste snaps her fingers like she just remembered something. "I talked to the girls about bringing it up at AASA. I think a lot of people would be on board."

"Just being real," says Tiya, "we've got no clue what to do with the stories yet, but having them would give us more options."

"Do the stories have to be written?" asks pink-sweater girl. "I'm in the video journalism class and I was thinking I could make a video. Or even put together a bunch of videos if people want to send those in."

"Yes!" Tiya claps her hands. "I mean, yes to the video idea. Not yes, it has to be written."

Celeste says, "What about art? I don't know how that would work, but I would love to draw something or make something for this."

Yumi adds, "I could also ask Poli if she'd let us make a special edition of the magazine."

"Yes to everything!" Tiya starts body rolling with her hand in the air and sings out, "We're really gonna do this, Mayday."

"Heeeyyyy . . . ," I say, throwing up a hand and rolling my body in sync with hers. I can't tell if the energy in my stomach is from excitement or worry. My heart says this is the right thing to do, but my brain says the right thing doesn't always lead to the right results. I haven't told Tiya about my mom's job yet, and now's not the time, so I just keep rolling.

When we come back from Thanksgiving break, Ava invites me and Tiya to a student council meeting with her. We debate whether we should go.

"Ava's cool, but student council is a bunch of white kids trying to pad their college applications. We don't need their stories. This isn't about them," says Tiya.

"But maybe if they get on board, we could get more than stories. Maybe access to equipment for whatever we end up doing. Microphones and speakers and stuff." I shrug all the way to my ears and raise my palms up like the emoji.

"We *are* reaching out to AASA, BSU, and the magazine and video journalism classes. I guess student council is just another student group?" Tiya muses.

"Yeah, but with more power."

"I dunno if planning dances and prom is power, Mayday."

"Ava gets to drive around the golf cart sometimes," I counter.

"Oooh snap, yeah. That *is* power right there."

"I wish I had that cart right now, so I wouldn't have to walk my butt home." I drag my feet dramatically across the sidewalk.

"Girl, me too. Stupid basketball practice stealing our chauffeur."

Stupid basketball is right. I'd rather be sitting with Marc in his car. I freeze and stomp out my thought; what the hell is wrong with me? Marc is Tiya's brother. Which means he's practically my brother. He was Danny's best friend. Which means he's doubly my brother. I slap my forehead a couple times.

"You okay, Mayday?"

Definitely not telling her what I was just thinking.

Tiya pats my back and keeps talking. "Just feels a little weird asking student council before we've even asked the AASA or BSU. BSU meetings are postponed until next semester so we can focus on finals. I bet AASA is the same. Student council probably has to keep meeting to plan all the study breaks and stuff." She folds her fingers together and says, "Let's say we invite the student council and they try to take over the whole thing? The whole point of this is to take back our narratives, so do we really need theirs? Their stories are the ones erasing ours."

"Truth." I tap my lips. "Hmm . . . but if they're like Ava, it might be okay? Maybe we should feel it out at the meeting and then decide."

"I guess if we're gonna do it, we might as well do it now and see what we think."

A few days later, we are a little late to our first student council meeting. We hover just outside the door and hear Ava say, "We all know Sequoia Park is white-privilege central. I think what May and Tiya are doing is important and we can help them make change. It's our responsibility as campus leaders to show solidarity here." A few people snap their fingers when she finishes.

Ava's standing at the head of a long oval table. Around the table sit three people from each grade—a class president and two representatives—and also the student-body officers. I don't remember all their official titles. She runs over and hauls us to the table. "I invited May and Tiya here to fill us in a little more. Does everyone know what's been going on?"

A freshman I don't recognize looks at me and says, "I heard stuff about Josh McIntyre's dad being racist against your family at the Junior Jam. Is that what this is about?"

Ava jumps in before I can respond. "He basically said Asians are the reason we're all stressed out. He said they're the reason there have been so many suicides in Sequoia Park recently. Then he specifically blamed May's parents for Danny's death."

A few student council members close their eyes and *pffft* air out of their mouths. Tiya adds, "May wrote a couple really beautiful responses in the *Sequoia Park Weekly*—you should read them if you haven't—and Mr. McIntyre wrote back something pretty predictable and racist."

"So Tiya and May are collecting stories to show that people like Nate can't twist other people's stories to serve their own agendas." Ava stands with a hand on her hip.

I nod. "There's been a lot of pushback on me and my family . . ." *Your mom's job is on the line, Maybelline Chen. What the heck are you doing at this meeting?* I push the intrusive thoughts aside for now. "We hope if more people step up together, it will be harder to tear down one person's story."

The freshman pipes up again. "So, what are you going to do with all the stories you collect?"

"To be honest, we're not sure yet. We're still planning."

"I think that's where the student council might be able to help out," says Ava, clasping her hands and smiling.

245

The freshman speaks up again. "I'm all for helping out a good cause, but I want to make sure we won't do anything that will get us in trouble. I don't want to get suspended and have it go on my record or something."

Ava laughs and tosses a baby carrot at him. "Don't worry, Jackson. We won't plan anything that will get us in trouble. Don't forget, colleges love to see students who show leadership. Standing against injustice is a great opportunity to do that."

Tiya's eyebrow arches and mine press together slightly at this. We make eye contact. This isn't some volunteer project for people to put on their college applications. But I'm sure she didn't mean it that way. She was probably just trying to settle nerves and get Jackson on board.

48

When school gets out for winter break, the two weeks stretch out before me like I'm using a spoon to paddle an inflatable dinghy across the Pacific Ocean. Marc and Tiya went to Port-au-Prince, so I'm stuck at home with nothing to do. They almost didn't go; their extended family urged them to stay home, and their grandparents got upset with Dr. and Mrs. Duverne for even considering the idea. They said the whole family was foolish for going back when kidnappings were at epidemic levels, and it was particularly dangerous for Haitian Americans. I was secretly hoping they would cancel the trip because I didn't want Tiya or Marc to be hurt, but also because I didn't want to be alone over break. In the end, Dr. and Mrs. Duverne decided to go back because they wanted Tiya and Marc to know their roots before Marc went off to college. They promised not to go out after sundown.

Mom and I have reverted to our old conflict-resolution patterns. As in, we ignore the conflict and never resolve anything. We never talked about our last blowup. We just didn't talk until the anger and pain faded enough for us to function in the same space together. Whatever that means.

Everyone in my house retreats into our rooms during the holiday season. Even my dad pulls into himself. He doesn't change any lightbulbs for two straight weeks.

Christmas is a sorry affair. Nothing feels right. I'm trapped in some kind of no-man's-land between the numbers three and four, and no matter what I choose, it feels wrong.

Hanging three stockings instead of four accentuates the empty spot where Danny's should be. Hanging four instead of three makes me think of all the stocking stuffers he'll never open.

Setting three spots at the table on Christmas morning feels like I'm cutting Danny out of the family. Setting four highlights the emptiness in his chair. We've eaten meals together at the dining table since he died, but for some reason, holidays make everything worse.

My dad attempts to make Danny's famous chocolate-chip pancakes on Christmas morning; he even tries to make them into shapes. They end up in blobs but taste fine; they're just not the same as Danny's. I eat four to show my dad his efforts are appreciated. After breakfast, we make our way to the tree for presents.

Honestly, I'm surprised there are any presents under the tree at all. Tiya and I made a trip to Target before she left, and we picked up some last-minute gifts. I got my mom and dad matching furry robes—my dad really needed a new one, though I doubt he'll ever get rid of the old one now. I also saw a Star Wars flannel pajama set that Danny would have loved and bought it, even though I knew he'd never wear it. I just didn't feel right not getting him anything.

I thought my parents might forget about the holiday completely, but they didn't. They got me a new winter jacket, a journal, and some colorful gel pens. When we finish opening our gifts, we discover three wrapped presents tucked in the back labeled "Danny." One is the pajama set I bought. The others have been labeled in my mom's and my dad's handwriting, respectively. We leave them behind the tree. We pretend we don't see them, and we never talk about them. I wonder briefly if I should go open Danny's shoebox, hidden back in my closet again. But I can't get myself to do it.

I miss singing carols out of tune with Danny, miss watching him whoop and holler while opening presents, miss drinking hot chocolate and watching *Elf* together on the couch. Miss bumming around the house with him on wide-open vacation days.

I am glad when Christmas is over.

Glad when New Year's passes.

They remind me of all the big and little holes Danny's absence leaves in our family.

No one, not even the Wus, comes to visit. They cancel dinner plans last minute. I figure everyone has too much merrymaking and celebrating to do, and my family would kill the vibe. The one thing I'm grateful for is watching my mom leave the house each morning the week between Christmas and New Year's. She doesn't talk about her job, but at least I know she still has one.

I've never been so ready for vacation to end.

49

The first Friday after winter break, Tiya and I get our school spirit on at her house. We're going to cheer on Marc at his basketball game. I haven't been to any of his games this year and I know he's glad I'm going tonight. Almost like old times. Green and silver face paint decorates our cheeks, and Tiya found some matching ribbon to tie in my hair. She got her hair done into Nubian twists over break, and she's wearing a green Sequoia Park T-shirt that she cut up to drape at the neck and crisscross in the back. I forgot my school shirt, so she finds me one of Marc's basketball shirts with DUVERNE written across the back and ties it in a knot at my waist. She attempted to tie it just above my belly button, but I wasn't having all that.

It's the first basketball game I've been to since Danny died, and my stomach's got an ant farm inside it. Tiya and I walk into the gym, and I freeze just inside the door. I was so eager to get out of the house and excited to support Marc that I didn't really think this through. I've been coming to this gym to cheer on Danny's games since seventh grade. The familiar sound of scuffling feet and cheering fans, the smell of sweat and paint, the sight of banners hanging on the walls hit me and I stop breathing. Tiya pulls me to the side and puts her arm around me while I relocate my lungs. It's a lot of Danny and missing Danny to take in at one time.

The last time I was here was the night of Danny's final home game. It was senior night, and Tiya and I made signs to wave when they called him onto the court during the pre-game ceremony. Cheers for Danny were so loud I had to cover my ears. He beamed so proudly. It was an exciting back-and-forth battle, and Danny had a chance to tie the score with just a few seconds left on the clock. Marc passed him the ball, and Danny went up, up, up over the defender . . . and the ball hit the rim and bounced out. The other team got the rebound and won the game.

He slouched in disappointment on the court but didn't seem bothered after the game. That night, instead of going out with the team, Danny decided he wanted to chill at home, so Tiya and Marc came over for movie night. I don't remember what we watched, but it was a fun night.

When my heart slows down from the memories and emotions, we go to our spot a few rows up from our team's bench. Marc is out on the court leading the team in their stretches. His loose warm-ups accentuate the gracefulness of his movements. It's not helping my heart.

Celeste breaks away from her seat with Oliva, Yumi, and Grace—I finally learn pink-sweater girl's name—and makes her way over to us. "Hey, you two! You got here just in time!"

"Hi! How was your break?" I'm low-key wondering why they didn't come over for dinner that night over break, but I'm too distracted to ask.

Celeste starts to tell us about her āyí from Sacramento who dropped in unexpectedly. The game hasn't started yet, but it's already hard to hear over the noise.

". . . so my āyí and uncle kept asking my parents about your family, May. They didn't realize our families were close."

"Who were these people again?" asks Tiya, tugging at her shirt because it keeps slipping off her shoulder. The referee blows the whistle. Marc looks up at us, and Tiya and I wave our arms. The corners of his mouth turn up when he sees my shirt. I drag my brain back to focus on the conversation.

"My mom's older sister. She was driving to LA with her husband and kids, so they decided to stop over for a couple nights," says Celeste. She's wearing new silver hoops with scalloped details, and they wave in the air as she talks. "Anyway, even they've heard about the letters you wrote, May."

"Seriously?" I lean forward, but glance over at the court. Marc is on defense guarding their point. He steals the ball.

"Yeah, apparently news travels far in the Chinese community," says Celeste as Marc makes an early basket and the gym

253

erupts in celebration. I can barely hear over the cheering. "It got tense because they told my parents to put some distance between our family and yours, May."

"What?" Celeste has my full attention now.

"That's what I said too. My āyí and uncle were talking nonsense about how being associated with you might put us in danger. They said it could hurt my future or my parents' jobs. Or even make us targets for worse. A couple years ago, an older cousin of hers was kicked to the street and beat up when he was walking around his neighborhood in Oakland. He was hospitalized for a few weeks, so she's extra worried." Celeste glances at me with concern. "My āyí started talking in Taiwanese after I got mad, so I didn't get everything, but that was the gist."

"I can be a pretty bad influence." I try to lighten the mood with a crooked smile, but I'm thinking about my dad's words: *A few mean words? . . . men like Mr. McIntyre can hurt you with much worse than that.* The faded picture of Uncle Joe from our living room comes to mind. Am I putting my family in physical danger?

I flatten my mouth when Josh walks up the bleacher stairs near us. He's looking extra tan. Probably spent his break on a family-owned tropical island or whatever.

"Yeah, I know." Celeste laughs and takes a sip out of her Hydro Flask. "My āyí is the one who had the hookup at Google for that internship. My mom is making me do it because she doesn't want to look bad after her big sister went out of her way to help me. Also, college apps."

"Whoa, I had no idea," says Tiya. She shoots a silent question at me: *Did you know she didn't want the internship?* I nod.

"It came up because we were supposed to go over to your house for dinner that night. My dad and āyí got into an argument all night about it. That's why we didn't make it," Celeste explains. She takes another sip from her water bottle and it makes a pathetic gurgle. "Ah, I'm out of water. Be right back." She hops up and climbs over a few people to get to the aisle.

Our team calls time-out, and I put my head into my hands. I stare at the dried gum on the bleacher floors. This mess is isolating my family—my parents especially—even more. I didn't expect that. Why isn't the entire Chinese community rallying around them? Instead, people are cutting us off with caution tape.

"Hey, ladies!" Ava calls as she makes her way over. "Scooch over."

We make space for her and she sits down. I glance at the game. Instinctively, I want to scream, "Go, Danny!" and my eyes keep searching the court for my big brother. Instead, they find Marc. I notice how he's clearly the team leader but never hangs on to the ball. I can practically see him making deliberate calculations to ensure everyone on his team touches it.

"How was your break, Ava?" I ask, pulling myself away.

"I was in Hawaii with my mom. We lay on the beach a lot." She pulls the collar of her shirt to show us her tan line but doesn't elaborate. "How was Haiti, Tiya?"

"It was . . . an experience." Tiya doesn't elaborate either, but she reaches for my hand the way she does, and we both hold tight for a few seconds.

Celeste slips back into her seat and takes a big gulp of water from her bottle. It's been decorated, like everything else she owns, with black Sharpie designs. She smacks her lips and says with her head cocked to the side, "In case it wasn't clear earlier, I have no intention of following my āyí's advice. Oh hey, Ava!"

One of the coaches calls a time-out, and Marc sits on the bench to catch his breath. Celeste whispers, "Hey, look, Ms. D is over there by the entrance talking to Mr. Gonzalez. She looks pissed."

Like lemmings, we look toward the door at the same time. Mr. Gonzalez is waving his arms in the air and his mouth is moving about a hundred miles a minute. Ms. Daniels's weight is on her right hip and her arms are crossed. There is a tornado on her face.

When they finish talking, Ms. Daniels glances around with a menacing teacher eye that makes us feel like we should look back down and pretend to busy ourselves with schoolwork. She sees me up in the stands and waves me over. "I'm going to go talk to her," I announce.

"I'm coming too," says Tiya, getting up. Celeste and Ava stand up too.

The four of us make our way to Ms. Daniels, and she pulls us out into the hall. She gets right to the point. "The administration invited Mr. McIntyre to speak to juniors and seniors on May first. He's going to kick off a speaker series about careers. I wanted to tell you before they make the announcement on Monday."

"Are you serious? I had no idea. He never—" Ava cuts herself off, her eyes open wider than a Disney doll's. "Why him?"

"He probably made some huge donation so he could come brainwash people to the dark side," says Tiya. Celeste takes a sip of water but coughs it back into her water bottle.

"He probably didn't have to do that. The school's probably been begging him to come speak to us." I wrap my arms around body and squeeze my hands in my armpits. I feel so small knowing my own school doesn't care what that man's said and done.

Ms. D says as softly as she can with the game on full blast, "He's offering five summer internships. Students can turn in their résumés and cover letters at the end of his presentation. The admin probably think it's a great opportunity. "

"Opportunity for who?" I grumble under my breath.

"Whom," Ms. Daniels corrects without thinking.

"Let me guess who will get picked"—Tiya starts ticking off fingers—"Josh, Ava—no offense, but you know it's true—those two meatheads over there, and one token black dude for optics."

"What if Marc . . . ?" I tap Tiya's wrist. It could be a foot in the door to starting his own company one day.

"He would *never*," she whispers fiercely.

"I don't think it's a guarantee that I'd get chosen," Ava says under her breath. I'm standing right next to her, so I hear what she says, but no one else notices.

Ms. Daniels looks around as a group of students passes by loaded with nachos and soda from the snack bar. "If you want, come talk to me after class next week. Maybe I'll know more then." We watch her walk into the gym and boot the nacho-soda kids back into the hallway with their food. Tiya, Celeste, Ava, and I are left catching flies in our mouths.

"I can't believe the school invited him to come," I say.

"I can't believe it either. *But*"—Celeste looks up slowly—"this could be a perfect opportunity to use the stories we've been collecting."

"We can plan some something for the day he's here." There is an excited glint in Tiya's eye. "Like, literally turn off his mic and tell our stories instead."

"We could actually plan some kind of rally or protest! Get everyone to cut class!" Celeste jumps a little as she talks. She and Tiya wiggle their upper bodies like a shot of electricity just ran through both of them at the same time.

Tiya pats Ava's shoulder. "Good thing we've got the student-body president with us. If she walks out first, no one else will hesitate! Or get in trouble! Plus hookups to the school's AV equipment, here we come!"

Ava smiles slightly and wrinkles her nose.

Celeste coughs and clears her throat. She pauses the excitement to ask, "What about your parents, May? I know they don't want you doing more."

I don't think leading a public face-off with Mr. McIntyre at school is what my dad envisioned when he told me to find another way. It's probably the polar opposite of what he was imagining. If my mom's boss didn't like my poems, I can't imagine that he'll be pleased when he learns I led a rally against his college buddy. How can I risk my family's livelihood or their safety for this?

Tiya doesn't know about my mom's job situation, but her hand is back in mine. Her face is shining. It reminds me of that poster under the fairy lights on her wall, the one that says, *The hottest places in hell are reserved for those who, in times of great moral crisis, maintain their neutrality.*

Is silence neutrality if it protects my family?

Is it actually protecting my family if people like Mr. McIntyre are always allowed to control our stories and history?

Maybe it's Tiya's excitement, or the energy at the game, or the thrill of seeing Marc ball again. Maybe it's the gaping hole where Danny should be on the court, the painful wave of memories that I keep fighting back.

I look at the three of them and say, "I have some ideas."

50

We have about four months until Mr. McIntyre comes to speak. It sounds like a long time, but if you count holidays, ski week, spring break, plus, you know, actual classes and homework and tests and stuff, it's actually not that much time. Tiya and I talk constantly about the best way to do things. We debate whether it's important for people to be able hear individual stories, or if the symbolism of our stories drowning out Mr. McIntyre's speech is more valuable. We discuss how to reach people beyond Sequoia Park High. We go back and forth on actions that might have a lasting impact. We argue about whether anyone, or only people who have been historically ignored or silenced, should be allowed to share.

Marc comes by more and more since he's turned in all his

college applications. He coordinates the seniors and offers us suggestions and questions. He usually brings snacks. I tell him snacks are the best contribution he's made to the group, and he waves me away with his hand. I notice he doesn't sit too close to me when we're all working.

Ms. Daniels helps us edit narratives that people send in—in the name of improving our writing skills. According to her, she's just doing her job. As word gets around, more stories come in. One day after school, Ms. D says, "I should have thought of this idea myself. Look how many people are turning in work!"

Yumi approaches Ms. Polinski, the journalism teacher, about running a special "Take Back the Narrative" issue of the school magazine. We want to fill it with the stories we've collected. Turns out Poli and Ms. Daniels are close, and she's stoked about the idea. We swear her to secrecy too. Poli goes a step further and institutes policies worthy of Silicon Valley tech companies. No one is allowed into the magazine room unless they are directly involved with the project, and no one is allowed to talk about it outside her room. Everyone has to sign what she calls a non-disclosure agreement. I had to look up what that meant before I signed. Once it gets going, the magazine staff asks Celeste to draw something for the special edition, and she is thrilled. She's never shared her art publicly before.

This inspires her to follow through on her idea of sharing stories through art. Not everyone likes to write, she says, pointing at herself. But people can also tell stories in other ways. She starts working with some students from her art classes.

We also ask people to send us videos of themselves telling their stories. Grace gets some students in her video journalism class to start editing and splicing the clips.

Olivia and Wes are our social media team. They create accounts on all the main platforms, and they're slowly ramping up the hashtag #TakeBacktheNarrative.

Tiya and I are the control tower. We coordinate all the moving pieces and work on plans for the auditorium—where Mr. McIntyre is supposed to speak—and the rally to follow. Ava is hooking us up with the school's sound system.

The hardest part is keeping the whole thing somewhat secret. We can't make everyone sign a nondisclosure agreement, and as our plans grow legs of their own, more people are in the know. All we can do is emphasize secrecy and cross our fingers.

One afternoon, Tiya and I are in her room doing some dance/kickboxing/Zumba/aerobics video she wanted to try. In the middle of an impossible sequence in which we are supposed to kick our legs, shake our butts, then punch up, down, and to the side, she goes, "You know you're gonna have to make a speech, right?"

"What?" I ask distractedly. I almost got the moves now. High kick, back kick, jump in place, two-step, butt shake, punch punch punch punch. "What's that about a speech?"

"You're gonna need to make one."

I kick my leg up and fall over. "No way." The idea of all those eyeballs on me makes my skin crawl.

Tiya pauses the video. "You better not sit down for long or

you'll kill the workout," she scolds, hopping back and forth to keep her heart rate up.

"You know I suck at public speaking. Remember how I almost failed the final in seventh grade because I froze up and couldn't talk?"

"Mayday, that was eons ago. You've done hundreds of presentations since then."

"This isn't a presentation, Tiya Marie."

"It's more important than a presentation, Maybelline." She hasn't stopped hopping back and forth. "You're the one who had the courage to stand up to Mr. McIntyre in the first place. You *have* to say something."

I haul myself back onto my feet and shuffle back and forth like an amah. It didn't occur to me that I'd have to give a speech, but I know she's right. I feel like the train has left the station and there's nothing I can do to get off or stop it now. I nod reluctantly. I open my mouth to tell her about my mom's job, but she sees me nod and knocks me over again with a flying tackle hug. From my spot on the carpet, I see she's tacked a small Haitian flag on her wall.

Tiya jumps back onto her feet and turns the workout back on. "Mayday, it means a lot to me that we're in this together," she says, arms and legs flying all over.

"Me too, Tiya." I half-ass my workout moves as I try to learn the new sequence.

"When Marc and I were in Haiti over break, it was really hard. Nothing's been the same there since the earthquake. So many people are still living in tin shacks without running water. My family has a home. They're the lucky ones. We barely left the house because it was too risky."

We shimmy, kick, jump, and the conversation pauses as we focus on breathing. During the next fifteen-second break, Tiya hops back and forth and says, "I felt so helpless, like nothing I did could make a real difference." She stops moving. "Planning this makes me feel like what I do matters."

The workout starts again, and we both use our shirts to wipe sweat off our faces. In between my panting for air, I wheeze, "Immigrants . . ."

Tiya smiles as she bounces. "We get the job done."

51

A few weeks later, a copy of the *Sequoia Park Weekly* is in the driveway when I get home from school. I bring it into the kitchen and flip through it absentmindedly. Nate McIntyre's been in the news again recently—something about money and big business deals and that kind of thing. In his last interview, he said something about Josh and "teenagers these days" and how glad he was the "whole racist thing blew over." I want to know if anyone responded.

When I get to the Letters to the Editor section, my eye goes immediately to a title that reads, "Two Different Perspectives." The subtitle underneath suggests that these letters are in response to the "whole racist thing" and my back-and-forth with Mr. McIntyre. I start reading and my jaw drops.

Dear Editor,

I'm a Chinese man who moved to California when I was young. My family had nothing when we came, and now I have a thriving business here. America is the land of opportunity.

Asian people know the value of studying and working hard. We make painful sacrifices and invest in our future. We know we can build the lives we want in this country because the diligent and skilled rise to the top. That is why we are successful here.

I'm tired of people using race as an excuse not to try their hardest. People who play the race card are simply making excuses for their personal choices and inability to achieve. We can always create our own destinies if we are willing to work hard.

Sincerely,

Byron Wong

What the what? This Byron guy sounds like an Asian Nathaniel McIntyre. I move on to the next letter. Surely this one will give a different perspective.

Dear Editor,

Like Maybelline Chen, I am a junior at Sequoia Park High School. I'm shocked that she took it upon herself to speak as a voice for the Chinese community in Sequoia Park. With the exception of her brother, I have hardly known her to associate with any other Asian students.

The death of Maybelline's brother has absolutely high-lighted the racism faced by Asians in this area. However, centering this narrative around her personal story shows that Maybelline lacks real understanding of these issues.

As the president of the Asian American Student Association, I feel it is my responsibility to articulate a few of these concerns . . .

I skip to the signature at the bottom. *Alvin Lo.* Shoulder smack king with the tight shirt.

He writes about white flight, the bamboo ceiling, the "model minority" myth, and more, but I stop reading because all I can think about is his jab at my social life. Why does it matter who my friends are? Is he saying I'm not Chinese or Asian *enough*? And holy hell, I'm not trying to speak for the Chinese community of Sequoia Park. I was just trying to defend my family.

My brain fills up with farting balloons again. They *thh-hbbbppttt* around my head so fast I can't think.

I hear my dad pull up, so I grab the paper and run to my room. My parents probably knew that people in our community would keep their distance and even lash out. Maybe something similar happened after Uncle Joe was murdered. Maybe people avoided my nǎi-nai and yé-ye because they didn't want to be next. But I'm blindsided. I didn't see this coming. I didn't expect to be attacked by other Chinese people. It hurts worse coming from them.

I really thought we would all stand together, united in a

common cause. Now that seems so naive. My parents were right: I really don't understand anything. I worry about our protest plans. It is only a matter of time until Mom's boss finds out. It seems like we've been gaining momentum, but what if not many people actually join us?

It's one thing to stand up when others are standing with me. It's something else entirely when I feel so alone and exposed.

52

The next day, Tiya is out sick, and Celeste goes to the Asian American Student Association meeting at lunch. She's kind of going as a spy. Are they going to talk about our protest plans? Alvin's letter?

I wander around the school, still reeling a little from yesterday's paper. I saw Alvin in the hall this morning and wanted to throw my water bottle at his head. I kept walking instead. I have pretty bad aim and wouldn't want to hit some poor freshman in the face, which is definitely what would have happened. The way things are going these days, I'd probably get suspended and maybe expelled and then trampled by a herd of pregnant hippos. The silent disappointed kind my mom has at her disposal. So probably a good decision not to throw it.

I shove my hands into my coat pockets and feel a crumpled paper inside. It's Ms. Daniels's Post-it note. *Heart and minds are changed through stories.*

Maybe I should go talk to her.

I walk past the hugging oak and down to Ms. Daniels's classroom. I hope she's inside. I knock on the door and test the handle. It's open, so I barge in. "Ms. Daniels! I'm so glad you're here because I really need to—"

I freeze. Her room is full of Black students lounging in and on top of desks that have been rearranged into a loose circle. Some people are sitting on the floor. Marc's sitting on the beanbag, and Ms. Daniels is writing something on the whiteboard. She's wearing a purple patterned skirt and a denim jacket. Her glasses dangle from a beaded chain around her neck.

"May! Come on in! It's our weekly BSU meeting. You are very welcome to stay."

A few faces smile at me, while some look at me without any expression. I'm not sure I should enter their space; I totally forgot today was BSU. But I've already barged in. Will it be insulting if I leave? Marc, sensing my discomfort, pats a spot on the beanbag and motions for me to sit down.

I walk hesitantly over to the beanbag and spot Janelle Mitchell up in the front. She's a violin phenom. I remember Danny and Marc showing me one of her viral violin videos last year when she was a freshman. She's performed in concert halls all over the world. Janelle smiles and lifts her head in greeting. I trip over Ms. Daniels's charger cord, and Janelle opens her eyes with worry. No one else but Marc notices, but I still feel like every eyeball in the universe is glued to my back. Marc's ex, Ijemma Aku, is sitting close to the door. Her long legs stretch out under the desk, and her hair is shaved close to her head. Her big silver hoops catch the light when she turns to look out the window. Just to the side of Marc's beanbag, I see Ayanna and Mikayla sitting on desks. They smile and wave.

Marc pats the beanbag again. He whispers, "Sit down, May."

I sit down crookedly on the edge of the beanbag, trying to give Marc his space. Ms. Daniels finishes writing on the board and turns around. "Actually, May, it's wonderful that you're here. I don't mean to put you on the spot—but to totally put you on the spot—we were just about to start discussing Nathaniel McIntyre and your protest plans. We need to decide whether the BSU should show our support somehow."

The seconds stretch awkwardly as she looks at me. Then she laughs and blinks. "Oh, ha, I didn't ask you a question, did I?" A few people groan and mutter, "C'mon now, Ms. D!"

She brushes them off with a wave of her hand and we all smile. It's classic Ms. Daniels. "What I meant to say was, Tiya was going to present the Take Back the Narrative idea to the group today, but she emailed me saying she was out sick. I was going to have Marc explain more, but since you're here, maybe the two of you can do it together?"

I squirm when everyone looks at me, and Marc taps my wrist lightly, reminding me to breathe. I stand up and see Ijemma's eyes laser focused on my wrist. "Sure, it's, uh, it's, um . . . The idea came after the Junior Jam and my back-and-forth with Mr. McIntyre in the *Sequoia Park Weekly*. There was a lot of push-back to what I wrote."

"I read some of the comments. People are stupid," Janelle says. She folds her hands together and props her chin on top.

"To be honest, it started because I was so mad about what Mr. McIntyre said about my family."

I see a few nods around the room. Ayanna mutters, "I was at the Junior Jam. Someone needed to tell that man to sit his ass down."

"This whole thing has kind of grown in ways I didn't really expect . . . or want." The letters from Alvin and Byron come to mind. I rub my wrists and take a breath. "Basically, we're trying to gather stories, mostly from people who have been historically silenced or ignored. We figure people can't hijack our stories—like they've been trying to with Danny's—if we all speak up together." I sit back down, still careful not to squish up against Marc.

Someone snaps their fingers from the back of the room. Ms. Daniels smiles and nods at me.

Marc tries to sit up in the beanbag, but it keeps collapsing underneath him. He shifts to the left, then shifts to the right, but the beanbag just erodes under his butt and he ends up practically horizontal. Eventually, he stands up. "Most of you know Danny was my best friend and May is my sister Tiya's. We thought it would be cool if the BSU got behind this too, added some of our stories to the mix. I know we've got more than a few."

"We sure do," Mikayla says, snapping her fingers. There are more snaps and some nods. Ms. Daniels rubs her hands together and smiles. She turns to grab a marker from her desk when a voice from the back of the room speaks up.

"What's in it for you, Marc?"

Balloons start farting around in my head. I see Marc turn around, jaw clenched. "Come again, Hugh?"

"You heard me. I'm just trying to understand why we're wasting time during our BSU meeting talking about something that doesn't concern us." Hugh Mumford kicks back and props his feet up on a desk. His hair is faded at his temples, with curls loosely twisted on top of his head. I think he's a senior too. "We've got enough issues to worry about, and as far as I can tell, this isn't our problem."

Ijemma snaps her fingers.

"It's everyone's problem," I say, anger from all the accusations I've been hit with starting to bubble over. Marc studies Hugh and Ijemma; I can't tell what he's thinking.

Hugh looks at me like I'm a fly crawling over his lunch. "Yeah? And what do you know about Black people's problems? You have your first run-in with an old racist white dude and suddenly you're going to conquer racism? That's not how this works, sis. Mr. McIntyre said some messed up stuff, but nobody's dead because of it."

Ms. Daniels isn't smiling anymore, but she's not jumping in either. Hugh takes his feet off the desk, puts his palms down, and leans forward, gaze unwavering. "Where were you when they shot little André Johnson behind the 7-Eleven because some white woman thought he was touching her butt? No one believed him when he said it was just his backpack. Now he's dead. He was ten, May. We were all at the protest. Where were you?"

I look down at my hands. Hugh keeps talking. "I think André's murder was everyone's problem, too, don't you? I don't recall seeing you out there, though. In fact, I don't recall seeing more than a handful of Asians out there at all. I'm not saying this country doesn't have a history of racism against Asians, but nobody's pulling guns on you for walking down the street. I think being murdered is a helluva lot worse than getting your feelings hurt."

My first reaction is one of defensiveness. What about the Asian women murdered in the Atlanta shootings? Celeste's mom's cousin and so many other elderly Asian people who were knocked down, beaten up, even killed right here in the Bay Area? Asian people are being murdered too. Why does it have to take death for people to care?

But then I take a deep breath and really try to hear Hugh. He settles back into his chair to the sound of snapping fingers and I hang my head. No one speaks. There is truth in his words, and they weigh on me. He's right. When Tiya and Marc told me about André, I asked if he stole something and they stopped talking. I had an opportunity to learn more, and I didn't take it. That's why Tiya and Marc didn't even invite me to the protest. But why did I need an invite? I should have been there regardless. I was—I am—still so ignorant. My face heats up as I wrestle with a growing sense of shame. I can't look at Marc or Ms. Daniels or anyone, so I stare at the dirty smudges on the beanbag between my feet.

Mikayla cups her face in her hands as she watches Hugh. She opens her mouth to say something, but Hugh sits up, a new thought tugging his body. "Come to think of it, where were you when DeMarcus got expelled for 'fighting' in the bathroom last year? Everyone knows that white boy came at him with a knife and DeMarcus hit back in self-defense. No one was else there, so DeMarcus got expelled and white boy got to graduate."

The story doesn't even sound familiar, and that, I realize, is part of the problem. I stare at the beanbag smudges until they blur together into a huge blob. Hugh continues talking. ". . . some of the loudest white-boy supporters were Asian. It's no secret that Asians hate Black folks. So remind me again why we should step into this protest for you?"

My head pops up and I respond without thinking, "Tiya is my best friend! Danny and Marc were best friends! What do you mean Asians hate Black folks?"

"Don't come at me with your 'I have Black friends' business." Hugh waves his hand like he's heard it a hundred times before. "Tiya and Marc helped plan the Black Lives Matter protest for André. What kind of friend are you if you didn't have their backs like they've got yours now?"

That shuts me up real quick. Tiya and Marc *have* been there for me through my darkest days, and I didn't bother getting involved with something that mattered to them. I wasn't too scared to ask about André or Black Lives Matter or being Black; I never thought to do it in the first place. But here they are helping me plan this thing like Mr. McIntyre messed with *their* family. They *always* show up for me.

Someone says, "Preach, Hugh!" and I sink into the beanbag. The beads shift around and I end up pressed into Marc's side; I was so focused on Hugh I didn't even notice when Marc sat back down. His body is warm, he smells like soap, and part of me wants to snuggle in. I try to readjust my position, but I just keep sliding back. Eventually Marc puts his arm around me so I'll stop squirming. I turn into his chest to blink away the pressure building behind my eyes.

Hugh watches me, then he says softly, "Don't get me wrong, May. I'm sorry about Danny. We all miss him. But I still don't think we need to get involved here."

Mikayla puts both hands on her desk. "I agree with almost everything you said, Hugh. Everything except the conclusion. I don't think sitting back and doing nothing is the answer. Just because it seems like Asian folks haven't always shown up for us doesn't mean we should do the same thing. And honestly, I don't know if it's true they haven't shown up. I see them at protests. I see them online. I think we have more shared history than we ever learn in school. We shouldn't be fighting each other anyway. We should be fighting white supremacy."

"We don't need to take up everyone else's battles to fight white supremacy," says Ijemma, turning from the window. Her eyes linger on Marc's arm over my shoulder, then shift to my face. "Like Hugh said, just staying alive and fighting for our own justice is bigger than a full-time job. It's exhausting enough as it is. I personally don't have the energy to take up someone else's fight too."

Someone clears her throat from the back corner of the room and people turn to look. Natasha Lee waves her hand. Her eyebrows are up and her lips pressed together. "Hey, folks, Black and Asian aren't mutually exclusive, all right? Can you all stop talking like I don't exist? I'm sitting right here." Natasha is one of the girls in Marc's patio crew. Her mom is Black and her dad is Chinese and she went to elementary school in Malaysia; she speaks at least four different languages.

The room seems to absorb these words before Marc, collected and calm again, says, "I hear what you're saying, Hugh and Ijemma. I'm exhausted too. I also hear you, Mikayla and Natasha. Thing is, I agree with some of what *everyone* is saying." He lifts his arm and leans forward, clasping his hands. "The bottom line is that white folks have always had the power to control the stories that uphold their systems. Is staying quiet now going to help Black folks in the long run?"

"Let me jump in for a sec to drop another question. It might help you answer Marc's," Ms. Daniels interjects before anyone can respond. "May shared in our English class that the stereotype of studious, obedient Asian students was created by a PR firm hired by Chinatown leaders—"

"To protect themselves from police brutality and frequent home raids." I can't help filling in details.

"The government and media took this idea of studious, compliant Asian Americans and blew it up into the 'model minority' myth during the civil rights movement. Why do you think they did that?" Ms. Daniels has no problem waiting in the uncomfortable silence that follows as people noodle over her question.

Janelle speaks up first. "I don't get how those two things are related."

Marc begins talking slowly, sharing his thoughts in real time as his big nerd brain (as Tiya would say) processes them carefully. "It's gotta have something to do with undermining civil rights," he mutters as he rubs his forehead. "Making Asians the 'model minority' must have disrupted the movement somehow, right?"

Marc doesn't realize he's slowly sliding off the beanbag chair and pulling me with him. I wiggle out from under his arm and climb back on the beanbag because he's basically sitting on the ground massaging his temples now. He loses himself in his thoughts and the group waits. They know more is coming. When he finally looks back up at Ms. D, everyone leans forward just a little. "It's two birds, one stone," he says.

"Say more, Professor Duverne," she says, smiling as she tosses Marc her purple whiteboard marker. He catches it and flips it between his fingers.

"By making Asians the 'model minority,' the government could say Asians became successful despite racism and discrimination. They could use Asians against the civil rights movement by saying Asians already overcame the same problems Black folks were fighting." Marc scratches his neck with the whiteboard marker. "The 'model minority' myth gives white people an out. It lets them argue that laws and systems aren't the problem, Black people are."

"So what's the second bird?" asks Ijemma, tapping her lips.

278

Hugh answers, "It placates Asian Americans. Increases their proximity to whiteness and makes them more likely to drink the white Kool-Aid. Which many of them did."

"I hadn't thought of that. That's a good point," says Marc, starting to count on his fingers. "Now I think it's three birds, one stone. One, it makes Black folks, not the racist systems, the problem. Two, it makes assimilation more appealing for Asians. They drink the 'white Kool-Aid.' Three, it divides oppressed people so we won't unite against our oppressors."

Hugh and Marc look at each other and nod as some kind of mutual respect seems to pass between them. Ms. Daniels opens up the conversation and redirects the group's attention. "So, what do you think? Do we want to get involved? Why or why not?"

The room erupts in debate. I listen and try to learn. Everything that's been shared today is making me dig deep and ask myself questions that hurt. When people say "Asians," what do they mean? Why do Asians drink the "white Kool-Aid"? Why do we—is it all of us or just some of us?—buy into the "model minority" myth? We know anti-Asian discrimination is real; why are so many people satisfied with white-adjacency? Byron Wong's letter comes to mind again. Why doesn't more of my community speak up against issues of injustice? Why don't I know more about the people who do? If we don't even stick together when the injustice is against us, how will we show up for anyone else? Why have I allowed myself to be so complacent and ignorant?

And most painfully, what kind of friend am I *really* if I haven't had Tiya and Marc's backs like they've always had mine?

I make myself small and burrow down in my seat. Marc's

readjusted himself onto the beanbag and he looks over to check on me. He puts his arm around me again, squeezing to let me know he's there. More confused feelings shoot through my body.

When lunch ends, I stay in the beanbag until everyone leaves. Marc waits for me outside the classroom, but I see Ijemma grab his arm and pull him down the hall, talking rapidly. She looks upset. Ms. Daniels stands at the door, sending students off with a smile. I know I'm going to have to walk past her too. I can't ignore her, but I also don't want to talk. Which is stupid because wanting to talk was the whole reason I ended up at the BSU meeting in the first place.

In the end, I wait for her, clutching my backpack on my lap. When all the BSU students leave, she props the door open and comes over to the beanbag. It bulges as she squishes down next to me.

"Huh. This thing is pretty comfy," she says. "Maybe I'll try teaching from down here this afternoon." I smile wanly in her direction. She says, "It's my prep, so I got time to talk, Ms. Maybelline."

"Sorry I messed up your meeting today, Ms. D."

"You didn't mess up anything, hon. I'm sorry I put you on the spot like that; I know you've been through a lot lately. But I think it was important. Sometimes the things we need aren't easy to hear."

"I came in because I wanted to talk to you about Byron and Alvin's letters in the *Sequoia Park Weekly*. Have you seen them?" Ms. Daniels nods and rubs her eyes. I continue, "But now I don't even know what I want to talk to you about. Mostly, I just want to cry."

"You can do that too if you want. I have a nice shoulder and a crap ton of Kleenex in my cabinet." She rubs her shoulder invitingly. "I don't mind a little snot right here."

"I just feel like I'm doing everything wrong."

"What makes you think you're doing something wrong?" Ms. Daniels gets up and rummages in her desk.

"I wrote back to Mr. McIntyre because I wanted to defend my parents, but I'm just making them bigger targets. My mom's job is in danger, people from our own community are avoiding us, and other Chinese people are attacking what I wrote." I punch little dents into the beanbag with my fists. I pretend the bag is Alvin's face. Then I decide he's not worth it. I pretend it's Mr. McIntyre's face and punch until the beanbag is pocked with little round welts from the stuffing inside.

"Are you upset because your parents are being attacked or because you're being attacked?

Huh. She flipped that on me good. "Probably both, if I'm being honest."

"Well, did you think everyone was going to agree with you?"

"No." I lean back in the beanbag, feeling it crunch under my shifting weight. "I mean, kind of. Yeah, I did. It seemed so obvious that what Mr. McIntyre said was wrong. I really thought everyone else would see things the way I did."

"It's part of the learning process, May." Ms. Daniels procures a bar of chocolate and breaks off a piece for me, saying, "I keep these for emergencies. I think this counts."

I take the chocolate. I forgot to eat lunch during the BSU meeting, and now my stomach is very unhappy with me. I dig around in my backpack for Pocky and give Ms. Daniels a few sticks. She repeats, "It's part of the process. As I suspect you're learning, racial dynamics are complex. Understanding all the different perspectives can be overwhelming."

"This meeting was eye-opening and hard, and those letters to the editor really got to me. I just don't know if I'm doing the right thing."

"Why not? Because people are pushing back?"

"I feel like I'm making things worse."

"First, learning and changing is hard. Second, what's wrong with people disagreeing with, hating even, what you're saying? People will always fight against you when you take a stand. That doesn't mean you're wrong."

I quietly process what she's saying. She hands me another piece of chocolate and says, "I wonder if the questions you should be asking are: What am I hoping to accomplish? What do I need to do to get there? *And* what am I willing to sacrifice?"

"I thought I knew, but I'm so confused now."

"Think about it. Don't stop learning because there's too much to learn. Remember what I said before? This is a journey and you're just getting started. You're not doing it wrong, May. You're trying and learning and that's what matters."

I smile and savor the chocolate in my mouth.

Sometimes teachers are so corny. And that's why I love them.

53

After school, I find Hugh before he gets into his car. I've been stewing about him all day, replaying all the things I want to say and ask. When he sees me, he tosses his backpack into the back seat, slams the door, and turns around. He shoves his hands in his pockets and leans back, ready.

"Can we talk, Hugh?" His face is impassive as he nods.

I launch in before I change my mind. "I wanted to thank you for what you said today." His eyebrows high jump into his hair. I rub my stomach to calm my nerves. "It's making me reflect about a lot of things."

He swings his right arm in an arc, palm up, like, *Go ahead*.

I gulp. "You were right to call me out about André and DeMarcus. Tiya and Marc tried to tell me about André earlier this year. I asked them some ignorant questions and they stopped talking to me about it. I didn't even know about DeMarcus . . . which I realize is its own issue."

Hugh holds up a hand for me to stop. His shoulders relax. "Hold up. I've been thinking too. I realized DeMarcus was expelled soon after Danny . . . passed. You weren't even at school then."

"But I'm sure there are more examples like DeMarcus I don't know about. I *know* there are more examples like André. You were still right. I didn't care enough to do anything until 'an old racist white dude' came for my family, and I've been really naive about how this was gonna go."

He chuckles. "You thought everyone was just gonna get it, right? Like, you could just make people see racism and they'd stop."

My face flushes red. "Actually, yeah. I really did."

"We've all been there, May. Except I realized the world was against me on this when I was five."

"Five?" I step back and bump into the Tesla parked next to Hugh's car. What high school kid needs a Tesla? Only around here, I swear.

"That's when I started kindergarten. I was the only Black kid in my class. One day, my friend Billy and I were racing to the playground, and he fell and skinned his knee. Billy yelled that I tripped him. He didn't mean it; he was just mad I got to the slide first." Hugh tosses his keys between his hands. "But some kid went and told the teacher. When she called us in, I heard

Ms. Payne ask Billy a billion times who pushed him. He started crying and said he fell on his own, but I still didn't get recess the rest of that week."

"That's messed up. I'm sorry, Hugh."

"When I was five, I thought losing recess was the worst thing that could happen to me. But it gets worse as we get older."

A herd of freshmen bikes by, talking about some video game and making plans to play together online. I notice I'm still rubbing my stomach and shove my hands into my back pockets. "Is it okay if I ask you a couple questions?"

"Depends. I'll let you know if I won't answer." His cheeks pull upward, but the movement doesn't quite reach his mouth or eyes, so he could either be squinting or suppressing a smile.

"Do you really think Asians hate Black people?"

He studies my face. I hope he can see I'm not trying to argue. I really want to know. I bite my lower lip. He says, "Listen, I don't see a lot of evidence that says otherwise. But as Ms. D would say, there is a lot of evidence to support that claim."

"Like what?"

"You tell me."

I don't have to think too hard to come up with examples, but it's hard to speak them into the open: My mom being unsure of Danny's friendship with Marc and mine with Tiya until it was clear they were both stellar students. Cousins being told they weren't allowed to date Black people. Open talk between adults about the "dangerous" community in Sequoia Grove and the "bad" schools there. Relatives asking my dad why he doesn't try to teach at a school in Sequoia Park where students "care about learning." Loud opposition to affirmative action from the Chinese community. Once my brain starts churning, the evidence keeps on coming.

Hugh watches my facial gymnastics, but I can't get myself to share any of my thoughts aloud. What comes out is something partly defensive, partly hopeful. "But it's not all Asians." I picture Tiya's poster of Yuri Kochiyama. "There are many who have worked in solidarity."

"I don't doubt it. How many can you name?"

One. And that's only because my best friend has a poster in her room. "Okay, not that many, but I think that might say more about my ignorance of Asian American history than it does about Asian solidarity with Black folks." I tuck a stray hair behind my ear. "At least I'm hoping it does."

"Maybe it's time to study up, then."

"I know." I sigh. "It's wrong that we don't learn this kind of thing in school."

"Yup."

"Like, don't take this the wrong way, but maybe if you knew more Asian American history too, your perspective on Asians might change. I know mine has just from doing research on Chinatown for Ms. D's class."

Hugh scratches his chin. "You're right. I'll give you that one."

"But why do we have to look it up on our own? We should be learning *all* of it."

"Facts." Hugh nods his head and grins at me. "Is your next

campaign gonna be to decolonize our school curriculum?"

I snort. Hard. Like, it's possible a stray booger shot out. "I don't know if I'll get through this one. One at a time, I think."

"You can count me in on that battle, for sure." He pulls out his cell phone to check the time. "What else you got?"

I have a lot of questions, but all I can think of is the one that really hurts. I stare at the bold patterns on his shirt when I ask, "How can I be a better friend to Tiya and Marc? Of all the things you said, that part got me the most."

He leans back onto his car and tilts his head sideways as he looks at me. "I can't answer that one, May. You're gonna have to figure that out on your own." He swings his keys around his finger. "But I'll tell you this: Tiya and Marc are Black. If their Blackness isn't part of your friendship, your friendship won't last."

His words land like a locker full of textbooks on my head. I nod. "Okay. Thanks, Hugh."

Hugh opens up the driver's door. Before he gets in, he says, "I'm going to think about what you said. There's always more for me to learn too. Maybe this narrative thing is something I should consider, but I'm not sure yet. I'll think about it."

He shuts the door and I back up against the Tesla as he pulls out of the parking spot. He shifts into drive, then rolls down the window. "Hey, I hope you figure out that whole friend thing," he says. He winks. "My boy Marc might be interested in a whole other kind of friend thing with you."

He smiles crookedly and drives off.

54

M

A

Y

D

A

Y

!

I miss school for ONE DAY

ONE DAY

And you crash the BSU meeting?!

🙈

Never miss school again,
Tiya Marie

Did you see Alvin Lo's letter in the paper?

I went to talk to Ms. D about it and accidentally crashed BSU

We need to talk

Come over for dinner

You can show me all the work I missed today

No way!

I don't want your gross bacteria

I'll wear a mask!!

My mom made fried plantain and griot

Your loss if you don't come

Ooh, you play dirty.

Fine, I'll come

But only if you keep your mask on the whole time

How am I supposed to eat?

Not my problem

You figure it out

55

The Duverne home feels like a hug. The colorful paintings, the aroma of plantain and pork, the leather furniture and mahogany carvings pull me into their warm embrace. But a hug from an entire house is nothing compared to a hug from Mrs. Duverne.

"CHERIE," she says as she bundles me into her arms. "Let me put some meat on those bones."

I inhale the love that radiates from her body and let her guide me to the kitchen table, where everyone is already sitting and a place is set for me. Tiya is dutifully wearing her mask, as promised, and Marc sits between her and Dr. Duverne, across from me. I smother a laugh when I see Tiya, who is moving her head and neck and arms and hands to make sure I see her medical-grade face mask. I resist the temptation to peek at Marc.

As soon as I sit down, everyone at the table jumps into action offering me food. Mama Duverne prevails and somehow gets ahold of my plate. She fills it with heaping spoonfuls of rice and beans, plantains, griot, and pikliz before passing it back to me. She's picked out all the softest, sweetest plantains for me because she knows they're my favorite. I wait for everyone else to fill their plates before taking a bite, and the sweet plantain flavor fills my taste buds.

"Maman, this is goooood," mumbles Tiya after lifting up her mask and spooning a bite into her mouth.

"Of course it is," says Mrs. Duverne with a slight shake of her head. She reaches over and rubs my arm. "You like it, cherie?"

I nod vigorously, my mouth full of food. I can feel Marc's eyes on me, and my stomach flip-flops. I keep stuffing my face, trying to keep my dang organ in place by weighing it down. It's annoying to be so aware every time he so much as shifts his elbow.

"Did I tell you Mayday crashed BSU today?" asks Tiya, her voice muffled beneath the mask. She looks back and forth between her mom and dad. "I think she could have waited until I was there, too, don't you?"

"Tiya, take that mask off your face, I can't understand anything you're saying," says Dr. Duverne. "How're you going to eat your dinner?"

"Like this!" She lifts her mask and spoons a chunk of pork into her mouth. Then she lowers her mask and chews.

Dr. Duverne just shakes his head like, *I can't believe we're related*, but I catch him smiling as he reaches for the rice and beans.

"You can take it off, Tiya Marie." I wave my arm like a queen.

"Oh, thank you, Jesus." She rips the mask off and sucks in a lungful of air. "It's hard to eat with that thing stuck to my face."

"I can't believe you really wore it."

"Well, I promised." We cheese at each other from across the table.

"May, did you bring Tiya any work that she missed? Can't have her falling behind." Mrs. Duverne gives Tiya some serious side-eye. "She seems to be feeling fine now that you're here."

"I sure did," I say between bites.

"Gotta have that Plan B, C, D, E so she doesn't end up another starving artist trying to make it on Broadway." Dr. Duverne chuckles. Oh no, not this again. I tap Tiya's foot under the table.

"Ugh, Papa. Don't start with that now," Tiya groans, making a face.

"She's gonna be a star on Broadway, Dr. Duverne," I say.

"Tiya's already a star in our hearts, isn't she?" Dr. Duverne passes a bowl to Marc. "But I don't think being a star on Broadway—if she makes it—is a stable career, especially for a Black woman."

"Audra did it." Tiya's on a first name basis with her "goddess of Broadway."

"That's one."

"Renée Elise Goldsberry."

"*Hamilton.*"

"That counts, Papa!"

"*Hamilton* was an anomaly. A once-in-a-lifetime kind of hit." Mrs. Duverne takes a sip of water and says, "Most people only dream about getting a role like that."

"Tiya could do it. You've got to hear her really sing," I say.

"There are so many talented singers out there who never make it. Even if they get a part, what happens when they leave the show? If they don't get another part right away? Who pays the bills? What about health insurance?" Dr. Duverne puts down his fork and looks at Tiya. "Are you going to sing *Hamilton*, *The Lion King*, and *The Color Purple* your entire career?"

Tiya glowers into her plate and Marc says, "Pops, you heard May. You have to hear Tiya really sing. People are going to be creating roles just for her." The way he jumps in reminds me of the way Danny ran defense for me with my mom. I miss that.

"When you showed some talent with basketball, we stopped letting you watch NBA or college ball at home. Do you know why?" Dr. Duverne looks at Marc, pushing his son to think. It's clear where Marc learned his critical, questioning way of speaking. I never knew he wasn't allowed to watch basketball at home; no wonder he used to come over to our house to watch big games with Danny.

Marc shakes his head slightly and ventures, "You didn't want me to be distracted from school."

"We didn't want your head filled with dreams of playing in the NBA. A little bit of talent doesn't make a professional basketball player," says Dr. Duverne.

"We wanted you to focus on real dreams. Dreams that could actually come true," Mrs. Duverne scoops more food onto Marc's plate. "Eat more; you're still growing."

"You can't control our dreams, Maman!" Tiya tries to keep her tone in check, but frustration creeps in.

"Look at Marc. He's making practical decisions about his future. He's not thinking about basketball; he's thinking about a career, and Silicon Valley is where opportunity lies now. We aren't controlling your dreams, baby. We're helping you shape them." Dr. Duverne is unfazed. "We've talked about this, Tiya. You've got to have backup plans."

Marc bites his lips and looks down at his plate. He would never talk back to his father, even when he disagrees. I don't know how he will pull off an HBCU if he gets into an Ivy.

Tiya, on the other hand, can't help but speak her mind. "Can't get grades higher than As, Papa."

"Good."

"She's going to sing at the rally," Marc says casually. "You should come and watch her perform, Pops."

Tiya's eyes get bigger than her plate. She flings every sharp utensil on the table at Marc with her eyes. Then she looks at me and mouths, *What the hell?*

"You never told us that, Tiya Marie," says Mrs. Duverne, "When did you decide to put that in the plan?"

I say, "Oh yeah, when we get everyone out on the quad, she's gonna kick the whole thing off with her powerful pipes." I lock eyes with Marc and he grins.

Tiya settles back into her seat. "It was a surprise." She folds her arms all salty-like. Her whole posture says, *Two can play this game, Mayday.* "Right after I sing, Mayday's going to give the rally speech in front of the whole school."

I choke on my rice. *The whole school?* I was thinking a video or the auditorium with just the juniors and seniors. Before I can respond, Marc says, "You should come. Tiya and May are going to kill it."

Now I'm using my eyes to fling all the utensils plus the entire table full of food into his face. Tiya shimmies gleefully in her seat. "May's a brilliant writer, so you know her speech is gonna be fiiirreeee."

"You sure this rally isn't going to get you in trouble? I'm not just worried about your principal. You know that." Dr. Duverne's eyes are filled with concern. Then he smiles and says, "Maybe we'll try to come see you both."

"You've protested before, but you still need to be careful," says Mrs. Duverne. "We'll try our best to come."

Noooooooooooo.

Tiya stretches her arms before folding them dramatically across her chest. She looks over at me and beams.

After dinner, Tiya and I are draped over her bed, nursing our bulging bellies. I hang half upside down over the edge and point at her poster of Yuri Kochiyama. "That poster saved me today when I was talking to Hugh. She is literally the only Asian person I could think of who has worked in solidarity with Black movements."

"She's not the only one, Mayday! There's a long history of Black-Asian solidarity!"

"Yuri is the only example I knew, and it was all thanks to you. I know I need to study up."

"Don't wait to learn about it in AP History, that's for dang sure." Tiya pulls me upright onto the bed. "You need to tell me all the things! Starting with BSU."

I give her a mostly accurate play-by-play of the meeting and the points Hugh made. She listens without interrupting, and when I finish the parts about André and DeMarcus, she nods slowly.

"He's not wrong, Mayday."

"I know." Still, I'm surprised to hear it from her. "How come we've never talked about this stuff before?"

"I've tried."

"And I was ignorant." I flop over the bed again, arms and head hanging over the edge.

"I wasn't going to say it like *thaaaat*, but . . ."

"It's true, right?"

"Yeah, girl. Remember that day when we tried to talk to you about André?"

"Ugh, yes. I'm really sorry, Tiya." Lying upside down is forcing my food backward up my esophagus, so I pull myself up next to her. "I get why you and Marc didn't want to keep talking to me about all that. I should have asked better questions and listened more."

"Me too. But it's hard. You never know how conversations like that will turn out. Plus it's tiring." Tiya leans against the wall. "Especially with people you love."

"I'm sorry I made painful things even worse."

"You were going through it, too, though, Mayday. It was so soon after Danny . . ."

"I know. Still, I've been a fool, but I'm trying to learn now."

"Don't take this wrong, okay?"

My stomach sinks. I nod, eyes on her face as she finds the words.

"I want to be able to talk *with* you about race, but I don't want to be your coach."

"You know what Hugh said?"

"What?"

"He said if your Blackness wasn't part of our friendship, our friendship won't last."

"I think it's probably true, Mayday." Tiya exhales loud. "I'm a Black girl and that affects everything. How I experience the world. How the world treats me. If I can't talk to you about it, if you don't try to get it, that's a huge part of me I can't share with you."

I nod, slowly understanding. "Is it okay to ask you questions? I don't want you to have to be my coach, but what if I have questions?"

"Yes, and it also depends. There are some things I don't want to explain. It's why I can talk with Ayanna and Mikayla so easily— there are things that go without saying."

That makes sense. It's like when I talk with Celeste. There are things we just know. My heart starts to fall apart a little. Does this mean there are things I'll never instinctively understand about my best friend? Things she'll never understand about me?

Tiya sees my face and grabs my hand. She knows exactly what was going through my dome. "We're talking now, Mayday. There will always be stuff to learn about each other." She exaggerates a wink. "That's what keeps things interesting."

I nod. "I'm going to learn and be better, Tiya. Treat things that happen to you like they're happening to me." I squeeze her hand. "I'm going to be a friend to you like you are to me. I'm going to be an ally."

"Co-conspirator." She schools me and grins. "We're planning a protest together. You're about to give a big fat speech and I'm about to sing in front of the whole school . . . no thanks to you and Marc. You're not forgiven for ganging up on me." She snatches her hand away and shoves me off the bed. I hit the ground with a *thwump*. She peeks over the side. "Mayday! Are you okay?"

I curl onto my side and start fake crying like a baby. She throws a pillow at me and laughs. "Oh, stop whining. My point was, we're already in it together. I think we're gonna be fine."

I grab the pillow and climb back onto her bed, and we talk for another hour. The whole time I wonder: Is giving the speech the only way to show her I'm serious about trying to be a better friend and co-conspirator? Because not giving the speech might be the only way to show my parents I'm trying to be a better daughter.

56

When Tiya and I knock on Marc's door before barging into his room, he's typing rapidly on his laptop. He's already wearing sweats, a hoodie, and a jacket, with car keys nearby. Ready to give me a ride home before I ask.

"You could give May a ride home yourself if you'd learn how to drive," he teases Tiya.

"What for? You're the best personal chauffeur in the world." Tiya laughs as she gives me a quick hug. "See you at school tomorrow, Mayday."

Marc has given me rides home approximately a billion times before, but tonight I can't find words to make any kind of casual conversation. I sit shotgun, hugging my backpack, trying to shuffle through questions about the BSU meeting, Marc's talk with

Ijemma afterward, and Hugh's parting words in the parking lot. None of them seem like light conversation topics for a short ride home. Marc looks over at me, and the right corner of his mouth pulls up into a crooked smile. "What's on your mind, Mayday? I know that look. Spit it out."

I can't. I don't even know where to start. Or if I want to get it out. That could be super awkward. So I ask, "How are *you* doing, Marc?"

"Me?" He points at himself and raises both eyebrows. "I'm wondering the same thing about you."

"Don't dodge the question," I say. "How are you *really* doing?"

He puts on his blinker and turns right at the next stop sign. "Mayday, we'll be at your house in three minutes. I can't answer that in three minutes."

"Try."

"Where do you even want me to start? Classes? Danny? BSU? College? I can't keep it all straight."

"Class, then."

"Classes are fine. I have a paper for AP English due Friday and a huge test coming up in BC calc next week. You know I'm the only Black student in both those classes? I hate that."

"Do the teachers say anything?"

"In calc, I feel like he's always waiting for me to make a mistake, like he doesn't think I should really be in his class. In English, I feel like the teacher is silently patting the whole department on the back for diversifying AP."

"That's gross!"

"Oh, I *know*. I gotta perform or else it's not just a disappoint-ment to me but for everything that's riding on me." He slows to a stop at a red light and turns to me with a sly smirk. "So you and Tiya are gonna have to find someone else to shuttle you around, because I gotta study."

"Ugh. Fine. If it's just for a week, I guess I can bike my butt where I need to go." I groan dramatically. "I never had to bike before because Danny—" I stop. Marc squeezes the steering wheel tightly when he hears Danny's name.

"Because Danny used to drive you places." Marc finishes my sentence. I nod. He smiles sadly and says, "I know, because half the time I was stuck in the car driving you around too."

I pause as he makes a left turn. "How do you do it, Marc?

"Do what?"

"Fake it till you make it. If I didn't know better, I'd think you were totally over it."

His eyes open wide. "Really? That's news to me. I feel like miss-ing Danny is permanent. I don't think I'll ever be 'totally over it.'"

"What does missing him feel like for you?"

Marc pulls to a stop in front of my house and turns off the ignition. He blinks, surprised. I want to take his hand, tell him I understand. Instead, I wait quietly and hold my backpack. He says, "Like I'll never be whole and I'll always be sad. It feels like my fault. Sometimes I hate the world."

He brushes the back of his wrist under his eyes and says, "That track plays on a loop in my head and I can't turn it off. I can turn down the volume most days. But nights are the hardest because there's nothing to distract me from the sound."

"There's one in my head too." I stare out the window at my house. I can see the downstairs lights are all on.

"I know, May. I wish I could turn it off for you. I feel like I need to be strong for everyone, but especially for you." The moonlight and shadows soften the lines of his face. "I wish we could understand why he did it."

"Maybe we could have stopped him."

"Yeah." His hands are still gripping the steering wheel though we've been stopped for a few minutes. "But if we couldn't have, maybe it would help us heal."

I shift my body to face him. "What if we never understand, Marc?"

"I dunno. My therapist said—"

"You have a therapist?"

"Yeah, didn't Tiya tell you? We both talked to the grief counselors at school, but they weren't there permanently, and I was really struggling. My dad found me someone to talk to. I usually go every other week."

I had no idea. "What did your therapist say?"

"He said there might not be answers, but that it was still possible to move forward. He suggested I join a group for other survivors. He said it might help." Marc tugs at the strings of his hoodie. "There are groups for sibling survivors too, May."

I shake my head. "I'm not ready yet. Maybe one day."

"You can always talk to me until you're ready. You know that. Think about it, though."

I nod.

Marc turns and scans my face. "I'm conflicted about college, May. I'm ready to get out of this city. Head to an HBCU—if I get in and my parents don't die from disappointment that I don't go Ivy. I want a fresh start. But I'm worried."

"About what?" I ask. Marc presses his palms into his eyes, but a lone tear escapes and rolls down his cheek. I pull my hoodie sleeve over my hand and brush it off. He grabs my wrist as I pull my arm back.

"I feel like I should stay close." He gazes into my eyes. My heart starts to beat uncomfortably fast, and I forget to breathe.

"Why? You want to go to a school with more Black students. Somewhere you don't need to carry such a huge weight all the time."

"I know, but I feel like I should stick around to be here. Make sure things are okay for Tiya. For you . . ."

"What are you talking about, Marc? You need to go to the college of your dreams: Howard or Morehouse, or that one in Florida. You're going to get in." I pull my arm back and look away before I fall into him any further. "You don't need to worry about us. Tiya and I will be fine."

He stretches out his hand before rubbing it on his sweats. He laughs awkwardly, then recovers. "I don't trust the two of you for a second. If I leave, who's gonna drive you around and keep you from getting into trouble?"

"We can handle ourselves just fine, thank you very much." My phone buzzes in my pocket. It's probably my parents. "Hey, Marc?"

"What's up?"

"What did . . ." Should I ask? It's none of my business, and Tiya will probably tell me later, but I can't help myself. "What did Ijemma want after BSU today?"

"Oh . . . that?" Marc rubs the back of his neck. "She, uh, had some choice words for me about dating someone who wasn't Black."

"What's wrong with you dating someone who isn't Black?"

"May, we *definitely* don't have time to get into that right now." He massages his temples. "Sometimes all these expectations are suffocating. It's not just Ijemma. It's my dad, the teachers, every-thing. I don't want to disappoint people."

I want to respond to what he just shared, but my heart freezes as I suddenly process his initial answer to my question. "Wait, what? Rewind, please. Who are you dating?"

"You, apparently."

"Huh?" I need a pacemaker. My heart seems to have forgotten how to function properly. "She thought we were dating?"

"She did."

"Oh, ha ha." The sound hiccups in my throat, like it's try-ing to stop itself from coming out. "That's funny. Because you're like . . . like . . . my brother."

"Ha ha . . ." Marc forces a laugh. "Funny, right? Because I'm like a brother . . ."

"I hope you set her straight."

"Oh, yeah, don't worry. I let her know."

Our awkward laughs fade into awkward silence before I hop out of the car and head inside.

57

My parents are waiting for me in the kitchen.

"If you're still hungry, I made curry chicken," says my mom, gesturing toward the stove. I love curry chicken. I'm too full to eat more but peek into the pot anyway; the curry sauce and chicken fat is starting to congeal on top. Next to the pot, sitting in the small halo of light from the stove, I spy a small plastic-covered plate of stir-fried mustard greens and rice. My mom set out food for me even though she knew I was going to Tiya's. She's a guilt-trip pro.

"I'm full."

"Where is your jacket, Maybelline? You will catch a cold if you don't wear a jacket." She's wearing sherpa-lined slippers, a pair of Dad's old sweats, and an oversized sweatshirt.

"It's not even cold outside, Ma. I'm already wearing a hoodie. You don't need to remind me about wearing a jacket all the time." I grab a box of Pocky and try to hustle out of the kitchen. I'm not trying to stick around for this.

"Maybelline," says my dad, foiling my escape. He's in sweats too, but his actually fit. "We need to talk."

My whole body immediately goes on high alert, and I can feel the flames beginning to lick at my insides. "This feels like an ambush."

"Sit down, Yam." My dad pulls out a chair and gestures at it. He's got that teacher calm turned on, so no matter what I do, I can't ruffle his feathers.

"I'll stand. What's up?" If I stay standing, I can make a break for it. Sitting feels like a trap.

They look at each other. Finally my dad says, "Mom had her performance review today. For the first time in her career, the review was not good." Dad stays in his seat, eyes watching me. His whole body is still.

I'm guessing a performance review is kind of like a report card for adults. "So what does that mean?"

"It means her job is in danger."

"And you think it's my fault."

"I think her job is in danger because her boss is friends with Mr. McIntyre, who feels threatened by what you wrote."

"Same thing."

"It's not your fault, Yam. But the letters need to stop." My dad looks over at my mom and she nods.

I fold my arms over my chest. "I haven't written any more letters."

"Are you going to?" My dad narrows his eyes when I don't answer.

I change the subject and fix my gaze on my mom. "I don't understand why you want to keep working for someone who clearly doesn't value you or your work."

"Ai-yah. You think it's so easy. When I was growing up, we were so poor—"

"I know I know," I interrupt. "Amah and Agong worked the paddies their whole lives and you studied so hard to be the top student at Tai-Da, the number-one university in Taiwan—"

My dad cuts me off with his teacher death stare. My mouth is really on one right now. We've been so busy building walls to contain our grief, but they aren't strong enough to hold my anger and frustration.

"Just having this job is an opportunity your amah and agong could never have imagined for me. Parents work hard so kids can have a better life."

"But you could work somewhere that gives you a better life too, Ma."

"A better life for my family is a better life for me. I make sacrifices to do what's best for our family. For you." My mom sits perfectly still, hands still in her lap. "So should you."

I try to channel my anger through an ice-queen mask like my mom's. "Why is working for a racist man better for the family? In the long run, you're letting him win. That hurts all of us."

My dad says, "When you grow up, you'll understand. The real world will knock that idealism out of you real quick. I used to think the way you do, Yam. You think you can change the world, but the best you can do is watch your back and survive." My dad sounds like a stranger. Who is this jaded man, and what did he do with Bà?

"I *am* in the real world. And it needs changing. I thought *you'd* understand." Ice-queen mask has melted off. All my muscles are tensed and ready to fight or bolt.

My mom's attempts at patience wear thinner than my dad's scandalous robe. Which he's not wearing right now, thank goodness. She snaps, "Why is this so hard for *you* to understand, Maybelline? I could be fired. If I lose my job, where do you think we will live? What do you think we will eat? You think life is free?" She goes straight for the jugular. "Danny would have listened."

Tears sting my eyes, but I push them back. I haven't cried about Danny, and I won't cry about this. "If Danny were here, he wouldn't have to listen because none of this would be happening!" I jerk my arm over my eyes. "Have you read the *Weekly* lately? You've been so afraid about what *might* happen to you that you haven't bothered asking what *is* happening to me!"

"You never talk to us . . ."

"Why would I talk to you? You never listen to me!" I turn around and run up the stairs.

When I'm halfway up, my dad calls out, "No more letters, Maybelline Chen!"

"I'm not going to write any more letters!" I yell.

58

You ever fight with your parents and what comes out your mouth doesn't match what you're actually thinking?

All the time

Why?

Why do we do that?

I blame undeveloped gray matter

And hormones

I'm over here dishing attitude and anger

But I'm actually worried and scared

About what?

Everything

59

Celeste gives us the play-by-play of the Asian American Student Association meeting. Apparently Olivia led a mutiny against Alvin because of his letter.

"So then Olivia interrupted Alvin like, 'Hey, Alvin, am I Asian enough for this club?'" says Celeste, acting out the scene with her arms.

"I love that girl!" exclaims Tiya, scrunching up the papers on her desk in excitement.

"Yeah, she was like, 'I have three Asian besties; maybe that's not enough to qualify?' Then a bunch of people started talking at once and this guy, David Reyes, stood up like, 'Yeah, Alvin, where can I get that textbook you wrote so I can pass the Asian qualification test? Or are only East Asians eligible? Am I disqualified because I'm Filipino?'" Tiya claps her hands as Celeste launches back in.

"Then Andrea Martinez stands up and is like, 'Alvin, if we're not purebloods, are we not Asian enough for you? Do I have too much Mexican to be in this club?' And Natasha Lee—you know who she is, right?'"

"She's friends with Marc, she's hella cool," says Tiya. I remember Natasha speaking up at the BSU meeting.

Celeste nods. "Okay, well she goes, 'Drea, you and me gonna go start our own club. I don't think Alvin can handle either of us in here.' And it goes on and on like 'Do we have to eat stinky tofu and boiled pig feet to be real Asians, or do potstickers make the cut?'"

"Everyone just got on him like that?" I ask, feeling a little bad for the guy.

Tiya reads my expression immediately and says, "Don't you feel sorry for him. He brought it on himself."

"I'm sure that's what people are saying about me too."

"Not everyone was against Alvin. Some people tried to defend him," says Celeste. "Saying we missed his main points, which were about real issues."

"I mean, there *were* points about real issues. I think. I only skimmed because I was so mad."

Celeste looks at me. "What you started and what we're doing is getting people to talk about real issues we don't usually discuss. That's a good thing." She grins in a wicked way I didn't know she was capable of grinning. "And Alvin still deserved what he got."

I nod. I'm still thinking about my mom's job.

I don't stick around for protest planning after school today. I almost forgot it was my birthday, and it seems like everyone's so caught up that they actually did forget. I stroll slowly toward my house, paying close attention to all the details that usually blur into the background. In my neighborhood, spring brings sculpted rainbows of blooming daffodils, freesia, magnolias, wisteria, and cherry blossoms. There are flowers hanging like curtains overhead, and flowers bursting like fireworks at my feet. The scent of floral bouquets and newly green leaves floats through the air.

Spring feels like the new life I'm trying to breathe back into my lungs, but days like this remind me how far I have to go. Spending my birthday alone is a stark contrast to last year, when Danny pulled off the best birthday surprise ever.

Last year, Danny fooled me into thinking my mom wanted him to drive me to San Francisco for an info session about a summer math camp. I was so pissed I turned my back and went to sleep in the car as we started crawling up 101. We were a slow-motion speck surrounded by cars stuck in Friday-afternoon traffic.

When I woke up, he glanced at me with a big grin, his dimple crookeder than ever, and said, "You woke up just in time to breathe in stinky exhaust air, sleepyhead!"

I almost laughed but played visions of myself wasting away at a summer math program and thought, *I'm mad at him. Stay mad.*

But he'd been reading my body language and verbal cues since I was zero, so it was no use trying to fake anything with him. He laughed. "I see you trying not to smile, May-May. Your eyes crinkled in the corners. You can't stay mad at me forever. It's been almost an hour now."

I looked out the window so he couldn't see my face and retorted, "I was asleep for most of that hour. It doesn't count. I get a couple more hours at least."

"Not if I can help it. We're stopping at the next In-N-Out. I know how to win you over."

"We both know In-N-Out is *your* first love, not mine."

"May-May, you will forgive anyone who feeds you. Look me in the eye and tell me I'm lying." I can hear the smile in his voice even now. He knew I was about to cave. I tried to think of a clever comeback but had a massive brain fart. We both knew he was right. I miss how he could read me better than anyone.

We went through the In-N-Out drive-through and I tucked a napkin into Danny's T-shirt as he maneuvered the car back onto the highway. He was a serial food splatterer, and that day he was wearing a white T-shirt, which meant more sauce than usual would torpedo out of his burger.

"Thanks, May-May," he mumbled as a pepperoncini back-flipped for freedom, and I laughed as it landed on his jeans. It was impossible for me to stay mad at Danny.

Danny reached over and turned on the music. It was the Jabbawockeez playlist he made for my fourteenth birthday. I'd given up on my break-dancing dreams back when I almost decapitated myself in our living room, but I held on to a healthy obsession with the Jabbawockeez.

He cranked up the volume and we freestyled to the music when we didn't remember the original moves, which was often. We listened to a few songs, then moved on to soundtracks from our favorite dance movies. As we merged onto 280, we started singing so out of tune the car shuddered.

It's funny which details I still remember. I remember rolling down my window and letting the cool air run its fingers through my hair. I remember looking around as the highway eventually became Nineteenth Ave and we began the slow crawl through the streets of San Francisco, past Stern Grove, through Golden Gate Park, into the Presidio. Red-tiled roofs stood at attention atop white stucco buildings—army blocks converted into tourist attractions. The fading light tiptoed across the water beneath the Golden Gate Bridge.

I remember I looked at him and asked, "Are you lost, Danny? This does not scream 'summer torture camp information session' to me."

Danny ignored me and kept his eyes on the road. Finally, he pulled into the parking lot behind the Palace of Fine Arts.

"C'mon," he said. I was too confused to move.

"What are we doing here, Gē?" I asked.

Danny didn't look at me, but his mouth kept twitching. He swung his feet out of the car and said, "Hustle your butt, we don't have much time." He opened the back passenger door and fished something off the floor in the back seat, jammed his hands into his pockets, then turned on his heel and began walking toward the theater.

I raced to catch up and found Danny waiting by the entrance with his chest puffed and a dopey smile draped across his face. My eyes traveled from his face to the banner hanging directly above his head.

FLOW: JABBAWOCKEEZ ON TOUR

No way.

He pursed his lips and cocked his head. Then he started doing his annoying celebration dance. It involved some chest pumping, butt shaking, strange leg maneuvers, and shoulder brushing. Then he spun around slowly and pulled an actual microphone out from behind his back. He lifted the mic into the air.

He spun around, still holding the mic up in the air, and with his other hand he held up two Jabbawockeez tickets. My jaw dropped as he spiked the mic into the ground. It clattered to the pavement and rolled up against the curb. A small dent bent its waffled metal. I barreled into his chest, hollering, "No way, Danny. NO WAY!" and hugged him like I was trying to squeeze water from a rock. He smelled like fabric softener.

"Happy birthday, May-May, he said. "Let go already; we're going to be late." But he hugged back, his face scrunching underneath his smile. We took a couple selfies and made some goofy faces. Danny picked up the mic and made me take a selfie with him holding it up while I rolled my eyes. Then we went inside.

It was the best birthday—and the last birthday—I ever celebrated with him.

I scroll back through my photos to find Tiya's text messages from that night. I took screenshots of them because I wanted to remember every single detail of the best birthday ever. She sent me about ten thousand messages throughout the show and on the drive home. Apparently, she and Marc helped Danny plan the surprise.

I'm dyiiiingggggg. Mayday, text me back already

Imma blow up your phone until you respond

M

A

Y

D

A

Y

Don't keep me waiting

HUUURRRYYY UP OMG the suspense

I DIE

MAYDAY

Best. Surprise.
EVVVWEEERRRRRR

Tiya

Tiya Marie

Tiya Marie Duverne

TIYA MARIE

How hot were they?!

Asking for a friend

They all wear masks

LOL oh yeah

But their moves were hot

Drool

Where you at now?

Beats me

It's dark outside

Danny has all the windows down

I'm turning into an icicle

That boy can do whatever he wants

And you will let him

He could drive with his toes if he wanted

You owe him for life

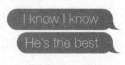

He is

And fine as hell too

Hahahaha jk

But not

What? You could be like, Marc is fine as hell

And I'd be like yeah girl he is

Because he is

They both are

Grooooossssssss

Not even

It's an observable fact

Just stating facts over here

Danny is the best

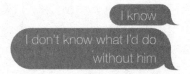

I choke as I reread my last text to Tiya that night. If I had only known what was coming. Life without Danny has been like . . .

. . . like . . .

. . . life without Danny.

There are no words.

I miss the big things: the birthdays and holidays. And I really, really miss the small things. The food stains on his shirt, our goofy dance parties, his mic drops.

I have so many memories of him singing "Lay Me Down" when I was sad, feeding me snacks when I was grumpy, and making faces at me when I tried to do my homework. He always took care of me first. I should have taken better care of him.

My heart constricts and I grip my chest.

I stop at the corner and wait for a car to pass, then as I step into the road, I hear a familiar voice yelling, "Hey, May! Wait up!"

I turn around and it's Josh.

60

I'm already in the middle of the street, so I ignore him and keep walking. No sense endangering my life to see what Josh has to say. I hear his feet pounding against the pavement as he runs to catch up, and I notice he's wearing his KT3s, the same shoes I saw in his room last fall. The same shoes I bought for Danny a lifetime ago. My mind flashes to the box tied shut in my closet.

"May," Josh puffs as he reaches my side. I keep walking without paying him any mind. "May, come on. Don't ignore me."

I stop and look at him like, *Really?*

"I waited for you after school. I really need to talk to you."

"I don't owe you anything, Josh."

"I know you don't, but can we talk?

I keep walking down the sidewalk, past the new-age house

that is all right angles and windows, past its neighbor with the Japanese rock garden. Josh keeps walking next to me. After we pass a few more houses, I stop and ask, "Why are you following me?"

"I want to talk to you, May. You're not making it easy."

"Holy hell, Josh. Why should I make it easy? You just expect people to fall all over themselves at your beck and call?" I stop and cock my head to get a good look at him. "Yeah, you probably do. It's what you're used to."

Josh starts rubbing his hands on his jeans. His palms must be getting sweaty. "I just wanted to talk to you about what you're planning."

I think *guffaw* would be the best way to describe the sound I make. "Why would I tell YOU about it? I'm not trying to hijack this whole thing before it happens. How do you know about it, anyway?"

"Everyone knows about it, May."

"Did your dad send you to intimidate me? Like he did my mom's boss?"

"What? No. What are you talking about?" Josh can't figure out what to do with his hands. I can't believe this guy is a big football star with excellent hand-eye coordination. He doesn't look at all coordinated right now.

"My mom's boss took her team out to dinner, and your dad was there. Apparently her boss is your dad's college buddy, and the new senior manager is his old intern. They threatened her job, but called it 'reorganizing' or something, and her dirtbag boss just gave my mom a bad performance review." I wave my hands around in the air like exclamation points. "So she might get fired."

"My dad was there?"

"I'm sure it was his idea, genius."

We walk past a house with a huge garden that looks like overgrown weeds, but I think they're wildflowers and they probably look like that on purpose. Then we walk past another house with glass art displayed around the lawn.

"Tell your dad he can't intimidate me. My mom's the smartest person I know. She'll be able to find another job, no problem," I say more confidently than I feel. The other day, Ms. Daniels asked me what I was willing to sacrifice. I'm not sure giving up my mom's job, my family's stability, and facing an eternity with the biggest hippo herd this side of the Nile is worth whatever small buzz we can generate from the rally. But I don't know how to tell anyone, not even Tiya, about my worries.

Josh stops in front of a house with a wall of bushes surrounding the yard and says, "I want to help."

I start laughing and study Josh's face, looking for the joke. He looks earnest and sincere. I ask, "Come again? You want to help Take Back the Narrative? You can't be serious."

Josh knits his eyebrows. There's some slight unibrow action happening that looks like it's been plucked before, but not for a while. "Why not?"

"I'm waiting for the punch line."

"That is the punch line." Josh throws his hands up and his eye glints. I think he's getting mad. "Why is it so hard to believe?"

My mouth falls open and I cup my hand over it before he can see the filling in my back molar. "Want me to list some reasons? One, your dad. Two, your defense of said dad. Three, your inability to think for yourself—"

A few blocks over, I hear the ringing of a crossing signal as it starts to go down. My lungs stop working.

Ding!

Ding!

Ding!

I forget about Josh for a moment because all I can hear is the train whistle as it speeds by, giant wheels rumbling over the tracks. The ground shakes under my feet.

"May? Did you hear what I said?" Josh waves his hand in front of my face.

"No, what did you say?" I'm still looking toward the tracks.

"I've been thinking about what you said last time."

"And?"

"You're right. I need to stop apologizing and do something."

"Yup." I start walking again.

"So I'm trying now." Josh stays in step next to me. "Cut me some slack, May. It's my dad. It hasn't exactly been easy for me."

I glare at him out of the corner of my eye and walk faster. He picks up the pace, too, his white shoes reflecting light with each step. "Wait a second, May. I didn't mean it that way. I just meant that it's not that easy to go against my dad, even if I know he's wrong. He's the only family I have. Would it be easy for you?"

That pulls me up short. No, it hasn't been easy for me to go against my parents, to worry about the consequences. To worry about everything. My mom's pregnant hippo of disappointment and its cousin, the rhinoceros of fear, are basically my roommates and make me question my choices every single day. I say through clenched teeth, "No. It hasn't been easy. But I'm here, Josh."

"So let me try to make things right." The glint in his eye turns to steel. I finally see the determination that must make him such a star on the field.

I think about everything Hugh said at BSU. It's true that I was driven to do something about racism only when it directly affected me. Hugh was unbelievably patient with my questions. Tiya has been a straight-up saint in that department. They both gave me chances after I'd been ignorant and hurtful. Who am I to judge Josh if I'm just starting to learn myself?

"Why now, Josh?" I focus on my feet as I walk between the lines on the sidewalk. We stroll past a house with a garden full of lavender. A few purple wands have bloomed early, and their sweet fragrance wafts through the breeze.

He looks at his feet as we walk. "I dunno. It's all of it. You. Your brother. All the letters. The comments section online. The discussion in Ms. D's class. It's not just one thing."

"Oh." I kick a rock out of my way. We walk in silence for a few blocks until we get to my corner. The silence feels like a water balloon, heavy with liquid that we can both see. Neither of us wants to make it burst, so it sags between us. Eventually, Josh says, "Let me say something the day my dad comes to school."

"Are you serious?"

"He'll listen to me, May."

"I don't know. I'll think about it."

He nods, and we stand awkwardly for a moment. Suddenly, honking horns and blaring birthday music come barreling down the street. Tiya is halfway out the car window waving her arms in the air. When the car pulls up at the corner, Marc calls, "MAY-DAY! You didn't stick around for planning today! We've been looking for you! Happy birthd—"

He stops when he sees Josh.

"Josh was just leaving," I say.

Josh nods and says, "Think about it. I'm serious." Then he turns around and walks back up the street.

When he's gone, detective Tiya practically gets a magnifying glass out to inspect every footstep. "What did *he* want?"

"To speak when his dad comes to school."

"What?" Marc almost drops the pastel teal box he's holding. "Oh, never mind, we can talk about it later. It's your BIRTHDAY!" He and Tiya bust out singing and dancing. "Happy birthday to ya . . . Happy birthday to ya . . . Happy biiiirttthday!"

When their song tapers off (it takes a while because I join in too), Marc hands me the SusieCakes cupcake box in his hand. When I take the box, his index finger ends up tangled around mine, and we both pull our hands back quickly. "There are four red velvets, your favorite. You can share with us if you want, birthday girl."

Tiya comes flying at me with a present wrapped in shiny gold foil. "Happy birthday, Mayday! I made this for you. Open it!"

I do as commanded. It's a framed collage of pictures of me and Tiya in all our most epic moments since middle school. That time she talked me into doing the talent show and I was the backup dancer while she sang. The two of us in the dressing room at Ross trying on the ugliest clothes we could find and checking ourselves out in the mirrors. The two of us burying our brothers in sand at a beach in Santa Cruz. Our first day of high school, holding up chalk signs like kids do when they start kindergarten. Our first high school dance when we thought it would be so cool to go all matchy-matchy.

Everything makes me want to cry, so I can't talk or the waterworks are about to get real. Tiya fidgets when I don't say anything. She asks, "Do you like it?"

I throw my arms around her. "I love it, Tiya Marie. Thank you!"

"Oh, thank goodness. Now let's eat your cupcakes!"

I look at the collage and cupcakes. Then I look at Tiya and Marc. My heart fills with warmth and peace and happiness. I let the feelings wash over me.

Today, I let the happy feelings stay.

61

The week before spring break, school is abuzz with talk about college visits to SoCal and the East Coast. People are also discussing trips to Paris, scuba diving adventures in Belize, and road trips to Jackson Hole. Growing up in Sequoia Park means navigating this strange alternate universe where people don't realize how out of touch and over-the-top their lives are.

I won't be visiting colleges or taking any fancy trips. My family never rolled like that, even when Danny was alive.

It's been almost a year since he died, and I've been avoiding my house. I can't handle the heaviness of home, so I find myself staying later after school each day. I want to keep my mind busy busy busy so I can't think of anything else. The magazine room has become our de facto command center for all things related to "the Resistance," as Marc started calling it. I bet Danny used to rope him into Star Wars marathons too. We only have a few more weeks until May, so it's crunch time.

Tiya is sitting with Hugh at a table, drawing a diagram on a sheet of scratch paper. Turns out my disastrous debut at the BSU wasn't a total waste; while not everyone decided to take part in our planning, some did. Tiya charged into their next lunchtime meeting and convinced a couple on-the-fence folks like Hugh to share their stories. He's become a pretty active part of our core team.

"People should stand here and here and here, spaced about this far apart," Tiya says. She's wearing a gray slub tee that says *I'M THE BOSS*. Hugh nods and snaps a couple pictures with his phone. He points to the paper and draws a big square.

"I think you and May should stand on the patio facing the grass," he says.

"Yeah, I think so too, but we should probably check with the student council about the sound system." Tiya arches her eyebrow at me with a very self-satisfied smile. "Gotta make sure *everyone* can hear Mayday's speech."

"And your singing," I retort before asking, "How are people going to get to the quad from the auditorium? It can't be a stampede. Somehow we have to get people out the door in a slow, orderly way."

We share some ideas, but eventually I fade out of the conversation. I'm having a hard time focusing. Tiya doesn't mention Danny, but I know the looming anniversary is on her mind too. I

329

wonder how Marc is doing and where he went.

I catch Celeste looking over at me, and once in a while, she holds up a drawing and smiles. The magazine people are in constant motion, absorbed in their work. After watching everyone for a while, I wander up to the leadership office to check on Ava and the sound system.

I find her sitting alone, scribbling something on a Post-it note; there are Post-its spread across the table in color-coordinated columns. Only one of the overhead lights is on, and shadows stretch across the other half of the room. Ava's wearing a denim jacket over a dress with a faded floral print, and she flashes her pearly whites when she sees me walk in. "May! I figured you might still be around campus."

"Yeah. I thought I'd come check and see if you were still here. What are you up to?"

"Just making notes of all the stuff we need to set up. It's going to take some coordination to get all the equipment onto the patio quickly," Ava says. "How's it going in Poli's room?"

"Tiya and Hugh are figuring out how to get people from the auditorium to the quad. Something that reduces the stampede."

"Anything I can do to help?" She looks out the window toward the quad. The sun is fading, but several classroom doors are still open.

"I think we'll probably need you and student council to be ready to jump in the day of. I figure all kinds of unexpected things will come up."

"Oh, I *know*. Nothing ever goes exactly according to plan."

Ava laughs and puts her pen down. "Remember the Last Chance Dance last year? When the power went out? That was a disaster."

I shake my head. I was still at home in bed, drowning in an ocean, at the end of the last school year. "I wasn't there."

She looks up quizzically. "But you never miss dances."

Actually, I haven't been to a single one since Danny died.

Ava covers her mouth as if she read my mind. "I'm so sorry, May. Of course you weren't there."

"I bet that dance got crazy."

"It did. Thank goodness no one got hurt." Ava pulls out her ponytail, runs her fingers through her hair, then ties it back up again. "I'm sorry I brought it up, though."

"I'm learning how to handle stuff like that. It's nice planning this event because it keeps my mind off things."

"I get that. When my dad left, I threw myself into school too. It helped me focus on something else."

"What . . . happened with your dad?" I ask hesitantly.

"He left for his secretary." She laughs, but I sense the pain isn't too far beneath the surface. "It's like a bad movie, right? I told myself I was going to graduate from Princeton and be so successful he'd be sorry he left."

"Seems like you're on your way." I watch her scribble something else. "Why Princeton?"

"I don't know. I probably heard someone say it was one of the best schools, so I got it into my head that I needed to go there. It's been in my head since I was thirteen."

I want to tell her Princeton won't make the hurt go away.

Getting into Princeton didn't help Danny feel better. Maybe having something to work toward is what helps. I look out the window. It's not quite dark outside, but the moon is already so bright it lights up the quad. All the classroom doors are closed now, and I can just barely make out a sliver of light from Poli's room across the grass. Tiya is probably waiting for me.

I snap my fingers. "I was supposed to ask you about the sound system. Everything good to go?"

"Oh yeah, Jackson's got it all figured out. Turns out that little freshman knows his AV equipment. His sister is a DJ or something."

"Tell him thanks for helping out even though he was nervous about his school record." I laugh. "I should probably head back."

"Yeah, I'm going too." I help her gather the Post-its and pass her a couple colored pens that rolled down the table. She puts the Post-its into a notebook and carefully slips everything into her backpack.

As we start walking out, I tell her, "Ava, it's cool to have Princeton as a goal, but it's not gonna make the hurt go away. You gotta know that it's definitely your dad's loss for walking out."

"I know you're right. I've just been working for this for so long, I feel like I can't stop now. It's all I have." Ava chews on her lower lip. "But thanks, Maybe."

I wander slowly back to Poli's room, pausing to watch my moonlit shadow stretch across the grass. One year ago this week, Danny was still alive. In a few days, I won't be able to say that anymore.

As I get closer to Poli's room, I smell pizza. The smell of pepperoni and cheese and grass brings me back to the night Danny found out he got deferred from Stanford. We had dinner with my parents, then I ordered Danny's favorite pizza and invited Tiya and Marc over for second dinner outside in our backyard. Danny was really disappointed, but he kept cracking jokes and trying to be positive. *Deferred isn't denied*, he kept saying. *There's still hope.*

We played H-O-R-S-E on the hoop in the driveway, and Danny kept forgetting which letters we were all on, which was unusual because he was usually so competitive. It was funny at the time but means something different when I look back now. He started to be more scatterbrained around this time: misplacing his keys, forgetting to stop at the grocery store, losing his Star Wars socks. He also started waffling on decisions, like the night when Tiya and Marc came over for movies and Dad made an appearance in his scandalous robe. That night, he couldn't decide on a movie, even though his go-to choice was always Star Wars. He didn't even change out of his basketball uniform until we forced him to go shower first.

I freeze halfway through the quad as I realize we did that movie night after Danny's last basketball game. The one where he missed the game-tying shot. He hadn't wanted to go out with the team, and we came home for a chill night instead. He didn't seem too bent up, but maybe he was and he just hid it so well. Are these all the signs I keep saying weren't there?

If I put them together with the times I walked into his room and saw him staring at the wall, or the couple times he locked his room door, or all the days he went to bed too late, or woke up midday, or seemed extra tired, do they add up to depression? Do they point to Danny's death?

Maybe I couldn't put all the pieces together because I was looking at the wrong puzzle. All those months, I thought I was living in a different one: the puzzle of Danny's exhausting but triumphant senior year. These pieces made sense in that jigsaw too. Looking back knowing what happened, the same pieces show an entirely different picture. I squeeze my head between my hands. I feel like it's starting to make more sense, and it still makes no sense at all.

I really should talk to a therapist like everyone has suggested. It's been almost a year, and that feels like a big milestone. A time to reevaluate. To remember Danny. To work out my own healing. I don't know how to process these questions yet, and I think I'm ready to try. I stop and pull my wallet out of my backpack.

It's worn at the edges and smooshed between a dollar bill and a receipt, but the business card is still there. Katherine Lo, Licensed Professional Clinical Counselor, is probably not answering phones at this hour, but I call and leave her a message before I lose my nerve. After I hang up, I inhale a lungful of the evening air and hold it as I count to three slowly. Then I exhale. I feel like I just took a big step.

When I walk into Poli's room, there are empty pizza boxes on the table, and Celeste brings me a plate with three pepperoni slices. I eat gratefully while I work. If Danny were here, he'd probably drop a pepperoni on his pants. I smile and hurt at the same time.

By the time we pack up to leave, it's almost ten o'clock and the streets are empty. Tiya calls Marc and he comes to pick us up. He's wearing basketball shorts and a sleeveless jersey. There's a white towel draped around his neck. The curve of his shoulder glistens with sweat, and the moon highlights the muscles on his arm. A half-empty Gatorade sits in the cup holder.

I bet he was shooting hoops over at the elementary school where he and Danny first started balling together. If I had known he was there, I could have gone with him. Tiya climbs into the front seat and I get in the back. Marc looks at me in the rearview mirror and his eyes glisten extra bright. I know he's missing Danny. Plus, college acceptance letters started rolling in this week. I know he's gotten into a bunch of UCs, Howard, Columbia, and Harvard, but I don't know where he's decided to go or if he's talked to his parents. I've been so torn up by the almost anniversary of Danny's passing that I haven't been able to ask.

There's a lot on his mind. I lean forward and put my hand on his shoulder. He reaches up and takes it. He doesn't let go until we get to my house.

62

Ms. Daniels squats between me and Tiya and whispers, "You need to go up to the office. Ms. Whittaker wants to see you."

The bottom drops out of my stomach and my lunch puddles around my feet. I've never been called to the principal's office before. Neither has Tiya. She turns around, grimaces, and draws a line across her neck with her hand. She asks, "Should we bring our stuff?"

"Probably, just in case. Why don't you wait outside for Celeste and Ava? They're going with you."

My brain falls through my stomach and squelches near my lunch.

The four of us are quiet as we walk across the quad to Ms. Whittaker's office. Ten thousand questions barrel through my mind. We haven't done anything wrong, so how does this work? Am I getting suspended? Expelled? Did they call my parents? What will they say? Is this about the protest? How did she find out? Who told her?

Then I remember my conversation with Josh, and I see red.

The secretary at the front desk silently points us to the back when we walk in. Am I imagining things, or does she look worried for us?

Ms. Whittaker's door is closed, so Ava lifts a shaking hand and knocks. A stern voice says, "Come in."

There aren't enough chairs for all four of us, so we stand behind the two chairs facing her desk. Ms. Whittaker finishes typing something on her computer while we watch her. She looks up at the clock, picks up the phone and says something to her secretary about her next meeting, then finally looks at us. I have a sudden urge to pee.

"I'm going to keep this brief, ladies," she says. A chime rings from her computer, and she clicks a screen closed. She folds her hands across her desk. "I've heard about your plans to disrupt Nathaniel McIntyre's presentation during College and Career Week. Let me be clear: if you carry through with these plans, you will all be suspended. You don't want that on your record when you apply to college."

Another chime rings, and she types something quickly. The four of us stand like statues. Celeste tries to stifle a cough, and it comes out sounding like a cat choking out a hair ball. Ms. Whittaker looks up like she's forgotten we are still in her office.

"Your parents have all been called. I trust you will make the right decision," she says. She points to the door with the pen in her hand. "You can go back to class now."

We can't get out fast enough. Tiya's out the door first, then Celeste, then me. Just as I leave the office, I hear Ms. Whittaker tell Ava, "I'm shocked you're a part of this, Ms. Prince. Your mother told me you vacationed in Hawaii with the McIntyres over winter break. I hope you're not dragging the student council into this. It would be a quick way to lose your position as student-body president."

Ava's face is pale as she shuts the door behind her. She can't meet my eyes as the four of us head back to class.

63

My mom is waiting for me when I get home from school. She doesn't even wait until I'm in the house before she lays into me. "You promised you wouldn't write any more letters, Maybelline!"

"I'm NOT writing more letters!" I walk into the house and fling my backpack to the floor before taking off my shoes. My mom follows behind me.

"你在幹嘛? What are you planning? Why did your principal call me at work?"

I stomp into the kitchen without answering.

"What are you planning?" she asks again.

I open cabinets like I'm looking for food, but it's more for distraction than anything else. I talk over my shoulder as I give her a sky-high overview of our plans. When I'm done talking, she says,

339

"So nothing Bà and I said mattered to you at all. You just kept on doing things we told you not to do. Not only didn't you stop, you did even *more*."

There's no good way to respond, and if I try, something slap-worthy will come out. I can feel my mom and her hippos behind me. She doesn't have to talk for me to know what she's thinking.

"Why, Maybelline?"

"I've told you why, but you don't listen!"

Her anger flares. "Why don't *you* listen to your parents? Why don't you care about your *family*?"

"I do care about my family! I'm doing this for our family! Why can't you see that?"

"How does losing my job help us? How does hurting your family show you care?"

"Because I'm trying to make things better for all of us. This is bigger than our family now." I am aware how pie-in-the-sky it sounds. I can hear my dad talking about right choices not leading to right results and how the world will teach me its lessons.

"Nothing is bigger than family!" My mom slaps her palm on the kitchen table.

I stare at the spot where her hand hit the table. She sucks in a deep breath and runs both hands through her hair. "Sit down, Mèi-Mei." I sit down and she sits across from me. She takes another breath and lets it out slowly. "When I graduated from Tai-Da, your amah and agong encouraged me to find a job in America. They knew they would not see me, their only daughter, and still they wanted me to come here. I did not want to come. I didn't want to leave them."

"Then why did you do it?"

"Because I listened to my parents, Maybelline. They knew what was best for me."

"It's not the same thing, Ma."

"Why isn't it the same? They made sacrifices for me, and I made sacrifices for them. And they were right."

"How? You could have gotten a good job in Taiwan. You were the top of your class."

"But Mèi-Mei. I met your dad here in California. I had you and Danny. You were worth every sacrifice." She hesitates for a moment and sighs deeply. "Maybelline, you think I don't understand, but you don't need to teach me about racism. I live it too. People tell me to go back to China, to go back to where I came from. They spit at me. I don't get the promotions I deserve. Just yesterday, someone pushed me so hard for no reason at the grocery store, I dropped the milk on the ground and it spilled everywhere."

"Mom! Why didn't you tell me?"

"I don't want to worry you. It's life here."

"It's not okay, Ma! You should have told someone."

"What for? What will they do? They won't do anything. It will just bring trouble to our family. To you. I need to protect you. You are the most important." She stands up. "Are you hungry, Maybelline? I can make you something to eat."

My heart feels so full and confused. "I'm not hungry, Ma. You don't need to feed me all the time."

She opens the refrigerator and pulls out a container of strawberries. We don't talk as she washes them and cuts out the leafy tops. She put them in a bowl and sets them on the table. Her voice is tired when she says, "We make sacrifices for each other. If you can't see why stopping what you're doing is best for the family, at least you should think about your own future. What will happen to you if you get suspended? What college will take you?"

"People can go to college after they've been suspended, Ma."

"Maybe not the best colleges."

"This is getting suspended for a good cause. I'm sure colleges will take that into account."

"Let's say you still can go to college after being suspended. Then I lose my job. How will you pay for school?"

"I'll apply for scholarships, I'll get a job—"

My mom stops me with her hand. "You're being selfish."

Tears well in my eyes, but I blink them away. "I'm *trying* to do what's best for all of us!"

"You don't understand, Maybelline."

"No, *you* don't understand!"

My mom gets up from the table and disappears into the living room. I hear her pushing books around on the bookshelf, muttering under her breath. Then she reappears holding an old brown photo album. She sets it in front of me without a word. I stare at it for a long time. I know what's inside.

"Open it," my mom says.

My hand trembles as I open the cover. My baby pictures fill the pages. Chubby, bald, onesie-clad photos of me drooling, eating, sleeping, playing—all with Danny at my side. "Ever since you were born, he watched out for you."

There's a picture of him squishing my face into his naked chest. My mom points at it and says, "He used to watch you nurse, so amazed that milk came from my body. One day I found him trying to nurse you himself. He couldn't understand why it wasn't working."

I can't help smiling at her memory. It sounds like something a two-year-old Danny would try to do. I flip the pages slowly, taking in the details of his beautiful, round little face. There's a picture of us at the park on top of a slide; I can't be more than eighteen months old. My mom says, "We told you not to go down that slide, but you saw Ge-Ge do it, so you had to do it too. You climbed to the top, then you got scared and wouldn't come down. Danny went back up and held you all the way down." She pats my hand as she remembers. "Then you ran around and wanted to do it again and again. He went with you every time."

I clear my throat. I wish he were here to hold me on this roller coaster now. "I miss him, Ma."

She takes my hand in hers and squeezes.

We look through the rest of the album together as she tells me more stories about me and Danny. When we get to the last page, she says, "This is what matters most, Mei-Mei. This family is all we have."

I nod. I let her close the photo album and put it back on the bookshelf. When she comes back in, she stands at the kitchen entryway and says, "You cannot sacrifice our family for your causes. This family is the most important. Especially now."

She lets her words sink in before she goes up to her room to change. Part of me wishes she would have just kept yelling and screaming at me. I can push back on her anger with my own. But this? This is much, much harder. I can't fight back against this.

Because I know she's right too.

64

May? It's Ava.

I can't do the protest anymore.

I'm pulling the student council out.

I'm so sorry.

65

Our little run-in with the principal doesn't slow down the planning. After Ava pulled the student council out, the school locked down the storage room with the AV equipment and confiscated student council members' keys. A few members approach us individually to see if they can still help out. Turns out that Jackson, Mr. Afraid to Get in Trouble, is quite the rebel. He talks to his DJ sister, who agrees to help us with the sound system. It actually works out better because we can handle everything off campus.

If anything, Ms. Whittaker added new fire to everyone's work.

Except mine.

I feel trapped with an impossible decision, and I don't know what to do. How can I keep planning this protest? How can I speak at the rally? I can't sacrifice my family's well-being, their safety, for this.

But I can't back out two weeks before the event. We've worked so hard. Tiya is counting on me. If I bail, I might lose my best friend.

This whole thing started so I could set the record straight about Danny. It's grown into something else entirely. I wish he was here to talk me through everything. What would he want? What would he tell me to do?

The last week of April, I disappear into the library at lunch. I find a semi-private corner and pile books on my desk to make a little wall. I nibble on zhōu and pickled cucumbers. Across the cubicles, I see Ava behind the backpack she's put on her desk. She's hiding here too.

She looks up and I look down before we make eye contact. A few minutes later, someone taps me on the shoulder. I turn around expecting Ava, but it's Josh. How does he always sneak up on me like that?

My jaw clenches and I ball my fists. "What do you want?" I whisper.

"You've been avoiding me. I need to talk to you." I turn away and shovel zhōu into my mouth. Josh taps my shoulder again. "Did you think about what I said last time? About me speaking?"

I try to disintegrate this fool with my eyes. "You can drop the act, Josh. I know you told Ms. Whittaker."

He pulls back like I'm a stinging jellyfish. "What are you talking about?"

"Give it up, Josh. Just leave me alone." I pack up my lunch and try to push past him, but he grabs my backpack.

"Wait a second. What happened?"

"Uh, you tattled to the principal about our plans? Or maybe you told your dad and he told Ms. Whittaker himself?"

"Maybelline. I have no idea what you're talking about."

I look at him and exhale. He should probably give up football and become a thespian. He's really good at this innocent-boy act. Before I can respond, I see a small pair of pale yellow Allbirds walk up behind him.

"It was my mom." Ava's voice is so soft, I can barely hear her. She looks at Josh. "I accidentally left my notebook open on my desk, and my mom found some of the Post-it notes I wrote with to-dos for the rally. She called your dad while we were at school. I'm pretty sure he called Ms. Whittaker."

Josh looks like he just got beaned in the face with a football.

"Why would she call Josh's dad?" I ask.

They look at each other. No one responds. Maybe they didn't hear my question. I start again. "Why would she call—"

"They're dating." Ava swallows hard and looks down at her perfect yellow shoes.

"What?"

"They started dating earlier this year, just before the Junior Jam. It didn't get serious until winter break," says Ava.

"You all went to Hawaii together," I say. "I heard Ms. Whittaker talking to you when we left her office."

Josh blurts, "You got called to Ms. Whittaker's office?"

I ignore him. I look hard at Ava. "Is that why you backed out?"

"Yes. I mean, no. Not exactly," she stammers.

"Then why? If they've been dating so long, why didn't you say something? Why did you keep going along?" It feels a little hypocritical for me to question her like this when I've been twisted up and going along too. If my own frustration with Ava is any indication, backing out of the rally will definitely cost me my closest friend.

"I wanted to be part of it. I believed in what we were doing," she says. "I don't know, I just thought we could pull it off without hurting anyone."

"How did you figure? We're going directly against your mom's *boyfriend*."

"They had barely started dating when this all started," she responds fiercely. "I didn't know it would get so serious."

"Then why back out now?"

"I didn't know they would last. But she's really happy. I don't want to mess that up; she's been through enough." She hangs her head. "And I can't get suspended, May. I'd get kicked off the student council. I can't risk it."

"Was this just one more thing to add to your college applications, Ava? Is that all anything is to you?" I bite my lips as I glare at her. "I hope Princeton is worth it."

Josh doesn't move as he whispers fiercely, "You of all people don't need to worry about getting into Princeton. You're a legacy."

"It's not like that . . ." Ava covers her face, and her body shudders as tears start rolling down her cheeks. We are whispering loudly enough for people to notice, and heads are turning in our direction. She mumbles, "I didn't mean to hurt anyone."

I ball my fists. "But you didn't plan on giving up anything, either. You quit as soon as it actually had an impact on your life." Ava's tearstained face just makes me angrier. I don't care if she didn't mean to. I don't care if she's crying. I don't care that I don't know what to do either. I'm not going to feel sorry for her.

Out of the corner of my eye, I see Tiya and Marc walk through the library doors. I bet they're looking for me.

Josh gently pulls me back a few feet. I didn't even realize I had stepped up to Ava's face while I was talking. He takes me by the shoulders and doesn't let my eyes look anywhere but his face. "Let me speak when my dad comes, May. Please."

I squirm away. I can feel Marc's eyes on me as he walks closer. "I don't need you to come in to save the day, Josh. This isn't about you."

Josh looks like he wants to say something more, but instead he takes Ava's elbow and walks with her out of the library. I start walking toward the door after they're gone. Marc takes my backpack and Tiya takes my hand, and they don't ask any questions, but I know I'll have to answer them soon.

66

Mrs. Duverne opens the door, and light and spice flood the entryway around me.

"Maybelline, cherie!" she exclaims as she kisses my cheeks and folds me in her arms. I love how she smells, and I snuggle into her embrace. "You haven't been over in so long. You doin' all right? How're your parents?"

I smile up at her weakly and she sizes me up in an instant. She pulls me into the house and shuts the door. "Okay, cherie, you just go up and talk to Tiya then. I'll bring some food up to her room."

Marc walks by the front door in lightweight gray sweats. He sees me and makes a driving motion with his hands. I make a small talking motion with mine and point upstairs. He nods.

Tiya is sitting at her desk in a hot-pink muumuu, listening to music and scribbling something on a sheet of notebook paper when I push open her door. As soon as I walk in, she spins around and asks, "You okay, Mayday? What happened today?"

I throw down my backpack and lie on the floor. "I thought for sure Josh was the one who told Ms. Whittaker. But turns out it was Ava. Kind of."

Tiya sticks her finger in her ear and makes an exaggerated cleaning motion. "Come again?"

"Ava's mom found some of her rally notes and called Mr. McIntyre while we were in class. He called Whittaker. Ava's mom and Nate McIntyre are dating."

"Ohhhhh shi—" The word dies on Tiya's tongue. Once, Mrs. Duverne actually made Tiya wash her mouth with soap when she heard Tiya swear. Tiya's been extra cautious at home ever since. "That's why she quit?"

"Kind of, yeah. Didn't want to mess things up for her mom. But mostly didn't want to get suspended and mess up her chance at Princeton." I fold my arm over my face.

"Isn't she a legacy?"

"Yeah, but you can never be too careful, I guess."

Mrs. Duverne brings up a tray of food and sets it next to me on the floor. "Thank you, Maman," says Tiya, blowing her mom a kiss.

"Thanks, Mama," I say, uncovering my eyes as my stomach growls.

"You're welcome, babies. Now eat up and don't spill." She closes the door gently as she leaves.

As soon as her mom leaves, Tiya says, "It's classic, really. As soon as sh— got real, she backed out. She didn't want to actually put anything on the line."

"I know." I push the food around on my plate with a fork. I'm hungry, but I don't have an appetite for what I need to tell Tiya next.

"Eat up. You know Maman won't be happy if we bring back bowls that haven't been licked clean." Tiya gestures to the food. Then she is silent for a moment before she says, "At least we have each other. We'll show them next week."

A boulder drops into the pit of my stomach. "I don't know if I should do it, Tiya."

As soon as the words are out, I wish I had a fishing pole to reel them back in. Instead, I watch them sail through the air. Tiya laughs. "Stop playing, Mayday."

"I'm serious."

Her head snaps up. Her face is expressionless as she asks, "What do you mean?"

"My mom might lose her job."

"What are you talking about?"

I tell her a little about my mom's boss and Mr. McIntyre, the dinner, and the bad performance review. Her face doesn't change. It freaks me out because she's one of the most expressive people I know. She shows all her emotions. "Say something, Tiya."

"You can't back down now, Mayday. We've worked too hard."

I feel like I'm blabbering when I respond. "I can't risk my mom's job. Our family can't afford to stay here on my dad's salary."

"This is for your family too! You started this whole thing to defend them."

"But it's making them bigger targets. The Chinese community is avoiding my parents when they need the most support. People are shoving my mom at the grocery store. My family feels like it's falling apart all over again—"

She interrupts, "If you back out, they win. Again and again and again. Like they always do."

"Her boss is going to choose his college buddy over her. She's going to be fired. They win anyway!"

"You have to make sacrifices! A job isn't her life. People give their lives fighting for what's right!"

She doesn't get to tell me what's right, or what I should sacrifice for this. She doesn't understand. My voice trembles when I speak. "My family has already been through too much, Tiya. This is hurting my parents even more."

"I don't know why you acted so mad about Ava," she snaps. "You're no better than her."

"That's not fair."

"Why not? You're doing the same thing." She presses her lips together. I stare at her, anger boiling in my stomach. I've never felt this way toward her before. She lifts her head defiantly. "Remember when you texted me about making decisions based on love or fear?"

I nod, dreading what she will say next.

"You think you're making this choice out of love. But this is fear, Mayday. All. Fear."

I force myself to swallow a few bites of food as Tiya gets up from her desk, walks over to her wall, and fiddles with the lights. She touches different pictures on her wall; one is a picture of us from our eighth-grade graduation. Both of us have enormous glasses. "You've already made up your mind, I can tell," she finally says. "You gotta do what you gotta do."

She doesn't look at me and I don't look at her. The silence between us is uncharted territory, a trail, an ocean we have never traveled.

I've never let myself out of the Duverne house before. Tiya always walks me out, gives me a hug and kisses my cheeks before I go. I feel bad not saying thank you, but I also don't feel like talking, so I sneak out when Dr. and Mrs. Duverne are laughing about something in the kitchen. I close the door gently and turn to see Marc sitting on the front step. He smiles and jingles his keys, but his smile fades when he sees my face. We walk to his car together.

We ride without talking all the way to my house. He keeps looking over at me as I replay my conversation with Tiya in my head. He knows I need time to process whatever just went down at his house. When we pull up in front of my house, I open the door and murmur, "Thanks, Marc."

He hesitates, then hops out too. He takes my backpack and falls in step beside me. The moon is waning, and a few stars are starting to wink from the sky. Marc touches my elbow lightly as we approach the house. "Talk to me, May."

The feel of his fingertips on my skin breaks the walls holding me upright. I lean into him, fighting back tears, and he folds me against his chest. His breathing and heartbeat steady mine. Marc rests his cheek on top of my head and asks, "What happened?"

My words crash and tumble over each other. I tell him about my mom's job, about Josh and Ava, about their parents dating, about my baby pictures. I end by telling him about Tiya. His arms tighten around me.

When I finish, he lets go and rubs his face. I find myself wishing he'd hold me again. "Whoa, that's a lot, Mayday. What's getting to you the most?"

"All of it." I cup my face in my hands and look at the ground. "It's like I only have wrong choices. I'm hurting people no matter what I do."

"What's hurting *you* the most?"

I step back a little. I've never thought of this before. "Fighting with Tiya." He steps closer, and my voice cracks. "What if . . . this is it?"

Marc shakes his head. "Tiya would never let that happen. You're her sister." We walk around the side of my house, and he opens the wooden gate to the backyard.

"I don't know why I'm doing this anymore. It was clear at first. I was mad at Mr. McIntyre, and I wanted to defend my parents. I wanted to set Danny's story straight." I stop on the grass on the edge of the light coming from my house.

"You're still doing that." He faces me. His eyes are soft.

"Am I?"

"*I* think so. No matter what you decide to do, you're choosing him first."

"How?"

"You tell me, Mayday."

I wrinkle my nose at him. "Don't get all Ms. D on me now. I need the answers spoon-fed, please."

He smiles and his lashes brush his cheeks. "Okay, you big baby, listen up. If you decide not to speak at the rally, you're putting family first by choosing what seems best for them right now. If you decide to go through with the rally, you're showing powerful people they can't use your family to spread their narrative. Either way, you're honoring Danny and putting him first."

"I've never thought about it that way." I take a step closer to him and he pulls me back into a hug.

"It was never going to be easy, Mayday. But instead of having two wrong choices, maybe you have two right ones." I lay my head against his chest and feel the truth of his words wash over me. Maybe instead of not being able to make a right choice, I actually can't make a wrong one. It doesn't make the decision any easier, but it changes things a little.

I tilt my face up to tell him what I'm thinking, and he looks down at me. Suddenly, I'm aware of his body against mine and my heart starts beating so fast I have to catch my breath. I can feel his heart picking up the pace to match. Instinctively, I look down.

Marc takes his finger and lightly traces the spot under my

chin before lifting my face back up to his. He asks, "Were you going to say something?"

The world disappears and I am lost, searching his eyes. "I don't—I don't know," I manage to say. I don't recognize his expression, but it is warm and deep, and I tumble in. My heart leaps into my throat, and my brain stops functioning. I feel like I tripped and am falling falling falling. He pulls me closer. As he leans over, he whispers, "May . . ."

When his mouth meets mine, I lose all sense of time and space. I don't know which way is up, or if my feet are still on the ground. All I know is there is a glowing sensation tingling through every nerve. My arms wrap themselves around his neck and he presses his hands into my lower back. Warmth rushes through me everywhere and I forget about everything.

But just for a moment.

Then it all crashes back down. What the hell is happening right now? What am I doing? This is Danny's *best friend* and Tiya's *big brother*. What would they think? What would they say? I'm in no state of mind to be kissing boys right now. Especially not this one.

I push Marc away. He steps closer but I stop him with my hand and a head shake. At the same time he says, "May, I shouldn't have . . . ," I say, "I'm sorry, I can't."

I'm not sure if I'm apologizing to him or to myself. This is too much.

Everything is too damn much.

I yank my backpack off his shoulder. Then I run in the back door and slam it shut.

67

I thought my words
were sword and shield.
I thought our words
would be an army.
But my words aren't any of those things at all.

They're a train
hurtling down the tracks
crushing everything I love.

I'm inside the locomotive
watching helplessly
unable to stop this relentless path of
heartbreak and pain.

68

I whirl up to my room and pace back and forth, kicking books and dirty clothes out of the way. I grab my pillow and walk in circles. It's hard to catch my breath. I keep seeing Marc's face, feeling his hands on my back, hearing him whisper my name. My lips are still tingling. I want to call him to come back, but I can't. It's not right.

What am I doing? Do I feel things for Marc because I'm trying to fill some of the holes Danny left behind? Do I really like him, or do I just miss having someone watch out for me? Did my heart choose Marc for Marc, or am I reaching for him because he was Danny's closest friend?

How would Danny feel about me kissing his best friend? What will Tiya say when she finds out? If I hadn't already messed things up with her, I've definitely done it now.

But I can't help tumbling back into Marc. I feel the warmth in his arms. The strength in his gaze. Then I force myself to push him away.

After this, I'm going to lose him too.

I'm losing everyone.

I wish Danny were here, and yet, how could I talk to him about *this*? I trip over a shoe that I kicked into the middle of my room and crouch to pick it up. Something pulls my eyes to the closet.

The shoebox.

No. I shake my head. *Not now.*

Something pulls me to the closet doors.

Now.

I throw clothes out of my closet and they go flying over my head, landing all over the room. A sweater drapes over my bed; a pair of jeans lands in the garbage can; T-shirts scatter all over the floor. I grab the shoebox and stare at it. It feels like it's alive.

My heart beats even faster and I can't stop my hands from shaking. I feel like I'm in a not-very-fun house and the walls of my room are closing around me. I have to get out of here.

I throw my jacket on—my mom would be so proud—clutch the shoebox in my arms, and run back out the door. I half expect Marc to be waiting for me outside, but he is gone.

I don't know where I'm going, but I start walking. I walk and walk, passing houses, rounding corners, crossing streets. Pale light melts off the moon and pools in uneven puddles over the neighborhood. Flowers that were so vibrant under the sun are now grayscale shadows that stand motionless in the dark.

Walking calms my heart, and it stops ricocheting around my rib cage. The even rhythm of my steps on the sidewalk lulls my breathing into a steady pattern. I walk in a daze, following my feet. I think it's my imagination, but it feels like Danny's shoebox guides me. I feel like Danny is with me.

Bright headlights and the sound of zooming cars tell me I've come to a busy street. I've walked myself to the crosswalk, and I look up to see the railroad crossing signal on the other side.

Danny's brought me to the tracks.

After Danny died, the city hired around-the-clock guards at every railroad crossing. He was the fifth suicide, but the third who died on the tracks, so people pressured the city council to do something more than offer condolences.

I hide behind the thick traffic pole, and when the guard on duty looks the other way, I slip into the shadows inside the fence that walls the railroad off from the busy street. Tall bushes provide cover as I walk. If I can make it a few hundred more feet, I will pass the station and the guard won't be able to see me. I'll be able to walk upright and blend into the shadows.

The box pulls me forward.

I walk along the stretch of tracks in the wide space between the rails and the fence. It is covered with large, uneven rocks, so I focus on staying out of sight and not falling. It only takes a few minutes by train from one station to the next, but on foot, it feels like forever. The metal rails catch the moonlight, then disappear onward into the dark.

I stumble more than once but keep going.

I trip along, unsure how far I've gone. I cradle the shoebox, nestle it into my chest like an infant. As the lights of the intersection dim behind me, I venture away from the fence and closer to the tracks. I press ahead in the darkness until my feet stop. I look to the tracks ten feet to my left and suddenly I know.

I am here.

I set the box at my feet and look around. I have seen this place so many times in my nightmares, I feel like I've been here before. I can't help picturing Danny standing here in this spot and all my emotions start to come in long waves. They start out in darkness, in the ocean, way back at the beginning, way down deep where the tears have long been buried. They roll in slowly. The waves build and build and build, growing taller, higher, stronger until they reach the shore. Until they reach me.

Then they curl up into peaks, hover for a moment, and crash. Wave after wave engulfs me until I'm sputtering and coughing and drowning in too much pain and missing and loneliness. The flames that I've barely contained all year flare up in a shower of sparks before they, too, are overwhelmed by water. And still the waves come.

The tears pour from my eyes. They are salty and they sting and they tumble onto the ground. I call out to Danny, "Why, Danny?! Why did you leave me?" A year's worth of tears fights its way into the world. "I needed you, Danny! I still need you so much!"

My body is racked with sobs so powerful I think I will break. Then red lights flash far away. I can see their pulsing glow in the darkness to my left. I hear the ringing of signals and imagine the red-and-white-striped crossing gates lowering on either side of the tracks. A single circle of light looms in the distance, growing rapidly as the northbound train races toward me. I don't move.

The Caltrain's horn blasts as it passes the signals, and I stumble backward. Then the train rushes past, speeding so quickly it creates a tunnel of wind that batters my body and whips my hair into a frenzy around my face. I scream. The gale catches my scream and scatters it into silence. And still, I scream. "I'm sorry, Danny! I'm sorry I didn't do more! I'm sorry I didn't know more! I'm sorry I couldn't help you! I wish you were here! I miss you I miss you I miss you!"

The train tears across the tracks, rips the night in half, then disappears. The ground rumbles as the train flies by, then suddenly it is gone and the night is still. I fall to my knees and collapse over the shoebox, soaking it with tears and convulsing with uncontrollable grief.

I sob with a part of myself that is ancient and animal. I sob knowing that only the stars bear witness to my sorrow. I sob grasping at the air for a brother I will never touch again. I don't know how long I sob, curled like a baby on the ground, but I lie there long after the sobs have trickled out and dried up. I lie there until the gasping stops and my sight returns.

When I hear the scurrying of tiny clawed feet on the tracks, I sit up and hold the shoebox with trembling fingers. I start talking to it like it is Danny.

I tell Danny about Mr. McIntyre and the letters I sent. I tell him about the students who were appreciative but spend much more time talking about those who weren't. I tell him about Josh and Alvin and Byron. I tell him about Celeste, and I say that he'd be so proud we're friends now. I tell him about Uncle Joe and Ms. D. I tell him about our plans to Take Back the Narrative. "You wouldn't even recognize me now, Gē," I say. Then I tell him about Ava and Ms. Whittaker. I tell him about Mom and her job and the photo album with our baby pictures.

I ask what he thinks I should do.

I look down at the box, expecting answers. It feels good to get everything out of my system, even if I'm only talking to a beat-up piece of cardboard. It is worn and the shoelace holding it together is frayed at the tips, but I feel like Danny's listening to me. I tell it about Tiya and hesitate before talking about Marc. My voice cracks when I finally do. Tiya and Marc pulled me to shore when Danny died. They helped put me back together and hold me up, even when I tripped over my own feet. Which I did. A lot.

I feel like I've lost them, and that is almost harder than anything else that has happened since Danny died.

When I look down again, the shoelace flops into my fingers.

It's time.

Gingerly, I tug on the shoelace, half expecting the whole thing to disintegrate in my hands. When it doesn't, I pull a little harder, loosening the knot. The rabbit went through the hole two times when this knot was made, the way Danny always used to tie his shoes. When the shoelace unravels, I roll it up in my fingers and slip it into my back pocket. It's one more piece of Danny I can't afford to lose. I take a deep breath, look up at the moon, then lift the lid off the box.

The first things I see are Danny's cell phone, headphones, and charger. My heart skips a beat. Why did he leave me his cell phone? I wonder if it will turn on after so long. I hold down the power button and the screen blinds me as it lights up. I blink a few times to clear away the light specks dancing behind my eyelids. Time moves sloth-like as my eyes adjust and the phone powers up. When the phone finally turns on, I see the directions Danny left for me on his background image. It says:

1) Play song on Spotify first.

2) Listen to the voice memo.

I find the Spotify app and open it. Danny deleted all his songs except one: Sam Smith's "Lay Me Down." I start crying as soon as I see the title, but I follow his directions like I always do.

I put on the headphones and listen. The first and second times through I just sob—I thought I cried out all my tears, but apparently there are plenty more where they came from.

It's not until the third time through that I realize this is the version featuring John Legend. Why did Danny leave me this version?

The fourth time through, I understand the song is like a conversation.

The fifth time through, I realize that I'm Sam Smith and Danny is John Legend. It's our conversation.

I listen again.

Sam—me—starts in their heartbroken tenor, *No words can explain the way I'm missing you* . . . The words echo exactly how I feel. When I hear Sam Smith singing, *The feeling's overwhelming, it's much too strong*, I start choking on sobs again.

Then John Legend—Danny—sings soulfully, *I'm reaching out to you, can you hear my call?* That's so Danny, reaching out to me despite his own pain. Worrying about me. Wanting to take care of me.

This hurt that I've been through. I'm missing you. I'm missing you like crazy.

Then they sing together, *Can I lay by your side? . . . And make sure you're alright?* Danny is still here, reaching out to me. Calling to me. Catching me. Missing me. Forgiving me.

Loving me.

I play it again and again, and I let the tears run. They flow from my eyes and split into rivulets that trickle down my face and drip off my cheeks. These are words I wish I could have sung to him. I wish I could have lain by his side and taken care of him. And it's like he knows. He loves me and he knows.

I lose count of the number of times I play the song. As I'm about to hit play for the hundredth time, I remember this was only step one. There is also a step two.

I scroll around to find the voice memo and don't give myself time to feel or think before I hit play. My heart stops when Danny's voice fills my ears. "May-May, have a Star Wars marathon once in a while. Eat an In-N-Out for me. Don't kick over any more bookshelves, but keep dancing. Hug Mom and Dad"—his voice falters—"and tell them I love them. The rest of this is for you when you're having a bad day. I made it for you, so you could have it when I went to college . . . but I'm giving it to you now . . . I'm sorry I wasn't stronger. I love you."

Then he launches into the most out-of-tune, horrendous-sounding version of "Lay Me Down" he's ever sung. It feels like he is here, alive, and it is the most beautiful thing I've ever heard. Danny left me his voice, and I feel like he will be with me forever. The phone battery is running low, so I only replay the memo one more time. It feels too sacred to play on repeat anyway. After the last warbling note of Danny's singing, I turn off the phone and hug it to my chest.

I carefully wrap the headphones around the phone and tuck it back into the shoebox. As I do, something hard rolls into my knuckles. I yelp, "Ow!"

I gasp when I look down. It's the dented microphone from Danny's spike-drop-worthy Jabbawockeez birthday surprise.

Danny *was* listening all along.

And he left me an answer.

69

When I get closer to the station, I hear a baby crying. A young woman is sitting on the bench, holding a wriggling bundle in her arms. Is she waiting for the train at this hour?

Late at night, the trains run about every hour and a half before they stop completely. I don't know what time it is, or if another train will come tonight. The microphone rolls around the shoe-box when I shift it to my left arm. I reach into my pocket with my right hand and fish for my phone to check the time. It's not there; I must have forgotten it in my room. The baby's screams echo down the tracks and I turn to look again.

A small duffel bag sits on the bench at the woman's side and she's wearing a thin jacket with a small blanket over her shoulder. She shivers and tries to soothe the little one. It gets chilly at night.

It's one reason vendors make a killing on those cheesy hoodies up in the city; tourists are never prepared for the cold. I squint for a closer look when her blanket wiggles and a tiny foot pokes out near her left elbow. She tries to cover it again, but two little feet kick like windmills until the soft covering falls away. The woman leans down and whispers as she throws the blanket over her shoulder and moves the baby underneath. It cries and cries and suddenly it stops.

She's nursing.

I turn away, embarrassed. Because boobs.

Filled with curiosity, I sneak another peek just as the baby pulls the blanket back off again. It's wearing a furry gray bear suit, and its arms and legs stick straight out from its body. The baby wiggles a little and the woman pats its butt.

Even from across the tracks, the woman looks exhausted. The light above her bench is harsh and highlights the dark rings under her eyes. She's wearing sweats, and her chestnut-brown hair is in a messy ponytail. Her mismatched flip-flops suggest she left her house in a hurry. She can't be more than twenty-five, maybe younger. What is she doing here so late?

The baby cries again, and its tiny hands reach up to its mama. In one smooth motion, she switches the baby into her other arm and moves the blanket into place. The furry bear stops crying when it starts nursing again. The woman nuzzles her nose into the little bundle and squeezes. When the baby kicks its feet, she reaches for her bag and rummages around before pulling out a worn sweater that she wraps over the fussy infant. She shivers, but her baby is warm and settles down.

I tug my jacket tighter around my neck. In my mom's world, being cold is like a mortal sin. Who knows how long this woman and her baby will be out here shivering before the next train comes?

If there is another one. I have no idea what time it is.

I really hope there is one. Soon, for her sake.

The baby has fallen asleep, and the woman pulls down her shirt as she kisses its nose. I wonder if my mom used to kiss me like that after nursing. It's hard to believe I was ever that small, that my mom ever smiled indulgently at me and tickled my nose. That there was a time before hippos.

As I watch the woman cradle her now-sleeping fuzzball, I have a small epiphany. When the baby cried, milk and blankets comforted it. Helped the little one fall asleep, even under the glaring station lights so far from home. I have no idea what's going on in this woman's life or why she's waiting for the train at this hour. Her small duffel seems hurriedly and sparsely packed, but she has the essentials. She has what she needs for her child.

Food and warmth are life.

That's why my mom is always hounding me about wearing a jacket and worrying about me catching a cold. It's why my mom packs me lunches and leaves me Pocky in a cup. It's the reason she cooks meals even when she's sad and saves food for me even though she knows I've eaten. It's why she constantly asks if I'm hungry and cuts up strawberries for me in the middle of a fight. I realize it's not a guilt trip. It's how she shows she cares.

I was once a helpless, chubby, tiny nursing bear too. There was a time when all I needed was milk and blankets.

And my mom.

Maybe when she pulled out the baby pictures that day, it was to remind us both that once, she was my world. At the time, I only saw Danny. Thinking back, I realize she was in almost every photograph. The ones without her are pictures where my face is scrunched in cries, and my arms reached up for her. Now, there is so much she can't control, so much she can't protect me from. But food and warmth are necessities she can still provide. These are things I will always need.

All this time, my mom has been telling me she loves me in the best ways she knows how. She's been showing her love this way since I was born. I just didn't see it until now.

I try to pick my way over the rocks more quickly because I need to get home. I need to hug my mom.

As I near the crossing gate, I remember to duck into the shadows by a tall bush when the security guard looks around. When he turns away, I hurry out onto the sidewalk and try to act like I was just out for a not-suspicious-at-all nighttime stroll. At the corner, I turn and glance back at the young mom and her bundled-up baby. The little bear is warm, but the woman is still shivering.

My yellow fleece rubs my chin. It's the jacket Danny brought for me to wear on the night of my birthday surprise. My favorite. I look back across the tracks at the woman's silhouette under the station lights. The signal across the street blinks to show it's safe to cross, but I make a quick decision and walk back toward the station instead. I pause just before I reach the platform and look down at my jacket. I pull it up to my nose and inhale. I rub its soft sleeves. I pull out the shoelace from Danny's box and stuff it into the back pocket of my jeans. Then I take off my fleece and hurry over to the woman and baby.

"Here," I say, holding out my jacket. "It's cold out."

She looks up at me, surprised. Her eyes are puffy and a little red. "Oh no, I can't take this," she says. "We'll be okay. The train will be here soon."

"Please take it. The train might not come for a while, and I live close. I can run home."

I hold the jacket out to her again. She reaches up and carefully takes my yellow fleece. She whispers, "Thank you."

"My mom's got it into my brain that there's nothing worse than being cold. I hope this helps." I hug the shoebox to my chest and jog back down the platform, across the tracks and back to the corner, where the signal has turned red. When it changes again, I jog across the street, my breath puffing out in wispy white clouds. Goose bumps crawl up my arms and I shiver. I keep jogging past grayscale gardens and looming houses. I jog until I'm almost home.

As I turn the corner to my street, I hear the train whistle in the distance. Its brakes squeal as it reaches the station, and I actually smile at the sound. I picture the woman and her baby climbing onboard and sinking into a warm seat.

For the first time since Danny died, I'm glad the train came again.

70

My house is ablaze with light; it shines from every window and pours out into the street. My parents must be waiting for me. They've probably been trying to find me, but I didn't have my phone. They must be on another level of worry now. I reach up to pull my jacket tighter, then realize all I have on is a loose white T-shirt with a blue pocket in front. I hurry into the house.

My mom is sitting at the dining table fiddling with her hands and tapping the screen of my phone, which is on the table. She must have found it in my room. My dad is pacing, adjusting wall fixtures, running his hands on windowsills. They look the way they did the night Officer Jeffries came to our house. Pocky is arranged in a cup, and there is a pile of lightbulbs on the table. I wonder if my dad's been switching out the bulbs to pass the time and distract his worry.

As soon as I walk in, they rush over, fear flying off their shoulders on wings. In four giant bounds, my dad reaches me and scoops me into his arms, pressing his cheek onto mine. I can feel his body shaking and something damp runs down my face. My mom is less than a second behind, wrapping herself around both of us, her arms reaching around me and grazing my dad's chest. They stand like this without moving, just breathing, for what feels like a very long time.

"We thought . . . we thought that you . . . When we heard the train . . ." She doesn't finish her sentences. She just kisses my head firmly over and over again.

My dad sets me down, grasps my arms, and flips them over. Seeing nothing but retreating goose bumps, he grips me and looks me over, making sure I'm okay.

"Ma, Bà . . . how could you think that I . . ." I can't find the words. I know what we've been through since Danny died. I could never make them go through that again. "I could never. I would never."

My dad pulls me back into a hug and my mom joins in the back. They press me between them like a Maybelline sandwich.

Moments later, my dad realizes that something is poking him in the belly and he looks down to see the shoebox I'm still clutching. "What's tha—" he starts, then stops as recognition dawns across his face. "Where did you get—"

My mom puts her hand on his arm, and he stops mid-sentence. She turns me toward her. "你okay嗎?"

I nod.

"Where did you go?"

"I was down at the tracks."

She nods like already knew. She hugs me again, then pulls back and rubs my arms. "You're cold."

I shiver in response.

"Where is your jacket?" She hurries over to the coat closet and grabs her shaggy brown upside-down-paper-bag coat. She comes back to the kitchen, wraps it around me, and guides me over to the chair. "Hungry?"

When I nod, she points at the Pocky she's set out, then goes over to the refrigerator and starts pulling out glass containers full of leftovers. I watch as she heats up food and fixes me a small plate. I don't complain or try to stop her.

They sit down and watch me eat. I fidget self-consciously, but somehow this doesn't bother me the way being stared at usually does. I can see a million questions behind their eyes, but they don't ask.

My dad and I start talking at the same time. "No, no, you first," he says with a wave of his hand.

I gulp and look at the shoebox. All the way home, I debated whether to tell my parents about it. But they've seen it now, and they want to know. They deserve to know. "Danny says to tell you he loves you." I stand up and give them each a long hug. "And he says to give you those."

Tears leak from the corners of my mom's eyes. Sometimes, when her emotions are drained, she doesn't have the energy to find words in English. "你怎麼知道?"

"It's in the box." I open the lid and take out his phone. "He hid this in my closet before he left that night. I point to the lid, where it says *For May-May* in faded Sharpie. "I didn't want to open it . . . until tonight."

We plug the phone into an outlet and watch as the battery signal turns green. I play them the beginning of Danny's message and stop it before he starts singing. Maybe I'll play the whole thing for them one day, but for now, I'm keeping his song for myself. They both inhale sharply when they hear him talk. He sounds so alive.

Like me, they want to play it again. And again. Tears stream down our faces as we listen to his voice.

"Sometimes I still think he's going to walk in the door." I bury my head in my arms and cry onto the table. "I miss him so much."

"Me too." My mom chokes up as she rubs my back.

My dad scoots his chair over and puts his arm around my shoulder. He lays his head on my back and I feel his chest heave in ragged breaths. "I miss him too, Yam. Every single day."

I don't think we've ever cried together for Danny. We've each been floating alone, suffering alone. I think we've tried to be strong for each other, but maybe we would be stronger if we could be vulnerable together.

Our tears flow like rivers emptying oceans, one tiny drop at a time.

* * *

As I wash the dishes and put the rest of the food away, my mom and dad sit at the kitchen table flipping through Danny's phone. They found the photos and have been alternately laughing and crying as they scroll through them all. My dad looks up. "Yam, why did you open the box tonight?" My expression makes him set the phone on the table and ask, "What happened?"

Warm water pours over my hands as I think over the last few days. Everything feels like it happened so long ago, but it was today, yesterday, the day before yesterday, and the week before that. I get lost in my thoughts and forget to answer until my mom comes over and turns off the water. She says, "Mèi-Mei, we can wash those dishes later. Come talk to us."

I sit back down at the table and, at first, the story comes out slowly.

I tell them almost everything. I tell them about going back to school and kids avoiding me in the halls. I tell them about Josh and Alvin and they frown. I tell them about Celeste and they smile. I tell them about Olivia, Yumi, and Grace. I tell them about the discussion in Ms. Daniels's class, the comments section, the BSU meeting, and the AASA meeting. I tell them about Mr. McIntyre's plans to speak at my school, and about our plans to Take Back the Narrative. I don't say anything about Marc, but I tell them about Ava, and finally, I tell them about Tiya.

Through it all, they just listen. Every time my mom opens her mouth with a question in her eyes, my dad pats her arm and she closes it again. Each time my dad starts to say, "Wait, what—" my mom kicks him under the table and he shuts up. When I'm done, they just sit and look at me, blinking. Then they look at each other before turning back to me.

"Yam," says my dad. "There are so many things we didn't know." My mom nods and he keeps going. "You were right. We were so worried about protecting you from what might happen that we never even asked what was already going on."

"You were dealing with so much." My mom takes Danny's phone and sets it back into the shoebox. She sees the microphone and asks, "Was this in the box too?"

"Yeah, remember how Gē was always doing those mic drops? Mostly for himself"—I smirk—"but sometimes for other people, like if they said something really funny or smart."

They smile as they remember. My dad picks up Danny's phone again and starts scrolling. "I saw a picture of you two and he's holding up that microphone. Here." He hands me the phone, and it's the selfie we took outside the Jabbawockeez show on my birthday. You can barely see my pupils because my eyes are rolled up to the middle of my forehead, and Danny is cheesing with the mic like he's about to drop it again.

I point at the dent in the picture. "See? It's the same microphone. I think—" I pause. Should I tell them what I really think? I don't want to kill this moment. But I don't want to hide more either. "I think it's Danny's answer to my question. About speaking at the rally."

My mom rubs her neck. "Maybelline, we were right about people twisting what you wrote. And how people would try to hurt you. And us." I gulp. Oh no, here we go. Then she continues,

"But you were right too."

Excuse me? I think she just said I was right. Must be something in my ears.

My dad watches me shove a finger in my ear to clean it out. He elbows me and grins. "You heard her, Yam. She said you were right *too*. That means we were also right, got it?"

I rub my hands together smugly. "Okay, okay, just making sure. Could you say that again, Ma? The last part."

"Ai-yah! I said you were right too la. 你們兩個。" *Oh, you two.* She shakes her head at us. She takes the phone and gently rubs her thumb over the picture of me and Danny. "This is our Danny. The real one. I want people to remember him like this. Not how Nate McIntyre talks about him." She squeezes the phone in her hands and gazes at my dad, then me. "I didn't understand what you meant when you said it was bigger than our family. But I see now."

I go for it. "I'm going to speak at the event, Ma."

"I know," she says, lightly touching the microphone with her fingers. "I think it's what Danny would have wanted."

71

Mayday

I'm so sorry

Can we talk?

Mayday

Mayday

Mayday

Mayday

Please stop ignoring me

I've been so wrapped up in this protest

I couldn't hear what you were saying

It finally processed through my thick skull

I'm ready to punch your mom's boss in the face

I shouldn't have said you

Whoops. Hit send early.

I shouldn't have said you should risk her job for this

Or that stuff about Ava

I'm really sorry, Mayday

Where are you?

I'm freaking out

I'm going to make Marc drive me over if you don't respond soon

I'll throw rocks at your window or something

If one is broken, it was probably me

We just came by

All your lights were on

You dad has been busy, those suckers were BRIGHT

Your parents haven't called me or Marc

So I'm assuming you're home safe

BTW, Marc told me what happened

I went off

But not gonna lie, if you two got married we could be sisters

No pressure tho

Please text soon

Love you, girl

I love you too, Tiya Marie

OH THANK GOD

I'm so happy you texted

I went down to the tracks

And forgot my phone

Just seeing your texts now

YOU DID WHAT???

I'm fine

Danny left me a shoebox with some things in it

WHAAA? WHAT WAS IN IT?

His phone with some music and photos

A mic

You gotta give me more than that, woman!

I can't do this over text

I need to see your face to have this convo

I HAVE QUESTIONS

ABOUT ALL THE THINGS

It was the mic he brought to my birthday surprise

And the Sam Smith song he always sang to me

> But the version with
> John Legend

> Tiya, I'm sorry too
>
> I've been so torn up about
> everything
>
> I should have talked to you
> sooner
>
> I didn't know what to do
>
> Felt like no matter what I was
> gonna hurt someone
>
> What you said was fair
>
> But I couldn't hurt my
> parents more

I know, Mayday

You do what's right for you

And your parents

> I'm gonna speak at the rally

DON'T PLAY, MAYDAY

> I'm serious

HALLELUJAH

72

It's May first. May Day.

My day.

This used to be College Day at Sequoia Park High. All the seniors would wear clothes from the colleges they planned to attend, but it got banned for the same reason we don't have vale-dictorians. Too much academic pressure.

Academic pressure that has too easily been blamed on "the Asians."

Today is the day Mr. McIntyre comes to speak at our school. It is the day we reclaim our stories.

It's *our* day.

There's a nervous energy around campus. Those of us involved in planning are buzzing with excitement, hoping we can pull this off. Students who haven't been involved know something's up and they whisper to each other, trying to find out more information. Teachers and security are on alert, cell phones and walkie-talkies ready.

I check in with Ms. Daniels before school. I want a pep talk or something from her, but she just looks at me and says, "I told you I expected a lot from you this year." When I linger, hoping for more, she boots me out of her room with the words, "You don't need me to tell you got this. You already know. Now go do it."

Somehow we get through our first three classes, and then it's time. Celeste and I head to our fourth-period pre-calc class with Mr. Gonzalez, sending last-minute texts and checking in on all the moving pieces. Everyone texts back thumbs-up signs and various smiley faces. Celeste and her team have art stowed in different places all around the school; they are going to display it around campus while we are in the auditorium with Mr. McIntyre. She made us promise to text her updates when it goes down in there because she'll miss that part while she's setting up.

When Mr. Gonzalez tells us it's time to head over to the auditorium, we all stand up and file out the door. Celeste slips around to the side of the building, and I hear her dainty feet fly down the hall as soon as she is out of sight. She has a lot to do.

As teachers herd several hundred juniors and seniors down the two auditorium aisles, I walk past Ava, who is careful not to crease the papers in her hand. Something on the ground has a commanding grip on her attention. I find Tiya and sit with her. My stomach somersaults when I see Marc in the row behind us.

I glimpse Josh on the other side of the auditorium and see many students holding papers to turn in to Mr. McIntyre. The room's acoustics catch our chatter and throw it against the walls; it reverberates and amps up the energy. Tiya and I whisper urgently, then we take deep breaths.

All we can do now is watch.

The lights turn off and the chatter quiets down but doesn't quite stop until Ms. Whittaker gets on stage to say a few words. She starts by saying sternly, "Welcome to the College and Career Week kick-off event! This is one of the most important weeks of our school year and will hopefully inspire your future paths. We've spoken to the individuals who are planning to disrupt today's presentation. Let me be clear that anyone who participates will be given consequences, so make smart choices. A suspension will not look good on your college applications." Then she flashes a smile and starts to introduce Mr. McIntyre. Blah blah, successful venture capitalist, blah blah, huge impact on the world's most innovative companies, blah blah, opportunity for you to learn, blah blah, maybe score an internship, blah blah, man of the community, blah blah, and father of our very own star quarterback, Josh McIntyre!

Josh stands up and waves. I start to get worried when he doesn't sit back down.

When Mr. McIntyre walks onto the stage, Ms. Whittaker hands him her mic, but she doesn't realize we've already disconnected it. I watch Mr. McIntyre's mouth move and feel an immense sense of victory when no sound comes through the speakers. He taps the microphone and frowns.

"Sorry, Dad," hams Josh, working the crowd. "Welcome to Sequoia Park High School, where many a formidable presenter has fallen to the unpredictable technological difficulty." He turns around and flashes a smile at the crowd. "I don't need a mic, though. Can everyone hear me?"

Everyone, even Mr. McIntyre, laughs. It sure is easy to charm a room when you're a handsome white guy. Especially if you happen to be the star football-playing son of a local celebrity. People just *want* to love you.

Mr. McIntyre gestures for help with the mic.

"No, Dad, it's my turn. I have a few things to say."

Mr. McIntyre smiles and steps back. He thinks this is a funny prank or something.

Josh turns around and smiles as if in memory. "All my life I've worshipped my dad. When my mom died when I was little, it was just the two of us, and we stuck together."

Marc leans forward and whispers, "What is he doing?"

Tiya and I exchange worried looks and lift our hands up in small shrugging motions. I am hyperaware that Marc is inches away. Since our kiss, I've been trying to act like nothing happened in order to focus on preparing for today's events. I still haven't talked to him about where he's decided to go to college or how things went with his parents. The truth is, being near him makes my heart skip so fast I can't possibly think straight.

But I think about Marc all the time; I'm all over the place. I don't know if I'm ready, and I don't want to screw things up. Tiya says she's all about it, but is that really possible? There are too many risks.

And yet, every time Marc is in the room, my nerves go on high alert, and I can't focus on anything or anyone else. I'm only aware of him. Even now.

Josh is still talking. "We were a team. He did everything for me, and he's given me everything. I know how much he loves me. He's a great dad." Mr. McIntyre is up onstage grinning. There are a few *awwwwws* from around the auditorium.

"Which is why this is so hard." Josh's smile fades. "What do you do when you find out your hero isn't perfect? When you are forced to see his weak spots, his blind spots . . ." Josh hesitates and glances quickly at his father.

Mr. McIntyre isn't smiling anymore.

"I didn't want to see it. I tried to deny it. But the thing is, I knew Danny Chen. We played ball together. He was kind of, you know . . . a role model for me. For a lot of us, actually. Also, I know May. I know a little about their family. They aren't the people my dad made them out to be. I told myself the things he said weren't a big deal. I thought the whole thing would pass."

Mr. McIntyre and Ms. Whittaker are both rooted to the stage as they watch Josh step out into the aisle. They don't try to stop him. "But it didn't pass. It got worse. And the only reason I knew is because he hurt someone I care about." Josh turns and looks right at me.

Marc clears his throat.

"I shouldn't have thought blatant racism could pass. And it

389

couldn't pass because you made things worse." Josh turns to face his dad, and Mr. McIntyre winces. "You turned people in the community against her and threatened her mother's job. And you did it after they lost Danny, in the middle of their worst nightmare."

Josh's voice softens. I think the room has disappeared for him and it's just the two of them. Like in all those pictures lining their hallway. "Dad, what if someone said it was your fault Mom died? I remember thinking we couldn't go on, but somehow we did. Imagine how much worse it would have been if everyone blamed you for her cancer." Mr. McIntyre pulls up a chair and sits down. He can't walk off the stage now, not with his own son speaking to him. "It *wasn't* your fault, Dad. But don't you see? This is what you're doing to the Chens. But what you're doing is worse."

Josh rubs his thighs, the way he does when he's nervous. It's those sweaty palms. "I know you want to make sure I have a smooth path, a good future. But the world you're trying to make for me—no, the world you're trying to keep the same for me—is not a better world, Dad."

The room is silent as Josh sits back down. Marc waits a second before standing up with the mic we prepared earlier. He turns it on and speaks with power. "Danny Chen was my best friend. My brother. Losing him was the hardest thing I've ever experienced. Watching what's been done to his memory and his family might be worse. His death has exposed the deep-seated racism in this supposedly liberal community, and we're here to say you don't get to twist our pain into your story, Mr. McIntyre. You don't get to rewrite our narratives."

Marc shifts the mic to his other hand.

None of the teachers made a move when Josh was speaking, but as soon as Marc starts to speak, Ms. Whittaker starts down the stage steps and several teachers stand up from their seats and start moving in his direction. One is speaking into a walkie-talkie. They look angry now. Entire rows of students stand up to make it harder for these teachers to get to the aisle. Several students move into the aisle to block the principal.

Marc ignores them all and surveys the room. When he speaks again, his voice fills the auditorium as he states each sentence with finality, then pauses to let it sink in before starting the next one. He builds off Josh's words. "We will never have a better world until all our stories are told. We will never have a better world until all our histories are known. We will never have a better world until all our voices are heard."

He pauses as students, and some teachers, yell out their support. Ms. Daniels smiles the biggest, proudest mama-bear smile I've ever seen. Marc passes me the mic. My voice doesn't sound nearly as commanding, and it trembles a little, but I try to match Marc's energy when I leap to my feet and say, "We're here to take back our narratives. Come see us outside!"

Students who helped plan this day jump up, whooping and clapping. Marc leads the way out of the auditorium, past two students we've positioned at the door to collect résumés for the internships. Students thunder out of their rows, many genuinely inspired and moved to action, others just excited by the drama and ready to snap pictures for their I-was-there-when-it-happened posts. Some teachers follow in support; others are swept up in the crowd shouting, "Get back here and sit down!" I see Ava in her seat, still clutching her crisp résumé. Everyone around her leaves, even the other student council members and all her sundress friends. Eventually, she gets up, too, and walks to the door. She gives her résumé to the girl collecting them before following the crowd out to the quad.

When everyone is outside, Josh takes the papers from the students at the door and walks alone back up the aisle and gives them to his dad. "Here are our résumés, Dad. Some in here might be the résumés you're probably expecting. But most . . . most are personal stories. How can you choose qualified applicants from a padded list of extracurricular activities and tutor-driven test scores if you don't know who they really are?"

He starts back up the aisle, then turns around again. Almost everyone has left, and I'm hovering in the back of the auditorium, one foot out the door. I really should go; this is a private moment. But the room's acoustics send Josh's quiet words all the way to the back of the room, and I can't help listening in.

"I'm sorry if I hurt you, but I'm not sorry I said something. I should have done it a long time ago. I know about your dinner with May's mom and about the threats to her job. I know Ava's mom called you and that you reported the rally to Ms. Whittaker. I read what you wrote, and all the comments from people supporting what you said." He rubs his hands on his jeans again but never stops looking at his dad. "I've always been proud to be your son, but lately, I've been ashamed." Josh uses his forearm to wipe his eyes before sticking his hands in his pockets.

As he turns away from the stage, Josh says over his shoulder, "If anyone needs to see what's happening outside, it's you, Dad."

I sneak out the door as Josh starts walking up the aisle.

73

Juniors and seniors pouring out of the auditorium are met by students of all grade levels spaced every twenty feet or so, creating a path that leads to the quad. Hugh is one of the first students positioned outside the door, and he launches into his story. He's been bussed to Sequoia Park schools since kindergarten through a special program that was started when a group of parents from the Grove sued to desegregate schools on the Peninsula. There is Ali, a freshman with muscular dystrophy, down the path from Hugh; she sits in a customized wheelchair and talks about giving up activities she used to love and the friends that cheered her on. Yumi and Olivia stand together holding hands, talking about the rejection they felt from their families when they came out. And on and on.

There are students positioned all over campus, sharing their stories and pointing people toward the quad. They keep talking whether people stop and listen or keep walking past. Occasionally, they start over, each time telling the story a little differently, remembering new details. Andrea Martinez is over by the history building, Natasha Lee by the math building, and Sione near the science building where his little sister is in class. Ayanna and Mikayla are both near the quad, telling everyone to sit down and face the patio in the center of the grass.

I text Grace, our video point person, to let her know that the juniors and seniors are out of the auditorium. Ms. Whittaker asked the video journalism team to live-broadcast Mr. McIntyre's presentation so the freshmen and sophomores could watch from their classrooms. Grace was more than happy to comply. After the entire school watched what happened, she had her team play the compilation of video stories they put together. When I texted, Grace stopped the video, flashed #TakeBacktheNarrative on screen and invited the underclassmen to leave their classrooms and join us.

Students didn't need to be invited twice.

They start pouring toward the quad, bewildered teachers following closely behind with cell phones in hand, trying to figure out what to do.

I check the hashtag, and people are already starting to post pictures and videos. I see a picture Celeste shared of a student sculpture she's displayed near the hugging oak. It shows a circle of girls holding hands. I feel a surge of strength; I know she put that there on purpose. Her team of artists did good. There is art hanging on walls, standing in planters full of flowers, and even chalked on the walkways. How they finished while we were in the auditorium, I'll never know. They were like magical elves that filled the school with splashes of color.

Stacks of the special-edition school magazines are dwindling quickly as students snatch them up. I see students flipping through its pages, reading stories, looking at pictures and gasping or laughing. "Look, Aaliyah! There's yours!" A girl yelps excitedly to her friend while pointing down at a page. "OMG! You're famous!"

Students find their friends and sit down in the grass. Some lay out hoodies or sweaters and sit on top of them; everyone chatters excitedly. The quad is a moving patchwork of color, and it soon runs out of space. Students start sitting on walkways and benches around the grass. Everyone wants to see what is going to happen next.

Tiya rushes around the patio, helping to work out sound-system kinks. Jackson's DJ sister didn't just provide equipment; she helped to set it up and stayed to make sure things ran smoothly. Jackson's sitting nearby looking pretty proud, and I give him a double thumbs-up.

Teachers mill around on their cell phones and walkie-talkies, talking excitedly or staring stonily into space. Some teachers, like Ms. Daniels, Mr. Gonzalez, and Poli, watch proudly from the sidelines, waiting for the next surprise. They help keep everyone calm. Ms. Whittaker is talking rapidly to a group of administrators who seem flummoxed by the whole situation. She's waving her hands while others shake their heads. I bet they're trying to figure out how to stop this mess and get everyone back to class. She's probably freaking out about a student riot or something. Why doesn't she turn around and look at all the young people sitting peacefully in the grass? This is not a riot.

We emailed a tip to the *Sequoia Park Weekly* last week, and I see a small camera crew, a reporter, and a photographer walking in from the parking lot. When one of the administrators in Ms. Whittaker's circle sees them, they all start whispering. Ms. Whittaker turns around, smooths down her shirt, and plasters a smile on her face. Apparently the reporters' presence makes the administration rethink their approach. I think they've decided to take the we're-supporting-student-voice path while the cameras are here—can't have anyone thinking they lost control of the entire school.

Out of the corner of my eye, I see Mr. McIntyre step out cautiously from the auditorium. He walks slowly toward the quad, trying to blend in.

Tiya waves me over to the patio. The sound system is ready. My heart is beating so fast I think it's going to pop out of my ears, and I feel like I'm walking on wobbly Jell-O. I can barely feel my arms and I really, really have to pee. That's what happens when I get super nervous.

But I can't back down now. I'm up after Tiya.

The quad is electric with anticipation, and Tiya stands near a speaker where most people can't see her, takes a deep breath, and starts to sing. Her voice blankets the crowd, and we all hush under its spell. Her voice soars and dips as she sings "Rise Up" by Andra Day. When she steps out from behind the speaker, all eyes turn up to watch her. She doesn't need to do anything dramatic to draw us in; she just stands with her feet planted like the earth itself is giving her strength. I've heard Tiya sing a million times. But I've never seen her perform like this. She lights up, and her voice pulls emotions from deep in our hearts. I can see her on Broadway one day, working this same magic on the stages of New York. I tear up, I'm so proud of her. Marc is so swelled up with pride he looks ten feet taller.

The song ends and no one moves. We're entranced and don't want it to stop. Finally, the crowd erupts in cheers. Tiya walks back and hands me the mic, but I shake my head. I brought my own—one with a little dent on the side. Jackson's sister helped me get it set up before school.

Tiya looks down and nods, then she shoves me out in front of the crowd. I almost turn around and walk off the patio in panic.

Tiya whispers, "It's May Day, Mayday. It's *your* day." I look back at her and nod.

I can do this.

I take a moment to gather myself. Then I begin.

"When I was in third grade, Danny got it into his head that we should dress up like Star Wars characters for Halloween. I'll never forget because my mom found a cheap costume for me online. Danny got to be Han Solo, but I had to be an Ewok."

I hear a few chuckles from students sitting in the grass.

"That night, I was so grumpy when we went trick-or-treating. Danny had this cool lightsaber, and I was just a glorified bear. My costume kept snagging on bushes and trees, and by the end of the night it was all shredded up. I was basically in regular clothes with a cloth and ears draped over my head. When we headed home, I tripped over my costume and all my candy went flying into a puddle in the gutter. I bawled my brains out right there on the sidewalk."

I look over at Tiya, who is laughing at the image of nine-year-old me losing it over ruined candy. "When we got home, Danny picked out all my favorites from his own haul—Reese's, Starbursts, KitKats—and made me a special bag. He was always doing things like that for me. It wasn't until I was older that I realized those were his favorite candies too."

The funny story is easy to tell. This next part is harder. "Danny was always a step ahead of me, watching out for me. He was my light and my anchor. Losing him was like . . . like . . ."

I stop. There are still no words. I squeeze my eyes shut as the tears push their way out. Tiya whispers from behind me, "You got this, Mayday."

I set my jaw and open my heart. "There are no words to describe what losing him has been like. There are holes that will never be filled. Questions that will never be answered. Things I wish I could do differently that I'll never get the chance to try. I feel like I never grew out of my third-grade self; I took everything Danny gave me and never stopped to think about what he wanted. Or needed."

Ms. Daniels is standing behind the seated students, all the way to the side. I can feel the positive energy she's radiating at me, even though her face is serious.

"Did you know he was wearing Star Wars socks the night he died? If you knew him, you're probably thinking, *of course he was*. Everyone knew he loved Star Wars. Sometimes I wonder if he loved it so much because he understood the battle between light and dark. To me, Danny was all light, but maybe he felt like he was fighting darkness alone. He hid his pain from everyone, and we never knew what he was battling. Danny suffered in silence until the end."

My skin prickles as hundreds of eyes rest on me, but I clench the mic and feel Danny close. "And I wish . . . I wish I had known. I wish I had made him sit in my room and talk to me instead of watching him leave for that party. I wish I had known to tell him to talk to someone, anyone. I wish I had one more chance to tell him to hang on. I would have told him it would get better, that I'd be there for him the way he always was for me."

My voice cracks. I grip the dented microphone tightly and feel its power run through me. I hear Danny singing, *I'm reaching out to you*. I let the words sink in and hold the mic a couple inches from my face.

"There is a silence that binds us. It ties our tongues when we need help. It muzzles our minds when we need to reach out and shackles our voices when we need to speak up."

Marc is walking away from the patio. Am I sucking that bad?

My heart drops, and suddenly it feels like all the eyeballs on me are boring holes through my body. My words disappear, and I look down at the wood under my feet. The crowd is quiet. When I look up again, I see Marc standing at the back of the crowd with four people. His parents are to his right; proud smiles lifting tearstained cheeks tell me they heard Tiya sing. On Marc's left is a small woman with her hair pulled back and a man with a soft roll near his belly button. *My* parents?

My heart swells for them. "When Nathaniel McIntyre attacked my family and threatened my mom's job, it seemed like silence was the safest path. If we could just put our heads down and let things blow over, what did it matter if he accused my parents of driving their own son to suicide?

"But I've learned that it matters." I look at Tiya and Marc and Ms. Daniels and Celeste. I look at my parents. "Danny's life mattered. And the stories we tell about him matter. I almost let fear stop me from sharing mine. I almost let fear silence me. But I've learned that silence is not the answer."

I hear some clapping and shouts of *Yaaas, girl!* And *Louder for the people in the back!*

I plant my feet like Tiya did and I feel another surge of strength. "Our silence gives men like Nate McIntyre the power to control the narrative. To revise our histories and shape our futures. But every time we speak out, it is an act of love. Love is how we overcome fear."

I step back and raise my right arm above my head. Some students throw up fists too. "We're not afraid and we won't be silent.

We're here to take back our narratives and step into our power!"
I look up into the heavens, searching for Danny, and whisper,
"This one's for you, Gē."

Then I drop the mic.

74

Tiya crushes me in a bone-pulverizing hug. "You were amazing," I whisper. "I can't wait to sit front row on Broadway watching you perform. You better get me free tickets when you're a star."

"Nah, Mayday. *You* were amazing. Turn around."

People are clapping. Some people are actually standing and cheering. For a second, I feel like a superstar.

Jackson's DJ sister takes over the sound system, and she turns on the music. People start dancing in the grass until Ms. Whittaker makes her way over and motions for the DJ to turn down the volume. She takes Tiya's mic and says she will allow the music to play through the end of lunch, at which point everyone must return to class as usual. Everyone whoops and the DJ cranks up the volume. I smile at Tiya like, *Can you believe we did this?* She smiles back like, *Yeah, girl, of course we did*.

We both mouth, *Immigrants*. And we smile.

I grab her and try to squeeze through the people standing in front of the patio. I text my mom and dad and tell them not to move. People keep trying to stop, hug, and talk to me, and I feel rude pushing through so quickly, but I need to see my parents.

Before I get through the throng, I see Ms. Daniels is talking to my mom and dad. When I walk up, she says, "I was just telling your folks how proud we are of you, May." She winks and squeezes my arm as she leaves. "I knew you could do it. See you in class."

My dad can't stop himself from dancing to the music, but my mom is smiling nervously, wide-eyed and baffled by the crowd of rowdy teenagers. Tiya's parents are wearing a similar expression. Marc holds his mom's and my mom's hands, presumably so they won't bolt. When Dr. Duverne sees Tiya, he hurries forward and engulfs her in his arms. He whispers something that makes her smile so big her eyes squeeze shut. Marc reaches over and tugs her ear.

"Ma! Bà! What are you doing here?" I yell as I bound up, sounding more mad than excited. I see Celeste on the other side of the grass hovering near some art and wave her over.

My dad points to Marc. "Marc called and said we should come."

Marc studies my face and I bite my lip. My stomach rolls around like a sea otter in water. There is so much to say, I don't know where to start. I lift my eyes to his and my voice comes out more quietly than I intended. "Thanks, Marc."

"Anything for you, May," he says. Only Marc could pull off that kind of line without a hint of cheese. It's totally sincere and I know it. I hold his gaze for a moment, hoping he can read everything I'm feeling.

Tiya breaks out of her dad's embrace and watches me and Marc. She mutters at me, "Y'all need to handle the tension. I can't take much more of this." I shove her to the side with one arm and she laughs. "I'm serious, though."

My mom smooths my hair and says, "I don't know how you can talk in front of so many people, Mèi-Mei. 嚇死了。 How come you didn't brush your hair first?" I shake my head and sigh. But when I look around for my roomie, the hippo, she's nowhere to be seen.

"I can't bother with my hair when I'm busy planning an all-school mutiny, Ma!"

My dad pulls me into his arms and says, "You made me cry, Yam. You were fire. Or is it lit? I can never get it straight."

I shake my head at him. "No, no, no, Dad. No more slang out of your mouth. Just no."

"Well, whatever the correct term is, you blew me away. You blew everyone away."

Tiya sings the line from *Hamilton* and adds a little flavor of her own: "You blew us all away . . . Mayday."

My mom takes my hands and squeezes. "I'm so proud of you, Maybelline."

My heart feels like it is going to burst into ten million glittering pieces of confetti. Then my mom says, "If Danny were here, he would also give you the microphone dropping. So you don't have to do it for yourself."

Celeste walks up just in time to hear this last bit and a snort laugh escapes her mouth before she can stop it. Tiya, Marc, and I start laughing so hard, we have to hold each other up. Even my dad starts cracking up. I gasp, "Mic drop, Ma! Mic drop! Not microphone dropping! That makes it sound like microphone poop."

My mom covers her mouth in horror, which makes us laugh even harder.

After my parents head back to work, Marc goes off to find his friends, and our little squad wanders around campus; Celeste snaps photos of artwork to post later, and Tiya scrolls through #TakeBacktheNarrative posts. There are a lot: pictures, videos, memes, quotes, reflections, and a lot of check-out-what-happened-at-my-school-today selfies. I make a mental note to not read any of the comments. Tiya holds up her phone to show us a picture of me speaking to a sea of students, then Celeste holds up her phone to play a video of Tiya singing. Tiya grabs the phone and says, "I sound *good*."

We jostle her with our elbows. I say, "Don't act all surprised. You *know* you sounded good."

Tiya spreads her arms and takes two steps back, like *What can I say?* Out of nowhere Celeste announces suddenly, "I'm going to turn down the Google internship."

Tiya and I look at her with open mouths. Tiya says, "Don't leave us hanging!"

"That's it. I'm going to turn it down. I've been thinking about it since I started doing the art for this whole thing; I really loved it. I figure, if May's parents can get over her speaking today—especially after everything they've been through this year—my mom can get over this five-week summer internship. I'm going to look into art programs instead."

"This will be more fodder for your āyí from Sac to tell you not to hang out with me," I say, laughing. "But whatever, that's amazing!"

"Ah, who cares," says Celeste. "Anyway, I just wanted you to know. I'm going to tell my parents this afternoon before I chicken out." We squeeze her and start walking to the hugging oak with our arms tangled around each other.

Grace uploaded the video she made, and it has already been viewed over five thousand times. That's at least one view for every student and teacher at Sequoia Park High School, and a thousand views from outside the school too. People are sharing the stories we told.

I survey the quad, where some students are still dancing but many others are engrossed in the magazine. I overhear a small group of students asking Hugh about getting bussed to our school. Taylor Harlow, the girl who tried to hug me on my first day back this year, tells him she had no idea. "Wait," she says to Hugh. "So you're saying most students from the Grove are being bussed to neighboring cities because there isn't a comprehensive public high school in your own town?"

"Yup," Hugh answers patiently.

Taylor wrestles with this information, trying to make it make sense. "Maybe it's better because students from Sequoia Grove get to go to some of the top high schools in the country . . . ?" She frowns as the sentence comes out of her mouth; she knows it doesn't sound right.

"You tell me, Taylor," says Hugh, winking at me as I walk by. He's trying to hide a sly smile before Taylor sees it. Oh man, she's in for it now. I chuckle. "Are you saying that a school of mostly Black and Brown kids couldn't become one of the top schools in the nation? Maybe you think people like me don't care about school?" Taylor shifts uncomfortably, but I know Hugh's just getting started. "What do you think would happen if kids from the Grove could go to a school, in our own community, with as many resources as this one? Have you ever wondered why we don't get those resources? Why we're still getting bussed in the first place?"

Taylor sputters as her head spins. To her credit, she doesn't give up. She sticks around and keeps asking questions.

As we near the hugging oak, we run into Grace, Yumi, and Olivia. Celeste breaks out of our arm tangle and takes them to see more of the artwork she hid around campus.

Tiya and I lie in the grass under our tree listening to the music that floats faintly from the quad. We don't speak. We bask together in contented silence. I feel like I'm soaring, and the sky is bright and full of light. Ms. Whittaker may come for us orches-trators of this all-school mutiny later, but I don't care. Our stories are everywhere.

Stories alive with color and shape, stories told through written words and printed images, stories shared from the tips of tongues, stories spreading in sound bites online. We're taking back the narrative, and people are listening.

Our voices are more than sword and shield.

They are bridges too.

I smell the soy-sauce chicken and my mouth begins to water as I bound through the front door. I picture the giant pot of drumsticks and eggs boiled in soy sauce, cooking wine, garlic, and a pinch of sugar. I can practically taste the sweet-and-salty flavor in my mouth. It's the kind of thing I used to be ashamed of in elementary school when my mom packed it for my lunch. Kids would always wrinkle their noses and say something like, "Eeew! Why are those eggs *brown*? That looks disgusting!" or "Gross! That looks like dog food!" Sometimes they'd even move tables to get away from me. But now when I have soy-sauce chicken, I have to bring extra to share. Mostly because of Tiya, though Wes and Sione can do damage on any kind of food.

It's been a week since the big event and I'm still riding the high. I kick off my shoes and they go flying past the entryway. I pick them up and take them to the small shoe rack by the door, but a large pair of brown leather oxfords I don't recognize is in my usual place on the top rack. I wonder who's here. I put my shoes next to the rack and call, "Ma! Bà! I'm home!"

"在這裡!" my mom responds from the kitchen.

My mom's nicest tea set—the gold one with colorful flowers from my amah—is out on the table. Steam curls from the lips of tiny matching teacups. My mom and dad are sitting at the table, laughing as they talk to our guest, who must be someone important if they busted out this teapot and the fancy tea leaves.

I walk into the kitchen and blink rapidly. I don't believe what I'm seeing.

It's Nathaniel McIntyre.

He's in my house. At my kitchen table. Talking and laughing with my parents like it's nothing.

Before I can bolt, my dad says in his teacher voice, "May, Mr. McIntyre came by to talk to you. We've been having a nice chat." His voice is friendly, but the undertone is both apologetic and stern, like, *Sorry to spring this on you without warning, but you better be polite.*

Mr. McIntyre turns around and offers me a smile. "Hello, Maybelline. I know this must be a surprise."

Um, yeah. I force a fake laugh. "You could say that."

Under the circumstances, it's the best I can do. What I really want to say is, *You have some cajones coming into my home, drinking my mom's best tea out of her best teapot!*

411

I hover in the doorway, torn by my desire to scarf down a giant bowl of soy-sauce chicken with rice and my hostility toward Mr. McIntyre. I hope my parents don't invite this man to stay for dinner; it is totally something they would do. My fingers are itching to text Tiya. Instead, I muster, "So, have you been here a long time?"

He looks down at the fancy gold watch on his wrist. It's an analog watch, probably some super-expensive brand. "I've been here about an hour." He smiles and looks to my parents for confirmation, and they nod. "I'm lucky your parents were home when I came."

Oh, the parents you basically accused of driving their son to suicide? Hey, by the way, that's my mom, the woman you tried to get fired. My mouth opens to say as much but shuts itself when I see the warning look my dad aims at me. Instead, I say, "Good timing."

After school today, I worked with Tiya and Celeste in the magazine room for a few hours. We were reading the *Weekly* coverage of our event and checking all the posts that have been put up over the last week. We suspect we haven't been suspended yet because the response has been mostly positive. Some media outlets are praising the way the school empowered its students. Ms. Whittaker probably doesn't want the bad press that would follow if she doled out punishments now. Also, if she suspended us, she'd have to suspend Josh too. There is no way she'd go there.

Students from Wisconsin, Arizona, and a few other Bay Area

cities have even been messaging us for tips so they can try something similar at their schools. Naturally, I don't mention any of this. I just stand against the wall, planning my escape route from the kitchen.

"Maybelline, finding me in your kitchen like this must be disconcerting at the very least, so I'll cut right to the chase. I've been thinking a lot about what was said during your protest, and I have some questions. I've tried talking to Josh, but he's not speaking with me right now." Pain pinches Mr. McIntyre's face and his cheek twitches. "I'm sorry to barge in on your family like this, considering the circumstances, but I didn't know where else to go. Josh mentioned he cared about you."

He sets my mom's fancy teacup gently back on the table. "I'm hoping you'll be willing to spare a few moments to talk to me. I know it's a lot to ask."

"A lot to ask" is quite the euphemism, buddy.

My dad offers to go upstairs with Mom to give us some space, but I gesture toward the front door. "Let's sit outside." Somehow sitting on the front steps feels a little safer than sitting in our kitchen. This way, I can bolt inside and slam the door if I need to.

My mom nods and hands me a jacket on our way out. I sense that she'll be hovering nearby, keeping her eye on us, and the thought is comforting. Mr. McIntyre lets me sit first, then he plops down without brushing the dirt away, which surprises me. We don't talk for a few minutes as we watch the light fade. A mom walks by pushing a toddler on a tricycle with a long handlebar.

"Look, May—can I call you May?" Mr. McIntyre starts in a

413

tone that sounds casual but is edged with power. "I'll be honest, when this whole thing started, I didn't really pay any attention to it. I figured it would pass. It sounds terrible, now that I've learned more about your family, but in the beginning, this was a blip on my radar."

I'm triggered already, so I bite my lip. Mr. McIntyre's shoulders fold in a little as he talks. "Josh and I have always been close, but over the past few months, he's been increasingly distant with me. I just thought it was school-related stress. I didn't know how much my words had affected him. Then, of course, your protest happened. I don't know what you did to get Josh to start things off, but it was a brilliant move. It made me listen."

"We didn't want him to speak. What he did wasn't part of the plan," I say, annoyed. "He did that on his own."

"Oh. I didn't realize." Mr. McIntyre blinks. He scratches a spot behind his ear. "I read through a few of the stories he gave me, and I promised that I'd read them all. I even got a copy of the school magazine. I'm trying, May. But Josh won't speak to me. I know you were friends." He looks at me hopefully, as if I can help him understand. I'm pissed he's here putting this on me after everything he's done. Don't come into my home, take advantage of my parents' hyper-politeness, and then dump your emotional baggage on me.

He takes my silence as an invitation to keep talking. "Why does it have to be one story over another? If I understand what you're saying, all our stories should be heard, right?"

I don't even know where to start with this. I hesitate, then just go for it. Speaking at the rally has given me new courage.

Or maybe I don't care as much that people might not like what I say. "You tried to whitewash my story and erase my family from our own narrative. Which, frankly, is what rich white dudes have done all throughout history."

"What do you mean?"

"Everything you think you know about history is rich white guys passing down stories the way they want to be remembered. It's practically fiction." I kick a pebble with my foot. "You're no different than them."

Mr. McIntyre looks confused. He starts to say something, but then clasps his chin instead. "I'm still not following." He looks at me like he wants an explanation.

I burn inside. "I'm not going to give you a history lesson, Mr. McIntyre. There are books you can read for that." I rub my knees and say quietly, "My brother was the most amazing person I'll ever know, and you turned his tragedy into self-serving sound bites. What did you gain besides approval from all the other closet racists in the Bay? Now you're sitting on my front steps, asking me to help you understand so you can make up with Josh, and you can't even see how wrong that is."

He doesn't respond. His mind is either reeling or building up defenses. I don't know, and I really don't care. I have more to say. "You didn't even need to do that much to keep your story heard over ours. You wrote a letter, maybe talked to some folks. Then a whole system of people did the work for you. You probably weren't even paying attention. Did you see what they said about my family online?"

He shakes his head.

I continue, "We had to sing, shout, draw, paint, write—literally shut off your mic—and you already admitted that it wouldn't have been enough to get you to listen. Your own son had to confront you publicly before you did that."

He puts his head in his hands and massages his temples. "I just want the best for Josh. What's wrong with that?"

Suddenly, the anger burns out and I'm exhausted. What's the point in arguing? I don't need to waste my energy on this. "It's time to hold up a mirror and take a hard look. You might not like what you find." I stand up and brush the dirt off my pants.

"How? I'm trying, May."

"You stop talking and you listen, Mr. McIntyre. You listen."

76

I get to school fifteen minutes early and clip my helmet into the U-lock I use in the bike racks. I started riding to school a few weeks ago, and I don't care if biking is for underclassmen who can't drive, or if I look like a mushroom with my helmet on. I like the fresh air. It gets me ready for the day, then clears my head when it's over.

I stop by my locker and smile when I see the little folded note taped to the front. Celeste has been leaving me little quotes and drawings each morning, and I've been attempting to return the favor. It's become a thing. I make funny little stick figure drawings for her, and she creates little masterpieces that should be framed, not folded up and taped to a rusty locker. Her drawing today is three super-fat kittens sipping boba out of thick straws. In big block letters it says, *BOBA GUYS AFTER SCHOOL?*

I tear out a sheet of notebook paper and do my best to draw the three fat cats passed out with straws and empty boba cups around them. I scribble, *Yes!* and start folding up the note, but a thought comes and I unfold it again. I draw arrows to the cups and write in block letters, *I don't share boba.* Then I draw a smiley face and fold the note back up. I run over to her locker and shove it in the vent. I hope it doesn't fall out.

It's kind of ridiculous because I'm going to see her first period and about a million more times throughout the day. But there's something fun about getting notes in our lockers, so we keep doing it.

Between Celeste's locker and Ms. Lawrie's classroom, people keep stopping me to chitchat, tell me about new #TakeBackthe-Narrative posts they've seen online, or just say hi and ask how I'm doing. I feel like a small moon, pulling waves toward me as I walk. I wonder if this is what it was like for Danny when he used to cruise through the halls at school. My chest still hurts when I picture him holding a basketball while high-fiving and chest-bumping his friends.

I walk by the quad and see posters the size of walls advertising junior/senior prom, and I realize with surprise that I can go this year. It had not even crossed my mind until now. This year, I've missed homecoming, winter formal, almost all the sports games, and a million other things. I used to love all that stuff. I feel a pang that tells me, given time, I might still love it.

Danny didn't make it to his senior prom last year. Of all the things he's missed since he's been gone, it feels stupid to be sad about this; it's just an overhyped high school dance. But if he had been alive, I know he would have loved it. I wish he could have experienced the flutters of dressing up, pinning a corsage on his date, faking proper etiquette at a fancy dinner, holding an awkward pose for pictures, and dancing until his feet hurt.

I've been thinking more and more about the things Danny will never do, taste, smell, try. I wish he could have been there to share his own story that day. I wish he could play basketball again. I wish he could drive through In-N-Out and splatter food all over himself. I also imagine him experiencing things that he will miss each passing year: going to prom, throwing his graduation cap in the air, road-tripping across the country with new college friends, sitting front row at a Warriors game, giving a funny toast at my wedding, pillow-wrestling with his own kids. There was still so much life ahead of him.

Dressing up and standing all night in uncomfortable shoes isn't high on my priority list, and I still have next year. I have time. I imagine getting all fancy-pants with curled hair and a long gown and putting my arm through my date's. I picture myself with Marc.

Then I realize Marc won't be here next year. He will be far away in college.

The thought hits me like a frying pan to the face, and I stop in my tracks in the middle of the walkway. I've known he was going to college. I even told him to go across the country to follow his dreams. Somehow, that did not translate in my brain; the reality of Marc moving across the country means he won't be here, nearby, every day. Someone runs into me from behind and I barely catch myself from falling.

A fog lifts from my mind and things suddenly seem clear. I need to find Marc. I don't have time to waste.

The rest of the day passes in a blur of thoughts flying a mile a minute. I try to picture high school without Marc, the Duverne home without Marc. Me without Marc.

I can't.

As soon as the dismissal bell rings, I grab my bag and head straight for the quad. Sometimes, Marc hangs out on the patio with his friends after school. When I round the corner of the library, I look up toward the wooden platform. Wes and Sione are already there laughing with a group of friends. I hover by the library, pretending to read the flyers stapled to the bulletin board and trying not to look like a stalker. Students leaving campus press by me, and lively chatter fills the air. I wait for an eternity, but he never shows up.

I head for my locker, where I'm supposed to meet Celeste and Tiya before we head to Boba Guys. I can't stop thinking about Marc.

77

Tapioca pearls expand in my tummy, and I feel uncomfortably bloated but so satisfied. I'm biking from Boba Guys to the elementary school, trying to hold a Hong Kong–style black milk tea with pearls on my handlebars. It's for Marc. Tiya said he's been going to shoot hoops a lot lately, so I'm hoping he's there today. If I have to bike any farther than the elementary school, I'm pretty sure this boba is going to end up splattered all over the sidewalk. I should have listened to the girls when they told me not to bring it, but I guess I'm more like my mom than I want to admit. Must have food offering.

There are a few late-afternoon stragglers at the elementary school, but most people have already cleared out for the evening. Cubbies line the outdoor halls. I can't remember being so small that my lunch and books and jackets and toys and knickknacks fit into those tiny rectangles. Life was so carefree then. My biggest worry each day was finding Danny after school so he could walk me home. I could never find the way alone.

I hear the echo of a basketball dribbling on the blacktop and see Marc, wearing basketball shorts and a blue-and-gold Warriors T-shirt, shooting around on the only tall hoop. It's just a ring with no net, and the lines on the blacktop are bleached and fading. He doesn't see me, so I stop and watch him play. He catches his own rebound, spins, and dribbles in for a layup. Then he takes the ball back to the three-point line and shoots a perfect arc that flies through the iron hoop without making a sound. He dribbles down the court, pauses, then runs back in, head-fakes some imaginary defender, steps back, and makes another shot. His motions are fluid. Graceful.

I find a little pint-sized picnic table and sit down. I used to sit like this to watch Danny and Marc ball. They played with one mind and one heart, like Steph and Klay. Like brothers. I can tell Marc misses Danny when he plays.

I watch for a few more moments, noticing the firm lines of Marc's calves, his strong hands, the beads of sweat glistening on his forehead. I almost chicken out of talking to him. I consider just leaving the boba and biking away before he sees me, but when I get up, I bang my knee on the little hobbit table and yelp. Marc turns around.

"May? What are you doing here? Are you okay?" He starts walking over, and I don't know where to look. It feels like a million butterflies are flapping their wings against my stomach lining and suddenly I have to pee. Awesome. I stare stupidly at Marc's feet as they begin crossing the blacktop toward me. Then I remember the boba. I grab the tall plastic cup and start walking quickly toward him.

"Here, I got this for you." I shove the cup in his direction, but I miscalculate the distance and accidentally slam it into his chest. Cold milk tea splashes onto his shirt. "Whoops, sorry."

Marc takes the cup and I realize I dropped the straw somewhere. I whirl around nervously, searching the ground. "I know I brought a straw, it's gotta be around here somewhere."

"How did you know I was here, May?"

"Tiya told me you might be here." I keep my eyes on the ground, hunting for the straw. I start to backtrack toward the tiny picnic table, but Marc pulls my arm gently.

"Don't worry about the straw, May. I can drink it without one, see?" He removes the plastic lid and takes a big gulp.

"But the zhēnzhū." I point at the tapioca balls at the bottom of his cup. "I mean the boba. You won't be able to get those."

He smiles. "It's okay. I don't need the calories."

"What? You look good." My hand flies to my mouth. I can't believe I just said that. Marc's smile stretches across his face.

"Yeah? You checking me out, Maybelline Chen?"

"No! I mean, not really? I just saw you shooting around, that's all." I feel the blush color my cheeks in broad strokes. I sputter, "You seem to be in good health."

Marc raises his eyebrows.

423

My brain just totally shuts off and I don't know where to start, so I pat his shoulder awkwardly and say, "Well, I'm glad you like the milk tea. Have a nice afternoon." Then I turn back around and head toward my bike.

"Whoa whoa whoa." Marc dribbles the ball once as he steps in front of me. "You came here just to drop off some boba and bounce? Really?" A little light twinkles in his eye, but in my current brainless state, I don't know if he's laughing at me or if he's pleased I'm here.

"Um, yes. I guess I did. See you around!" I try to step around him, but he holds his hands out a little to his sides. His fingers are strong and slender. How have I never noticed his hands?

"May, I know you better than that. I can tell your brain just shut off. I've seen it do this a million times. I just don't know what it means right now." He takes a step closer, his eyes searching mine. "I'm guessing you came here to talk to me about something."

"Maybe?" I think being at an elementary school is making me talk like I still go to school here.

He steps closer, instinctively dribbling the ball a couple times. Can't he tell every step closer makes my brain shut off more? He tucks the ball under his arm. "So talk to me."

"Well, I, uh, was walking through school today, and I saw these posters on the wall." Marc nods patiently, but doesn't say anything. The look on his face says he knows my brain will thaw and all the words will come tumbling out. If he talks, he will only slow down this process. It's embarrassing he knows me this well.

"And, well, there were these huge posters for prom, and I realized I could go to prom this year because I'm a junior. I'm not saying I want to go, but the idea that I *could* go was surprising, you know?" I don't even know what I just said. My hands are sweating. I rub them on my shirt. "I was thinking about how I missed all the dances and a lot of other things too." I peek up at him.

"Anyway, there was this huge poster for prom, and I told myself that I could go next year, but then—" I gulp and start talking really fast. "But then I realized when I thought about going to prom, I pictured myself going with you. And then I realized you won't be here next year because you'll be at Howard—congratulations on your scholarship, by the way. Tiya told me. I never properly celebrated with you before because, you know, everything. I wanted to tell you then that I'm glad you're setting your own path, not just living out other people's expectations—and, um . . ."

"Are you asking me to prom, May?" The corner of Marc's mouth twitches upward.

"What? No!" That came out more forcefully than I meant. "I mean, would you want to go to prom? Isn't it too late now? I mean, I didn't know you'd want to go to something like that. Not with me, I just mean in general . . . or with me." He keeps smiling in a way that says he knows I'll get to the point eventually. I think he finds this whole process rather amusing. "I was just trying to say I don't think I'm ready for prom this year, but when I thought about going, I thought about going with you."

Marc sets his bubble tea on the ground and steps even closer. He smells like cocoa butter and sweat. My heart beats through my chest, and I'm sure he can hear it thumping erratically. He still doesn't say anything; he knows there is more coming.

I continue, "And then I couldn't imagine not seeing you at school, or at your house, or just, you know, not having you around in general." My heart is beating so fast I'm sure I'm going to faint.

Marc runs his fingers lightly through my hair and tucks a strand behind my ear. I nearly lose my voice, but manage to whisper, "I'm sorry I freaked out before."

"I'm glad you're here." He cups my face with his right hand.

"I can't stop thinking about you." I press my cheek into his palm. "I just . . . I need time."

The basketball drops out of his left hand and bounces away. He reaches for my hands. Tingles shoot through my fingers and they curl around his. He lifts my arms over his shoulders and around his neck, then wraps his arms around my waist. Marc inhales deeply and holds me tight as I nestle myself into the crook between his neck and shoulder. He says, "We have time, May."

We stand there, holding each other, for who knows how long. I feel like I can stand forever in this space where we don't need words to share understanding. Where silence might be the beginning of something beautiful.

78

IT'S ABOUT DANG TIME

YOU TWO WERE KILLING ME
WITH ALL THAT AWKWARD

WE COULD BE SISTERS

FOR REAL!!

Nothing happened!

But I'm happy

YOU'RE happy??

Marc came home and practically
skipped around the house.

He did?

Don't tell him I told you that.

I'M SO HAPPY TOO!!!

First comes the love,
then comes the marriage . . .

THEN COMES MAY AND
TIYA ARE SISTERS FOREVER!

Haha. You're ridiculous.

I love you too, Tiya.

Love you, girl.

Immigrants . . . and all that.

Yeah, we get the job done.

We also get this done . . .

😂😂😂😂😂😂😂😂😂😂

💀💀💀

EPILOGUE

I put the finishing touches on the tiny pair of origami shoes I just folded. This is probably the eighty-seventh pair that I've made, but all the others have gone into the garbage can. I need this pair to be perfect, and I've been practicing for weeks using some instructions I found online. I take the little silver marker I bought just for this project and draw a wavelike line around the edge, just above the sole. Then I add a check mark on the front corner of each shoe. I examine my handiwork and nod, pretty pleased with myself. They could pass for mini KT3s. Danny is going to love these.

Today, we are going to sweep his grave in honor of Qīngmíng Jié, literally the Pure Brightness Festival. It's also sometimes called Tomb Sweeping Day, which sounds kind of morbid, so

I don't love that name. It's the day we honor our dead ancestors and loved ones. Technically, we missed the actual day, which my mom told me is celebrated on April 5 in Taiwan, and my dad told me is celebrated in China on the first day of the fifth solar term on the lunar calendar, whatever that means. Basically, in China, Qīngmíng Jié is sometimes April 4 and sometimes April 5. Either way, we completely missed it this year because it happened during all the stress about my mom's job and the rally.

My parents, especially my mom, felt really bad about missing Danny's first Qīngmíng Jié. I have a few memories of sweeping my grandparents' graves, but it's not the same here as I imagine it was for my mom in Taiwan, where it's a national holiday. I think traditions have a way of getting diluted when people move away from home.

We load up the car with stacks of paper money, food, and flowers and drive up to Half Moon Bay. The wide lanes of 280 curve through sloping hills and past a blue reservoir that looks like someone threw a handful of glitter across its surface. In the distance, the sun is pulling a thick layer of fog off the hills. My dad winds up the highway as we merge onto 92, then pulls up a slightly hidden road that leads to Skylawn Memorial Park. We're lucky the fog rolled back early today; from the memorial park, we have views of the Santa Cruz Mountains, the Pacific Ocean, and the bay.

When we find Danny's resting place, we unpack all the goodies we brought for him. There isn't actually much to clean here because the grounds are maintained in pristine condition, but my parents go around and readjust plants that look out of place and wipe down Danny's headstone. Then my dad sets up a little stove for burning money while my mom busies herself laying out the food. She brought all of Danny's favorites: beef noodle soup, oranges, even an Animal-Style Double-Double from In-N-Out. I brought him a box of Pocky, plus the folded surprises I have wrapped up in my backpack. I dig out the tiny incense burner we bought in Chinatown last week and find the red-and-gold incense sticks. I lay it all near the food until we're ready to begin.

While I wait for my parents to finish up, I start folding paper money into Chinese ingots. Keeping my hands busy distracts me from thinking about my brother's body, buried right here. I don't want to think of him that way.

I make sure every crease of the red-and-gold-foiled paper is sharp, and I fall into a methodical rhythm as I fold. Eventually a pile of boat-shaped money builds up beside me. My mom gathers the folded money into a large garbage bag so it won't blow away. None of us has uttered a word since arriving; we are lost in our own thoughts.

My mom taps my shoulder and hands me three sticks of incense. She helps me light mine, then she lights hers and my dad's. Its fragrant smell reminds me of my Taiwanese grandparents. They always burned incense on a small altar with a flowing, graceful Guanyin and different fat-bellied Buddhas. I remember Danny and me pretending to bàibài, copying our grandparents' fluid movements as they knelt in front of the altar.

My mom steps in front of Danny's headstone, holds up her

incense, and pauses with her hands in midair as she gazes up at the sky. A tear rolls down her cheek as she slowly bows three times. My dad follows after her, then I take a breath and step up too.

I hold up my incense and think of Danny's face. I bow once and talk to him in my head. *I miss you, Gē. I miss you so much it's hard to breathe. Wherever you are, I hope you're happy. Like playing-basketball or Star Wars–movie-marathon happy.*

I bow again. *Thanks for the song and the mic. It was perfect, as always. You sound like you're still alive somewhere. Are you strumming a harp singing out of tune in some angel choir? They probably kicked you out already with that squawk for a voice.*

I raise my incense and bow low a third time. This time, tears roll down my cheeks too. *I wish I could hear your voice again. But I know you're out there, watching over me. I know silence from the heavens doesn't mean you're not there. I just need to listen differently now. I didn't show it enough before, but I'm here for you too. I miss you, Danny. I love you forever.*

I open my eyes and realize I'm still folded at a right angle, tears dripping onto the grass. My mom comes over and helps me straighten up. I turn into her shoulder and cry. "I hate this, Ma. I wish he were here."

"Me too, Mèi-Mei. We will always miss him. Always." She rubs my back. After I called Katherine Lo, Licensed Professional Clinical Counselor, we started attending family therapy and individual therapy. It's not just helping us work through grief, it's helping us talk so we can actually hear each other. We're not great at it yet, but we're trying. "Let's make sure he knows."

She gestures to all the stuff we brought for him. The food has been arranged in beautiful bowls at the foot of his headstone. Even the burger. It's all there for him to eat, wherever he is. It occurs to me that food is the language of our love, even when one has passed to the next life.

My dad steps in, gripping the bag of folded money. "Let's do this. There's nothing like showing love by burning a giant bag of fake money." He winks at me, and I grin in spite of my tears.

We kneel by the small stove and start to burn the money. Supposedly, once it's burned, it will go to Danny so he can use it in the afterlife. I wonder what they need money for over there.

I'm not sure what I really believe about life after death. I don't know if Danny will actually get—or want—all the stuff we burn for him, or if he's happily using his angel wings to dunk basketballs on some heavenly hoop. Maybe both. I figure I better do this in case it works.

My mom and dad start folding more money while I burn it. I hear them talking softly about the job interviews she has next week. After the rally, she went back and quit her job. Then she came home and freaked out about her uncharacteristic burst of impulsivity. But word got out, and people started reaching out about new job opportunities. It feels good knowing that our event might help my mom find a better position somewhere she is valued. Mr. McIntyre even reached out with a few job prospects, but my mom turned him down. She's taking her time trying to figure out the best place for herself. I'm proud of her.

I am mesmerized by the smoke that curls upward from the burning paper. I stare as it stretches up through the air until my dad scoots over and pulls out two handwritten recipe cards from his pocket. "What're those?" I ask, peering over his shoulder.

"Just a couple copies of Nǎi-Nai's dumpling recipe." He holds both over the fire and lets them burn. "I figured maybe Joe and Danny could each use one. Maybe they'll find each other faster this way."

"Finding each other through their stomachs is definitely the Chen way to go." I grin.

"Yeah, we brought extra food and set some out for Joe too. They can feast together. Though I'm not sure Danny will share the burger."

"Next time, we can bring Uncle Joe his own. Oh! I almost forgot!" I get up, grab my bag, and pull out the tiny KT3s and a little ball I folded and decorated like a basketball. I light a corner of the ball and watch as a bright orange spark catches the edge. The paper glows, then curls inward as the fire eats it up. I whisper, "Thought you might want these so you can keep balling up in heaven, Gē."

"What's that?" My dad looks up to see the glowing edges of the ball.

"Oh, just a little something I made for Danny," I say, embarrassed.

"Is that a basketball?" He sets down the money he's folding, and leans over to take a closer look. He spies the little shoes. "Are these KT3s?"

I nod. He takes them out of my hand and examines them before handing them back. "Wow, Yam. These are awesome." He struggles to finish. "Danny's going to love these."

"I hope so. Do you want to—?" I lift the shoes toward him.

He hesitates. Maybe the shoes are too much. Danny's actual KT3 is still upstairs in my parents' room. My dad takes the shoes out of my hand. "You sure?"

I nod. My dad gingerly lights the tip of one shoe. As we watch it burn, he says, "Next time you'll have to make a pair for Joe too."

"Okay, but Danny's not gonna like someone having a newer release."

My dad laughs. "Do you remember the way he used to lace up his shoes? Always the right one first? Always rabbit through the loop twice instead of a double knot?"

I didn't know he always did his right shoe first, but I go through the loop twice instead of double knot because of Danny. My dad keeps talking as he lights the second shoe. "I remember teaching him to tie his shoes when he was small. He had a hard time remembering how to do it. Then suddenly one day he was big and had figured out his own way. He always did that . . . added his own Danny flair to everything."

My mom brings over a few more folded ingots and stacks of shiny, unfolded paper. She sits down on my left. "Do you remember the time he accidentally put làjiāo on his eggs because he thought it was ketchup? He drank almost twenty glasses of water because it was so spicy. He made a funny face . . . like this." She crosses her eyes and sticks out her tongue and we all laugh. She points at a little jar of làjiāo and the water bottle she set out for him. "I left him a little surprise too."

"I don't remember that."

"Oh, you were still very small. I think maybe you had run away from the table because you didn't want eggs that morning." She nudges me playfully before adding, more seriously, "Danny was always trying to make us smile."

I hug my knees. "There was so much I didn't know about him."

My mom rubs my back. "He loved you so much, Mèi-Mei. He used to put his ear on my big belly and listen for you. He loved when you rolled around in here." She pats her stomach. "He used to talk into my belly button and tell you about all the toys out here waiting for you. He thought if you knew about the toys, you might come out faster."

"He used to bring extra snacks to school for me in case I got hangry." My parents shake their heads and chuckle. "I used to text him, and he'd swing by my classroom to make a drop-off. He was always watching out."

"So that's why we always ran out of snacks so fast!" My dad slides closer and hugs me. "He's still watching out for you, Yam."

"I know."

They both nod, as much to me as to each other. With that, we start burning money again. After we run out of folded ingots, we start putting stacks of gold-foiled paper into the small flame. We watch all the money turn to ashes and float up to heaven in the smoke. My parents wrap their arms around me and we sit quietly, remembering Danny.

We have so many beautiful memories; I just wish we'd had time to make more with him. There is an emptiness that will never fully heal and a pain that still tugs me toward darkness, though not as powerfully as it once did.

I know Danny's still with us somehow. Maybe as an actual spirit. Maybe just in spirit. I don't know. But I feel him nearby. And lately, I've felt sure that I'll see him again. I'll get to hug him again one day.

"Maybe next time, we could bring him some paper Star Wars DVDs. In case he gets bored," I say.

"I'm going to fold him a jacket," says my mom.

"I saw a miniature passenger plane at the paper money store," says my dad. "I bet Danny would love his own private jet."

I laugh out loud thinking of Danny flying a 747 around heaven. I slip my hands into my parents' open palms, and they lace their fingers between mine. We stand up together.

An ocean breeze wraps itself around us and ruffles our clothes. There is still so much to say, but we hold on to each other and breathe slowly as we gaze at the sun-kissed view. The hills and the clouds and the ocean seem to extend into eternity.

In this moment, I feel close to Danny. Close to my parents. This silence we share is one that connects us. It is a bond of heartbreak and healing. Sadness and hope. Darkness and light.

And most of all, love.

AUTHOR'S NOTE

I started the story that would become this book in the summer of 2017. It was born from the desire to tell a story about anti-Asian racism. I wanted the world to know it was real. I wanted to explore Asian American history, Black and Asian solidarity, reasons we stay silent, and what it takes to speak out.

Never, not once, in the years that it took to imagine, draft, and revise this novel did I imagine that the term "anti-Asian racism" would become a phrase widely used in newspaper headlines, social media posts, or in any kind of collective dialogue. I never imagined a global pandemic. Atlanta. Attacks on our elderly. I could not have fathomed that one day, anything related to Asians in America would become a topic of collective conversation. It had simply never happened at this scale in the decades I have breathed on this planet.

The world showed interest in a truth that existed long before, but the world's attention lasts but a brief moment.

This story was born from the teenage suicide epidemics that racked my community for years, the effects of which still reverberate to this day. It was born from a group dinner I attended where a wealthy white man stated the pressure and stress and suicides in our community came from the Asian families that lived here. It was born from a Lyft driver who told me the same thing less than a week later. It was born from the invisibility of being Asian. It is an invisibility that runs so deep people don't see me even when I face them across a dinner table or when I'm the only passenger in their car.

It started out as a story about anti-Asian racism, but racism doesn't exist in a vacuum. This is a story about family, friendship, mental health, fear, power, hope, healing, and love. It is a little bit of my truth. It is one of many stories that can and must be told.

Thank you for picking up this book. May we each find the love and courage we need to speak our stories and truths so boldly the world can never turn away again.

ACKNOWLEDGMENTS

Every book is a work of love woven together from threads contributed by a vast community that spans time and place. I am incredibly grateful for the generosity of the community that made this book possible. I am indebted to more people than I could ever hope to name in these pages; without you, none of this would be possible.

Julia Tachibana, you are a wonder in this world. Thank you for opening your heart, for sharing your experiences, for allowing me a glimpse into the journey that continues each day. You are a warrior that carves your own path and shapes the lives of those around you. I'm grateful to be in your sphere.

Thank you to my agent, Caryn Wiseman, who has redefined the word *champion* in my life. Thank you for seeing the soul of this story when it was just eight messy chapters, and for advocating for it with such sensitivity and love. Thank you to the ABLA team; I'm grateful to be part of the family.

Thank you to my editors, Clarissa Wong, Alyson Day, Eva Lynch-Comer. Thank you, Clarissa, for always understanding my heart and pushing me to write it in truth; for helping me shape characters and story with deeper complexity and nuance. Thank you, Aly, for your vision and your eye for detail; for shepherding this story into the world with so much passion and insight. Thank you, Eva, for the tireless hours poured into this story, for the thoughtful questions and piercing eyes. Without this team, this book would not be what it is.

Thank you to the entire team at HarperCollins; I know there is a whole world I never see and so much that happens to bring a book to life. I am filled with gratitude for each and every one of you. Thank you to my copyeditors, Erin Hamling and Nicole Moreno; you really are magical elves with magical eyes. Thank you to my marketing team, Audrey Diestelkamp and Lisa Calcasola, and to my publicists, Lena Reilly and Ro Romanello. Thank you all for helping this story find its readers. Thank you to associate art director Joel Tippie for the details that make such a difference. Thank you to production manager Annabelle Sinoff for holding this whole circus together.

My deepest awe and admiration to Victo Ngai, whose art is otherworldly and brilliant. Thank you for the stunning cover.

Thank you to my critique group: Claire Bobrow, Molly McDonough, Natalie Mitchell, Stephanie Lucianovic, and Helen Taylor. It is an honor to work with you. Thank you for helping me find my way to finishing.

In writing a story that explores so many complex and traumatic topics, I tried my best to do it in a way that felt true without being retraumatizing, without romanticizing pain, causing more harm, or reinforcing stereotypes. As one story, it cannot possibly capture all the lived realities of so many who experience anxiety, depression, and/or other mental health struggles. It cannot capture the lived realities of all Asian youth. It cannot cover all the complexities of interracial history or relationships. I am grateful to the people who read this story through all of these lenses, who helped me rewrite over and over and over again. Thank you to mental health experts Kathleen Allen MS, DNP, Michelle Lee, MA, LPCC, and Nandini Ahuja, whose insights and expertise helped me understand grief, survival, healing. Thank you to all the readers, including Nicole Overton, Elodie Leroy, and Shasta Clinch, who tackled this story through perspectives of race and cultural background. You showed me how easy it is for implicit biases and stereotypes to show up in a story, even as I tried so intentionally not to let them, even as I've been dedicated to a journey of anti-racism and liberation. I am grateful not only for the ways you pushed my writing and my story, but also for the ways in which you helped me reflect and grow as a human.

Thank you to Kelly Loy Gilbert, Abigail Hing Wen, Tiffany Jewell, Stacey Lee, Nic Stone, Misa Sugiura, and Randy Ribay for reading this first novel. I'm just following in your wake, trying to light up the world the way you do. Your words of encouragement mean the world.

Thank you to my family and friends. You are the circle that holds me up, that gives me strength and shows me the way. You know who you are. I hope you know how much you mean to me, how much I love you. When I say you give me life, I am not exaggerating.

Dave, every example of brotherly love in this book is based on you. Daren, thank you for being the big brother I always wanted. Ning, you deserve thanks for more than I can list, so I'll just thank you here for being my text thread muse.

Harv, thank you for being my personal encyclopedia of Chinese history; for finding every answer I needed to understand my own roots and language and culture; for being the only person in the family I allowed to read the book in all its messy stages. It needed you, as do I.

Mom, this book, the woman warrior, the *wear a jacket* and *show love through food* is all you. You are my whole world and always have been. Thank you for showing me love in so many ways. I'm still learning to see them all.

Carter and Aila, everything I do and everything I am is because of and for you.

RESOURCES

If you or someone you know needs help, please
reach out to the following organizations.

National Suicide Prevention Lifeline Phone Number:
1-800-273-8255

National Suicide Prevention Lifeline Website:
www.suicidepreventionlifeline.org/

National Suicide Prevention Lifeline Website for Youth (Teens):
www.suicidepreventionlifeline.org/help-yourself/youth/

Youth Suicide Warning Signs:
www.youthsuicidewarningsigns.org/youth

You Matter:
www.youmatter.suicidepreventionlifeline.org

Active Minds:
www.activeminds.org

Ditch the Label:
www.ditchthelabel.org